IDLE HANDS

DS JAMIE JOHANSSON BOOK 3

MORGAN GREENE

ALSO BY MORGAN GREENE

DS Jamie Johansson Prequels

Bare Skin

Fresh Meat

Idle Hands

The DS Johansson Prequel Trilogy Boxset

DI Jamie Johansson

Angel Maker

Rising Tide

Old Blood

Death Chorus

Quiet Wolf

IDLE HANDS

1

THE SOUND of Bach's *Partita number two* echoed mournfully down the tunnel.

She stood there, eyes closed, playing from memory, the bow sawing back and forth on the strings. The knuckles of her left hand protruded at sharp angles, the calloused pads of her fingers hammering the strings against the worn neck.

The notes punctured the air and resounded off the concrete. The white walls had been tagged with graffiti, the stark paint of the walkway decorated with the bubbling anger of the city.

She kept time in her head, the sounds of the footsteps coming towards her not even registering as she played.

The piece lasted seventeen minutes and forty-five seconds. Not a moment shorter. Not a moment longer.

She was one of the few people who could play it, and one of the select few of those who could do so with the kind of precise grace that only the masters ever manage to attain.

Her hair shimmered in the halogen bulbs as she moved side to side, the short, messy strands twisting and flicking as she played.

A couple in their fifties approached. They were on the way home from a late dinner. George Bennet had lied to his wife, told her he had booked a table. In fact, he had forgotten that he had agreed to go out at all.

So when they got to the restaurant, George told the waitress that he had made a reservation. He knew that his wife knew, but wouldn't give up the ruse. He was stubborn like that.

They had to wait more than an hour before they were seated and didn't receive their starters until nearly nine-thirty.

It was now well after eleven, and Nicola Bennet was walking quickly, dragging George along, because he refused to let go of her arm.

He did hate it when she stormed off.

As such, he had his leather-gloved hand clamped around his own forearm, his right threaded over the crook of Nicola's elbow.

He didn't think she was furious, but there was a coldness coming off her that wasn't anything to do with the cool May air.

George did this sort of thing often.

Nicola didn't know why she expected more.

Each reflected on that as they walked, unaware that the music they were hearing wasn't as discordant and slap-dash as they might have first thought. That each note was carefully chosen and placed, and hit with impeccable accuracy. That it was one of the most complex and beautiful pieces of music ever written.

That they were in the presence of one of the most talented violinists in the country – if not the world.

That to stand and give her even a moment of their time would alert them to this fact.

And that the man standing in front of the violinist in the zipped-up hoodie, his hands firmly in his pockets, fists balled, hood pulled up over his head, was about to kill her.

Nicola moved around him and George went with her, his shoulder grazing the man's arm.

He didn't flinch.

He was enthralled.

In that moment, there was nothing else in his world.

His eyes were fixed on the violinist's fingers. The delicacy and adeptness of them. Their strength, their elegance.

Their beauty.

The corner of his mouth twitched, his eyes narrowing, jaw quivering as she built to crescendo.

George and Nicola Bennet were fifty feet away and still moving.

Still ignoring the music.

Still ignoring each other.

The notes began to chime, Bach's double stops barking in the darkness.

The last weeping vibrato sustained and then faded, and she dragged the bow across the strings, playing that final, wailing cry.

And then, as her eyes opened, he lunged.

2

IT WAS midnight at the headquarters of the Metropolitan Police in London, and five people were sitting in a locked room.

The door had no window in it, no one could see in, and the room was all but soundproof, designed for this sort of thing.

Inside was a large, beech table, and around it were twelve chairs.

Detective Chief Inspector Henley Smith sat at the head, massaging the corner of his jaw with the knuckles of his right index finger and the pad of his thumb. He was listening intently as Detective Sergeant Paul Roper spoke.

After he had finished, Smith sighed and sat up straighter. He looked as tired as they all felt. No one wanted to be in the office at midnight. But they had to be sure they wouldn't be caught.

'So basically,' Smith said, trying to keep the curtness out of his voice. 'You've found nothing.'

DS Roper shifted uncomfortably on his seat and winced. Though he was back on his feet, he was still slow and couldn't walk without a cane. The knife had missed everything vital, but the wound was still deep, and had cut through the thoracolumbar fascia, as well as about three other muscles, which meant that he had a long road to recovery ahead of him.

He couldn't even remember the name of the muscle that was damaged, but that didn't stop him from bringing it up every time he couldn't be bothered to get out of his chair to get something.

'That's about it, yes,' he said tiredly. 'They've been smart about it, I'll give them that.'

Smith tapped his pen on the table and made an *mmnnn* sound. 'And what about you, Johansson? Any news?'

Detective Sergeant Jamie Johansson was five-six, with ash blonde hair and blue eyes. She let out a slow breath, looking across the table at her interim partner, Captain Nasir Hassan, who, unlike Roper, had made practically a full recovery after getting shot during their last operation.

He looked at the table.

'No,' Jamie said plainly. 'I'm looking into it, but Amherst and Brock have looped the HMRC in on the Grigoryan case, as well as the Ministry of Housing, Home Office, and the MOJ.' She shook her head. 'Grigoryan has his fingers in so many businesses, import-export deals, property, stocks and bonds… There's probably not a single law he's not in violation of somehow. And Brock and Amherst are building a case with all these other agencies and governing bodies, it'll take years. They're *actively gathering evidence*,' she said, using air quotes, 'so that they can take him down. But in reality, they're never going to make any serious progress. Not with everyone falling over each other. There'll never be an end to what they find – clever, really. They'll keep putting together small violations, keep saying they need more evidence to really nail him, while he does some truly heinous shit behind our backs. And the worst thing is that if anyone goes near him – even types the name Jonathan Grigoryan into a government database – it'll flag on someone's radar and get right back to them. He's untouchable.'

Smith threw the pen down. 'So we're basically fucked then?'

Jamie resisted the urge to shrug. She'd spent the last three months trying to find dirt on Amherst and Brock – the likely leak that had made their last operation go so spectacularly sideways – but couldn't find anything. Roper had been digging into them too, from the other side, and had also come up with exactly nothing.

The Department of Professional Standards had launched an investigation themselves, but after just three weeks, had said there was no evidence to suggest wrongdoing, and had dismissed the case.

Which in itself stunk just as bad as Amherst and Brock did themselves.

They were the only ones who knew about the operation at the port who had the sort of reach and seniority that would be any use to men like Jonathan Grigoryan and Ho Zhou – two high-level scumbags with ties to trafficking, slavery, corruption, and everything else that would make your toes curl.

Smith hadn't liked it one bit.

Which was why they were carrying on the investigation themselves.

But Grigoryan, Zhou, whoever else was out there, pulling the invisible strings… They were smart, well-funded, better connected, and seemingly untouchable.

If it wasn't a wall of solicitors and barristers preventing them from getting close, it was their own damn detectives and officers barring the way.

Smith's team was infected.

And probably so was every other in the Met.

Even the DOPS were rotten. Or they'd seemingly become inept at the very thing they were made to do. Which didn't strike Jamie as likely.

And now, everyone was growing tired.

They were getting nowhere, and they were losing steam.

On paper, everyone was as clean as a whistle. And they had to be careful how hard they pushed this. It was being done behind closed doors. In secret. If anyone found out that Smith was launching an investigation into his own detectives on the premise that the DOPS were corrupt… Apart from a PR shit-storm, it would have much further-reaching consequences.

No one knew what would happen, but then again, no one knew who anyone was really working for.

Smith rubbed his eyes and stared down the length of the table at the fifth and final member of their team. 'What about you, Fischer? Please tell me you have some good news?'

Gretchen Fischer was an up-and-comer in the cybercrimes department and Smith had poached her for this investigation. She was twenty-seven, petite, and had glasses that were far too large for her face. She had to keep pushing them up her nose every ten seconds.

She looked up from her laptop screen, the white reflection swirling in her lenses, and pushed her thick black fringe out of the way, only for it to fall immediately back into place resting on her eyebrows.

'What?' she said, having not been listening.

Jamie cracked a little smirk. Hassan did too.

'Amherst, Brock,' Smith said. 'Have you found anything?'

She leaned back in the chair and laced her hands behind her head, elbows out. She let out a low whistle, seemingly unphased by Smith's authority, or the look of frustration on his face. Though she was like that. She didn't do well with social cues, and rarely let anyone's mood or station prevent her from acting exactly how she always did. 'I can tell you what kind of porn they like.'

Smith grit his teeth. 'Is it the illegal kind?'

'No,' Gretchen said.

'Then what use is that to the investigation?'

She actually did shrug. A big emphatic shoulder raise and then a casual drop. 'Dunno,' she said. 'But these guys have had help. That much is clear.'

'What do you mean?' Smith asked.

She cleared her throat, hawked, and then swallowed it. Roper and Hassan both grimaced. Smith held one back. Jamie thought it was sort of funny. Her mother would have been aghast. That's probably why she was trying not to laugh.

'Well, no one is this clean online,' Gretchen continued, going back to her laptop. She started tapping again, and Jamie didn't know if Smith could make it out, but she was close enough to see in the reflection on her glasses that Gretchen was scrolling through Reddit, and not working. 'They've had a cleaner in to make sure everything's hunky-dory.'

Smith drew a slow breath. If there was one thing that agitated him it was when people didn't speak concisely.

'I mean, these guys are *clean.* No credit card debt, no weird online purchases, no dodgy web history. No phone records or texts to say they're doing anything wrong. No money trail. No deposits into their accounts. No *hidden* accounts as far as I can find… At least nothing tied to them by name. They've been schooled in it – I can tell you that much. Taught how to stay invisible, and scared into staying that way.'

Smith stared at her, looking expectant that she might finish the observation.

She didn't.

'I don't suppose you know who by?' He was talking through his teeth now.

'Nope,' Gretchen said. 'But whoever is paying them on the sly isn't a novice at it. They know how not to get caught,' she mused. 'It's no wonder DOPS dropped the case. There's literally nothing to say that Amherst and Brock are anything except good, clean, hard-working detectives.'

Smith ran his hand over his bald head. 'What about the night of the operation? Anything there?'

'Nope. No incoming or outgoing calls to either of their phones, no pings off any of the towers, nothing to say that they sent any sort of message or signal to anyone outside the operation.'

Smith was growing more tense. Jamie could see the vein bulging in his temple. 'So if you had to make a guess about how they *might* have got the word out? How would you have done it?'

She shrugged again, made an *I-uhhngo* sound and kept her eyes on her screen. 'Sat-phone?' she added after a few seconds. 'Though you'd need an encrypted signal not to show up anywhere – so either your own private satellite, or the ability to piggyback off a comms satellite without them knowing about it. But that's some serious shit. And without alerting the MOD to what we're doing by hacking into their sat-network to look up the positions of comms sats on the date in question – there's really not anything else I can do.'

Jamie didn't know if it was the news she was delivering, or the seeming casualness of the delivery which was annoying Smith more.

Though she didn't seem phased by his demeanour, which seemed to have a defusing effect on Smith, somehow. Every performance needs a receptive audience, she guessed.

Jamie made a mental note of it and checked her watch. It was nearly ten past twelve and she was flagging.

'Right,' Smith said, reading the room. 'Go home, get some rest, keep working… We'll reconvene in two weeks. Okay?'

Everyone nodded.

'You're released,' he said, leaning on the table.

They all pushed back and Jamie stood up. 'Nas,' she said to Hassan.

He looked at her, pushing the chair in. 'Yeah?'

'You still okay to help in the morning?'

He nodded. 'Sure. Eight, you said?'

'Unless you want to come earlier?' Jamie replied.

He laughed. 'No, that's okay' — he held his hands up — 'I've got to get the kids up and ready for school. If I book out earlier, the wife will just think I'm sticking her with it.'

'Fair enough.'

'So I'll be there for seven,' he added, laughing.

Jamie gave a courteous chuckle, not having the energy for a true belly-laugh. Hassan made a lot of jokes about his wife and home life. About his supposed fleet of girlfriends – which Jamie knew didn't exist. But still, it was beginning to shift from playful to cry-for-help, and she didn't know how she felt about that.

'Eight is fine,' she said, making sure she wasn't causing any more marital distress.

Hassan nodded in confirmation.

'Hey,' Roper cut in. 'What about me? Don't you want my help?' His face twisted painfully as he shuffled the chair back under-table.

'Roper,' Jamie said with a sigh. 'I wouldn't be able to get you to lift boxes even if you were in good health.'

'Lifting stuff is bad for your knees,' he said airily. 'And plus, don't they have services for this sort of thing? Professional movers?'

Jamie pressed her lips into a line. They did, but the truth of it was that she wanted as few people to know she was moving as possible. So far, it was only Hassan, Roper, Cake, and now Smith and Gretchen – both of whom she trusted with her life. Smith was proving to be an honourable and stalwart man and senior officer. And Gretchen – apart from not caring what went on in anyone else's life – seemed utterly incapable of deception or reprehensible behaviour.

Though it wasn't *everyone else* she was trying to keep her move from. It was *him*. Elliot Day. The man whose grasp she never seemed to be able to escape.

After finding him in her apartment three months ago, things hadn't been the same.

She didn't feel safe anymore.

And while no one knew the real reason she was moving, she was glad they were happy to help. Hassan and Cake would do the heavy-lifting, and she already had a van rented and ready for it.

They all began to move towards the door.

Gretchen had already gone. Probably slipped out the moment that Smith said they could leave.

Jamie took the Glock 17 semi-automatic pistol off the desk and clipped the holster onto her belt.

Since their last operation – at Felixstowe port – there was an elevated threat. Jamie and Hassan had taken two of Ho Zhou's soldiers off the board and derailed a major source of income for him. And Zhou had already had her beaten up once to get her off his back – and Elliot had killed his head bouncer at the Jade Circle in recompense. Now that there was blood in the water, Smith didn't think Zhou or Grigoryan would be above stepping things up.

And with Hassan not cleared for active duty with Armed Response yet, and Roper nowhere near fit enough to be her partner again, Smith had made Hassan her temporary partner. And had cleared them both to carry a firearm until the investigation was complete or the threat-level had dropped sufficiently.

It didn't look like either of those things was about to happen any time soon.

And with an infatuated serial killer and a host of vengeful crime-lords with her in their crosshairs, she couldn't say that carrying it didn't make her feel just a little better.

'Wait,' Smith said suddenly, just as they reached the door.

Jamie knew that tone. She stopped, hung her head and turned.

He was standing in front of his chair, reading off his phone screen.

'What is it?' Jamie asked.

'Murder,' Smith said plainly, squinting at the details. 'Just came in – body was discovered in an…' He trailed off, scrolling down. 'Underground walkway.'

Jamie set her jaw.

Smith checked his watch and looked up at her. 'Feeling fresh, Johansson?'

'Always,' she lied.

'Good – it's above your pay-grade,' he said, looking down reading on, 'but I don't think anyone else will be up at this time and you can be on the scene in fifteen.' He didn't seem thrilled with giving it to her. She was just a DS after all, even if she did seem to have a nose for murder cases.

But she was there, she had Hassan with her, and they could both be there faster than anyone else.

And the faster you could get to a crime scene, the fresher it was. And the fresher it was, the better start you had on the case.

'I'm on it,' she said, before he changed his mind.

Her bed couldn't have been further from her thoughts, suddenly. She was wide awake.

'Johansson,' Smith added, getting to the bottom of the notice, looking grave. 'Be careful.'

'Always am, sir.' She smiled briefly.

'I mean it – it's a bad one.' He put his hands on his hips and looked at the ground.

'Sir?' Jamie felt herself stiffen, reading his posture, one hand on the door handle.

'They cut her hands off.'

3

JAMIE AND HASSAN pulled in at the curb in silence.

Three police cars, an ambulance, and a crowd of people were all huddled around the entrance to the tunnel.

It led down under the road and stretched to the other end of the intersection. They were common in the city, popular with kids, homeless people when it rained, and anyone looking to get out of the open air.

What circumstances led to this kill, Jamie didn't know.

They were going into this one blind.

She glanced at Hassan, who was already scanning the scene.

He wasn't a detective, never had been, but he'd been a uniformed officer for four years, worked traffic for seven – completed all of his advanced driving courses and aced every firearms test they had – and then put in for Armed Response. So while he wasn't Roper – he knew the job, knew the city, and had a sharp enough mind to be of continual use.

As bad as Jamie felt about it, she was glad to have him with her.

She and Smith both knew that he was physically fit enough to be cleared for active duty again, but by the sounds of it, his wife liked the idea of him not charging into gunfire, and though he wouldn't admit it,

Jamie could see he liked playing detective. And his experience and rank definitely elevated her standing.

Smith never would have given this to her if Roper was her partner.

But he was glad he could go home to bed, so she guessed that made it – what was it called? No harm, no foul?

'Come on,' Jamie said, pushing the door of her car open with her kevlar-toe-capped trail boots. Hassan opened the door on the other side and got out, the seat appearing from underneath him as he exited.

Her small hybrid hatchback wasn't designed for someone his size, really. Not that he was overly tall or inordinately massive. The car was just small.

It rose two inches on the springs as he got to his feet.

The May air was cool on Jamie's skin.

After a long, cold winter, the spring had finally arrived. Late as it was.

The days were humid and warm, the air that ripe mixture that only London can produce, and the nights cool and crisp.

Jamie shivered once and then zipped up her chocolate-brown suede jacket, the woollen hood immediately warm against her neck.

Her boots squeaked as she stepped up onto the curb, surveying the small crowd that had gathered at the police line.

Tape was affixed to a lamp post on one side, a railing on the other, and stretched around the entrance to the tunnel.

One uniformed officer was stood at the entrance, his hands clasped in front of him, the blues from the patrol cars and the ambulance dancing off his hi-vis jacket. Behind him, a translucent sheet had been stretched across the opening and taped in place to obscure the view.

There were ten people gathered at the tape and two of the uniformed officers were working their way around them. Asking questions, taking statements. Five were teenagers on bikes, come to see the show. There was an older woman trying to see into the tunnel. She had shopping bags in her hands, and was moving her head around to see if another angle would give her the ability to see through the sheet.

There was also a young couple, a guy in his forties talking loudly on his phone – saying something about the scene, telling a friend to get down there – and finally, an elderly Asian woman who didn't seem to know what was going on. At first glance, it looked to Jamie like she was standing in a queue. Then it occurred to her that maybe she thought she was.

Either that or she liked the aftershave the guy on the phone was wearing, and maybe the curve of his ass too, judging by how she was holding her head.

Jamie shook it off.

Nothing stood out to her.

'Let's go,' she said to Hassan, doing a quick check of the surrounding buildings. All commercial – some apartments over shops. Not a bad part of the city by any stretch. Though just from the few words that Smith had said, this didn't sound like a spur-of-the-moment thing. Not an altercation gone wrong.

This was something else entirely.

Jamie flashed her warrant card at the officer at the sheet and he nodded, pulling it aside.

As they ducked to get into the tunnel, the outside world faded away.

In front of them two paramedics were kneeling down, putting things into their kit bag, talking to one of the officers who was making notes.

Behind them, another uniformed officer was interviewing two people – a man and a woman in their fifties. Both looked shaken.

Witnesses.

Beyond that, another sheet had been taped to the ceiling. Though you couldn't see through it, the lights beyond were throwing a reflection off a dark shape that Jamie knew had to be a pool of blood.

Her stomach knotted as she pushed forward.

Hassan didn't seem bothered. He approached scenes with the same stalwart reserve that he did an operation.

Unflappable was the word that Jamie found suited him best.

The first sheet was to keep people from seeing into the tunnel, the second was to keep whoever was inside from the scene itself.

Jamie had no doubt that it would be the same on the other side, too, boxing the murder into a little room for them.

She slowed as they approached the couple, and looked at them in turn, smiling as brightly as her face could muster at half-past midnight.

The officer stopped talking and lowered his notebook.

'Hi,' Jamie said. 'I'm Detective Sergeant Jamie Johansson with the London Metropolitan Police.' She wondered how many times she'd said those words in her life. And how many more she would.

Neither of them smiled or returned the greeting. Jamie knew why, and understood.

'Did you see what happened here?' Jamie asked them, reading their faces.

Hassan hung back, letting Jamie work. That was another thing she liked about him over Roper.

'No,' the woman answered quickly. 'We didn't see anything – which is why we don't need to be here.'

Jamie bit her bottom lip, hearing the bite in the woman's tone. 'Okay,' she said, smiling again. 'I know it's late, and I'm sure you've already been through everything—'

'We have,' the woman said again. 'And we don't know anything, didn't see anything – just heard that god-awful music, then screaming. That was it. Next thing we know…' She trailed off, staring into space, and then shivered animatedly.

Jamie cast Hassan a look.

'She was on the ground,' the man interjected absently, his eyes seemingly trained on the same invisible thing the woman's were. No doubt the image of it was burned into their minds. There were a few seared in Jamie's, too. 'So much blood,' he muttered.

Jamie nodded, processing. They were within earshot of it then – they must have seen something. Heard something.

She glanced down at the officer's notebook and could see that he'd taken a statement already.

But she'd still need to question them herself.

'Would you mind hanging on for a few more minutes?' Jamie asked, making her voice soft.

The woman answered again, the bite in her voice getting sharper. 'We already told Officer…'

'Davies,' the officer said, helping her.

'… what happened. I'm not going through it again.' She started shaking her head, closing her eyes at the thought.

Jesus, they did look shaken.

'I'd really like to hear it for myself if I could,' Jamie said, and then turned to Officer Davies before the woman could reply for a third time. 'Why don't you take them outside? Get some fresh air.' Jamie touched Davies' arm and dropped to a whisper. 'Don't let them leave before I come back out.'

Davies nodded and herded the couple towards the first sheet, and the cool night air.

They went like sheep and Jamie looked after them for a moment, fishing a pair of nitrile gloves out of her pocket on autopilot.

She took a deep breath, tasting the faint scent of copper on the air, and then turned towards the scene.

Hassan was at the inner sheet already. He nodded to her. 'You good?'

She returned it. 'Yeah, open it.'

Jamie gestured to the sheet and he took hold of the plastic, pulling it back with a big hand, his dark skin a stark comparison to the ghostly white barrier.

The smell of rust hit her, the unmistakeable stench of blood like liquid in the air.

She set her teeth, locked down her throat, and stepped inside.

Hassan was at her elbow a second later, the sheet falling into place behind them.

They were in a box. Two concrete walls on either side, and a sheet in front and behind.

Just them and a girl lying on her side on the floor, dead, in a pool of her own blood.

And Smith was right.

Her hands were missing.

4

'SHIT,' Hassan said, his voice quiet.

Jamie was silent.

They both stared down at the girl.

If anything, it was more unsettling that Hassan was rattled by it than the crime was itself.

Since they'd been partnered up, it was mostly smaller-time stuff. A few gang-related incidents, robberies and larceny, a body showing up in the Thames – which proved to be an accidental death.

This would mark both Jamie and Hassan's first truly grizzly murder.

But she was ready, whether it was happenstance that put her here or not.

She glanced up, seeing her father standing at the far side of the body suddenly. He had his hands in the pocket of his heavy pea coat. He was smiling with something like pride hidden in the wrinkles of his face.

He gave an almost imperceptible nod, and Jamie returned it, looking away.

When she glanced back, he was gone.

'You good?' Hassan asked, clocking her staring into space.

'Yeah,' Jamie said. 'I'm good.' She laced her fingers together and pushed her gloves tightly onto her hands before crouching down, noting everything she could see.

The girl was lying on her side in a foetal position, her elbows together, wrists in front of her face, her arms stacked one on top of the other, stumps just in front of her nose.

She could only have been nineteen, maybe twenty. Her skin was tanned, her hair dark, short, and naturally curly. Jamie would have said she was maybe three-quarters caucasian. A grandparent on either side black, possibly. She pursed her lips – she didn't think this was racially motivated. But you could never quite cross it off the list, no matter what colour someone's skin was.

The girl's skin was bright, though, unblemished. She looked after herself.

She had a piercing in her nose, a small silver stud. Nothing fancy.

And there were dimples in the skin below her bottom lip, one at either side. They'd been pierced before, but the holes were healing. Snake bites, they were called. Two rings that curved over the lip and into the mouth.

Her hair was cut short on the sides and pulled back over her ears, quaffed into a bunch on top.

She was attractive, but not conventionally so. She had a wide nose, almond-shaped eyes that were heavily made up, and full, pink lips.

Though it didn't really look to Jamie like she was trying to show herself off.

Her clothes were comfortable, not feminine, not masculine. She was dressed for the night – a pair of skinny jeans and black Dr Marten classic boots.

She was wearing a knitted long-sleeve top that was pushed up her forearms.

On top, she had a heavy grey cardigan that hung loosely, too. It didn't have any buttons – more of a cape with arms, than anything else.

A strange mixture of clothes – not exactly fashion. But she had her own style. That much was clear.

Jamie's eyes kept moving, ignoring the bruises on her throat, the severed hands, and the pool of blood that she was doing her best not to stand in.

She was tired of cleaning it off her boots.

Behind the girl was a violin case.

It was laid flat on the floor, on top of a towel.

Jamie's eyes lingered on it. The towel was old and tatty, and so was the case. It was real leather, but frayed at the seams and beaten up.

Jamie couldn't see any branding.

Why would the girl bother to put a towel down if the case itself was worn out?

Jamie stood up and stepped around the blood pool, towards it.

Hassan watched carefully, studying what Jamie was doing in silence.

He had the will to learn.

Jamie lifted the lid carefully. It was closed, but not latched.

Inside was a violin.

It looked to be antique, that perfect, warm reddish colour that only string instruments could be. It sat on a plush red velvet interior, the neck supported by a cradle, the body snug against the sides.

Jamie leaned the top of the case against the hinged stopper and inspected it.

The bow had been placed back into its holster in the top half.

Jamie lifted the corner of the violin, seeing that the back of the neck had a depression where you would hold it. It had been played half to death, but lovingly looked after.

She peeled it out of the case entirely and looked at it, making a note of where it was before she did.

The SOCOs would need the scene as untouched as possible to dust for prints, collect DNA, look for evidence.

'Looks old,' Hassan said, taking a step closer.

'Mhm,' Jamie replied, looking at the intricacy of the grain, the obvious build quality.

She'd played the piano as a child – been pushed into it. She'd always liked the violin but her mother had said, *What? So we can listen to you strangling cats all hours of the day and night? No thank you.* Jamie didn't know much about them, but you could always tell you were holding something expensive just by the way it felt in your hands.

Hassan watched how carefully she was holding it, his eyes moving over the body of the instrument, seeing the quality of the case and how it was on a towel so it wasn't on the bare stones. He didn't need to touch it to come to the conclusion that it was a pricey piece. 'Stradivarius?' he asked aloud.

Jamie curled a smile and looked over her shoulder. 'You know violins?'

'Am I right?'

'Hofner – nineteen-oh-nine by the label inside,' Jamie said, tilting it so that the light caught a curled and browned piece of paper visible through the F-hole. 'But close,' she added, giving him a quick smirk.

'Eh, took a punt,' Hassan said, trying not to look at the girl on the ground.

'I'm impressed.'

'Don't be, it's the only brand I know.'

Jamie put the violin back and stood up, looking at it.

'What are you thinking?'

Jamie moved her mouth back and forth as she weighed it up. 'I'm thinking that this is an expensive violin.'

'Okay.'

Jamie looked at the body again. No watch, no jewellery. Jamie knelt again and reached over, lifting the corner of the victim's cardigan. She could see the rectangular outline of a smartphone pushing through her jeans.

Jamie pressed on the bottom of it with her finger and slid it out carefully until it was half exposed. It was an iPhone – not the latest, but a midrange model, maybe two-years old.

Still worth stealing though.

'This wasn't motivated by money.' Jamie stood and folded her arms. 'The violin, for one, is worth probably a few thousand. Antique, high quality. I'm not sure on value – we'd need an expert to say – but it's definitely worth something. You've only got to look at how she treated it to know that. And her phone is still here, too – could definitely sell that for a bit.'

Hassan nodded slowly.

Jamie went on. 'There's no wallet,' she said, scanning the girl's other thigh for the telltale lump in the pocket. She leaned over the body, checking the back pockets, too, lifting the hem of her top to check. Jamie let out a slow breath and lowered it, going over the rest of the victim, inch by inch. 'She's got no jewellery – but you can see that there's a slightly paler band on her left wrist – so she wears a watch, usually. Probably takes it off to play. Either way, I don't think it was stolen, the wallet either. Not by whoever did this.' Jamie bit her lip and looked around. 'I think she knew this area, knew that there was a chance she'd get mugged – so she didn't bring anything with her. Just the phone and her violin.' Jamie stood now and checked the floor around her feet, around the violin case. 'She wasn't busking by the look of it – no hat or plate, and she wouldn't let people toss coins into her case.' Jamie furrowed her brow. What the hell was she doing down here then? And with an antique violin, too. Jamie closed her eyes for a second, heard the faint whispers of voices echoing down from the street, reverberating in the tunnel.

The acoustics.

She had just come down here to play.

That was it.

Hassan folded his arms and looked at her. 'How did she die? How do you see this playing out?'

Jamie didn't like conjecturing at this stage, but Hassan was struggling to visualise how this went down.

'I'd say…' she started, tentatively. 'This doesn't strike me as a spur of the moment kill.' She narrowed her eyes at the body. 'But it doesn't quite have a planned precision, either.' She pointed at the girl's neck. 'You can see there's a hand mark there, fingers – sunk in deep at the right side – her left – killer's right hand – but also a welt at the front of the throat, here,' she said, touching her own neck, just under the soft patch of flesh below her chin.

Jamie swallowed and stepped around to the side, looking at the back of her head.

'Yeah,' she said, carrying on. 'There's a little bit of blood here, too – hard to see, but look.'

Hassan moved to the other side and squinted down.

'See how it's dried there in the hair?'

He nodded.

Jamie turned to the wall behind the victim. 'Yeah, here,' she said pointing and standing up. There was a faint mark on the wall at about head height. 'This is where she hit her head – not hard enough to crack the skull – there's no blood – but enough to daze her, for sure.'

Hassan took note of that too.

Jamie was already back in front of her. 'I'm going to say cause of death is blood loss.'

Hassan made a face like he didn't know if that was supposed to be some sort of joke considering the huge pool of blood that spread out in front of the girl.

It wasn't. 'Single stab-wound to the abdomen,' Jamie said, crouching to get a better look. 'One, hard motion – deep. Looks like a big knife.'

'Big enough to cut someone's hands off?'

Jamie said nothing. She hadn't come to the hands yet.

She closed her eyes and stood, visualising it. 'He's standing, watching,' Jamie mused, backing up until the girl was directly between her and the mark her head had left on the wall. Right where the killer would have stood. 'He waits for her to finish – to put the violin away, and then comes at her.' Jamie lifted her right hand. 'He charged, grabs her by the throat, drives her back into the wall. That explains the impact mark on her neck, the blood on the back of her head.' She raised her left hand now, gripping an invisible knife. 'He takes the knife out, and stabs her once – roughly. With his off-hand.'

'And then?'

'Then…' Jamie opened her eyes. 'She falls to the ground – bleeding – a lot, and he takes the knife to her hands.' That didn't sound very concrete.

'Didn't the witnesses say she screamed?'

'Yeah. That's what alerted them.' Jamie bit her bottom lip and knelt again, finally looking at the girl's wrists.

She was still trying to be careful not to move or remove anything, and whatever she touched, she put back. The violin, the phone, the way the hems were draped around her thighs.

The girl was on her side, her knees raised to around naval height, her feet slightly tucked under her legs. A natural position to curl into, if you were dying, Jamie thought.

But the arms were positioned just so – placed in front of the face, wrists stacked, stumps together.

The girl's face was blank, the stare vacant, eyes open.

Jamie was low now, leaning in over the blood to look at the wrists.

They were roughly cut. Hacked was the word that came to mind. More with force than precision.

If the couple were within earshot, then they were close by. The killer did this quickly, in case they came back. Maybe they did? Jamie would question them when she got outside.

For now, she had to look at the scene.

There were no bloodied footprints, And the blood pool was wide now.

Her arms had blood on them, but the streams had run upwards, towards the elbows.

Her hands had been held aloft when they were removed.

Jamie closed her eyes, visualising it, and went back to the girl's stomach.

It was soaked with blood – from the stab wound – that made sense.

She moved upwards now, towards her collar again.

She couldn't reach it – the blood pool was too wide.

Jamie made a little growling noise and drew a breath. 'Hassan,' she said, calling him over. 'Take my hand.'

She held her left up and he took hold of her wrist, her own hand curling over his forearm.

'Got my weight?' she asked.

He nodded. 'Sure?' One of his eyebrows raised, but he didn't question her.

She leaned over without saying another word, suspended above the blood pool, and reached out for the girl's collar. With her index finger, she pulled it down and saw what she expected to, bruising. In the shape of the toe of a shoe.

'That's good,' she said, and Hassan reeled her in with one arm.

She regained herself, blew a puff of air out of her mouth to get a strand of hair off her face, and then couldn't help but think how Roper wouldn't have – or couldn't have done that.

She was liking Hassan's quiet and obliging detective style more and more.

'The killer,' she said, getting more of a picture of things now. 'Rushes at her, grabs her by the throat, drives her back into the wall.' Jamie touched the back of her head. 'Smacks her head. He stabs her once, hard.' Jamie glanced at the girl. 'Right in the middle of the torso, here' — she touched her midriff, just below the solar plexus — 'hits the aorta. By the time she realises what's happening, she's on the ground – manages to scream.' She let her eyes close, raising her arms until they were above her, hands together. 'He grabs hold of her hands, holds them up, puts his shoe on her chest to keep her down, and then cuts them off.'

'Both at the same time?' Hassan asked, trying to play it out in his own head.

Jamie pressed her mouth into a line. 'Maybe? Or one at a time. She'd be weak, losing lots of blood, probably going into shock. I don't think she'd put up much of a fight at that point.'

'Damn,' Hassan said, looking down at her. He blew out a long breath of air, and ran his big hands over his slicked-back black hair. 'Brutal.'

Jamie nodded. 'Yeah – but he knew he was rushed – did it quickly. Had to.'

'Must have been a big knife,' Hassan added.

'Yeah,' Jamie said, looking at the wrists – at how mauled the skin was. 'Or a saw. Something serrated. Look at the cuts.'

Hassan glanced down. He obviously wasn't squeamish, but this was a far cry from what he was used to, and Jamie could see that looking at her was tough.

She thought he had a daughter. A girl and a boy, if she remembered right.

He probably found it hard not to draw that comparison.

It took her a long time to be able to distance herself from the bodies that lay before her. But she'd gotten there in the end, and so would he.

'So,' Hassan said, clearing his throat. 'Was this premeditated? If he's walking around with a knife or saw in his pocket…'

Jamie clicked her teeth together. 'I don't know – but it doesn't strike me that way. I think he's been thinking about it for a while maybe… But I just don't know. If I had to make a guess…' She drew a slow breath. 'I think this is his first time. His first kill. It was messy, rushed… I don't think it went how he imagined… The urge just took him.'

Hassan processed that. 'So what now?'

'Now,' Jamie said, checking her watch and sighing. It was closing in on one a.m. 'We question the witnesses, wait for the SOCOs to arrive, and then… with some luck, make it home in time for the sun to come up.'

He sighed with her, pulled out his phone. 'Guess I should text my wife,' he said sullenly.

'Probably,' Jamie said, not bothering to check her own phone. She knew no one would have texted her.

She swallowed hard and cleared her throat heading for the sheet again.

The smell of blood faded away behind her as she walked back up the tunnel, glad that she could focus on work.

Behind her, Hassan was tapping away on his screen.

Jamie picked up the pace, pulling away from him, letting the sound of his thumbs fade among her footsteps.

She went back to the girl, in her mind – the way that it had all gone down – and settled on one question that Hassan hadn't asked, and that she didn't have an answer for. Just why had he taken her hands in the first place?

And perhaps worse – what exactly did he intend to do with them?

5

JAMIE PULLED the second sheet to the side and stepped back into the early morning air.

She immediately clocked Officer Davies and the miserable looking witnesses and walked over.

When she was within a few metres, she could hear Davies telling them that they needed to wait for the detective to arrive before they could leave.

They were jostling from foot to foot, shivering a little.

Jamie knew that they wouldn't be too responsive, but a night of sleep and talking about it to each other would only fog the details in their mind.

She didn't doubt the officer's note-making ability, but it was always best to hear it straight from the source.

Jamie came up on Davies' shoulder, making sure to position herself so that the witnesses had their backs to the crowd.

She put out her hand to the both of them – the woman first, reading the relationship dynamic – and waited for her to shake it.

The woman clasped it quickly, jiggled it rather than shaking, and made a point of looking away.

'Detective Sergeant Jamie Johansson,' Jamie said, smiling warmly.

'I want to thank you for waiting for me. Sorry that it took so long.' Jamie wasn't sorry.

'Mm,' the woman said, still looking into the distance.

'George,' the man said, smiling back at Jamie. His eye contact was making up for the both of them. Jamie struggled not to look down. 'And this is Nicola,' he said sullenly, gesturing to his wife with a sideways nod that told Jamie everything she needed to know about them as a couple. 'Bennet,' he added.

Jamie nodded, stored it, and then sighed emphatically, putting her hands on her hips.

She shook her head a little, looked down, and then back up at George, meeting his eye. 'I'm sorry, George, I really am,' she said, brushing an errant strand of hair behind her ear. 'I wish I didn't have to ask – I know you've been through this already, but I really need your help.'

He flushed a little. 'I…' he started, then cleared his throat, dropping his voice a few notes. 'I'll do what I can,' he said confidently.

Jamie knew that Nicola would do nothing except be difficult, and that George was rarely called upon – and when he was, he wasn't thanked. They didn't strike Jamie as a happy couple, but she knew that George would jump at the chance to be useful.

To someone.

'Good, good, thank you, George,' Jamie said, ignoring the audible tut from his wife.

He nodded, puffed out his chest a little, and then nodded to show he was ready.

Davies watched intently from Jamie's shoulder, studying her rather than the witnesses. He was aspiring to be a detective, Jamie thought. Though she didn't have the time nor the energy at this time in the morning to look at him, let alone ask him what his hopes and dreams were.

Jamie cleared her throat, kept her eyes on George's, counted to three in her head, and then began. 'So you were there, you said – you walked past, and then you heard screaming?'

George thought on the event and then nodded. 'Yes, we were

headed home from dinner. She was playing – we walked past, and then as we got to the end of the tunnel, we heard her scream.' He nodded again, to confirm his statement to both himself and Jamie. Nicola continued to look away.

'Did you see anyone else down there? Apart from the, uh, violinist, I mean.' Jamie had to be careful not to use the word victim. Often witnesses tended to compartmentalise events like this and using words like that could break down those fragile walls.

He blew out a long stream of sour, coffee-scented breath, and then screwed up his face. 'You know, I don't know.'

Jamie narrowed her eyes a little.

'Maybe? We were walking quickly, talking – you know,' he said, laughing nervously.

Nicola snorted but didn't look around.

'I understand – it can be difficult to remember, sometimes. It's okay.'

Nicola muttered something under her breath that Jamie didn't catch.

She needed to focus on George.

He closed his eyes and then reached to his left shoulder with his right hand.

George clasped at the fabric there and tugged. 'Wait,' he said, opening his eyes and looking at his hand. 'There was someone. I bumped into them.'

He looked up at Jamie, seemingly pleased with himself.

Jamie's chest tightened but she kept her face straight.

Suspect? Witness? The killer?

'That's great, George. Can you remember anything else about them?'

He pursed his lips. 'I don't – maybe a man. I think? I remember they felt solid. Were wearing a coat, maybe?'

Nicola tutted again and looked around. 'God, you are useless,' she said cuttingly. 'It was a man. In a black hooded sweatshirt.'

Jamie let her eyes drift slowly to Nicola, who was shaking her head at her husband.

'You bumped into him as we walked past.'

Jamie processed, wondered if Davies had that in his notes already or if Nicola's overwhelming need to belittle George had jogged her memory. 'Is there anything else you can tell me about him? Did you see his face? Hair colour? What else he was wearing?'

'No,' Nicola said. 'He had his hood up, hands in his pockets, I think.'

'I think—' George started before being cut off by his wife.

'You don't think anything.' She gritted her teeth. 'If you can't remember to make a simple dinner reservation, you certainly can't remember anything of use about someone you weren't even sure existed ten seconds ago.'

Jamie bit her lip.

George shrunk.

She wanted to get them apart – needed to, but she couldn't squander this momentum.

'Nicola,' Jamie said, turning to her. 'Can you tell me exactly what happened, once more. Just so I have it straight in my head. Please – it would be really helpful to the investigation. So we can map out a timeline.'

Nicola's jaw flexed, her skin shining in the glow of the streetlights. Her face was lined, her eyes coloured with a purplish eyeshadow that made her look like a peacock. 'Of course. Someone needs to be of help.'

Jamie smiled politely.

'We were walking through the tunnel,' Nicola said. 'The girl was playing that music – god-awful. Tuneless – and then it stopped, and there was screaming. We froze – couldn't quite see what was happening – we were already out of the tunnel and up the slope. Then it stopped.' She swallowed, rattled by reliving it. 'And then we stepped back down to see – and called the police as soon as we saw the blood.'

Jamie kept her eyes on Nicola. 'Good. Thank you.' Something was niggling at her. 'Was there a long pause between the music stopping and the screaming?'

'Hmm,' Nicola said, furrowing her brow. 'I don't think so. Maybe a few seconds.'

'A few? Two, five?' Jamie pressed, hearing Hassan coming up behind her.

'I don't know. A few. Not long at all though. It seemed like as soon as she stopped playing, there was screaming.'

'Was it one scream? Disjointed? Did you hear any other voices?'

Nicola was shaking her head. 'No, nothing like that – it was just music,' she said, chopping the air with her hands. 'A couple of seconds of silence, and then the scream.'

Jamie went over it in her head again. So the girl is playing, she finishes, puts away her violin, stands back up, and he charges at her. But how long would it take for her to put her violin away? He waited for her to finish playing, but why? He liked the music. He waited for her to put the violin away. Why? He respected the instrument. Did he talk to her? Did he ask her something while she was putting the violin away? She gave an answer he didn't like, he decides to kill her then?

No, that didn't add up. Nicola said a few seconds, then a couple of seconds. Two, three, four at a push? That wasn't much time to elapse. Especially not for conversation.

So the violinist finishes playing, puts the violin away, turns around to face the killer, and…

No, that would take too much time if Nicola's story was anything to go by. Especially when you factor in the fact that she was driven back against the wall, too. She wouldn't have made a noise – didn't, according to Nicola – but then as he took his hand off her throat and wrestled her down, foot on the chest – she let out the scream.

So the killer waits for the violinist to finish, then lunges at her. She hits her head on the wall. The killer releases his grip. She screams. One, two – yeah, that worked time-wise. But that would mean that she still had the violin in her hand.

There weren't any marks on it though – it wasn't dropped.

Did she hold onto it the entire time? It meant a lot to her. But how would it end up back in the case? Did the killer put it back in there? Did he pull it from her hand and put it in the case?

That would explain the screaming – she'd have time to scream if he was doing that.

If he did, then it meant that he cared enough about it to make sure it was safe. More so than stifling her scream. But if he cared about it so much, why wouldn't he steal it? If he knew what it was, what it was worth, why not just take it – to sell it, or even to have?

And why the hell would he take her hands?

Whatever the reasons, she couldn't assume that he was operating on the same wave-length as her or even a sane human being.

If the crime was illogical, then that pointed to some sort of mental instability. If that was the case and there was a documented history of it. Of violence, or treatment, even, then it wouldn't be too difficult to find some suspects – they'd all be in the government databases. Especially if he'd received NHS treatment.

'Jamie?' It was Hassan, at her shoulder.

'Yeah?' She snapped out of her train of thought and looked around at him.

He gestured to George and Nicola Bennet, who were both staring at her, as was Officer Davies.

She'd been silent for longer than she'd meant to.

A wave of fatigue washed over her suddenly and she glanced down at her watch. Nearly one.

She blinked a few times and cleared her throat. 'Thank you,' she said to them. 'Officer Davies,' she said, turning to him. 'Make sure to take their contact information – and give them the number of the support line, too.' She turned to the Bennets. 'If you need anything, or want to talk about what happened – events like this can be traumatic – then call the support line. And if you remember anything else, or would like to discuss what happened, then call me directly.' She already had a card out of her inside chest pocket on autopilot, presenting it to them.

Nicola took it and folded it into her hand. 'I will,' she said, not even glancing at George's outstretched hand. He was going for the card too.

He retracted it and bowed his head.

'Officer,' Jamie said, nodding to Davies. 'Mr and Mrs Bennet.'

They let Jamie go without another word.

She turned and headed for the car, Hassan in tow.

'What do you think?' he asked.

Jamie sighed, pulling Smith's number up on her phone. 'I think it's a weird one.'

'What's your first thought? Where do we go from here?'

Jamie's thumb hovered over Smith's name. 'My first thought is that this guy is dangerous.'

Hassan pressed his lips together.

'That there's something more going on here – that he knew the victim. That he knows music. Classical music. That he knows instruments. Maybe even that one specifically. Maybe he's a musician, too. There was something about her – or that piece – that set something off in him. That drove him to murder here, in plain view of whoever might be happening by. Regardless of the consequences.'

'So this was, what, a rage killing? He didn't like the music?'

'I think it's the opposite.'

'Jealousy?'

Jamie bunched her face up. 'No, it doesn't strike me as angry like that.'

'Angry?' Hassan raised an eyebrow. 'You don't think shoving someone back against a wall, stabbing them in the chest with a knife, and then cutting their hands off strikes you as *angry?"*

Jamie drew a slow breath, scanned the crowd again. 'No. Passionate, yes. But angry, no.' She was searching for the right word. 'Frantic.'

'What?'

'The kill seemed frantic – rushed. Not planned. A heat of the moment thing. He had tunnel vision. The couple was close by, the risk was huge for him. But he couldn't resist it. The kill was frantic.'

'Okay, so where does that leave us?'

'It leaves us with a lot. But nothing to do tonight. He was rough, rushed with her hands. It dawned on him that time was short, that the risk was high. That he needed to get out of there fast. But whatever drove him to do this wouldn't let him leave her hands behind.'

'So you think it was more about the girl's hands than the girl?'

She was afraid to say.

'Fetish thing, you think?'

'I don't know.'

Hassan ran his hand over his head again and exhaled, pushing his hair to his scalp.

Jamie dialled for Smith and he picked up on the second ring. 'Yeah?' he said. 'What's the situation?'

'It's a strange one,' Jamie said, leaning back against her car. 'Single stab wound, hands hacked off. Witnesses don't have anything concrete – male, no description, hooded sweatshirt. Nothing else to go on from them. But we have a timeframe, can scrub through local CCTV,' Jamie looked around and spotted three cameras overlooking the street already. 'See if we can't track him coming in.'

'Is that all?'

'I have a few hunches. Nothing definite. But something to start running down if you want me on this.'

Smith was silent, thinking.

It was definitely something Jamie had never tackled before. And without Roper to help, she was more than in at the deep end. Though she didn't think she was in over her head. She always hated how those two things seemed to be synonymous. Still, it wasn't her choice, and she was just starting to get on Smith's good side. She didn't want to jeopardise that. 'I can stick around, wait for the SOCOs,' she said, not waiting for him to speak. 'I've got my laptop in the car – can write up a prelim for whoever takes over if you want—'

'No, no,' Smith said, sighing, still thinking.

Amherst and Brock usually took these kinds of cases, but Smith wasn't keen on passing them anything too big for obvious reasons. And the other senior detectives on his team were wrapped up with other cases.

'Can you handle this?' Smith asked, directly.

'I can,' Jamie said without hesitating.

'Okay.' There was no emotion in his voice. 'Then it's yours. For now. But Johansson, this is a big case, and remember that if you screw this up, it reflects directly on me.'

'I understand.'

'If I'm the DCI who assigns a DS to a murder case like this and they catch the guy – then it makes me look good. But if I assign an inexperienced, young, headstrong, stubborn, defiant, impetuous DS to a case like this – and they shit the bed…'

'I understand.'

'Good. Just so we're on the same page.'

'We are.'

'Okay. So you're going to do your dog-with-a-bone act, right? Same as you did with the Jade Circle case?'

'I'm not sure I know how to do it any other way.'

He drew a slow breath. 'Keep me posted.'

'Will do.'

He hung up.

Hassan eyed her.

'What?' she asked.

'You're grinning,' Hassan said.

'No I'm not,' Jamie replied, grinning.

'You really like your job, don't you?'

Jamie watched as the headlights of passing cars reflected in the high-vis jackets of the uniformed officers, as the silent blues on top of the patrol cars played off the buildings opposite.

How the police tape fluttered in the breeze.

How the plastic sheeting hanging over the mouth of the tunnel hid a bloody murder scene.

And thought that yes, she did really like her job. And that suddenly, she didn't really care if she watched the sun come up or not.

If she was there all night, there were worse places to be.

And that the feeling of catching whoever did this was worth it, a hundred times over.

'Yes,' she said, a look of determination spreading across her face. 'You're bloody right I do.'

6

THE SOCOs WERE there by one-fifteen, Jamie was off the scene half an hour later – things well in hand.

By four her phone buzzed to tell her that the body had been removed and the coroner had taken receipt of it.

By six, her alarm was going off because she forgot to unset it.

She was skipping her session with Cake that morning in favour of him helping her move.

Jamie stayed in bed until seven, which was a lie-in as far as she was concerned.

Her apartment was now all boxed up.

The bedroom was empty except for the bed and a neat stack of boxes against the wall.

As she sat on the edge of her mattress, for the last time, she stared around.

Ever since Elliot had broken in a few months ago, it hadn't felt like home anymore.

Jamie didn't know if it had before.

She'd had the locks changed and had an extra deadbolt put on, but she wouldn't put it past him to get in again if he wanted to. And he knew that Jamie's place would never be under surveillance, because she wouldn't tell anyone. She couldn't, without compromising herself.

Which meant, if he was so inclined, he could walk in any time he liked.

And while he seemed to be more inclined to help than harm at the moment, if the mood took him, he could get in there and slit her throat in the middle of the night and there was nothing she could do about it.

Since that night, three months ago, she hadn't seen or heard from him. No postcards to add to her wall, no messages of any kind. Nothing.

And not knowing his whereabouts was almost worse.

She sighed and looked at the wardrobe – the well-built, custom, mirror-doored wardrobe that hid her secret: her project wall with the pins and postcards that chronicled and tracked Elliot Day's journey.

And now it lay dormant, unfinished.

She hadn't taken it down yet. It was the last thing.

Jamie pulled her eyes away from the mirror, a tired and unfamiliar woman staring back out of the glass suddenly, and wondered if she'd put it up again in her new apartment. Or if Elliot had seen it, realised that she was hunting him – would always be hunting him – and had decided that the risk wasn't worth the reward.

That he would finally just leave her alone and move on with whatever semblance of a life he was now living.

Somehow, she didn't think she'd heard the last of him.

Jamie exhaled, picked up her phone, and opened the app that was linked to her coffee machine. She hit the button and it started grinding beans in the other room, ready to make a fresh pot.

Thirty minutes after that, Jamie was kneeling in the wardrobe in silence, putting a rubber band around the postcards, her coffee steaming next to her. She slipped them into a large envelope, sealed it, folded the empty space at the top over, and then wrapped that in a rubber band, too. She slotted them into the top of the box that she'd brought in with her, burying them among her winter clothes – thermal base layers – that she rarely used unless she was headed out of the city hiking or if the weather was severe.

She couldn't remember the last time she'd gone hiking.

She supposed there was a social element to it that she was lacking.

Jamie cleared her throat, spooled the yarn she'd used to link the pins in the map together, and then pushed that into the box too.

She took all the pins out and popped them into the plastic cup she'd double-side-taped to the wall.

That went in, too.

Then came the map.

She folded it as neatly as she could and placed it into the box, pushing the creases down to stop it from unfurling itself.

Then, there was just one thing left.

Jamie swallowed and reached for a shoebox in the bottom of the wardrobe. The last one there. The one she'd intentionally missed.

She lifted the lid and stared down at a small black flip-phone, it's monochrome display dark.

Jamie picked it up, holding it like it was about to explode, and then put it face-down on top of the map, willing it to stay silent forever.

She grabbed the lid quickly, stripped off a length of packing tape in silence, and secured it shut.

And then it was done. She was packed.

It seemed like no time after, Cake was there with the van. She'd arranged to hire it, but had given Cake the cash and asked him to use his name and pick it up.

He'd obliged her. Could tell it was important, or at least that she wouldn't ask if there wasn't a reason.

He didn't pry.

She appreciated that.

By eight, Hassan had arrived, too.

Roper showed up late, as usual, to 'supervise'.

As little help as he was going to, or could be, he'd seemed insistent on coming.

Jamie thought that there was a two-fold reason for this. Firstly, because he'd never seen the inside of her apartment, and he wanted to see how Jamie lived. And secondly, because he was afraid of being left out.

He didn't have a lot of people in his life – and was good at pushing the ones he did have away.

With Hassan filling his shoes – and doing a pretty good job – he was trying to make sure Jamie remembered who her *real* partner was. His words, not hers.

Hassan and Cake ferried boxes up and down the stairs, chatting idly – mostly about how they knew Jamie, what they did for a living, and then suddenly, about boxing. Both of which they seemed to have a deep-seated love for. Jamie knew Cake had always followed it, but Hassan had never mentioned it.

Though she supposed that she hadn't really spent that much time talking about anything outside of work – and with his wife and kids waiting, he always rushed off after his shifts.

The three of them moved through her apartment, touching her things, taking them away, and she realised that she didn't really know any of them.

And that they were probably her closest friends.

'Bit slow, aren't they,' Roper said, coming up on Jamie's shoulder, slurping at a cup of coffee. He nodded at Hassan and Cake, both of whom were moving towards the door, carrying Jamie's sofa between them.

She was standing at the kitchen counter, the last of her utensils, cutlery, and other bits and pieces in a box next to her.

Jamie glanced at it, then at Roper, smiling. It faded quickly. 'Where did you get that cup?'

He dipped his head over his shoulder at another cardboard box on the counter. It had been pulled open and a strip of bubble wrap laid crumpled next to it.

'I just packed that,' Jamie said with a sigh.

'Should have left a cup out, then.' Roper shrugged.

'Your cup is right there.' Jamie pointed to the opposite counter.

'Oh,' Roper said, trying to be endearing. His boyish grin didn't suit him.

Jamie didn't think that she meant that much to him – or anything, really. But here he was, trying to make a charming nuisance of himself for the sake of memorability.

'Just rinse it out and put it back when you finish,' she said with a sigh. Somehow, she wasn't in the mood to joke around.

She looked down at the picture in her hands. She'd been holding it for five minutes straight.

There wasn't much in the way of memorabilia in her apartment – especially not from her childhood. There were only two photos in the entire place. One that usually sat on the book case behind her TV, a picture of her father in dress uniform, taken when he'd been promoted to *Kriminalinspektör,* the equivalent to a Detective Inspector. It was as high a station as he ever reached.

She'd heard that he had turned down a promotion – didn't want to get stuck behind a desk running a unit. Always said he'd belonged on the streets, hunting down criminals like the animals they were.

That picture was taken two years after she was born, and was already boxed up.

It had been given to her at her father's funeral, by one of his colleagues who had brought it from his desk at work. Said she should have it.

The one she had in her hand now was the only one she had of them both together.

She was six – and they were a hundred miles north of Stockholm.

Her father was kneeling behind her, grinning, one hand on her shoulder. Jamie was standing on the bank of a river, her hands next to her head, suspending a river pike that was nearly as tall as she was.

A *gädda,* it was called.

She still remembered that day.

Her father had coached her through it, helped her land it. She'd begged him to take the rod, to help her, but he had refused.

You do it on your own, or you fail on your own.

He'd never been much for helping. Never been a hands-on father.

But he taught her a lot.

Everything she knew.

Her fingers curled around the photo and she looked at it.

Her mother had the rest of them – hidden away somewhere, Jamie thought. She told Jamie she'd lost them all and every time Jamie brought it up, her mother picked an argument over it.

And short of raiding her attic, she didn't know what she could do. Her relationship with her mother was hanging by a thread anyway and doing that would sever it altogether, she thought.

What passed between her parents in those final years Jamie didn't really know. She was shielded from it. But her mother was still raw.

Guilty.

Sorry.

Angry.

Angry that Jamie's father could do so much wrong to her and then still come out as a noble martyr.

Jamie didn't see it that way – not exactly.

He'd killed himself.

Jamie didn't think there was any nobility in that.

But her mother thought there was. Or at least claimed it so she had one more thing to be angry at him for.

He may have started it all, but she was no saint, either.

Jamie was just sad that she couldn't speak to him in those final years, not really, and that she hadn't been allowed to. That she was told by her mother he didn't want to know her. Didn't want her.

That she was all Jamie had.

But it was a lie. He'd wanted to be in her life.

Now that he was dead, Jamie knew it was the truth.

And that hurt worse than anything.

'Nice photo,' Roper said, standing awkwardly next to her, looking over her shoulder. 'Trout?'

Jamie exhaled slowly. 'Sure.' She dropped the photo into the box, covering it up with bubble wrap, and then closed the lid, interlocking the flaps so it stayed closed.

'I went fishing once,' Roper said.

'Oh yeah?' Jamie answered, looking around to see what else there was to pack.

'Didn't catch anything though. The guy I was with – Andy his name was – forgot to bring bait. Brought a cooler full of beer instead.' He started laughing to himself. 'So we sat there with baitless lines in the water, got a bit worse for wear and then decided we should try and catch it like those – you know, the tribe that's… Where is it? It doesn't matter – but we took off our shoes and socks and waded in up to our knees, tried to grab a fish right out of the water with our hands.' He continued chuckling. 'Though the only thing I caught was tetanus as I managed to stand on my own fishing hook. Probably should have reeled them in before we tried it!'

Jamie looked around at him. 'Funny story.'

Roper read the look on her face and cleared his throat. 'You probably had to be there.'

'Probably.'

Jamie took her own car, the box with the picture in it on her passenger seat, and led the way.

It was just before nine when they pulled up outside Jamie's new apartment.

The building was an old, narrow townhouse on a treelined street built some time around the turn of the twentieth century. It was two stories with an attic conversion and had been turned into a duplex.

A Polish family owned it and had lived there since the seventies. All of the children had now grown up and left, and the owner had died, leaving it to his widow.

She didn't want to move from the house – refused to leave was more accurate – and released capital by converting the top two floors into another apartment, and lived on the ground floor.

The upstairs apartment needed work, but Jamie didn't mind. What she liked most about it was having to go through two doors to get to the main stairs.

The front door let into an old hallway which led to the staircase. The door to the right, before you got to it, which had originally let into the living room was now the main door for the ground floor apartment.

The stairs were blocked off from the hallway by Jamie's front door.

Anyone coming through would have to get through both doors, and Jamie liked that a lot.

Though what sold her most of all was the fact that the woman who owned it was in her eighties, didn't speak a lot of English, and definitely wasn't prepared to hand over a lick of her income to the government.

There was no tenancy agreement, no standing bank transfer, no paper trail.

Every month, she would put an envelope of money through Mrs Iwankowski's door – pronounced *I-van-kowski* – and that covered her water, heating, and rent. The only thing she'd need to get sorted out was her internet. She thought she could live without a TV license and make do with Netflix and YouTube and keep her name and new address out of that too.

And while she got the internet thing figured out – she was hoping that if Mrs Iwankowski didn't have it, she could register it in her name and just tack it onto the bill – she'd bought an extra twenty-five gigabytes of data for her phone and would hotspot it until then.

She pulled in at the curb and got out, heading for the front door.

Cake pulled in behind her, followed by Hassan and then Roper. Hassan was driving a mid-range BMW four-by-four – and Roper was of course in his last-legs Volvo.

Mrs Iwankowski was on the doorstep before Jamie even got to it.

She was all but bald, a coloured scarf wrapped around her head, a few wisps of white hair poking from under it.

Her body had curved over like a dandelion and a cane had been used to prop up the part leaning over.

She clung onto it with both hands, the knuckles hidden somewhere inside the shawl-cum-curtain she had draped over herself.

Both Cake and Hassan came up behind Jamie and stared up at the building – which by all accounts, was falling into disrepair.

'Mrs Iwankowski,' Jamie said brightly. 'Good to see you again.'

The old woman looked from Jamie to Cake and Hassan and back. 'You said you live alone,' she droned with a heavy accent, narrowing her eyes.

'I do – I am,' Jamie said. 'They're just helping me to move.'

She said something in Polish, flapped one arm at Jamie, and then began to turn slowly away. 'Key in front door. Don't lose – only one.'

Roper hobbled up finally as the woman crossed the threshold. 'She seems nice,' he said.

Hassan elbowed him. 'Maybe you two can swap walking sticks, eh, mate?'

He tottered, grimaced, and then swore under his breath. 'Piss off.'

Jamie couldn't help but smirk at that one. 'Come on you two, you can fight upstairs.'

She led the way into the hall and unlocked the front door. She wasn't the first tenant to rent the duplex, but she couldn't get a straight answer as to what happened to the last one.

She'd found the listing in the newspaper of all places. Jamie figured if there was one way to stay off Elliot's radar it would be doing it this way. The situation wasn't ideal, but she'd definitely sleep better knowing he couldn't find her. Feeling the city around her like a shell, shielding her, hiding her from his reach.

The convoy trudged up the creaking staircase and onto the first floor.

Directly at the top was the bathroom, and to the right of it the stairs wrapped around onto a landing, with the next flight going up overhead.

The two bedrooms which had been on this floor had been knocked into one large room.

Both doors still remained. One at this end, and one at the far end of the landing.

At the front, a pair of windows looked down into the street, a sizeable beech tree obscuring the view.

The floor was bare boards, the walls peeling wallpaper.

An old fireplace sat facing into what used to be the front bedroom, the grate built right into the brick.

There was a draft coming through it already and it wasn't even windy.

At the back was a shabby, cheaply installed kitchen that looked to be pushing a decade old judging by the discolouration of the tops.

It clung to one wall, a free-standing cooker its rusted centrepiece.

In front of that was an old table and chairs that the previous tenant had left. Worn wood.

And behind that was a glass door and pair of windows that let out onto a steel balcony and staircase. It wound down to the ground, into a small, enclosed back garden hemmed in by crumbling walls.

Mrs Iwankowski also had a door that led onto it, but never used it. It was too much for her, and the arcing brambles were now too much for anyone to tackle without the use of power tools, or at least far too much time to waste.

It made the garden impassable from the outside. Which was perfect. No way in. Although she thought Jamie thought she could leap from the balcony over the neighbouring wall and land in their garden if it really came to it.

Jamie saw it as a potential escape route.

Just in case.

A long way down and a long way over, but she'd risk breaking an ankle if it was life or death.

Upstairs was a large, open-plan bedroom in the eaves of the roof. It had a pitched ceiling and a pair of big skylights.

'So…' Jamie said, breaking the silence that had fallen over the guys.

They all stood frozen in the rear doorway to the living room.

'It's, uh…' Cake started, not able to find the words.

'A shit-hole,' Roper finished, not pulling any punches.

Jamie pressed her lips into a line. It was definitely a project. But Mrs Iwankowski said she could do whatever she wanted to the place. Well, her actual words were, *I don't care what you do, so long as you're quiet.*

'Jamie,' Cake started, laughing nervously. 'When you asked me if I'd mind helping you out with a few bits around the new apartment, I didn't think it would be such a…'

'Shit-hole,' Roper reiterated.

Hassan scratched the back of his head. 'Yeah, uh – why *are* you moving here, Johansson? If you don't mind me asking.'

Jamie turned to him and shrugged. She didn't think saying that it was to escape a psychotic, obsessed serial killer would help the situation. 'It's closer to work, closer to the gym, it's bigger. The rent is cheap. Plus, the landlord is hiking up the rent at the end of my agreement at the last place.'

Hassan nodded slowly. 'Right.' He didn't seem convinced. And he definitely wasn't impressed. 'It's just that your old place was so…'

Clean? Neat? Modern? She could see him saying all of those.

'Nice…' He screwed his face up a little. 'And this place is so…'

'Shit-hole-y.' Roper said again.

'I was going to say, *not.*' Hassan furrowed his brow at Roper.

Jamie sighed. 'Yeah, well,' she said, wishing they'd all just stop talking and carry some boxes. 'Mrs Iwankowski's family all hate her, so when she leaves the building to me, I'll be the one laughing then.'

She breezed past them and down the stairs, going for the van.

It was true that the place was a shit-hole.

But it was a lie that Mrs Iwankowski's family hated her.

Though they didn't exactly *like* her. She'd gotten that much from the viewing when they'd all milled around in an angry silence offering her no help as she scuttled around with her cane in hand. But then again, how could they? She was a sour old woman who smelled like boiled cabbage and seemingly subsisted purely on a diet of vodka and bigos, judging by what was spilling from the recycling bins outside the front door. Which, understandably, didn't do a lot for her mood.

She sat in her front window all day and night, scowling at the world, glaring at everyone who walked past.

But Jamie thought that made the whole thing ideal.

The perfect guard-dog.

She'd love to see Elliot try and sneak past that.

The place needed work, but it could be made liveable – just – and it *was* decently priced. And Cake had already agreed to help get the plumbing up to scratch, as well as do a little job for her that day. And the electrics weren't too bad. With a little elbow grease effort, it would be okay.

And to Jamie, that was more than a fair enough trade off.

She got to her car and turned to look back up at the building, the beech tree leaves rustling gently above her.

She drew in breath and then let it out, wondering if this would ever be home. If she'd ever find somewhere that felt like that.

Or if, saddest of all, she'd know how it felt when she found it.

7

'WHAT HAVE YOU FOUND?'

Those words rang in Jamie's ear at the worst possible time.

She answered the phone to Smith just as Cake and Hassan were hauling her memory-foam mattress up the second flight of stairs.

'Uh,' Jamie said, watching as they came through the door. The three people who were supposed to be working the case were there in that apartment.

She cleared her throat instead, hoping he'd say he had to go or was getting another call. 'Turned up nothing so far – the girl had no wallet, no ID. But we're on it.'

'Mm,' Smith said, not buying it. 'And I suppose your lack of progress has nothing to do with the fact that Roper, Hassan, and you all have this morning booked off?'

'We'll be in soon,' Jamie said, not sure why she was feeling guilty. She was entitled to her holidays. Same as everyone else.

'You know, if you're trying to convince me I made the right choice letting you run this thing, you're not off to a great start.'

Oh yeah, that might be why. She unclenched her jaw and breathed in a dusty lungful of air. 'I've got this,' she said, turning to see Cake and Hassan standing next to the bed looking at her. 'We've got this.'

She gave them both a smile and they returned it, not sure what further physical labour they were blindly consenting to. 'SOCOs will have the report from the crime scene over today probably, coroner too.'

Hassan's face changed in realisation and he mouthed the word, 'Smith?' to her.

She nodded in confirmation.

'Good,' Smith said, still not buying it. 'And Johansson, if you need anything – you tell me, okay? We're on the same team, remember.'

'I know.'

'So if there's anything I can do to help things run smoothly, then I'll do it. It's important that—'

'Gretchen,' Jamie said quickly.

'What?'

'I want Gretchen. Fischer.'

'I know who you meant. I'm just surprised. Why?'

Jamie didn't really have that good of an answer, other than that Gretchen was the best cyber she'd ever worked with, and she wanted to surround herself with people she already trusted. 'She's good. The phone is all we have to go on unless the SOCOs turned something up at the scene. And it also gives us plausible deniability if anyone sees us together – when we're working the murder, or anything else.'

Smith drew in a slow breath, knowing that she wasn't wrong. 'She's tied up with a big tax-evasion case at the moment.' He paused for a few seconds. 'But I'll see what I can do. And when I call back, I expect you to have something.'

'We will,' Jamie said blindly.

Smith hung up and Jamie tapped the corner of her phone against her chin, looking at Cake and Hassan.

'Do we need to go?' Hassan asked.

Jamie thought for a second. 'Have you carried the TV up?'

'Not yet.'

'Then we've got time.'

. . .

Jamie waved goodbye to Cake as he climbed into the cab of the rental truck and pulled away from the curb.

She dispatched Roper back to HQ to link up with Gretchen, dig into the officers' reports from the scene, chase down the SOCOs, and to find out what CCTV covered the area – and then to get hold of it.

He didn't deal well with orders, certainly those coming from the person he used to outrank, and definitely not when they were stacked up like that.

Jamie and Hassan were headed to the coroner's office to check out the body. The initial assessment had been done, and Jamie wanted to get the coroner's take on what had gone down.

The report hadn't been filed, but Jamie needed to see for herself, to hit the ground running with this.

The trail was still fresh, and now that she had Elliot out of her head, she could focus.

She closed the car door and bathed in the solitude. Hassan had the address, she'd meet him there.

Twenty minutes later, she pulled in at the curb opposite the coroner's and got out, realising she'd sat in silence the entire way. She hadn't even had the radio on.

Her mind kept going back to the victim. Jamie didn't feel right about the scene. She was missing all her jewellery, and had no wallet. And there was nothing to say she was busking, either.

Could this have been a simple robbery and murder? Maybe they were sending a message by cutting off the hands. Some gang affiliation or even an initiation, maybe? It was gruesome, but it wasn't out of the question.

Hell, maybe they just hated classical music.

Hassan pulled in behind her and they crossed the road.

The air was humid, the sky turbulent and grey, but dry. There was no rain in the air. Just an eerie closeness that seemed to press in on Jamie's ears.

The clouds didn't move overhead. They just hung there. Silent and still.

Jamie and Hassan crossed quickly and went up the steps into the coroner's office.

The reason they were there was two-fold. As well as hearing it from the pathologist, she also wanted to pick up the victim's phone. All the belongings would be catalogued here, along with the violin, and swept for DNA and further evidence, before going to the evidence lock-up at HQ.

Jamie wanted to take another look at the instrument – and hopefully with Gretchen on the case, find out the value, and where it came from. Expensive instruments always had a history, and a history meant a trail. And any leads right now would be invaluable.

Though the violin was just one part of this puzzle that Jamie was yet to place.

Inside, the interior was cool and clean, an AC unit above the door blowing a stream of air down onto the faded tiles.

This office was a little more modern than the one Jamie and Roper had visited a few months earlier, but the lingering smell was the same. Bleach and formaldehyde.

The smell of dead things.

They approached the counter and Jamie lifted her warrant card reflexively. 'Detective Sergeant Jamie Johansson,' she said on autopilot. 'This is Detective Sergeant Paul—' She stopped, looking at Hassan. 'Sorry,' she said, to both the receptionist and her new partner. 'Force of habit.'

Hassan smiled charmingly at the woman behind the counter, his straight white teeth gleaming in contrast to the thick and perfectly groomed facial hair around his mouth. 'Special Officer Nasir Hassan,' he said, eyes flashing. 'How are you today?'

The woman flushed. She was in her fifties, her hair curled and bunched above her head in a red tangle, held there by a series of clips and bobbles. She grinned and then shook her head, her hair wobbling one way, the loose skin under her chin going the other. 'Oh, I'm fine – you know, same old, same old.' She laughed shrilly and Jamie winced a little.

Hassan chuckled disarmingly and Jamie felt her own cheeks warm.

'I'm glad to hear it,' he said, leaning forward, elbows on the counter. 'I was wondering if you could help me today?' His voice was like melted chocolate.

The receptionist nearly fell off her chair.

'Of course,' she said, finding her voice somewhere deep in her heaving bosom.

Jamie let him do… whatever it was that he was doing. He was handsome, sure, and muscular. Well groomed. Confident. Smooth-talking.

Not her type, but it seemed to have an effect on most women when he laid it on thick.

Which Jamie found that he often did.

Maybe it was the smile, maybe the deep brown eyes. Maybe it was the fact that his shirts were all one size too small. Or maybe it was the way he said 'Special Officer'— because he did like to say it a lot.

That was what Smith had dubbed him so that he didn't scare the shit out of anyone by introducing him as *Captain of Armed Response Nasir Hassan.*

Jamie didn't mind him working his charm on whoever he wanted to – it was a nice change of pace from Roper's dour insistence that he only needed a warrant card, and that manners without one would get you nowhere, so why bother using them when you've got the former in your pocket?

'We're looking for a young woman – she was brought in last night, no ID. Do you know who I mean?' Hassan asked, making the sort of face that indicated he hated to ask.

She bit her bottom lip, staring up at him over the counter like a headlight-struck rabbit. 'Hmm. I'm not sure. Sadly, we get more than one of those a night sometimes.' She looked up at Hassan with her version of doe eyes. 'Do you have any other information?' she asked dreamily.

Jamie expected she didn't see many people who looked like Hassan in here. Most of the coroners and pathologists she'd met in her life were of a type, and that didn't tend to be charming and desirable.

And the rest of the people in here were dead. She didn't expect that the receptionist was into those much. Especially considering it looked like Hassan was a single smile away from her launching herself over the counter at him.

Jamie couldn't stick it anymore. 'She had no hands.'

The receptionist's head swivelled towards Jamie and Hassan cocked his own, not lifting from the counter. He was looking at her as though she'd just yelled the worst swear word she knew.

Jamie cleared her throat. 'The victim. She had her hands cut off,' she said a little less forcefully.

'Ah,' the receptionist replied, giving Hassan a quick, nervous smile. 'That one. Let me get the information for you now.' She began tapping on her keyboard. 'Nasty business, that.'

'Terrible,' Hassan said. 'But don't worry.' His chest puffed a little. 'We'll catch the guy who did it. I promise you that.'

The woman's cheeks flushed again.

Jamie rolled her eyes.

She never thought she'd say it, but she was starting to miss Roper.

And that was saying something.

The body was in examination room two. The post-mortem was yet to be carried out, but initial assessment had been done.

The receptionist – who introduced herself as Lindsey as Hassan had started to move away; 'I'm Lindsey, by the way,' she'd said. 'You know, just in case.' She'd smiled longingly at him.

'Thanks, Lindsey,' he said, making serious eye contact with her. 'I'll let you know if we need anything else.'

Jamie let go of whatever mild irritation she had pent up and walked steadily towards room two.

The door was magnetically locked and needed a keycard to be opened, but the receptionist – Lindsey – assured Hassan that the doctor was in and that all they had to do was knock.

Jamie did so without hesitation and after a second, the door buzzed open.

She pushed inwards, the wood smooth beneath her fingers, and found the smell of bleach and bare metal thick in her nose. She grimaced a little at it, and then pressed forward.

Jamie expected she'd have to get used to that smell working murders in the city.

Examination room two was small.

The whole building was small, in fact.

This wasn't one of the largest in the city, but it was the closest to the murder site, and Jamie could see the pathologist had a few years of experience under his belt.

And a few pounds of skin hanging over it.

He was sixty-ish with a bald pate and grey hair pushed back over his ears. His nose was long and wide, like he was wearing one of those fake glasses-and-nose masks. Except he didn't have glasses. He barely had eyes.

They were pale green and hidden away behind thin folds of eyelid skin that a bloodhound would be jealous of.

'DS Jamie Johansson,' Jamie said. 'This is Special Officer Nasir Hassan.'

Hassan nodded but said nothing, back in detective mode. Observing. Learning. Like a switch had been flipped now that there were no women in the room.

She wondered for a second what that made her.

The pathologist was standing on the far side of a slab, the victim from the night before laying naked in front of him, a cloth covering her from the naval to the mid-thigh. Her skin was pale, grey almost in the harsh lighting. The heavy makeup of the night before, the shadowing on her almond-shaped eyes, the lipstick, it was gone. Wiped clean.

The pathologist looked out at them from his hidden eyes, hands loosely clasped in front of him, a tray table filled with scalpels, forceps, and a rib spreader.

'You're a little early,' he said in a droning voice. 'I haven't started yet.' There was no hint of anger or frustration in his voice. Just a simple, bored statement of fact. As though the young woman in front of him without any hands was of no interest at all.

Jamie could see now the gaping wound at her sternum, the dark, furious bruising around it from where the hilt had impacted the skin.

She dragged her eyes back to the pathologist. 'That's fine – we don't need the full report. Just wanted to check in, collect the belongings for evidence, see whether anything jumped out at you.'

'You mean besides the fact that someone had hacked her hands off?' He raised a bushy eyebrow.

'Yeah,' Jamie said, putting on a polite smile. 'Besides that.'

He looked at Jamie for a while and then lifted his hands, sighing as he did. He held them under his chin and drummed his thumbs together just next to his stubbled, draping neck. 'The victim,' he began, as though dictating for the file, 'Is approximately twenty to twenty-two years old. She is in good health, appears to be well-fed, not dehydrated.' He drew another breath and stared down at her. 'Cause of death,' he began again, his right hand moving out, index and middle fingers outstretched until they hovered above the sternum. 'Single stab wound to the chest. Single-edged blade approximately five centimetres in height, fifteen in depth. I suspect a hunting knife of some kind due to the shape of the wound and the bruising caused by the hilt. The blow severed the aorta cleanly, causing massive internal haemorrhaging. Her chest cavity would have filled in seconds, crushing her lungs.'

'So she suffocated?' Hassan asked, folding his arms, pinching his chin.

'No,' the pathologist replied flatly. 'She bled out far too quickly. With a cut like this, she would have lost consciousness in fifteen, maybe twenty seconds.'

Jamie played it over in her head. It fit with what George and Nicola had said – the scream. It has sustained for a while.

But then, as his boot came down on her chest, stifled it – then she passed out, and her lungs were crushed by her own blood. How long had she been awake for? How long had she known what was happening to her before she was allowed that reprieve of darkness?

'You can see here,' he said, moving on, 'that there are a series of bruises, in parallel lines.' He swept his fingers back and forth between her breasts. 'This kind of bruising pattern is congruent with a foot being placed against the skin and a large amount of weight applied steadily.' He looked up at them and Jamie's eyes moved from the thin, even, plum-coloured bruises to his face. 'Rather than a forceful impact.'

'He rested his foot on her chest?' Jamie confirmed.

'Placed it there, yes. His right foot, judging by the curvature of the tread marks.'

Hassan chimed in. 'Can we determine the boot size? The make? That will help us narrow it down,' he finished, turning to Jamie.

Jamie glanced over at him, keen for the pathologist to press on, and put a lid on it. 'It'll be a size nine or ten which narrows it down to ninety percent of the guys in the city, the tread-pattern will be almost impossible to match definitively to any specific shoe, and it wouldn't stand up in court anyway.' She wasn't trying to be unkind, but there was a lot of ground to cover, and she couldn't afford a single misstep.

Hassan didn't seem to take it personally. 'Alright,' he said. 'Sorry to interrupt.'

She felt bad anyway.

The pathologist continued unperturbed, moving from the chest. 'The bruising on her left wrist suggests that he grabbed hold of her arm with his left hand here, at the bottom of the forearm.'

Jamie looked at the girl's left wrist. There were clear fingermarks there.

'The cuts are different on each hand, curiously,' the pathologist said, moving his still outstretched fingers from one hand to the other. 'The left, as you can see here is much rougher – sawed through. But the edges are jagged, the cut not clean. He had to readjust to get around the bones – and there are some nicks in the flesh here and here where it seems to move off-line.' The pathologist looked up again and shrugged casually. 'Though I suspect that was partially down to the victim struggling against him and moving her hand as he was cutting.'

Jamie and Hassan both grimaced in unison.

'The way that he was trying to do it was completely inefficient,' the pathologist observed. 'There would be no steadiness to it. No tension in the wrist while he cut through it as he was holding below the cut, here, see?' he asked, gesturing to the girl's wrist and then holding his own arm upright, his hand flopping around atop it as he wiggled his elbow.

Jamie clenched her teeth, trying to ignore the ease with which he was making the statement, and the movement.

'Though he seemed to learn his lesson quickly,' he pressed on. 'The second cut, on the right wrist, here,' he said gesturing to it. 'Is much cleaner. And you can see the absence of bruising on the arm.'

Jamie and Hassan both had to lean over the slab a little to get a good look.

'The slight roughness you see here on the epithelial tissue, is congruent with tearing, rather than sawing. So I would think that he had the sense to hold onto her hand this time, and then with his boot on her chest, created that tautness in the wrist.' He clasped his hands together again. 'It would have made for a much easier and faster cut. Especially as she tried to pull her arm away from him – as the torn tissue suggests she did.'

Jamie tried to compartmentalise. 'Would you say your findings are congruent with this being a first kill?'

'Do I think the killer has done this before?' The pathologist's eyebrows bristled as he bent his loose face into a look of thoughtful reflection. 'No. I don't think he has. But do I think this is his first kill?' He paused, seemingly for dramatic effect. 'That I can't say. The single stab wound to the chest, right into the aorta? To the hilt of the knife, with this much definite force? It would strike me as odd to find out that this was his first kill. Perhaps his first human kill, but I believe he has experience using a knife, at the very least. It would take a strong stomach – and some imagination – to do this your very first time out of the gate.'

Jamie let her eyes unfocus as she tried to paint a picture of this guy in her head. Sociopath, possible psychopath? Criminal history? History of violence at least? Not a doctor or anyone who had any surgical knowledge, she didn't think. It was too brutal for that. Too haphazard. And she'd also seen what a psychopath with the skill to wield a scalpel could do. And how precise that was. She shuddered, driving her mind away from Elliot once again. So who was this guy then? What had put him in this position, to believe himself capable, and then convince himself to do it? The pathologist had said he'd used a hunting knife. Did he hunt? Did anyone in the UK? Maybe he fished. There weren't many places close to the city where you could fish and gut your own. Especially not where there was anything large enough to need a knife that size.

But she was just reaching now. She didn't know enough yet.

Her eyes drifted from the pathologist to the counter behind him, to the large, clear, ziplock bag resting there that contained the girl's clothes.

The girl.

Hell, she didn't even know her name yet.

No wallet, nothing to go on until they could get into that phone.

'So what is it about this girl that made the killer want to maim her so badly? That made him want to do *this* to her?' Hassan asked, maybe to the pathologist, maybe just out loud, looking down at her, the sadness clear in his eyes.

The words rang in the ether and Jamie's mind churned, a few pieces snapping into place suddenly.

The cuts.

The way he wanted to improve.

To do it better.

More cleanly.

To preserve.

'It's not about the girl,' Jamie said, her stomach twisting itself into a tight, nauseous knot. 'For him,' she said, looking up at Hassan. 'It's about the hands.'

8

Jamie and Hassan headed back to HQ.

The evidence bag rode on the seat next to Jamie, an inventory sheet stapled to the front of it.

All the victim had on her were her clothes, her phone, and the violin. That was next to the bag.

Jamie kept glancing at it, feeling like the answers were close at hand. But still just out of reach.

The SOCOs had dusted everything down before removing them to the lab for testing and now that the pathologist had swept them for DNA and trace particulate, taken all the samples they could, they needed to be logged in evidence.

She got there before Hassan and took the stairs up to the second floor, to the evidence room – a massive lock-up that occupied a large space right in the middle of the building that you couldn't get to without going through about fifty officers.

Jamie approached the window, the bag in her left hand, the handle on the case of the violin crunched into the plastic, the residual print-dust darkening her palm. She already had the file open on her phone, the case number showing on screen.

The woman at the window was maybe around the same age as Jamie, her hair pulled back into a tight ponytail.

She looked up from her computer screen, confined to her little booth.

She didn't seem thrilled with the posting.

'Checking some evidence in,' Jamie said, sliding her phone and warrant card under the window in front of her.

The clerk pulled the former towards her, checked the file number and then tapped it into her keyboard. 'Fill this out,' she said, pushing a clipboard back, along with Jamie's phone and warrant card.

Jamie pulled out the pen tucked under the clip and began writing into the boxes.

After she'd inputted the clothing, she wrote down the details of the phone, and then stopped.

Just simply writing *violin* didn't quite feel right. This thing was worth a lot of money. And was important enough for the killer to spend a few vital seconds putting it safely back into its case before he killed the girl.

Jamie swallowed.

The violin was *important*. To her, and to the case.

Antique violin.

It would have to do.

She sighed and put the pen down, pushing the clipboard back. 'I'll need to keep the phone, though – it's going straight to forensics,' Jamie said, opening the hatch next to the window and putting the bag and case on the tray inside.

The clerk checked the list over. 'We need to log it in the system, first.'

'Okay, how long will that take?' Jamie asked, knowing you couldn't just cut through the red tape.

The clerk looked up at her. 'I'm pretty busy. An hour maybe?'

'Can we do it any quicker?'

'I doubt it.'

Jamie held back her scowl. Maybe Roper would have something by now. 'Fine,' she said, taking a card from her jacket pocket and pushing it under the glass. 'Can you just call me when it's ready?'

'I don't know, like I said, I'm pretty busy.'

Jamie exhaled, feeling her fist clench at her side. 'Just call me, okay? It's important.'

'I'll try.'

'Thanks,' Jamie said, not meaning it.

She turned and walked away, knowing she'd have to check back herself.

She just hoped Roper did have something for her.

Though she doubted it.

It was Roper, after all.

9

As much as she hated the hold up, Smith hadn't given her the green light yet to get the phone over to Gretchen, and she was determined not to screw things up this early on.

She trusted Smith to go to bat for her – he'd said he would. So she just needed to let him grease the wheels. Whoever was in charge of Gretchen wouldn't want to lose her.

She was that good.

Jamie would just have to wait.

She checked her watch – it was nearly one now and her stomach was tight and gnawing on itself. She hadn't had lunch yet, and didn't bring anything with her.

Jamie paused on the stairs and looked over her shoulder.

She was headed to four to meet Roper – to ask him what he'd dug up so far.

But she needed to eat. And the longer she held off, the more time he would have to scrub through the CCTV and find something useful.

She pulled out her phone and opened the messaging app, opening her conversation with Roper. 'Found anything on the CCTV yet?' she wrote, hitting send.

The cafeteria was on the ground floor – and while Jamie generally avoided it – mostly because she hated waiting in line for anything and large groups of people weren't really her thing – the selection of healthy foods was getting better.

Looked like Jamie Oliver wasn't so bad after all.

Jamie exited the always-empty stairwell onto the ground floor, and immediately considered going out to get something instead.

She stuck to the wall and headed for the cafeteria at a quick walk.

The place was a zoo. Uniformed officers bustled, civilians thronged. It was open to the public too – or at least those who weren't actually police officers. Which included everyone who worked there and everyone visiting. Which always seemed to be a lot of people. Including school trips.

Jamie grimaced, lifting her elbows, and waded through a sea of white polo shirts and charcoal trousers, feeling their sharp shoulders and grubby hands rubbing across her jacket.

Why did children have no manners?

On the other side, she queued up for food and took a tray from the stack.

She let her eyes wander, and then stopped, freezing for a second.

She definitely should have gone out for food.

'Johansson.'

'Brock,' Jamie said, forcing a smile as Amy Brock, another female Detective in her unit, and one of the people she was investigating under Smith's command, clocked her and jogged over.

It looked like she was chatting to another officer, and as luck had it, hadn't grabbed food yet either. She snatched up a tray, beaming at Jamie. 'How's it going?' she asked, seemingly thrilled to see her. 'I don't think I've ever seen you in here before.'

'I usually bring my own,' Jamie said truthfully. Though she didn't know what else she could say – or how much she really should considering the investigation.

But then again, Brock, at first pass, had been clean as a whistle. Gretchen had said so. And was being too innocent a crime?

She didn't know.

But Jamie definitely wasn't getting a good vibe from her.

The friendliness was almost pantomime.

'Ah yeah,' Brock said, laughing a little. 'Not surprised. Too many calories in this shit, huh?' She gestured casually to the food that awaited them, steaming away in big steel trays.

One of the servers scowled at them, clutching a ladle.

'Something like that,' Jamie said, measuring Brock.

She always forgot how tall she was until she was standing right in front of her.

Brock was around five-nine, and a little broader than Jamie. She had strong shoulders, and carried herself powerfully, the muscles in her legs outlined in her tight black jeans.

Jamie wondered how many squats she did a week.

A million, she guessed, judging by the two clearly defined knuckles of muscle sitting side by side above her knee.

Brock had short, dark hair, and tanned skin. A strong jaw.

But her posture was relaxed, trying its best not be imposing.

'So, work getting the best of your schedule, huh?' she asked.

'Why'd you say that?'

'Well, no time to make your lunch this morning – and it's obviously important to you what you put in your body.' Brock looked Jamie up and down quickly and she felt a little vulnerable.

Jamie turned away so Brock was sort of at her shoulder, and shuffled forward in the line. 'You should be a detective or something,' she said, giving a quick smile.

People had begun to back up behind them now and there was no way Jamie could get out without it being obvious.

Brock laughed. More loudly than the joke warranted.

She was definitely trying to butter Jamie up. 'Hey, I'm sorry we never got to follow through on the whole De Voge—Kosiah bust. Wanted to see how that whole thing shook out. Heard you handled the hell out of it though. Hassan took a bullet, but you nailed De Voge on your own, right?' She let out a low whistle. 'He was a nasty piece of work. That's impressive.'

Jamie resisted the urge to say, *you would know*.

She looked at Brock for a while and then turned back to the lunch queue. 'Thanks,' she said, keeping it casual.

'Whatever happened to him, do you know?' she asked lightly, picking at a hangnail.

'Who? De Voge?'

'Yeah, well, Kosiah ate a few bullets by the sounds of it. But De Voge? Unless you put one in the back of his head, he seemed to drop off the face of the earth.' She shrugged nonchalantly.

'Yeah, I don't know,' Jamie replied, eyeing the food in front of her. There was something that looked like mashed potato, but it was an undulating, creamed yellow slab that didn't strike her as appetising. And there were pork steaks all layered up, swimming in their own juices that looked more like rubber than meat.

She spotted some salads in sealed containers, felt a little better, and eased forward.

'Just weird, is all. Was a big collar for us. Was hoping to read the interrogation notes – expected you to be handling it all things considered.' She chuckled again, and then lightly punched Jamie in the arm. 'What, did Smith pull you off it for being inexperienced? He's such a dick.'

Jamie pressed her lips into a line, seeing what Brock was doing. 'I think he was a witness in another case,' Jamie answered, throwing her a bone to try and get her off her back. 'Smith told me to leave it alone.'

She caught Brock eying her. 'So you did?'

'Yup.'

'You?' She raised an eyebrow. 'Who hounded me and Amherst to work our case when she wasn't even assigned to it? You let the biggest collar of your life go? Just like that?'

'What can I say?' Jamie said, pulling a salad onto her tray. 'Guess I learned my lesson about sticking my nose where it doesn't belong.' She smiled at Brock now, who was trying her best to read Jamie's expression.

Brock looked at Jamie and broke into a grin, revealing straight, narrow teeth. 'Yeah,' she said, brushing it off. 'You don't cross Smith more than once, amarite?'

Jamie nodded. 'Mm. He doesn't strike me as the forgiving type.'

'No – no,' she said, an audible pause between the words. She looked thoughtful for a moment. 'You're probably right there.' She drew a quick breath and then stopped, reaching to her hip. She laid her hand there. 'Oh, that's my phone,' she said.

Jamie couldn't hear it buzzing.

'I have to take this,' she pulled it free, not looking at the screen. 'Let's uh, get together some time. Grab a drink,' she said, stepping backwards out of the queue.

'I don't drink,' Jamie replied, still smiling.

'So order an orange juice.' Brock shrugged, dancing backwards towards the swelling crowd. 'And I still want that sparring session – you're a handful in the ring I hear,' she continued, rising to a light shout to penetrate the din. 'And I want to see what you're made of.'

Jamie watched her go, narrowing her eyes just a little. 'Yeah,' she muttered to herself. 'I want to see what you're made of, too.'

'Please tell me you've got something solid for us to go on?' Jamie pulled a wheeled office chair from an empty desk next to Roper's and sat down.

Hassan was on one of the guest desks a few over.

Jamie could see he was looking at knives online – trying to find one that matched.

Much like the boots idea, finding the right knife would be little to no use. Not unless they knew exactly where it was bought and when. And even then, they'd have to find the murder weapon itself. Which Jamie didn't expect to without finding the killer first. So it wasn't really much help. But it was keeping him busy, and right now, Jamie didn't have the mental capacity to police him, as well as the case.

Having Hassan as her partner did give her the room she needed to spread her wings, but in terms of actual investigating, the lion-share fell to her. Conversely, Roper challenged her at every turn, but was capable of doing some investigating on his own.

Though she was beginning to doubt that, considering what he'd found so far.

'Well, it's more than nothing.' Roper sighed. 'But not a whole lot.'

He leaned forward and tapped on his screen.

CCTV footage pulled from a lamppost cam showed a dark figure crossing the street.

The road was empty, and in the distance on the right-hand curb, the pixellated white mouth of the tunnel stuck out of the darkness.

The figure moved quickly, hands in his pockets. He was wearing black jeans, a black hoodie with the hood up.

As he walked, he didn't look around, didn't falter.

He moved with purpose towards the mouth of the tunnel.

'This him?' Jamie asked.

'Yep,' Roper said. 'Far as I can tell.'

'This is the first camera I've clocked him on. There's a lot of them rippling outwards from here, so it'll take a while to trace him any further. But it's a start.'

Jamie checked the timestamp. About fifteen minutes before the crime took place. 'Do you have him coming out?'

'Yeah,' Roper said, tapping on the keyboard with his index fingers. He took a few seconds to navigate to the right clip, and played it. 'This is all I've found so far.'

The footage played – it was four seconds long – and showed arguably the same figure running past a grainy camera from left to right, one hand pumping, the other stuffed inside his hoodie – presumably holding onto the hands he'd just severed.

Jamie bit her lip. It was nothing. Unless Roper got a full facial shot or managed to track the killer back to wherever he'd come from, there was little they could do.

Gretchen would still be their best bet with the phone.

'Okay, keep going with the CCTV, find out what other cameras are around this one – get a map of the area, see if you can figure out where he was running to.'

Roper looked at her for a second and she read his face.

'Please,' she added.

Desk-bound or not, he was, or at least had been, her superior officer for a long time.

'Sure,' he said. 'Not like I've got anything else to do.'

She grinned and slapped him on the shoulder. 'That's the spirit,' she said. 'You manage to take a look at the crime scene photos yet?'

He nodded grimly. 'Yep. What a mess.'

Jamie bit her lip. 'What do you think?'

'I think this a serious one.' He looked at her, his face conflicted. Something like worry, and jealousy mixed in there.

She could tell he wanted to be out there with her – helping, watching her back. But Jamie knew him well enough to know that deep down, he felt he should be leading this. It could have been his redemption, a big case like this. A real comeback.

She couldn't blame him. But she also needed his help. His years of experience were irreplaceable. And he wasn't a half-bad detective when he wanted to be. She needed to make sure he felt inclined to be of as much help as he could.

'Anything jump out at you?' She asked it hopefully. 'Anything you think I missed?'

'I read your prelims,' Roper said, nodding, puckering his lips and rocking on his chair.

'That's not an answer.'

He drew a slow breath for effect. 'No,' he said after a while. 'I don't think so – only – maybe…'

'What is it?'

'Just the way she was arranged. Killer did that, I guess?'

'Coroner's findings were congruent with her being on her back when he took her hands, one at a time. Boot on her chest.'

Roper took that in. 'Right – I suspected that maybe he'd laid her hands one on top of the other like that to cut them both at the same time – cut down to the ground, you know?'

'Yeah, that was my first thought, too.'

'But if he didn't, then why arrange her like that?'

'Foetal position?' Jamie mused. 'Mother issues, maybe? Childhood abuse manifesting itself?'

Roper scrunched up his face and shook his head slowly. 'That's not how it strikes me. She wasn't curled tight enough to be foetal. It was more like… prayer?'

'Prayer?'

'Yeah. Body was curled – bent over, but not balled up. Legs bent back at the knees, elbows down in front of the stomach, wrists at the chin, laid on top of each other. If her hands were there, and you put her upright, she'd look like she was—'

'Praying.' Jamie finished it for him.

He shrugged. 'Just a thought.'

'You think there's a religious element at work here? Cult maybe? Some sort of sacrificial thing, or a rite of passage?'

He blew out a coffee-sour breath and rocked upright. 'Too soon to tell. But maybe.'

'Okay,' Jamie said, filing it away in her mind.

She was about to thank him and tell him he'd done a good job, but just then, her phone started to vibrate.

She pulled it out and saw Smith's name flash up on screen.

Her eyes went to his office.

The glass windows showed no one inside.

The door was closed.

She answered quickly, with more confidence this time. 'Hey – Roper's scrubbing through CCTV, we've got new information from the pathologist, and I'm going to be chasing down the violin this afternoon—'

'I'm not calling to check on your progress, Johansson,' he said, something cold in his voice.

'Oh,' Jamie said, a shiver running down her spine. 'What is it?'

'The hands,' Smith said, the words out of shape on his tongue. 'They've turned up.'

10

'HEY,' Jamie called, pushing the phone back into her jeans. 'Get your coat.'

Both Roper and Hassan turned towards her and got up onto their feet in unison.

Roper hissed and then swore, cradling his back.

Hassan looked from him to Jamie.

'Sorry,' Roper said, lowering himself back down. 'Force of habit.'

'You'll be back at it soon,' Jamie said to him reassuringly. 'So long as you're keeping up with your physio.' She said it like a statement but inflected like a question.

He looked up at her and scowled. 'What do you think.'

Hassan was next to him in a second, his thin black jacket in his hand. 'Where we going?'

'That was Smith,' Jamie said. 'The victim's hands have been found in a bin about three-hundred metres from the scene.'

'Shit,' Hassan said, surprised.

'Maybe they're someone else's hands,' Roper mused, shrugging and turning away.

Hassan looked at Jamie for confirmation.

'He's joking,' Jamie said, motioning for Hassan to head for the stairs. 'I hope.'

Hassan asked twice why they were taking them as they headed for the parking garage.

Twice she gave the same answer. Because she preferred it.

He didn't seem sold, but didn't protest.

Jamie didn't know why she had to explain everything she did to everyone. Brock – why didn't she come to the cafeteria more often? Hassan – why didn't she take the elevator? Cake – why didn't she try fighting competitively? Her mother – why didn't she find a man?

She never asked anyone else why they did anything. She didn't see why her decisions were such a big deal.

'You okay?' Hassan asked as they headed into the cool interior of the underground parking garage.

'Fine, why?'

'I don't know. You seem off. Tense, I guess.'

Jamie paused and drew in a long breath. He was right. She wasn't being very pleasant. And whether he was going to be a help or a hindrance on this case, he had the best intentions, and at the end of the day, was watching her back.

The guns on their hips weren't for show, after all.

And Brock had already proven that she'd been locked out of the De Voge case. She was sniffing around for answers.

Smith had the sense to hand De Voge over to Interpol quietly. And Zhou, Grigoryan, whoever De Voge could flip on wanted to know where he was.

It only furthered Jamie's suspicion of Brock and Amherst being the moles.

And on top of that, the case was getting worse.

One incident – one murder – one severing of hands. Hell, that could be an isolated incident. A moment of weakness on behalf of the killer. Or a fantasy being lived out.

But for them to turn up, in a bin? Discarded?

She didn't like it at all.

It told her that the killer didn't want them anymore. So either they weren't of importance after all, which made this just something he did for the hell of it, or…

'Jamie?' Hassan said, stooping a little to look her in the eye.

She'd stopped in the middle of the lot, her mind whirring.

'Sorry,' she said. 'About everything – I know I'm being weird.' She shook her head, tried to laugh it off. It didn't feel right. 'Just a lot going on, you know? This case, the Brock and Amherst thing, moving… It's all a lot.'

She didn't even want to think about what the consequences would be if Elliot found out she'd moved and then tracked her down.

Angry? Vengeful?

Jesus, if that wasn't a can of psychotic worms she wasn't keen to open.

'I get it,' Hassan said, not a hint of condescension in his voice. 'This job's not easy – not for anyone. You wouldn't be human if it didn't take its toll.'

She looked at him and found comfort in his face.

'Come on,' he said. 'I'll drive.'

Jamie nodded, relieved that he'd offered. 'That'd be good.'

When Jamie and Hassan arrived at the scene, things were getting rowdy.

There were four police cars parked in a loose circle around the bin – two on the curb, and two on the street, and uniformed officers were directing people around the scene.

The bin was on a road that was unremarkable. Mostly apartments, some shops.

It looked like the residents had come out in force.

They were thronging around the police cordon, and hanging out of their windows overhead, trying to get a good look.

There wasn't a tent set up – no time. This was fresh.

Jamie pulled on a pair of blue gloves and crossed the scene with Hassan at her shoulder.

'Police,' she announced, approaching the crowd. 'Please, move aside,' she commanded, holding her warrant card up.

The five-deep mass parted slowly for her, and then swept apart when they clocked Hassan behind her.

She glanced back and saw that he was doing his game-face, which turned him from teddy to grizzly-bear in an instant.

A uniformed sergeant was standing at the centre of the madness, filling in his notebook, back from the crowds, next to the bin itself, over which a translucent sheet had been thrown.

The bin itself was black metal, strips stood upright around a round receptacle.

'DS Jamie Johansson,' Jamie said, flashing her warrant card.

'Special Officer Nasir Hassan,' Hassan added.

The sergeant looked at them one at a time, his pen hovering above the page. 'You two the lead officers on the murder case?'

Jamie and Hassan nodded.

'Good.' He nodded once, definitely. 'DCI Smith said you'd be along.' He made a face like there was a bad smell – and there was – it was coming from the bin. 'Right, suppose you want to see them then.'

He didn't wait for them to confirm before he turned to the sheet.

'When did this get called in?' Jamie asked.

'About forty minutes ago – a lady went to put a fast food cup in, noticed a handkerchief laid on top of the rubbish,' the officer said. 'She said it was spotted with blood – so she stopped, looked a little closer, and could see a finger poking out.' He turned the corners of his mouth down, and then shuddered.

Jamie nodded, processing. She looked into the bin, and could see the handkerchief in question – white, not silk, but a tight weave. Soft. Plush. But not extraordinary. The kind of thing you'd use to polish a violin, maybe? Still she couldn't tell until it was laid out flat and she could take a proper look. But that would have to be after the SOCOs had taken their pictures.

As it stood, it had been pulled aside, revealing all of one hand, and half of the other.

Jamie tried not to breath through her nose. The smell was already starting to manifest, the warm May air doing nothing to keep them fresh.

'Did the woman do this, or did someone else?' Jamie asked, moving her finger in a cyclical motion above the hands. She wasn't focusing on anything just yet. She didn't want her mind to jump to the wrong conclusion about anything.

'Do what?' the officer asked.

'The handkerchief.' Jamie looked at him. 'Who moved it?'

'Oh, er – what do you mean?'

'You said there was just a finger poking out when the woman arrived. But the hands are nearly completely uncovered.' Jamie did her best to talk quietly, but the din of the crowd was forcing her to raise the volume.

'It wasn't me,' the officer said, as though absolving himself of guilt. 'Must have been her – pulled it back to see, I bet.'

'Is she still here? The woman?'

'Of course,' the sergeant said, nodding firmly. 'She's in the back of one of the patrol cars, er' — he stopped, turned, and scanned the four around them — 'that one,' he finished, pointing to one at the curb, just a few metres away.

Jamie nodded. 'You took a statement?'

He held up the notebook. 'Of course.'

Jamie looked at the bin, and then at the sergeant. It wasn't that he looked horrible at his job, but Jamie needed all the information she could get, and she didn't know that she trusted his note making implicitly. 'Hassan,' she said, turning to him.

He lifted his chin diligently.

'Can you speak to her for me? I want to specifically know how this looked when she got here, okay? As much detail as possible. Whether she saw anyone standing nearby when it happened – anyone wearing dark jeans and a black hoodie. Or even not – just anything unusual like that.'

'Other than finding hands in a bin?' the sergeant chimed in.

Everyone was a bloody comedian.

Jamie fired him a merciless look and he folded his lips back into his mouth.

Hassan gave more of a reassuring nod. 'Got it. You think the killer stuck around to see them found?'

'Maybe,' Jamie said neutrally, looking around the crowd. Nothing jumped out. Just people out for the matinee. 'Seems odd to present them like that – not tossed in, not stuff down inside or hidden in something – unless he wanted them to be found.' Jamie glanced at the hands themselves now. 'They were displayed by the look of it. He wanted them to be discovered – the question is why. So like I said—'

'All the information she can give.' Hassan gave a quick smile. 'Don't worry. I got it.'

He melted away behind her and she returned to the bin itself, stepping closer.

The sergeant hovered like a wasp.

Jamie ignored him and honed her focus.

The hands were covered. So the killer wanted the handkerchief to be seen first. Or at least for them to be covered. Like a funeral shroud.

There was definitely a ceremony here. Some sort of remorse at work.

The finger was poking out – enough to alert someone this wasn't just a normal piece of rubbish. But the rest were covered respectfully. That word seemed odd, but it clicked into place in Jamie's mind as she tried to form a picture of what had happened.

The hands themselves were laid on top of what looked to be a piece of cardboard – the bottom piece off a value pack of tinned – Jamie tilted her head to read the writing – beans.

It was placed squarely in the bin, equidistant from the sides, the hands laid on top, side by side, thumbs nestled together, tips just touching.

Symmetrical.

Yep, this was definitely deliberate.

Carefully done.

Why this bin though? It was full – meant the hands would be clearly visible. Had the cardboard there, ready to become a plinth.

She answered her own questions as she went.

Jamie looked around at the street. It was busy, but not bustling. Not that far from the murder scene. Not too close either. She squinted at the sky, visualising the city in her head. It was headed towards the centre from the murder site – so if this was on the way to wherever he lived, it didn't narrow it down much.

But then again, why had so much time elapsed between the kill and them being dumped?

No, that was the wrong word.

Displayed. That was better.

This was all for an audience.

So why the handkerchief then? If the hands were the prize to display, why cover them up?

Is that what this was? A trophy to display?

Odd place to display it if they were.

And if they were, why display them at all? Why not take them home and do whatever nefarious thing he had planned? Why go to the trouble of cutting them off at all if he was just going to abandon them?

No, this didn't seem right. Didn't feel right. Didn't fit the modus operandi of a kill like this.

You don't take a trophy and then get rid of it, do you? Not without reason.

She thought back to what Roper had said. About the victim. About how she was arranged. In prayer, maybe.

She stepped back from the bin and looked at them from a wider perspective.

You stop at a bin on a busy street, knowing you might get caught, and take the time to arrange a piece of cardboard to sit on top of the other rubbish, and then remove the two severed hands you're carrying from your jacket and place them on top of a makeshift dais. You arrange them neatly – carefully – and then cover them with a handkerchief. Why?

Jamie closed in again and looked at the hands for the first time, in detail.

There were no rings on her fingers. And they looked shiny – sort of.

Jamie frowned and leaned in a little, sniffing the air.

Among the smell of rubbish – faintly – coconut? No – not quite. Thicker in the nose. More vanilla than that. Cocoa butter?

She wasn't imagining it.

Moisturiser on the hands.

Weird.

She looked closer, inspecting every pore.

The fingers were slim, the tips calloused. Not surprising for a musician.

But above that the nails were filed short.

Some shorter than others. And one of them was cracked a little across the line of the nail bed, and another looked like the tip had been snapped off – or at least torn off. The others were filed to the flesh. The broken ones – damaged during the filing? And the cuticles – they looked raw. Pushed back from the nail-beds into deep curves. But a few of them had little nicks – there were some pieces of skin peeling, too. Damn. She wasn't gentle with her hands.

Jamie processed and moved upwards to the cuts.

The right hand was neater – that was for sure. But that gelled with what the pathologist had said about the way he cut them.

But Jamie couldn't see any of that torn epithelial tissue like the pathologist had pointed out on her wrist.

She looked more closely. There were bruises on the right hand – a thumb mark on the knuckles where he'd held her hand in place during the cut. But the cut marks themselves were clean – sort of.

Jamie blinked, making sure her eyes were telling her the truth.

The edges looked worked on,

Like the killer had cut into the skin after the fact. Like he'd tried to shape the edges to make them neater.

She inspected the left hand now too, and the work was clear there, as well.

Hassan came up behind her and leaned in until his face was level with hers.

'What do you see?' he asked, barely above a whisper. He must have been finished with the description – but Jamie didn't take her attention away to ask.

'The edges here, they're chamfered,' she said, pointing to the cut marks. Whether the killer had done it with the same hunting knife or a different one, she didn't know. But he hadn't done a great job if neatness was what he was going for.

'I'm surprised,' Hassan said, standing up a little straighter.

Jamie stood up next to him. 'That he chamfered the edges?'

'That you know what the word chamfered means.'

Jamie frowned. 'Why, because I'm a woman?'

'Because it's hardly a common word,' he said, his face telling Jamie he thought it was weird she made it into a gender thing. 'I don't think it's used outside of carpentry, really.'

'I think you're wrong there,' Jamie said, shaking her head and stooping back down to look at the hands. 'Point and case.'

In reality, it was her father who'd taught it to her, like most of the random tidbits of knowledge she knew. He was always handy – would never pay to have something fixed that he could fix himself. And the opportunity to escape Jamie's mother and disappear into the workshop at the bottom of their garden – equipped with a fridge full of beer – was always too good to pass up.

'Killer cut into the hands after he took them?' Hassan asked, bending over again.

He seemed to have to bend a lot lower than Jamie did.

Jamie nodded. 'Looks like. Tried to make them pretty.' She put two and two together suddenly. 'And he also worked on the nails, too, the cuticles.' She pointed to the fingers. 'Even moisturised them by the looks of it.' She sighed, choking on the stench of flesh, rubbish, and cocoa butter. 'But dead skin won't take moisturiser in the same way, and I don't think he's had much practice – in giving manicures, or in trimming flesh.'

'Is it making you feel any better that this is his first time?' Hassan asked.

'Not in the slightest,' Jamie said, a sense of dread creeping up inside her. 'I know what this is,' she said stiffly, standing up.

'What?' Hassan asked – half professionally curious, half nervous to hear it.

'It's an apology,' Jamie said, her eyes going to the handkerchief. It was in a heap just at the side, still covering half of the right hand's fingers.

'An apology?'

She nodded. 'Yeah. Roper said that the body was arranged in prayer – but it wasn't prayer in a religious sense. More like…' She searched for the right word. 'Pleading, I guess? Hands together' — she put her hands together in front of her, palms flat, fingers extended upwards, and turned to Hassan — 'like this.' She let her eyes widen with innocence. 'Please, please forgive me.'

Hassan looked at her, expression grave.

'And this,' Jamie said, dropping them and looking at the bin. 'This is as good as a funeral pall. He wanted them to be found – wanted them to be returned. He's sorry.'

'Sorry he killed her?' Hassan wasn't sure he was following.

'No,' Jamie said, sighing. 'Sorry he screwed it up.'

'Damn.'

'He wasn't planning on killing her – but he did. And he took her hands, but made a mess of it. Then he tried to tidy them up, make them look perfect. He trimmed the cuts, filed the nails, tried to do something with the cuticles. But he made everything worse. Made them—'

'Unusable,' Hassan said, finishing her sentence.

'Exactly. Whatever he had in mind requires perfection for him. He needs them to be perfect, otherwise, whatever he's intending, it's not going to work.' She drew in a long breath and tried not to think about how sick she felt. Jamie told herself it was from the smell coming out of the bin, but it wasn't. 'And this is his way of saying sorry. He didn't want to kill her, I don't think. It was just a necessary step to obtaining his prize.' Jamie narrowed her eyes for a second, looked at the hands again. 'He realises, to some extent, the gravity of this. He's not immune to the feelings that come with murder.' She looked at Hassan. 'I don't know if we're looking for a psychopath here.'

'Then who are we looking for?'

She sighed again, and took a step away from the bin. 'Honestly, I have no idea.'

11

The SOCOs arrived and tagged Jamie and Hassan out.

'Make sure to bag the handkerchief,' she said to a guy in a white jumpsuit carrying a hard-case full of equipment.

He rolled his eyes. 'Whatever you say, detective.'

It was an obvious request, sure. But the hands were in a bin. At what point did they stop just bagging rubbish for evidence?

Jamie headed for Hassan's car and pulled Roper's number up on her phone. She wanted to keep him looped in. And it was his prayer observation that had got her mind churning on the apology angle of all this.

But they still didn't know a lot of things – one, namely who was doing this. But they were starting to build a profile. And secondly, who the victim was.

But she was hoping that Smith had Gretchen on board by now. They were losing ground with every second, and Smith knew that.

'Roper,' Jamie said as he answered.

'What's up, boss?' he said, his playfulness bordering on sour.

'I think you were right about her being arranged in prayer – but it's not a religious angle. I think the killer's praying for forgiveness.'

Roper was silent for a second. 'Interesting. I'd ask if you needed a hand over there, but…'

'Very funny,' Jamie said, getting into the car and putting him on loudspeaker. Hassan slotted into the driver's seat and she put the phone on the dash so he could hear. 'You'll be glad to know I've got a crapload more CCTV for you to sift through. The guy arranged the hands on a makeshift altar – dropped a handkerchief over them and everything. I'm hoping he's not smart enough to have checked for cameras.'

'Handkerchief? If you run, maybe you can still catch him. He must be at least a hundred.'

Jamie tried not to sigh. 'It's from the violin case, I think. To clean the instrument.'

Roper made a mildly interested noise but didn't bother to form a word.

'Anyway, we're heading back,' Jamie said. 'Any word from Smith about Fischer?'

'For the internal case?' he asked, dropping his voice as he said it.

'No, for this – I asked Smith to put her on it.'

'I've heard nothing. Want me to follow up?'

'Nah, it's okay. Last thing I want to do is piss him off. Especially when I don't have anything solid to distract him with.'

'Welcome to being a lead detective,' Roper said dryly. 'Fifty-percent wondering what the hell's going on, and fifty percent trying to avoid your SO until you finally know.'

Hassan cracked a wry smile next to her, but said nothing.

'Okay, we're heading back then,' Jamie said.

Roper hung up without saying goodbye and Hassan turned the ignition.

Jamie let him pull away without saying anything else. She was internalising.

Knowing what was going through the killer's head was a start, but it was also coming with a growing sense of dread as to what was looming.

If his first kill was unusable, then sorry or not, it meant that there was a greater purpose that he was serving. And that presumably, he still needed to serve it.

And that only meant one thing.

That this was his first kill.

But it wouldn't be his last.

By the time they got back to HQ, Jamie had received an email from Gretchen that she'd been instructed to work on their case by her SO, and that she'd be at Jamie's desk at three o'clock with what she'd found.

It was five-past by the time Jamie mounted the final stair and stepped onto her floor.

Roper was sat at his desk, with Gretchen sat behind Jamie's to his right, tapping on her keyboard. He lifted his hand and tapped his watch at her.

She was getting tired of his humour already. Jealousy, or whatever this was, didn't look pretty on him.

God she hoped Gretchen had something that would send her straight back out onto the streets.

She didn't disappoint.

'Gretchen,' Jamie said, walking up.

Gretchen turned around from Jamie's computer and smiled at her, her eyes magnified behind the large lenses, her fringe sitting thickly along the top of them.

She was playing solitaire. 'Detective,' she said, turning back to the game.

Roper snickered in the background.

'Make yourself at home,' Jamie said.

'You know,' Gretchen started, dropping an ace of clubs onto a two of diamonds, starting a cascade of cards. 'You really shouldn't use a family member's birthday as your password.' She narrowed her eyes at the screen, looking for her next move.

'Wait, you're logged into my account?' She came forward quickly, ready to snatch the mouse from Gretchen's hand.

'I just wanted to check,' Gretchen said lightly.

'Check what?' Jamie asked indignantly, mindful of the fact that she was about to elbow out of the way the one person who was going to put their case on-course.

'Whether you had more sense than him,' she said, looking at Roper.

His smug smirk froze, and then slid off his face. 'What's that supposed to mean?'

'Your ex-wife's name and the number of the house you two lived at?' Gretchen rolled her eyes. 'Come on guys. You're both a hacker's dream.'

'It's not my birthday,' Jamie snapped, a little louder than she'd hoped. 'And no one would know when he was… you know what, it doesn't even matter. Because I'm changing it.'

'Good,' Gretchen said. 'You should. Like, immediately. If you haven't been hacked already, that is. And if you have – it's a little pointless.' She stuck out her bottom lip. 'Of course, you'd need to be logged in from HQ – have a secure connection to the intranet here before you could even access your account. But you know, considering what and who we're' — she made two clicking noises with her tongue — 'investigating' — and then she winked — 'getting access to an HQ computer isn't exactly an issue, right?'

Jamie ground her teeth.

Roper laughed nervously. 'I only use that because I always have – I didn't change it since the divorce.' He cleared his throat. 'It's just easier to remember, you know?'

'No one cares, Roper,' Jamie growled, turning back to Gretchen. 'I'd appreciate a little more focus on the task at hand, okay?'

Gretchen held her hands up. 'So-rry,' she said, not sorry at all. 'Was just trying to help you out here.'

'By violating my privacy?'

'By showing you how easy it is for anyone who wants to get your information to, uh, get it.'

Jamie's jaw flexed.

'And anyway,' Gretchen went on. 'You've got nothing to be ashamed of in your account.'

Jamie narrowed her eyes.

'Not like him,' she said, nodding at Roper again.

He paled a few shades.

Gretchen slowly shook her head.

Roper didn't have a comment to make on that one.

'But come on,' Gretchen said. 'I had to know who I was throwing my lot in with for this investigation. For all I knew, you two were the ones—'

'It's fine, honestly,' Jamie said, putting a hand up. She didn't want to probe further. She already felt like her life was violated enough. She didn't need the details. 'Do you need me to get you a requisition form for the victim's phone?'

Gretchen raised an eyebrow. 'You think I'd trudge all the way up here for that?'

Jamie felt tired suddenly. 'No,' she said with a long sigh. 'I suppose you wouldn't, would you.'

Gretchen beamed at her, totally unaware of the tension between the three of them. 'Okay,' she said brightly, turning to the computer and using a keyboard command to pull up a window. It showed a picture of the victim, front and centre. The photograph looked professionally taken and the girl looked younger, smartly dressed in a white shirt, and she was smiling broadly.

'This is Alyssa Doran.'

Jamie looked at the photo carefully. There was no mistaking her. She had little make-up on, and must have been around sixteen or seventeen in the photograph.

Gretchen hit another command and the photo zoomed out to show that she was sitting on a stool, holding a violin in one hand, and a bow in the other, both resting on her lap.

'This was taken four years ago after she made first chair for the Westmorland County Orchestra. She was sixteen.'

Jamie nodded. 'Okay, so that puts her at twenty now.'

'She was born and raised in a little town called Penrith,' Gretchen said. 'Grew up there with a normal family, nothing to report – after she finished sixth-form, she was offered a scholarship at the Royal College of Classical Arts and Music here in London – and moved to the city.'

'Alone?'

'Yeah, her parents still live in Penrith – they run a business there together. A small boutique furniture showroom.' Gretchen hit another button and another window un-minimised itself, showing a simple website for the showroom in question. She hit the button again and it disappeared.

'Do they know yet?'

'About Doran?' Gretchen glanced up at Jamie. 'No, I haven't gone to anyone else with this yet.'

'Okay,' Jamie said, making a mental checklist. 'Can you get their contact information for me, then forward it to Roper?' She turned to him. 'Can you inform them?'

Roper's face dropped further than it already had. 'I'd rather not.'

'If you can do a sit-up, I'll ask Hassan to do it.'

He glared at her.

'Well, you'd be able to if you'd been doing your physio.'

His glare burned hotter.

Jamie turned back to Gretchen. 'You got all this off her phone?'

She nodded. 'Yeah, sort of, once I was in, I just grabbed the IMEI number and then requisitioned the contract details from the provider and went from there. The Westmorland Orchestra website keeps a record of all its members and how they did in competitions – that sort of thing. Was easy. I basically Googled her name.'

'Good,' Jamie said, hoping that meant that more information would flow freely to Gretchen's fingertips. 'Do we have a contact for the college? Any friends she went with, where she stayed? Anything like that?'

Gretchen shook her head. 'No, not yet. And this is where it gets weird.'

'Weird is bad,' Jamie muttered.

'Mm, yeah – so she's been enrolled at the college since September two years ago on a three year music degree – Classical Theory and

Performance – standard stuff. Looks like she was doing well, too.' Gretchen leaned forward, navigated to the college's website, and then clicked swiftly into their photo-yearbook of the players in their orchestra.

Jamie didn't see Alyssa's name or face there.

Gretchen opened a command console in the browser without even a cursory glance at the keyboard under her dancing fingers, and started dredging through the raw code until she found what she had already found earlier. She clicked on it and the page reloaded.

A blank grey square appeared with a red cross in it, the words "IMAGE NOT FOUND" appearing inside it. But the name underneath read Alyssa Doran, followed by a list of achievements and qualifications – of which there were a lot. ABRSM Performance Diploma Violin, Grade 8 Viola, Distinction in all her examinations. Primary school orchestra first chair, secondary school orchestra first chair, sixth form first chair. County youth first chair, county seniors first chair. National youth orchestra first chair.

'Looks like she was a prodigy,' Jamie said. 'I don't get it – where's her photo?'

'Well, this page was taken down about seven months ago – in October. They removed her photo from their server and took the link off the main site, but the page is still active.'

'Seven months ago? What happened?'

'I can't see the list of active students without getting in touch with the school – unless... you know. But hey, we're supposed to be on the right side of the law, right?'

'Right,' Jamie said.

'So we're still waiting on a response from them regarding that. But I can say with pretty much certainty that in October of last year, she dropped out of school, and did everything she could to scrub herself from the face of the earth. And the internet, too.'

Jamie stuck out her bottom lip. 'Any ideas why?'

Gretchen scratched her cheek, belched for no reason other than that she needed to and didn't care what anyone thought about it, and then continued. 'Still working on that. The phone's new – or at least new since October. And it's empty. No photos of friends, no active link to the Apple Cloud, no email inboxes set up. No social apps. Nothing. It's like she didn't want to be found. At least not through her phone or the internet. It's basically as empty as a phone could be. There's only a few contacts saved. Mum, dad, a couple of takeaways. No friends, nothing like that. And no contact with the college either. But here.' She opened another browser window she had minimised – all still in Jamie's account – and showed off a Facebook page which said "This Account Is No Longer Active".

The URL read *AlyssaDora7,* and Gretchen already had another three tabs cued up. 'The backend of the page shows this as having been displayed since October twentieth. And in these photos,' she said, clicking on the other tabs, which showed group shots of friends in bars, playing instruments, just generally living life, all including Alyssa, 'have her tagged, but the tags are all dead now. Which only happens when a profile gets taken down.' Gretchen took a second for Jamie to process that, and then skipped over to both an Instagram and Twitter account, both bearing the same deactivation message. 'These were taken down around the same time, by the looks of it.'

'Any reason you can see?'

'Not yet.'

'So you know she took down her socials and was taken off the school register. Do we know for sure she wasn't still enrolled there more recently than October?'

Gretchen went back to the photographs of the friends. 'This girl here,' she said, pointing to a smiley young woman with dark skin and golden, curly hair, 'is called Chessie Fowler. Real name Francesca, but she goes by Chessie. She was Alyssa's roommate in the dorms. But in October of last year – on the twenty-second – she put up a post saying that the room felt empty and she didn't know how she felt about living with someone new after all this time.' Gretchen had that already loaded and flicked over to it. The picture showed a blank wall and a single bed with a bare mattress, light streaming in through a window on the left. Over the bed, little spots of adhesive tack were left on the paint, like someone had taken down posters.

Under the photo, there were lots of sad emoji faces, and a bunch of hearts. The words 'Miss you, wherever you are,' finished the post.

Jamie drew a slow breath, watching as Gretchen continued down the rabbit hole.

'And this girl,' she said, going back to another group shot and pointing at a girl who seemed to be in the background of most of the pictures, 'is named Mimi Paganelli.'

'Mimi?' Jamie arched an eyebrow.

'Yeah,' Gretchen said, pulling up her profile.

The girl was pretty – a mix of heritage. She had dark, wavy hair that looked almost Hispanic, but her features told Jamie she was at least half-Asian. Chinese, or Korean, she guessed.

As if reading her mind, Gretchen said, 'She's here on a violin scholarship, too, same as Alyssa was, from a school in South Korea. Super talented, by all accounts. Father is Italian, mother is Korean. They live just outside Seoul. Looks like her and Alyssa were friends – but not close. And I'm not surprised.'

'Why do you say that?' Jamie asked.

'This world is cut-throat. Music at this level.' Gretchen looked up at Jamie. 'It's not really that well-paid, and players have a long shelf-life. Only maybe the top orchestras in the world pay enough to sustain their players, and when you split it between a hundred and two of them…'

'A hundred and two?'

'The number of players in a full symphony orchestra.'

'Right.'

'The pie gets even smaller. To make the *real* money, you have to be first chair. Something special. And orchestras head-hunt the best. So unless you come out of school first chair, you're not looking at a big pay-day.'

Jamie felt like Gretchen was going somewhere with this, and let her speak.

'And up until mid-October, guess who was first chair?'

'Alyssa?'

'And then after she disappeared?'

'Mimi.' Jamie nodded.

'Check this out,' Gretchen said, pulling up the final tab in the browser. It showed Mimi's profile, and was open to a specific update she posted on the twenty-fourth of October.

It read:

Wow! Wowowowowowow! I can't believe it! I know it's a sad time, and I miss her too... and we're all wondering how we're going to do it without Lys – but I wanted to share the news that I've just been told I'm going to be the new first chair! I promise that I'm going to work super hard, and that I won't let you all down. I can't be Lys – no one can – but I'll do everything I can. And I know we're going to be stronger than ever xoxox

The post was liked by a bunch of people, and lots of comments said things like, *You deserve it!* and *Congrats! I know you'll do great.*

'Seems like Mimi was popular,' Jamie said.

'Platitudes, man,' Gretchen said, shaking her head in semi-disgust. 'Just everyone trying to look nice online.' She seemed sour about social media in general. 'I bet,' she said, carrying on, folding her arms, 'that Mimi couldn't have been happier that Alyssa was out of the way. There's only room in the spotlight for one. Only one first chair. And with Alyssa gone, Mimi's on course now to have the kind of career that she probably wouldn't have if Alyssa was there.'

Jamie licked her lip slowly, looking at the grinning face of Mimi Paganelli, wondering if she could imagine this happy young girl hacking off the hands of her rival. That would be a pretty big screw-you. And if this world was as tightly-wound as Gretchen said. As high stakes... then maybe...

Jamie drew a breath. 'You think that's motive?'

Gretchen shrugged and looked up at her. 'I dunno, you're the detective. You tell me.'

12

JAMIE DIDN'T REALLY THINK this felt like a jealousy killing.

But she wouldn't be a good detective if she didn't run the lead down.

It was after five when Jamie got to the Royal College of Classical Arts and Music, or Ro-Cam, as Gretchen told her the students called it.

Hassan had clocked off for the day – headed home to the wife – his words, not hers. *She's been bunking off with the kids since four – and* someone's *gotta cook dinner.* He laughed as though it was an inside joke of theirs, but Jamie could see in his eyes that unless he was out the door at five on the dot and home no more than twenty minutes after, life wouldn't really be worth living.

She would have liked him to be there, but she understood his priorities. She didn't have any others, and the thought of going home to her cold, run-down apartment didn't really thrill her.

So here she was, on her own. Lone wolfing it.

Jamie shook her head. No, that was a silly thing to think.

She was simply acting on good information as soon as she could. By tomorrow, the trail would be even colder.

And anyway, she was just questioning some students, seeing if she could check out Alyssa's dorm. Hoping that she could speak to some of her tutors, see if she couldn't figure out why she'd disappeared. Was she unhappy? Did she crack under the pressure of it all? From Gretchen's description of the life ahead of her, there wasn't much room for screw-ups.

Jamie pulled into the staff car park, near the main building, and opened her door into the clear May air.

The clouds had parted and the air had thinned.

The sun was still warm, but there was a chill on the breeze.

Jamie sighed, took her Glock off the passenger seat where it was laying and put it in the glove-box. It was uncomfortable to drive with it on her hip.

And there was no reason she'd need to carry a firearm into a school.

She exchanged it for her park-anywhere badge, pulling it out, flipping it open with her fingers and dropping it onto her dash in one movement, in plain view of the parking warden who would swoop in like a vulture no doubt.

She could already see her, circling on the far side of the tarmac, eyeing Jamie's hybrid-hatch with a sort of cruel justice in her eyes.

Just try it.

She repositioned it to the side of the windscreen the warden would approach from, and then got out, locking the car and checking the handle.

Jamie had called ahead and told the administration that she'd been coming.

They hadn't had a positive ID yet on Alyssa. There was no doubt that it was her, but they still needed to have the next-of-kin confirm.

Roper still hadn't made the call.

They were never pleasant.

But that wasn't going to stop Jamie running down leads, even if she couldn't use the definite statement that Alyssa Doran was dead.

Jamie approached the administration building, the heels on her walking boots clicking softly on the concrete.

A pale strip of paving slabs led to the glass door between two well-manicured lawns.

The campus seemed quiet to Jamie, though she guessed classes were over for the day.

A few stragglers were meandering down the main drag between the buildings, and a few students were sitting on communal greens, stretched out, enjoying the last of the afternoon before it got too cool to relax.

She slowed her pace as the door neared, eyeing one group. There were five of them, a guy in the centre lying on his back, one heel on the opposite raised knee, hands laced behind his head showing off his narrow arms.

He had curly ginger hair, and a broad mouth. He was laughing loudly. Jamie knew the type. The one who always had to be the centre of attention.

Jamie scanned the others, remembering her time in uni. She didn't miss it.

Too much social pressure for her liking.

She didn't keep in touch with anyone from her classes. For a brief second, she wondered where they were. And then realised she couldn't have cared less.

Around the boy were three girls and another guy. One girl, to his right, was sitting cross-legged in a pair of denim shorts that came only about an eighth of the way down her pale white thighs. She was picking petals off a daisy, casting glances at him through her hair.

She liked him, that was obvious. She was laughing along with him, and more animatedly when he glanced over.

Another girl was talking to the other boy, a backpack in front of them. They seemed to be discussing notes.

And finally, the last girl, with dark hair, was sitting with her arms around her knees, staring away from the group. Smiling and turning her head only when she was aware the others were looking in her direction.

She was disinterested in them. In their jokes. In their social circle. She was making an outcast of herself, linked only by proximity – probably in their classes, or fell in with them in first-year and never left.

She could leave and they wouldn't notice. And she wouldn't care.

She was just there because she felt that she should be – not in her room, alone, reading the book she was thinking about or going for a run…

Jamie felt an affinity with her. Wanted to go over, lower her hand to the girl and pull her up – say, *it's fine. You don't need to do it for them. They won't care anyway. Just be you. You'll get by fine on your own.*

Jamie was fine. Wasn't she? She wasn't alone?

The door swung open in front of her, the handle smacking into her outstretched fingers.

She jolted back to reality, pain lancing through her hand, and she realised she'd been standing right in front of it with her hand halfway out.

Jamie blinked, retracted her throbbing hand, and looked at the person standing there in the doorway.

'Oh, sorry,' he said, a boy of no more than twenty-two or twenty-three. He was thin, with bristly brown hair, his face angular, beard wispy and thin. 'I thought – are you…? The door wasn't locked, but you looked like – uh…' He trailed off, reading Jamie's stern expression.

The boy had a university badge and lanyard around his neck and Jamie could see he was a member of staff, but also there doing a post-grad. The badge said as much. 'Scott Waldron,' he said, smiling suddenly with slightly crooked teeth. He put a hand on his chest. 'Oboe. Third chair.'

'Jamie Johansson,' Jamie said. 'Detective Sergeant with the Metropolitan Police.'

'Oh,' Scott replied, looking a little taken aback.

Jamie supposed in her jeans, walking boots, and long sleeve t-shirt, she didn't look much like a detective just then. Especially since she'd been standing aimlessly outside the door staring into space.

'Is, er,' he started, scratching the back of his head. 'Is everything alright?'

'I need some information, if possible,' Jamie said, pulling her warrant card from her back pocket for the sake of protocol and holding it up. 'You mind if we go inside?'

'Sure,' Scott said obligingly.

Jamie stepped past him and into the foyer of the building. There was a hardwearing black carpet on the floor and a lot of veneered wood panelling on the walls.

A crescent shaped desk curved into the space from the back wall, where the words 'Royal College of Classical Arts and Music' rose from the surface in a regal silver. Underneath, in cursive text, the words '*ars longa, vita brevis*' were inscribed.

Vita was life – Jamie knew that. *Longa*? Long? *Brevis*… brevity? Short?

'Art is long, life is short,' Scott said, following her eyes. 'True art endures the test of time, but—'

'I get it,' Jamie said, watching as he walked around the desk and sat at the computer. 'Do you have access to student records?'

Scott looked at her for a second, narrowed his eyes a little. 'No – at least not the ones you're probably looking for. I can see what classes people have, help them reset their password, or I can send emails…' he said, reeling off the list of things he was able to do. None of which were useful.

Jamie inhaled, and then blew out the air, thinking. 'And I don't suppose anyone with that access is here right now?'

'What is this about – I might be able to help anyway?' he said hopefully. He was looking up at Jamie in an intense way – like he wanted to keep her there. She wasn't really experienced enough with guys coming onto her to tell whether it was an amorous stare. They rarely seemed to go for the girl in hiking boots with no make-up. Jesus, she was reliving uni all over again being here.

Jamie swallowed and looked away.

Whether he was or not, it made her squirm a little. But she had to get back on track.

'Do you know Alyssa Doran?' Jamie asked, being careful of the tense. She didn't want to let on that anything had happened to her. Not yet at least.

'Alyssa?' He seemed to brighten instantly. 'Of course – where is she? Is she okay? Is she coming back?'

Jamie measured his frantic words. 'I can't really discuss the particulars of the case,' she said diplomatically. 'But I'm just looking to gather some information at this point, speak to some of her tutors, her friends, maybe. How do you know Alyssa?'

'Everyone knows Alyssa,' he said, snorting a little bit. 'How could you not? She's… She's…'

'She's?'

'Amazing.'

'Right.'

'Losing her was a huge blow to all of us.'

'What do you mean losing her?' Did he know she was dead?

'Losing her from the orchestra,' Scott said, smirking as though he'd heard a funny joke at Jamie's expense.

'Of course,' Jamie said as self-deprecatingly as she could. 'It must have been difficult.'

'Players move on, of course. They graduate, they lose their edge – there's a million reasons.'

A million? Jamie counted two. Though she didn't say anything. He was still giving her his version of charming eyes. And besides being ten years her junior, there were a *million* reasons why she wasn't interested. 'Oh yeah?'

'Of course. And Alyssa was irreplaceable. *Is* irreplaceable.' He corrected himself.

'What do you mean "was"?'

'Just that we all sort of hope she's still coming back.'

Jamie nodded. 'Ah.'

'I mean, after what she did… You'd think she'd never be able to. But we'd take her back. At least I would. You know?'

Jamie just raised an eyebrow.

'Of course, it's not right, you know – what she did…'

Jamie often found that saying nothing was better than asking questions. If a witness was happy to talk, she was happy to listen.

'Gilberto is still really mad – but I think if he could hear her play again, he'd change his mind.' He was near babbling.

Something struck a chord in Jamie's mind. 'What exactly is it that Alyssa did?'

'You don't know?' His eyebrows raised now, creasing his blotchy forehead. 'I thought that was why you were here.'

'Enlighten me,' Jamie said, forcing a smile.

'She stole Gilberto's Hofner,' he said, as though it were the worst tragedy to befall man since we got up onto two legs.

The antique violin. 'Ah. Bet he was upset about that.'

'Upset?' Scott laughed. 'I've never seen someone so angry – he was saying that when he found her' — he started to do a weird sort of butchered Spanish accent and made his eyebrows point down in the middle. His hand also rose into a point and he waved it madly — 'I'm going to pull off the E string and cut her effing head off with it!' He finished and then started laughing at his own impression.

Jamie felt her spine stiffen a little.

Scott read her grave, interrogating expression and his own smile faded.

He began to realise then the possible gravity of the situation.

Jamie watched as his Adam's apple rose up and then plopped back down in his throat. 'Is, uh – is Alyssa okay?'

Jamie stepped a little closer to the desk. 'Is Gilberto a student?'

'N-no,' Scott stammered a little. 'He's the arranger – the conductor – for the orchestra.'

'Okay, good. And Alyssa stole his violin?'

Scott nodded slowly. 'Yeah, but that whole thing about cutting her head off,' he said, laughing nervously. 'He wasn't serious.'

Jamie nodded. 'No, of course not.' She thought about all the countries where criminals who stole had their hands cut off. Gilberto was a Spanish name, she thought. She'd have to check what their historical punishments were like there. But if Mimi wanting first chair wasn't motive enough, a passionate, disgruntled arranger who just lost his lead violinist, and his prized violin along with it, might be a prime candidate.

Revenge trumped jealousy in Jamie's mind.

'So, how much was the Hofner worth?' Jamie asked.

'You can't put a price on something like that,' Scott said, suddenly conscious of what he was saying – and who he was implicating.

'But I'd guess a lot?'

He just gave a brief smile. 'I really wouldn't know.'

'No problem.' Jamie looked around a little. 'Was Gilberto in today?'

'Uh, yeah, I think so – he's actually here now.'

'Really? I'd like to speak to him.'

Scott glanced at the computer monitor. 'They're in rehearsal until six.'

'Who are?'

'The orchestra,' he said, giving Jamie a look that suggested everyone else on earth knew that the orchestra practiced on a Thursday at this time.

'Of course. And why aren't you there, Scott, oboe, third chair?' Jamie asked casually. She had no interest in him as a suspect, but as a witness, he was fragile enough to spill his guts about everyone.

'I'm working,' he said, looking sorry for himself. 'I had to cover someone. But they won't miss me.'

Jamie drew a long breath, hoping she wouldn't have to get into his musical woes. 'That's a shame. Is it far from here?'

'A few minutes' walk.'

'Can you draw me a map?'

Scott nodded. 'Yeah, but it's easy to find.' He pointed his hand in the direction the students had been on the grass. 'Second building on the right. Can't miss it.'

'Thanks, Scott,' Jamie said. 'What time are you here until? I might have more questions.'

'Nine.'

'Well, don't work too hard.'

'I never do.'

'Humph,' Jamie said, cracking a smile and heading for the door. 'I couldn't have guessed.'

13

JAMIE WALKED QUICKLY towards the building that Scott had indicated.

The practice wouldn't finish for another twenty minutes or so, but she wanted to be waiting when it did.

The building itself was old, brown stonework, and regal. Everything on campus was.

As she stepped through the automatic glass doors that had been built into the original frame, the sound of classical music greeted her.

It hung in the air, a distant and ominous echo, seeming to come from both of the corridors in front of her, and through the walls itself.

She closed her eyes and let her ears do the work, following the network of deserted, tiled corridors until she found her way to the main hall – which Jamie presumed was the only room big enough to fit a one-hundred-and-two-piece orchestra.

She stopped short of the double doors there, reading the paper notice that said 'Practice In Progress!' as if the music ringing through the wood wasn't hint enough.

Jamie stood back a little so that her nose wasn't pressed to the glass and angled herself to see in.

The room was set up like a theatre – tiered rows of audience seating rising towards the back wall, and a deep stage filled with chairs, stands, and musicians, all sawing away and tapping their instruments.

In front of them, she spied the maestro – a guy who must have been fifty. Maybe a little more.

He was thin, tanned, bedraggled almost.

His hair was bushy and wild, about a hand-span long. It was black originally, but was now speckled with grey.

His roughly stubbled chin bobbed and weaved as he moved up and down like he was on springs, folding and casting his arms through the air fluidly.

Every few seconds he would focus on a specific section of the orchestra and move his hand in a certain way, motioning them to get louder or quieter, to back off, slow down, and sometimes, he'd move it in a cyclical motion, a look of frustration and anger seizing his lined face. Jamie guessed that meant they weren't keeping tempo.

This must be the infamous Gilberto.

He didn't look like a killer.

But he was definitely passionate. She could see that much in him as he shaped the music through the air with his hands.

Jamie checked her watch. Just quarter to.

And she suspected, judging by the way Gilberto was puppeteering them all that they wouldn't be allowed to leave a second before six.

Jamie turned her attention now to the string section, seeing if she could spy Mimi Paganelli.

She was right in the middle – unmissable.

Mimi was half a head shorter than everyone else, sitting bolt-upright on her chair. She was playing furiously, her face a mess of concentration lines, and she was looking at Gilberto so hard Jamie expected him to burst into flames.

The pressures of first chair, she guessed.

Was that why Alyssa left? Did it all just get too much for her?

Jamie could see Chessie Fowler sitting to Mimi's left, her arm moving solidly back and forth on the cello strings.

Jamie could pick out the sombre, throaty hum among everything else.

She didn't know much about classical music. And she certainly didn't recognise the piece, but it was beautiful. Rising and falling like an ocean.

She would have liked to have gone inside, found a seat, and watched them.

But she was working.

And a girl was dead.

And she didn't think that languishing in the sweet music of the could-be killer was appropriate.

She checked her watch again, feeling very tired suddenly.

She had been up nearly all night, and was working off about three hours sleep.

And there was no denying it then.

Jamie had passed a coffee machine on her way in.

She would go back and get one.

That would kill the time, too.

Jamie turned from the door and headed for the machine, pulling her phone out as she did.

At three minutes past six, Gilberto took one last breath, raised his hands, and then flattened them out like he was fighting down a bedsheet blowing in the wind.

He pressed the sound of the orchestra into the floor and then stamped it out with a flick of his wrists.

His bottom lip turned out in reasonable satisfaction, and Jamie wasted no time pushing through and into the hall.

Gilberto Delgado was fifty-three years old, and had immigrated to the UK from Spain to work as a music teacher and arranger for the college in 2011.

He'd grown up just outside Bilbao and had been first chair for the Spanish national orchestra for seventeen years before making the switch to teaching.

He played violin.

Gretchen had found all of that out in about thirty seconds on her laptop at home as Jamie approached the machine, jabbed the button for an americano, and then waited for it to brew.

She'd taken one sip, tipped it back into the waste tray, and then binned the cup.

It tasted like shit.

'Mr Delgado,' she said clearly, her eyes heavy, as she approached.

The raking of chairs and the murmur of voices echoed in the room.

Gilberto turned and looked at her, eyes narrowing, going from her face to her boots and back. 'How may I help you?' he asked, not sounding very helpful.

Jamie flashed her warrant card. 'DS Jamie Johansson – London Met. I was wondering if I could speak to you for a moment?'

He stuck out his bottom lip a little, arranging his sheet music on his lectern and turning back to look at it. 'Unless you're here to tell me that you've got my violin, and have arrested that thief for stealing it, I don't have the time.' He slotted the sheets all together in his hands and picked them up. 'Well?'

'We do, actually,' Jamie said, forcing a smile. His demeanour wasn't exactly inviting. 'Though no arrests have been made.' She needed to be tactful. She wanted to read his reply – see whether he would hint at her death.

'No?' He raised an eyebrow. 'And I suppose you want me to turn evidence, do you?' He scoffed. 'Go on record that she stole it from me?' He folded his arms now, his crumpled white shirt creasing further around his stomach. 'I suppose she's spun the story that I gave it to her?'

'I'm not able to discuss the particulars of an investigation,' Jamie said curtly. 'But I would like to continue this conversation somewhere a little more…' She looked around the room at the dozens of students all packing up.

By the time she looked back around, he had his hand outstretched, a business card in it. 'Please,' he said, jiggling it.

Jamie took it and the second her fingers closed around the paper, he was moving away from her. 'I have another engagement,' he said. 'But I'll be at home until just after ten tomorrow morning. Call before you arrive.' His voice carried to her as he closed the distance on the door on the far side of the room.

Jamie glanced down at the thing in her hands and when she looked up again, he'd melted into the crowd and disappeared.

She swallowed, curling the card into her fist, unsure whether she'd just let a murderer walk away from her, and whether when she turned up at his door in the morning, she'd find an empty house.

For a second she considered running after him, but her body seemed unwilling to spool up, her muscles aching and seized.

She turned her attention to the class instead. There was more than one person that she wanted to talk to here.

Her eyes scanned the strings section, where she could see a girl with a shock of golden curls putting a cello into its case. Chessie Fowler. But there was no sign of Mimi Paganelli. She must have already slipped out.

Jamie approached quickly, half weaving, half shouldering through the throng of students wanting to get home, the scent of stale sweat coming off them.

Delgado had been working them hard.

'Miss Fowler?' she called out, watching as Chessie clasped her case.

The girl looked up, wondering who'd called her name, and then locked onto Jamie as she appeared out of the mess of bodies. 'Hi,' she said, unsure of the situation. She turned her head and the glow of the lights overhead shone off her forehead, her smooth brown skin lightly sheered with sweat. 'Can I help you with something?'

'Chessie Fowler?' Jamie confirmed, finding a smile come to her face more easily now than it did with Gilberto.

'Yes?' She answered unsurely.

'My name is Detective Sergeant Jamie Johansson, I'm with the London Metropolitan police. I was hoping I could ask you a few questions about your old roommate, Alyssa Doran?'

Chessie's jaw set suddenly. She looked at Jamie, her eyes filling. 'Oh my god,' she said, falling to a whisper. 'She's dead, isn't she?'

14

Jamie stiffened.

No one should know that. No one *could* know that.

'Why do you say that?' Jamie asked, matching her volume.

'It's true, isn't it?' Chessie urged. 'My god, I told her. I *told* her!' Chessie welled up truly now, stifling a sob.

Jamie felt her throat constrict and her fists curl. She needed to get Chessie out of there – away from the crowd who were beginning look over, stopping their exodus to see who this stranger was that was making their cellist cry. 'Hey,' Jamie said, stepping closer, reaching out for Chessie's arm. 'Why don't we get out of here, huh? Go somewhere and talk?'

Jamie's fingers grazed her skin, and the girl erupted into tears.

She threw her arms in the air, snatched her cello up, forcing Jamie to dance backwards out of its path – or sacrifice her knees to the steel clasps – and watch as she shoved her way down the steps and towards the door.

Jamie held her hand up, ready to shout after her, but she was already three-quarters of the way to the door and Jamie knew that the corridors were tight here.

She let her go. She'd be no use in this state anyway – Jamie could catch up with her tomorrow. She'd speak to the college in the morning, find out where Chessie lived, and then pay her a visit after she'd seen Delgado.

But how she already knew Alyssa was dead was a mystery. Unless they'd been in touch, and she'd confided something in Chessie before she died?

Jamie stood still, watching the students file out of the room.

Mimi Paganelli was gone. Delgado had rushed off to another engagement. Chessie had run out crying. And she was left with exactly nothing.

Nothing except a damp, empty, sad little flat to go home to. Which was nothing more than a hiding place from the psychotic organ harvesting serial killer that had a less than pleasing obsession with her.

Jamie sighed, waiting for the crowd to thin, and wondered how her life had got like this.

She thought about how things were easier when she was investigating larceny and domestic disturbances.

And then she finally went home.

By the time she pulled up outside her new apartment – which took almost twice as long as it should have – as she had pulled up outside her old apartment first, realised, and then had to drive on, it was dark and growing late.

Mrs Iwankowski's curtains were drawn, a lamp burning orange behind them.

Jamie parked up on the other side of the road and crossed quickly, opening the door and letting herself into the downstairs corridor as silently as she could.

She'd never paid any mind to her footsteps when she lived in her other apartment, but here, she seemed to feel like she needed to creep.

Jamie turned and locked the door behind her, then walked across the tattered carpet, opened her own front door, and locked that behind her too, making a mental note to get a better lock when she had a chance.

It took her about thirty minutes to find the towels, and by the time the water grew hot and she'd thrown her clothes next to the tub and climbed in, it was almost nine.

The day had been a blur – a long, tiring blur and her mind wouldn't quit. It was like an idling car after a race. Burning hot, churning through the fuel left in her tank, dying to suck on empty and sputter out.

She hoped it would soon.

15

It was just after four in the morning when she sat bolt up in bed, sucking in a sharp lungful of air.

She twisted over onto her front, one knee bouncing on the mattress, the other foot hitting the cold wooden floor, and reached for the Glock on her nightstand, silhouetted in the moonlight.

Her phone screen was flashing red and yellow, a large number '2' strobing as it vibrated violently on the cabinet.

Motion alert.

She touched it with her off hand, silencing it, turning to face the closed bedroom door, muzzle snapped to attention.

It was warm in the room, and she was wearing a loose pair of shorts that just reached her thigh and a tank top, but a sweat had already broken out under the line of her jaw, down her spine.

Her heart beat hard.

She steadied her breath, flexing her fingers around the grip.

The work that Cake had agreed to do – plumbing, some electrical, some decorating, even. That could all wait, it was inconsequential.

The thing that couldn't, though, the one job she'd asked him to do before he left, was install a pair of motion sensors she'd bought.

One at the top of the stairs, one over the fire escape at the back of the kitchen.

And number two, the fire escape sensor, had been tripped.

Jamie held her breath, pricking her ears for any sound. Breaking glass. The crunching of wood as someone breaks a doorframe. The squeak of a floorboard underfoot.

But there was nothing but silence.

Silence, and the blood roaring in her ears.

She let out a breath, told herself it was nothing, and then padded towards the bedroom door, pistol raised, finger resting nervously on the trigger.

No one else has a key, she told herself.

No one should be in here.

No one but me.

She reached the door, her hand moving towards it without her eyes moving from the sights, and missed the handle.

Jamie swore under her breath, took it in her fingers the second time, and dragged it slowly open.

It swung over the boards sending a wash of cold air over her toes, and she moved out onto the landing, watching the stairs fall away from her.

There was nothing but darkness ahead, the narrow flight leading down to the landing, and then wrapping around towards the living room before continuing down to the ground floor and front door.

She couldn't just stand here. She needed to move, to be on the offensive.

If someone was coming up, she wanted to be the one surprising them.

Jamie willed her legs to move and like an iron mechanism seized with time, she bucked off the rust and began to walk. Cautiously.

She put her feet on the outsides of the steps, making sure they didn't creak. Waiting for them to take her weight before she stepped down.

One, two, three. She counted them out in her head, eyes fixed on the corner.

She'd cross the hall, into the living room, get a line of sight on the balcony door. Stick close to the wall.

Then she'd move in, close the gap quickly. Ten steps. It couldn't be any more.

If someone was at the door, they'd not know she was there until they had her muzzle in their face.

She was halfway down the stairs now.

Next to the kitchen light switch there was one for a security light positioned over the fire escape that covered the back garden.

It was overgrown with brambles and other shrubs, but if someone really wanted to get in without being seen…

She was on the landing now, moving quickly. Like a cat.

Her heart had silenced itself. Either beating so fast she couldn't hear more than a hum, or having stopped itself altogether.

Jamie's mouth was dry now as she got into the living room, staring into the darkness.

The blind over her shoulder blotted out the streetlights and the beech trees did the rest, allowing only pinholes of dim orange brilliance to pierce the black.

Jamie tried to focus, her eyes failing her, and listened as the faint click of the gun shaking in her hand echoed around.

She wanted so badly to just pull the trigger.

She knew where the door was – could visualise the glass panel.

Could already see *him* there, standing right behind it, hand on the glass, looking in.

Looking for a way in.

And she could put a bullet in him. Two. Mid-chest. Hell. Seventeen. Empty the damn magazine. Watch as he stumbled backwards, tumbled over the rail and fell, prostrate, limp, and punctured down to the ground. Never to haunt her life, waking or sleeping again.

She was at the threshold now, within reach of the light switch.

Yes. She would do that.

Turn it on, see his face, the shock there. One of his hands on the lock, the other on the handle, trying to pick his way in. Silent, and slimy. Cunning. Evil as he was. Ready to slither up her stairs and into her bedroom.

She shuddered, feeling the grip sweaty in her palm, and took her left hand off the butt, spidering it over the wall towards the switch.

She groped for it, feeling the droplets of sweat bead on her forehead, run into her eyebrows, tickle the sides of her nose as they ran along the seams of the bags under her eyes, and then streamed down her cheeks like tears.

Her fingers met plastic and stopped.

This was it. The end.

The end of Elliot Day and the grip he had around the throat of her life.

She exhaled once, blinked slowly, letting the fear drain out of her, and then flipped it on.

Light exploded from the security lamp above the door and flooded into the back garden.

It blinded her momentarily and she resisted the urge to jerk her finger back into the stock.

She blinked hard, shoving herself against the doorframe for support, for cover – for she didn't know what.

Her eyes untwisted from her face and she stared through her lashes, squinting in the light.

Her pupils constricted and then loosened, fighting for focus, and grabbed onto it just in time to see the slinky grey body of a tabby cat leap down from the railing of the fire escape, landing on the adjoining wall, and then plunging into the thicket below.

Jamie's chest ached and she moved forward at pace, ignoring it, until her nose was against the glass, pistol lowered, pointing at the ground.

Her heavy breaths misted on the cool surface, obscuring her view as she roved across the back garden, enclosed and impenetrable as it was.

The cat was gone.

And there was no one else there.

Jesus.

She ran her hand through her hair, felt it wet under the pads of her fingers, and thought about how she almost just discharged seventeen rounds into a stray cat.

Fuck. That would have been a lot of paperwork.

Jamie turned her back to the door and slouched against it, sinking to the tiles.

They felt cool on the back of her clammy thighs.

She put her head between her knees and cradled the back of it, stretching her neck, feeling the corner of the magazine pressing into her skull.

Jamie let out a low, miserable laugh and then picked her head up, feeling her eyes burn, blurry with tears.

She was a damn mess.

She stared, vision distorted, up at the large dark welt of her father.

He knelt in front of her, heavy coat hanging around his knees, and pressed his mouth into a concerned line. *This life,* he said, shaking his head slowly.

He said nothing more, just rested his hand on her knee.

She rested hers on top of his, the pistol pinned between, and felt nothing but the cold metal in her grip.

And then, he was gone, and Jamie was once more on her own.

It took her five minutes to get up, at which point she got herself a glass of water, and stood staring into the back garden, still drowned in light.

When she got back to bed, finally, it was getting light out.

She put the pistol on her nightstand, grip angled towards her, and looked at it, fully loaded and ready to go.

Was this really what her life had come to?

Sleeping with a loaded pistol next to her pillow?

Jamie swallowed and screwed her eyes shut.

Yes, it had. But she would rather have it there and not need it, than need it and not have it.

And if she wasn't sure of anything else in the world, she was sure of that.

The next time she saw Elliot Day, there'd be a loaded gun between them.

She just hoped that she would be the one holding it.

16

Jamie solved the problem of being dog-tired two days in a row by doubling the amount of coffee in her drip filter.

She slurped it out of a travel mug as she headed down the stairs, ready to head straight back to the college.

She'd looked up the number as soon as she'd gotten up and put in a call to arrange a meeting with the Head of Student Services, a woman named Eleanor Phillips.

Eleanor hadn't sounded thrilled to fulfil the request, but then again Jamie did give her a list of things she needed access to, and told Eleanor to have them ready when she arrived. When she said that she didn't know whether she could give that information, Jamie did what she hated doing – and threw her weight into it.

'Listen, Eleanor,' she said, not un-derisively. 'This is a murder investigation. Which means we can either do this just you and me, or I can put in a call to the DCI, get a warrant ordered, pull judges into this, get the head of the college on the phone, and march in there with a dozen uniforms and requisition it all. It makes no difference to me, whatsoever.' Jamie was met with silence after. She took it as obedience. 'I'll be there in about thirty.'

Today, she just wasn't in the mood.

The sky overhead was a grey sheet when she pulled into the car park, glaring at the circling traffic wardens.

It was just a quick stop here, and then onto Gilberto Delgado's. But before she left she needed both Chessie Fowler's address, as well as Mimi Paganelli's. And from there, she didn't really know.

One step at a time.

That's all she could do.

Jamie swallowed, checked herself in the mirror – saw a tired, scowling face staring back – and then shouldered her way out of the car, tossing her park-anywhere badge onto the dashboard as she did.

Her phone started buzzing ten steps from the car. 'Hassan,' she said, sighing, pulling it to her ear. 'Where are you? I've been calling you.'

'Yeah, I know, I'm sorry,' he said breathlessly. Jamie could hear crying children in the background, the roar of tyres on the road. He was driving.

Jamie checked her watch. It was nine-twenty already.

'I've just got to drop the kids to school and I'll be right there,' he said, the noise deafening in Jamie's ear. She held the phone away as the pitch rose to a piercing shriek.

'Little late for school, isn't it?' Jamie asked.

'Yeah,' he sighed. 'The missus was supposed to run them down but Angie threw up in her cereal and then over Josie when she tried to clean her off – and then Rami got explosive…' He trailed off, made a grumbling sound, and then took a breath. 'Long story short – Josie had to shower and re-dress, and I had to sort the kids. I'll be there A-S-A-P.' He paused for a second. 'Where are you? HQ?'

Jamie gritted her teeth, adding those things to the mental list of the reasons she didn't want to have kids. 'I'm out at the college,' Jamie said. 'But don't worry – I won't be here for long. I'm heading to do some interviews with the conductor of the orchestra that Alyssa played in, as well as her old roommate.'

'Okay,' Hassan said. 'Shall I meet you there?'

'No, it's fine,' Jamie said. Hassan could be intimidating, and Delgado already struck her as the power-hungry type. Hopefully, if he didn't see Jamie as a threat she could get him talking. And when it came to Chessie, if she was as fragile as she was the night before, then Jamie wanted to handle that alone, too. 'You head to HQ when you can – I'm sure Roper is going out of his mind. I want you two to dig into Gilberto Delgado – he's one of the lecturers here and that expensive violin that Alyssa had – well, turns out she stole it from him.'

'Ouch,' Hassan said. In the background the kids were still screaming. 'Okay – are we looking for anything specific?'

'No, I just want to know who this guy is and everything we can find out about him.' Jamie drew a breath, pulling up just shy of the door she entered through yesterday. 'And have Gretchen check Alyssa's phone again, see whether she can find any communications between her and Chessie Fowler, Alyssa's roommate.'

'You think she's involved?'

'I don't know – I doubt it, but you can never say for sure.' Damn, was she really getting that cynical? 'But when I approached her last night, she asked me if Alyssa was dead, and then ran off crying.'

'What did you say?'

'I didn't say anything – I didn't get chance. It was more like, *she's dead, isn't she?* rather than, *is she dead?* Like she already knew.' Jamie bit her lip, staring in through the glass door.

Scott was sitting behind the desk, and he waved brightly at her.

'Just see what you can dig up,' Jamie said, hoping to get away from the sound of screaming children as quickly as she could. 'And check if Roper's contacted the family yet. And if he hasn't, make him.'

'Make him?'

'I'm authorising the use of deadly force if necessary.'

Hassan laughed a little. 'Sure thing – keep me posted.'

'Will do. And Hassan?'

'Yeah?'

'Good luck – sounds like you need it.' Jamie hung up and stepped inside.

'Officer,' Scott said, grinning. 'Good to see you again.'

'Detective,' Jamie answered, smiling briefly.

'But I'm not a—' Scott started, before cutting himself off, realising

Jamie meant herself. He blushed violently, his cheeks swelling like radishes. 'I'm sorry,' he said quickly. 'I didn't mean to…'

'It's fine,' Jamie said, holding her hand up. 'Easy mistake to make.' She wouldn't even usually correct someone – she never cared about titles. But today she just had no patience, and a headache was starting to develop behind her ears.

Scott laughed, looked at her, eyes twitching a little as he studied her face, and then moved down to her waist.

Jamie narrowed her eyes at him a second, wondering what the hell he was looking at, and then realised she'd not unhooked her pistol. It was still on her hip. Shit, she'd driven with it on, too. Hell, was she that tired? No, her mind was just occupied.

Hard night.

She instinctively pulled the hem of her jacket over it and held onto the corner at the zip-end. 'I'm here to see Eleanor Phillips,' she said, trying to drive the conversation in the right direction.

'Oh right – yeah, I'll call her now.' He grinned at her, and then picked up the phone, dialled an extension, and waited.

He waited a while.

Jamie drew a slow breath, rocking onto the heels of her boots, watching Scott out of the corner of her eye.

He scratched nervously at his unkempt – and unwashed – brown hair, running his tongue over his bottom lip, the thin strands of hair around his mouth bristling. He looked like he was about to say something Jamie hoped he wouldn't, and then he did.

'I'm really sorry about the whole officer-detective thing,' he said quickly, almost garbled.

'It's fine, Scott,' Jamie said, producing the closest thing to a smile she could.

'How about I buy you a coffee or something? As a way of saying sorry.' He gave a wide grin, then brought his mouth down to a more earthly width. Then he swallowed hard, and looked at the desk in front of him. 'It's the least I could do.'

Jamie exhaled slowly, unable to sustain her smile, and clasped her hands together in front of her instead. 'That's a sweet gesture, but you really don't have to.'

'I want to,' he said, a little more force manifesting in his voice now.

'It's not really appropriate,' Jamie said, wondering how long that phone was going to ring in his ear for – or if it even was ringing.

'It's just that the girls here aren't... What I mean is that I've always been mature for my age, and I think you're really—'

'Look, Scott,' Jamie said, coming forward a step. 'I appreciate the thought, but beyond being totally inappropriate, I'm in the middle of a murder investigation here.'

'Murder?' His eyes widened suddenly.

Jamie clenched her jaw. She shouldn't have said that. 'Yes,' she replied measuredly. 'So I really can't—'

'Is it Alyssa? Did he murder her?' Scott asked, the surprise in his face apparent. His thick eyebrows were very expressive, Jamie noted.

She tweaked. 'He? Who's *he?*'

Scott opened his mouth to reply and then froze, the cogs in his head turning. 'I...' he started. 'I don't... remember?'

Jamie narrowed her eyes at him.

'I'm sure I will...' Scott said slowly, measuring his words. 'But it could take a while...'

Jamie's jaw flexed.

'Say... the amount of time it takes to drink a cup of coffee?'

She drew a long breath and then let the anger welling inside her ebb away. She didn't even know what to say to that. But if Scott did have some information, she needed it. Though she wasn't prepared to rent her time out in exchange.

'You do realise,' Jamie said, coming forward to the desk now, 'that if you have information that could be useful in an active murder investigation, knowingly withholding it is grounds to be arrested for obstruction of justice?'

Scott swallowed hard, lowered his head, and looked up at her from under his thick, crumpled eyebrows.

'And that trying to blackmail a police officer is also a crime that carries a heavy sentence?'

'I…' He began, his bottom jaw flapping, tongue quivering behind his teeth.

Jamie felt a twinge of guilt, but if she let off now, she'd just have to deal with the aftermath of his grovelling apology.

'So who is *he?*'

'Uh, I don't know if I should…' He looked around nervously.

'Name, Scott, now,' Jamie said, feeling the corners of her eyes twitch.

'Don't tell him I told you… It's…'

'Today, Scott.'

'Mr Delgado.'

'The conductor?' Jamie tried to keep the surprise out of her voice. She'd thought he was squirrelly and the violin was motive, but had not really pegged him as the murderous type.

He nodded.

'Why do you think he murdered Alyssa?'

'I mean, I don't think – I don't know,' he said, shaking his head now.

'Breathe, Scott.'

He forced one into his lungs.

Scott was visibly sweating now.

'Tell me what you know. Was it over the violin?'

'No – maybe – he was definitely angry about that, but… but it was because they were…'

'They were what?'

'You know.'

'I really don't.'

'Together.'

Jamie's eyes narrowed to slits, her pulse quickening. 'Together?'

He licked his bottom lip, still clutching the receiver to his neck, the back of his thin hand showing to Jamie.

'Romantically?'

'I think… everyone was saying it. It was a rumour,' he said apologetically. 'You know, because they spent so much time practicing together – but then I saw them leaving, once… It was late, after practice. They stayed sometimes, to work on Alyssa's parts – the concertos, mostly.' He was speaking quickly again and Jamie could see his pulse thundering in his neck.

'You saw them leaving?' Jamie filled her chest. 'Elaborate.'

'They left the practice hall just before nine.'

'And?'

'And they were holding hands.'

'And?'

'She was laughing, and leaning against him – he kissed the side of her head, whispered something in her ear.'

'When?'

'Last year – the spring, maybe? Before everyone went home for summer.'

Jamie took that in. So they were having a relationship? Her nineteen at the time, him fifty-odd. Her a student, he a teacher. Her teacher. Her mentor.

Crime of passion? He oozed that when she watched him last night. To lose not only his star violinist, but also a lover? Did she take the violin just to spite him? To drive a knife into his chest? Did he do the same to her?

'Thank you, Scott,' Jamie said. 'You've been very helpful.'

'You're welcome,' he said, albeit reservedly.

Jamie homed in on the phone he was still holding onto. 'No answer, I guess?'

He glanced down at it, then back at her, smiling sheepishly.

She wasted no time in reaching over and snatching the receiver out of his hand.

His fingers opened like it was a hot coal and Jamie held it to her ear.

It was there an instant before she registered the dull bleep of the off-the-hook tone.

He'd never even dialled the extension. Just tapped some random button.

Jamie growled and slapped the receiver down on the counter. She didn't like being screwed with. Especially not when her patience was as thin as this. 'Eleanor Phillips' office. What number is it?'

Scott shrank into his chair. 'Uh, three-oh-three.'

Jamie was already moving.

'The lifts are—'

'I'm taking the stairs,' she called back, hip-checking the door open and disappearing into the stairwell.

'I'm sorry!' He called, his voice reverberating off the concrete blocks just before the door snapped shut behind her.

Scott's voice died in the echo chamber as she ascended to three, her headache worsening, and prayed that Eleanor had the information ready. If not… Well, her mood wasn't exactly getting better by the step.

'You're later than I expected,' Eleanor said as Jamie knocked on the open door and stepped into her office. 'DS Johansson, I presume?'

Jamie nodded and moved into the middle of the room.

The walls were a tired shade of robin's egg blue, and the ficus in the corner looked desperately in need of watering.

Eleanor was in her forties, her hair tied back into a low ponytail behind her head, her features sharp, lipstick a sickly shade of cranberry red. She gestured to the wire-framed chair in front of her desk but Jamie lifted her hand to decline and then folded her arms. 'Yeah, I got held up at the front desk,' she said moodily.

'Oh,' Eleanor said, rolling her eyes and making a little *tut* sound. 'Scott can be a talker.'

'Isn't he just.'

'So…' Eleanor started, gauging Jamie's demeanour. 'I expect you want to just get right down to business?'

'If you don't mind.'

'Of course,' Eleanor said, smiling politely. Though the creases at the corners of her eyes told Jamie she wanted to be done with this as quickly as possible.

That made two of them.

'These the files?' Jamie asked, nodding to a short stack of manilla folders on the desk.

Eleanor gestured to them and then clasped her hands together on the desk in front of her, seemingly unable to even muster the energy to confirm verbally.

Jamie picked them up and opened the top one. Chessie Fowler. This was her student record – including her current address, contact details, next of kin, emergency contacts. Everything Jamie wanted and needed.

She closed it and switched them in her hands, seeing Mimi Paganelli's name on the second top page.

Jamie nodded to herself in approval and swung them down under her arm so that they rested against her hip. 'Thank you.'

'Is there anything else I can help with?'

Jamie thought for a second. 'Yes, actually.'

Eleanor's smile twitched, like it was a mask whose glue had just dislodged. It looked ready to fall right off her face.

'Can I see the information you have on Gilberto Delgado – employment records – that sort of thing?'

'You didn't ask for—'

'Yeah, yeah, I know I didn't,' Jamie said quickly. 'But I'm asking now.'

'Well,' Eleanor said, letting out a long exhale, 'It will take a while to dig it out.'

'That's fine,' Jamie said, checking her watch. 'Just email it over when you get a minute.' She dug a card out of her jacket pocket and held it out to Eleanor.

She seemed reluctant to take it. 'Is, er,' she started, 'Mr Delgado involved in the… *case?'*

'We're just gathering information at this point,' Jamie said diplomatically. Jamie had to disclose that their investigation was to do with a former student – Alyssa Doran – but otherwise, she'd divulged nothing.

'Right.' Eleanor nodded.

'Why? Do you think he might be?'

'No, no,' she said quickly. 'It was just a question.'

Jamie wiggled the card. 'I have another meeting to get to, but thank you for these,' she said, lifting the files a little. 'If I need anything else, I'll be in touch.'

'Of course,' Eleanor said, taking it finally.

Jamie read her face, studied how fast she'd said that she didn't think Delgado was involved. How sure she seemed.

Jamie lingered, waiting for Eleanor to speak – to see what she'd say. She looked like there was something she wanted to.

Jamie relaxed her posture, lowered her head slightly, put on a softer tone. 'And if there's anything you think would be of use to me or the case, don't hesitate to call. My number is on there as well.' She smiled briefly. 'Call me any time.'

'Okay,' Eleanor said, holding the little white card in both hands, looking at it.

Jamie checked her watch again. She'd be late if she didn't leave now, and she didn't want to miss Delgado. Especially as he was becoming more central to the case by the minute.

But there was something else there. Eleanor knew more than she was letting on.

Jamie paused at the threshold, wrestling the seconds, and checked the corridor for anyone coming. She turned back. One last try. 'Have you known Mr Delgado for a while?'

Eleanor looked sheepish suddenly. 'A little while. A few years. Why do you ask?'

'No reason,' Jamie said, sighing. 'What's he like? Is he nice?'

'Yes, I suppose,' she said, measuring her words, not sure where Jamie was going with this.

'Is he single?' Jamie asked, scratching casually at a bead in the paint on the frame.

She watched Eleanor stiffen out of the corner of her eye. 'I don't know.'

But she did know.

Jamie may not have had many female friends, but she could read women like a book. 'Handsome, isn't he? The Spanish look – tall, tanned…'

Eleanor swallowed, stuck her bottom lip out, and then began straightening papers. 'If you like that sort of thing.' She was being aloof now.

Jamie restrained a smirk. She'd hit a nerve.

If Eleanor wasn't involved with Delgado, she wanted to be.

By the sounds of it, he got around.

'Thanks, Eleanor,' Jamie said, moving through the door. 'You've been a big help.'

More than you know.

17

JAMIE CLOSED in on Gilberto Delgado's house just before ten.

He'd asked her to call first, but she'd not wanted to give him any notice.

She wanted him rattled.

Especially since, by Scott's account, he was sleeping with Alyssa.

Jamie stared at his house.

It was a modest townhouse – three stories, narrow, but expensive. More than what a teacher at a university should be able to easily afford, at least.

She drew a slow breath and pulled her phone up, keeping one eye on his front door. She texted Gretchen. 'Delgado – can we find out his income? Whether he's got anything squirrelled away. What he made while he was touring with the national orchestra. Family money. Anything like that.'

She texted back almost instantly. 'We?'

Jamie's jaw tightened. 'You?'

'On it.'

Jamie sighed and put her phone down, kicking her legs out of the car. She had a little time before ten and Delgado said he wouldn't be leaving until after.

She crossed the road, the worst of the city's traffic having already eased its way to work, and climbed the stairs to Delgado's front door.

Jamie adjusted her holster so that it was further around her hip – less intimidating that way – and lifted her hand to knock.

She froze, the sounds of the city fading to white noise behind her.

Her right hand moved on autopilot, going to the place her pistol usually was, and then sliding around her belt to the grip.

Jamie's heart bounced in her chest, the black door with the tarnished brass knocker in front of her sitting slightly ajar in the frame.

She swallowed, scanned the street, and then laid her left hand on the paint, her right resting on the grip of her Glock.

The slab of wood swung inwards on its hinges, creaking softly, and revealed a dated but clean interior.

Hardwood floors, pale, painted walls, and decorations that spoke of Delgado's Spanish origins. A quaint side table sat against the wall before the stairs, a picture of himself as a younger man hanging above it. He was standing on the peak of a craggy mountain, his arm around another man. His cheeks were sunburnt, the golden lenses of his sunglasses glowing in the blazing sun.

The words written in the corner, in handwriting, said *Mulhacén, '03*. She didn't know if that was the name of the mountain or the person that Delgado was with.

A clock ticked somewhere in the interior, but Jamie could hear nothing else.

She stepped forward slowly, listening for the sound of anyone in the house, any sign of anything amiss.

There were none.

A ceramic bowl sat on the side table and Jamie could see car keys in it.

She didn't like that.

It meant, for one thing, he hadn't left in the car. And the distance to the college campus was too far to walk. At least comfortably. No more than three or four kilometres – an easy run. But an hour's walk, probably.

Sure, he could have taken public transport. There was always that chance. But the car keys had his house key on it too.

She exhaled, settling herself, and approached the door on her right that led to the front room.

Jamie's fingers closed around the handle and she pushed down softly, letting it swing inwards.

The clock ticked louder – an antique grandfather sat next to the fireplace.

There was a brown leather sofa, a woven rug with blues and yellows in a circular pattern on it, and a large television. It was scant on decoration otherwise – a lonely photo of a shaggy dog on the book case – which only seemed to be filled with music books and what looked like a few old thriller novels.

It felt like a bachelor's pad to her.

But where was the bachelor?

As she moved deeper inside, hand still resting on the grip of her pistol, she wondered at whether or not this was cause enough to enter? She could if she thought someone was in immediate danger… then again, the door was open. But what did that mean?

Had Delgado left for work, forgot to close the door, and now she was trespassing?

Had he rushed out last night the second he'd got home? Thrown some things in a bag, and was now across the Channel and fleeing into Europe, another killer escaping her clutches?

She set her jaw, hoping not.

Or was she about to find him dead, his hands cut off? Like Alyssa.

Who was he in this mess? Victim? Killer? Bystander?

The kitchen lay ahead, through an arch, and she stepped in, barely breathing.

The spartan decoration continued here. There was nothing on the worn wooden counter tops except one jar of utensils and a coffee machine.

Jamie sniffed the air, looking at the pot filled with black liquid.

She could smell the bittersweet aroma of a fresh brew.

A quick check over her shoulder let her know she was still alone, and then she crossed the tiled floor quickly and rested the back of her hand against the glass.

Still hot.

And there were no cups in the sink.

Shit.

She didn't like this. Not one bit.

Jamie swallowed and looked around, searching for anything amiss.

Her eyes roved, and then stopped.

The microwave was flashing – zero-zero, zero-zero.

She approached it with more haste now, the tension in her shoulders making them ache.

A buzzing had developed in the back of her skull.

Jamie reached out and pulled the handle open.

There was a cup in there, drowned in the bright yellow interior light.

She rested the backs of her fingers against it, the porcelain warm against her knuckles.

She must have just missed him.

Shit. He'd been warming milk, ready for his morning coffee. And then something had happened.

Something bad.

Jamie felt the tell-tale click of her pistol coming free of the holster and slowly raised it in front of her, her heart beating on the inside of her ribcage now.

She could feel it in her throat, in her wrists.

In a blur, she was back through the living room and into the hall, heading for the stairs, pausing every moment or two to listen for footsteps above.

Nothing.

Jamie approached the bottom step, reaching out and pushing the open front door close to the jamb before going upstairs.

The carpet on the stairs dulled the sound of her soles pressing into the steps, a mix of caution and haste in her gait.

She led with the muzzle of her weapon, sweeping across the landing.

Nothing.

No one.

There were three rooms upstairs – a bathroom and two bedrooms. And much like in her own apartment, another staircase led to the second floor.

All the doors here were open.

The bathroom was clear, the back bedroom clean and empty, too – a guest room.

The front bedroom's door was half-closed and the smell coming through the gap told Jamie that it was where Delgado slept.

The smell of a body. A slight odour of sweat. Of aftershave.

She nosed the door open with her gun and then pushed it with her elbow stepping in and doing a once-over with the pistol.

The bed was unmade on one side, but nothing else was amiss.

Shit. He wasn't here.

Jamie could see the side of a suitcase under the bed, and just to cross it off the list, she stepped in and headed for the wardrobe.

She reached out and paused, her hand hovering in the air.

Slowly, she reached up and tugged the sleeve of her top down over her knuckles, and then took hold of the wardrobe handle, pulling it open.

For all she knew, this could be a crime scene.

The wardrobe was full – no empty hangars. At least not enough to suggest that he'd torn clothes from them and shoved them into a bag.

She checked the drawers next.

All full of pants, socks, undershirts.

He'd not packed anything.

Which to her said that he hadn't left of his own volition. At least not with the intention of fleeing.

Jamie exited swiftly and went for the stairs, keen to check the last room off her list and call this in.

The house was as silent as death, and she was more and more sure that Delgado wasn't here. He'd been taken.

The attic room was a narrow, pitched space that Delgado had turned into a practice room.

The floor was carpeted thickly, and across the back, bare brick wall, sheets of music had been pinned up between photographs of him playing as a younger man. He was standing amongst the orchestra in some, shaking hands with people in others. He had his arm around a woman in another. All of them shot at one of his performances. Marking occasions or milestones.

He was sentimental, if nothing else. And proud of what he'd achieved.

A music stand was positioned next to one of the skylights, and a violin sat on a perch, gleaming red in the dim brilliance coming through the window above.

Dust motes floated aimlessly in the shaft, unaware of Delgado's fate.

Jamie sighed and dropped her gun to her side. 'Shit,' she muttered, inventorying the room with her eyes.

Nothing seemed out of place to her, but then again, she didn't know Delgado from the next person.

She was about to turn away when she paused, and glanced back at the wall, something catching her eye in the seeming chaos of pinned-up sheets and poorly arranged photographs.

A blank spot.

Jamie went over, her boots sinking into the thick, noise-deadening carpet, and reached out, running her fingers across the bricks that seemed to stick out between the papers, a perfect square of space.

She looked at the pads – clean.

The rest of the photographs were covered in dust. She could see it resting on the tops of their frames.

Jamie lifted the bottom of the sheet of paper pinned to the wall above it – the weathered front page from Mozart's Concerto No.5 for violin, signed by someone Jamie presumed was involved in the orchestra that performed it – and saw what she expected: a single, lonely nail.

A picture had been here.

Until recently.

Either Delgado had taken it, or the person who had taken him had.

Jamie didn't have enough information to go on either way. But she didn't like this one bit.

A second later, she was heading down the stairs, her phone already at her ear. 'Roper,' she called between breaths as he answered.

'Hey boss,' he replied, glib as ever. 'What's up?'

'We got a problem. I need you out here now – Gilberto Delgado, the victim's teacher and the conductor of the orchestra – he's missing.'

'Missing? Missing how?'

She grunted, her feet hitting the ground floor. 'Like he's not here, Roper – and he should be. Door open, keys on the side-table, fresh coffee in the pot and milk in the microwave.'

Roper drew a slow breath. 'You sweep the house?' he asked pragmatically.

'Yes.'

'Signs of struggle?'

'None. But someone else was here – a picture has been taken from upstairs.'

'Of the killer?'

Jamie's scalp prickled. 'I don't know.' She hadn't really thought that hard about it. But if the kidnapper had taken it, then it made sense. Especially if it was someone who knew Alyssa. 'Just get out here – and bring SOCO. I want this house swept, and I want Delgado's life picked apart piece by piece.'

'Okay. Hassan's not long turned up, you want me to bring him?'

Jamie drew a breath and looked at her watch. 'No, I'm going to head to Chessie Fowler's. Alyssa's old room-mate, see if I can't find out exactly what happened last October. Hassan can meet me there.'

'Oh,' Roper said, dejected suddenly. 'Okay. I'll put in a call and see what uniforms are around, get someone to hold down the scene for you.' He cleared his throat. 'Keep you updated.'

'Thanks, Roper,' Jamie said, but by the time the word came out of her mouth, the line was already dead. She exhaled hard, trying not to feel bad about throwing Roper the scraps – if that's what you could call an active crime scene – and headed down to her car.

She slotted into the driver's seat, keeping an eye on the ajar door of

Delgado's house, and pulled the folders onto her lap. She needed more information. About Alyssa, about Delgado. About what they were doing together.

Shit, Delgado could have staged his own kidnap, she supposed? A double bluff to let him get away clean?

Why did she want it to be him? It would make it neater. She could just hunt him down, catch the son of a bitch, and that would be it. Or better yet, if he'd fled the country, toss the case to Interpol and be done with it.

No. She shook her head. That wasn't her. She wasn't that sort of detective. She finished what she started.

Her head swirled as she thought of Elliot, lurking out there somewhere.

Jamie exhaled, forcing her mind straight, and opened the file, scanning down to Chessie's address.

It wasn't far.

But then she paused, and remembered one of the other pages that she'd seen when she leafed through in Eleanor's office.

On page three, there was a class schedule.

It said that Chessie had class from ten until twelve that morning. And it was already ten. Jamie rubbed her eyes, feeling tired, and then leant her head back against the headrest.

She pulled up Mimi's file instead, saw that her apartment was even closer than Chessie's, and then checked page three.

Mimi wasn't in class until one.

She had time.

Finally, some good news.

Her phone buzzed next to her. It was Roper – who famously never text. And yet he had. Damn, he must really be pissed to be left out. 'Uniforms en route. Be there in two.'

That was something at least.

'Thanks,' she typed back. And then added. 'Have you contacted Alyssa's parents?'

She stared down at it for a second, and then deleted it, sending the single word instead.

He didn't reply again.

Jamie called Hassan instead, glad to hear a more friendly voice, and gave him Mimi's address. 'I'll meet you there.'

'Got it,' Hassan answered diligently. 'See you there.'

Jamie let the phone fall from her ear, and tapped it gently against her chin, staring up at Delgado's door, trying to fix it together into some sort of coherent shape in her head.

But so far, she couldn't.

She was missing too many pieces and she couldn't tell what the puzzle was a picture of.

Jamie checked her watch again and felt her heels jig in the footwell, springing up and down against the carpet under her pedals, a creeping sense of dread curling through her guts.

She wanted to get to Mimi's as quickly as she could.

But it didn't matter how fast she got there.

Because it was already too late.

18

JAMIE PULLED UP A STREET AWAY.

She'd circled through Mimi's, but it was full.

The buildings looked sort of industrial, like they were originally warehouses or factories. Hewn from red brick, with big, Georgian-esque windows and weeds growing out of the mortar.

Hassan texted to say he was a few minutes out when Jamie got out of the car. She'd been leafing through the student information on Mimi. She was here on a full performance scholarship, and had plenty of experience as first-chair in her previous ensembles. Jamie wondered how she took that – coming from the other side of the world, South Korea, to be the star of the college's orchestra. Only to be snubbed by a local girl.

She had impeccable grades, too. Firsts across the board. Jamie made a mental note to check up on Alyssa's school records. That was something she hadn't done yet.

Jamie locked her car, checked the handle, and then straightened her jeans. The holster always had a way of making them sit a little funny. It hooked onto her belt, but it seemed to force her t-shirt up over the grip, and somehow push the corner of her underwear just a half-inch too low on her hip.

Wearing one made her feel a little safer. But the continual discomfort was definitely a price to pay.

She sighed, covered it with the hem of her jacket and headed around.

As she approached the concrete steps leading up to the entrance hall Hassan came jogging down the pavement from the other direction.

He looked out of breath, a little sweaty.

'Sorry,' he said when he was about ten feet away. 'I had to park a street over. This place is a nightmare.'

Jamie swung her eye over the parking situation – cars bumper to bumper on both sides of the road. He was right. It was. But streets like this full of apartment blocks were always the same.

'It's fine,' Jamie said, keen to get upstairs. 'Let's just get on with this.' She could feel the tension in her voice. Delgado's disappearance had rattled her. And she didn't want to miss another key witness.

Jamie approached the door – modern glass with a metal strut in the middle. The glade was frosted, the interior murky beyond.

'Locked,' Hassan surmised, looking at the fob-lock needed to get in.

The door was magnetically sealed. Jamie had seen plenty like it in student accommodation. It helped to keep unwanted visitors out.

But there was still a buzzer system, and Jamie wasted no time in pressing the button for 4C, Mimi's apartment.

The chime rang out and Jamie let off after a second. Pressing it again, and then again. Just to make sure she was heard.

She could feel her patience wearing thin.

There was no response.

Jamie exhaled, straightened her belt again, and then pressed for a fourth time.

Nothing.

She scowled and clicked her incisors together, the same sense of dread that had never quite left since Delgado's creeping up again.

'Now what?' Hassan asked, squinting up at the building like he was going to spider his way up there.

'Old detective trick,' Jamie half muttered as she ran her fingers down all the buttons. The chimes all rang out in a thick cacophony and Hassan raised an eyebrow.

After a second, there was a crackling, and a voice came out of the little speaker box.

'Hello?' it said. It sounded like a guy. Tentative.

Jamie wasn't sure which apartment it was from. But it didn't matter.

'This is Detective Sergeant Jamie Johansson with the London Metropolitan Police. We're here enquiring about an active murder investigation and we're looking to speak to Mimi Paganelli. Can you buzz us in, please?' she said formally, but assertively.

There was silence on the line, but Jamie could hear his faint breathing through the quiet crackle of static.

'If you refuse, that could be considered obstruction of justice. A chargeable offence in—'

The line went dead and the door buzzed, the magnetic lock disengaging.

Jamie reached out and pushed it open with her foot, gesturing for Hassan to lead. 'After you.'

He smirked a little. 'I'll remember that one for next time,' he said, pushing the door wide with his large hand.

There was no lift inside, but the stairs didn't bother Jamie. She went up them like a mountain goat.

Hassan, on the other hand, had a lot more bulk to heft than she did, and by the third floor, he was squeezing at his quads with his hands, grunting a little with each step.

'They don't keep you fit in AR?' Jamie joked, trying to lighten the apprehension that had swallowed them up.

The stairwell was dead quiet.

'AR keep us fit,' he said, his breathing ragged. 'But three months of R-and-R, and my wife's home cooking isn't doing me much good.' He slapped his own belly. What little there was of it, at least.

Jamie hadn't noticed that he'd put on any weight, but studying his form lugging its way up the stairs behind her, the chiselled torso bulging through the shirt that she'd taken note of a few months earlier had had some of its corners rounded off.

Even under the Harrington-style jacket he was wearing, anyone could tell he was a muscular guy. But it took serious work to keep your fitness high enough to carry all that extra weight.

On four, Jamie slowed the pace, letting Hassan catch up and grab his breath.

She spotted 4A on right, B on the left, and then another door about twenty feet down the corridor.

Jamie cast a quick glance over her shoulder at Hassan, who nodded, filling his lungs, and then motioned her on.

She walked forward, tweaking her ears automatically, the sounds of music coming from the door on the right. The one on the left offering nothing.

A faint smell of stale alcohol hung in the air, the dark grey carpet blotched darker in places.

The walls were scuffed.

Somewhere on the floor below, there was laughing and shouting.

It echoed dully through the building.

Students.

Jamie thought back to her own student years.

She barely went out. Didn't drink. Didn't 'party'.

Between her father's old habits, and then his death, it didn't exactly put her in the party-hearty mood.

Jamie shook it off, slowed at 4C, and turned back to Hassan.

She caught his eye, saw that he'd gotten his breath back, and then knocked the door with her knuckles down low, next to her thigh. 'Let me do the talking, alright?' Jamie said.

'Sure,' Hassan replied, smiling. 'Wouldn't know what I was asking about, anyway.'

Jamie studied his face, wondering if that was a jab at her for not including him in the investigation enough so far.

She'd met Delgado the night before at the college, and then gone there first thing alone. But otherwise, he was up to speed? She didn't have time to hold his hand through this, that much she knew for sure. He'd need to sink or swim.

Jamie swallowed, and then cursed herself for being so harsh. Hassan was a good man, and a good officer. He was definitely out of his element here, more used to having a rifle in his hands than a murder investigation.

She forced a smile back. 'I'll lead the questions – you keep an eye on her reactions, look for anything out of place. And if I give you the signal, give the apartment a once-over.'

'The signal?'

Her and Roper had this sort of thing all worked out. But she didn't have time to run Hassan through it all. 'I'll touch my right ear,' she said, the motion coming to mind first.

He nodded. 'Alright. The old one-two. You keep her busy, I'll go through her drawers.'

She laughed a little – one muted note. 'You can keep your fingers out of her underwear. Just check for anything that's out of place.'

'If you say so,' he replied, holding his hands up innocently.

Jamie shook her head a little, and quietened herself, listening at the door.

No movement inside.

She knocked again, harder this time. 'Mimi?' she called. 'Mimi Paganelli?' Maybe she was asleep. Heavy night, perhaps. It wasn't out of the question. She'd rushed off somewhere the previous evening – maybe it was to a party.

Jamie exhaled and stepped back, glancing up and down the corridor. Maybe she was just out.

'Jamie.'

She looked up at Hassan, who's voice was hushed, his eyes widened a little.

Her hackles rose and she followed his eyes down past her left hip, to the doorframe.

She'd been standing in front of it, hadn't noticed.

A handprint on the white frame.

Four fingers, a smeared palm.

In blood.

She stiffened, staring at it, and stepped close to the door again.

Bloodied handprint coming out? That wasn't good.

Jamie pressed her ear to the surface, listened for anything inside.

There was nothing.

Dead silence.

Jamie's fingers twitched, wanting to reach for her pistol.

She closed her fist now and banged on the wood. 'Mimi Paganelli, this is Detective Sergeant Jamie Johansson. If you're in there, let us know.'

Jamie could feel her jaw flexing, the skin on the back of her head bunching, her scalp prickling.

She stared down at the dark carpet between her boots, studied the worn fibres. The dark spots.

Speckles. Droplets. Blood? There was no way to tell.

'Shit,' Jamie said, standing back and looking at Hassan. She weighed probable cause in her head. If Delgado was gone from his house, he could be in there right now with her, knife against her throat.

Jamie looked at the handle – it wasn't a key fob this time. She swallowed hard, reached for it with her left hand, dragging her Glock from its holster simultaneously.

The metal was cool under her grip, the spring inside the mechanism whining gently as the handle hit the bottom of the arc.

She didn't know if she wanted it to be locked or unlocked.

Her stomach was churning either way.

The latch clicked open and the door swung inwards on its hinge, the sickening metallic tang of blood thick in the air.

She remembered it well from the tunnel where Alyssa had been killed.

That same rusty stench.

Jamie looked down, the hardwearing carpet turning to cheap, beach-coloured laminate, the unidentifiable droplets on the carpet now stark red splatters leading in a trail from the doorway, swinging inwards, out of view behind the door.

She looked at Hassan, his pistol already out, too, and then stepped in, cautiously.

Jamie tip-toed right and then left, stepping over the trail of blood, keeping her eyes moving up and down to make sure she wasn't surprised.

The apartment was small – barely bigger than a studio.

On the left was a wraparound kitchen with a small table, a lonely cup sitting on it.

In the middle was a living space – a sofa and a desk against the back wall, modest TV against the inner wall. And on the far side of it, a door into what had to be the bedroom. It was closed, and the blood trail led between the sofa and a coffee table, straight under it.

Jamie shuddered, the trail thickening as it got closer to the bedroom, and steadied herself, the pistol half raised.

It quivered in her grip.

Hassan came up on her right and touched her shoulder, motioning her forward.

Jamie tried to move, but her legs had seized.

She knew what lay beyond that door.

Or who.

Mimi Paganelli.

Hassan tapped her again.

How could she have been so stupid? She knew that the killer was going to want to strike again – do it right this time. Mimi was a prime target if he was after a talented violinist.

She should have been quicker.

Hassan took the lead now, stepping past her, and gestured to his eyes, and then to Jamie. *Watch me.*

She lowered her head, drew a slow breath, felt the bulk of her father looming over her suddenly. *It's not your fault, Jamie,* he said, his voice low, husky. She could almost smell the whisky on his breath, the roughness of his fingers as he brushed them across her temple, moving the ever-errant strand of hair off her forehead behind her ear. *It's just the job, and it doesn't get any easier.*

She looked up, her father gone, and homed in on Hassan.

Steeling herself, she moved forward again, closing the distance between herself and the door.

Hassan was already there, leaning against the frame.

He switched hands, holding his pistol aloft in his left now, so that his elbow was against the door, his body aimed out at Jamie.

She watched as his fist closed around the handle, and then he paused.

Jamie hovered in front of it, straddling the blood trail, and met his eyes.

He was waiting for her mark.

Jamie filled her chest, tried to slow her heart, and nodded before she lost her nerve.

Hassan pushed down and shoved the door inwards, swapping hands again like the professional he was, and Jamie stepped through, covering the entire room with her muzzle in a second.

No sign of the killer.

But his work was evident.

Jamie let her gun fall to her side, her guts knotting up inside her.

Hassan stepped in next to her. 'Damn,' he muttered under his breath.

Jamie's forearm came to her face and she held her sleeve against her nose, trying to block out the smell.

The bedroom was small, but the mess wasn't.

Though the body lying here in front of them wasn't Mimi Paganelli.

Jamie pulled her phone out and called Roper, turning away from the gruesome scene in front of her.

'Yeah?' he asked, his voice bouncing as he walked. 'I'm almost to Delgado's now – SOCOs are about ten minutes out.'

'Don't bother,' Jamie said gravely. 'Delgado's can wait, tell them to come here instead.'

'What?' He stopped, his heels clacking on the pavement. 'Why? What about Delgado?'

Jamie let out a long breath and turned back to the bedroom doorway, to the scene beyond. 'He's here.'

Hassan was kneeling down, looking more closely at Gilberto Delgado. He was sitting up, slumped against the bed, his chin resting on his chest, his legs splayed in front of him.

His hands were on his thighs, fingers facing the ceiling, set like claws, soaked red with his own blood.

Delgado's stomach was a mess of ragged fabric and deep, angry looking gashes.

Stab marks.

Three, maybe four by Jamie's count.

Her blood ran a little cold and she turned away again, Roper's voice swimming back in her ear.

'He's there? Going after Mimi? Did you arrest him?'

'No, Roper,' Jamie muttered, her voice cracking. 'He's dead.'

19

THEY COULD HEAR Roper coming from the third floor.

He took an age to get up the stairs, and though he arrived before the SOCOs, by the time he reached the apartment, they'd already over-taken him.

Jamie and Hassan were standing back from the bedroom, letting the officers do their work. Taking photos, collecting blood samples.

They were both transfixed, trying to work it out in their heads.

But right now it was like someone had taken the puzzle pieces and dumped them out on the floor. And then stolen the box so they didn't even know what they were building.

'Jesus,' Roper said, limping through the door, his face red and blotchy from the climb.

He stopped and looked over the apartment, following the trail of blood with his eyes to the propped-up body of Delgado against the bed.

Jamie went over, suddenly glad to have his eyes here. His mind.

Roper had been a mentor to her, whether she second-guessed everything he said or not. And she always appreciated his input and his summations.

And Hassan was obviously feeling the pressure, too. He'd not said a word since they'd found Delgado. This was a far cry from

Armed Response. And a quick-study or not, this was serious. Two deaths. And now Mimi Paganelli was missing. And her life was definitely on the clock. The killer seemed to be wasting no time. But why Delgado? Why was he dead? And why did he still have his hands?

Jamie tried to clear her mind, turning to Roper. 'Officers holding down Delgado's house?' she asked, dispensing with the formalities.

Roper nodded. 'Yeah, two of them there, waiting for SOCO.'

'We'll send them over after this, see what they can pull.'

'They might be a while,' Roper said, expression grim, as he stared into the bedroom.

'Mm,' Jamie replied, not wanting to look at it just then. She knew she'd have to get up close soon enough. But the air out here wasn't too repugnant and she wanted to drink it in while she could. 'What about Chessie Fowler. She been picked up yet?'

'Two uniforms on the way to the college as we speak.'

'Good,' Jamie said, sighing with relief. Her two key witnesses had already been taken from her. She couldn't risk Chessie's life, too. Alyssa was the start, but there was entanglement here. Alyssa and Delgado's relationship… Alyssa and Mimi's rivalry… Alyssa and Chessie's friendship… The killer was someone close to them. Someone who was inside this knot of love and relation. 'I want her in custody as soon as we can, and held for questioning.' She paused, thinking about it. 'I don't care how it looks. I want her pulled out of class and in the back of a police car ten minutes ago.'

Roper nodded in agreement, but didn't take out his phone to communicate that to the officers en route. Maybe he didn't realise she was asking him to pass it along. Maybe he'd already expressed a similar sentiment.

Jamie opened her mouth to interrogate it, then quit on the idea. She wanted Roper's attention exactly where it was just then. On the apartment. Not on whatever little power-spat was bubbling between them.

She exhaled hard. 'Smith's going to want an update, and something solid for us to go on. And I'd like to give it to him.'

Roper rubbed his neck. 'Then let's get to work.'

Jamie smiled at him. 'Like getting the band back together, eh?' she said playfully, trying to build a bridge.

'If you say so,' Roper replied, sticking his bottom lip out and stomping right through the middle of it.

He stepped forward towards the bedroom and Jamie moved alongside him.

They hovered by the door, two SOCOs inside in white suits, kneeling over the body. One was measuring the wounds and the other was taking photographs.

Jamie had a strong suspicion they'd match the knife used on Alyssa. The killer liked the gut it seemed. Liked to get up close and personal. He'd rushed Delgado in the same way he'd rushed Alyssa. Driven him backwards, blade in his belly.

Jamie stared down at the wounds. Multiple stabs.

Anger came to mind.

Alyssa had one wound. One, hard, necessary strike.

Delgado had deserved more.

Maybe he fought back more?

Or maybe the killer just wanted to feel that knife go in again. And again.

'Stabbed him a few times,' Jamie said aloud now, nodding to the body.

'Four,' one of the SOCOs said from behind his mask, looking up at her. 'Best we can tell so far.'

Roper sucked his teeth. 'Entry wounds look jagged – really put that knife into him, didn't he. Wanted to hurt him.'

Jamie felt her shoulders relax a little. As dire as the situation was, having Roper here made her feel a lot more at ease. 'Personal connection.' She nodded to herself. 'Revenge.'

'Could be. How'd he get him here?'

'Must have been important enough to make him run out of his house without his car keys. The coffee in the pot was still hot.' Jamie was just talking aloud now.

Roper furrowed his brow, thinking about it. 'So the killer lures Delgado here and then kills him?'

'Looks like.'

Roper touched the nearest SOCO on the shoulder – the one with the camera —and gestured to Delgado. 'Check his pocket – he got a phone on him?'

The SOCO patted Delgado's soaked jeans and slid the phone in his left pocket out, offering it to Roper.

He patted his jacket pockets, looking for the thing Jamie knew he didn't have.

She was already handing him a pair of gloves from her own. She'd taken to carrying a spare pair on account of Roper never having any with him.

The box in her car was surprisingly full these days, now that he wasn't taking out of it.

He noticed them, glanced up at her, and then took them. 'Thanks,' he muttered, pulling them on and taking the phone from the SOCO. He clicked it on and the screen lit up, a dull smear of dried blood clinging to it.

An alert was visible on the screen. It said, 'Study Of Modern Classical: Milko Kelemen.' The line underneath said. 'Started 21 minutes ago.'

Roper tried to unlock it but it required a code.

Jamie checked her watch. It was now ten-fifty-one. He said he'd be out just after ten, and this looked to be a reference to his teaching schedule.

But what would have made him run out of the house without his keys in such a blind panic?

That was the phrase that came to mind. Blind panic. To drop everything and what, *sprint* here? Jamie screwed up her face. No, it wasn't that close – and even in rush-hour traffic, she would bet that ninety-nine out of a hundred people would take the car.

She exhaled.

'What is it?' Roper asked, reading her face.

'Don't know, something doesn't fit here.' Jamie closed her eyes. The how could wait. What mattered the most was *why* he was here.

Jamie thought back to Alyssa. What did she know? Scott had said they were in a relationship. But Alyssa had fled the school, deleted her socials… She guessed that ended the relationship.

She knew that Delgado now had his attentions on Mimi. She was his new first chair, after all. And though perhaps not conventionally attractive, her half-Korean-half-Italian heritage made for an interesting look. She had the smooth skin, almond eyes of her mother, the tanned complexion and thick, curled black hair of her father.

Jamie narrowed her eyes and looked around the bedroom.

Clean. Neat. Fastidiously so. Everything was placed perfectly. Nothing out of shape or place.

The pillow behind the SOCOs head had a welt in it – the baggy creases of someone having slept there. The bed was perfectly made. But the sheets weren't fresh.

'You got a blacklight on you?' she asked the SOCO with the ruler.

'Er,' he said, turning to the hard case beside him. 'Yeah.'

'Pull back the duvet – check the sheets.'

Roper scratched his chin. 'You thinking Delgado?' he asked. 'And the girl?'

Jamie clicked her teeth together, watching as the SOCO pulled back the cover gently, the other officer lifting Delgado's body slightly so the fabric could come free.

The first ran the lamp over the bottom sheet and the white semen splotches glowed under its purple haze.

'I'd put money on it,' Jamie said. 'They both rushed off last night from practice. I'd bet they were meeting up.'

'The student and her teacher,' Roper mused, shaking his head. 'Can't believe this shit still happens.'

Jamie nodded. 'Mm, well Delgado's definitely the type. The head of student services has a thing for him, too. And he and Alyssa were supposedly involved, as well.'

'Oh?' Roper arched an eyebrow.

'Scott, a student who works the front desk of the admin building – he said it was common knowledge, practically. That their late night one-to-one tutoring sessions included a lot more than bow work.'

Roper began to smirk. 'You know you could have used fing—'

'Don't.' Jamie cut him off. 'Have some class, Roper. The guy is dead.'

He shrugged, moving his mouth from side to side like he wanted a cigarette.

She was proud of him for quitting. And prouder he was sticking with it.

'So Alyssa disappears,' Roper said, using his hands to gesticulate. 'Delgado's star player and main squeeze is gone. Mimi Paganelli steps up to first chair, and onto Delgado's radar, too.'

'Sounds about right.'

Roper processed it. 'So this morning, the killer, what, breaks in here, holds a knife to Mimi's throat, then… calls Delgado? Sends him a picture of it? Tells him to get here right now or she dies?'

Jamie reached out and took the phone out of his hand. 'Guess we'll find out,' she said, shaking it gently. 'I'll get Gretchen to take a look at it.'

'So Delgado rushes over here, comes through the door, and bang, takes a knife to the gut.' Roper moved his hand in and out with the sort of detached coldness that only a detective with as many years under his belt as he did could have.

It was even more surprising considering he himself had felt the cold touch of steel just a few months before.

He kept moving his hand. 'One, two, three, four, as he's pushed backwards, and then dumped here – facing the open door.'

'The door was closed when we got here.'

'Right,' Roper said. 'But the blood trail going backwards is continuous. Smeared a little with footprints,' he added, pointing to the little slips visible on the laminate, 'but not puddled at the threshold like it would be if they stopped at the door. So the door *was* open.'

Jamie was surprised at the deduction.

'He was dumped backwards, left there in the doorway to watch.' Roper lifted his hands and turned around, back towards the apartment.

Hassan was standing in the middle of the room, watching them intently.

Roper limped out, heavy on his cane, and past Hassan, approaching the kitchen table. The lonely cup that sat there with pale pink flowers on it.

Jamie followed. 'Where was Mimi during this?' Jamie asked. 'The killer is in her apartment, he calls lover-boy, gets him over here. How does he deal with both Mimi and Delgado?'

Roper squinted around the apartment and Jamie took to looking more closely, too.

She didn't know what she was looking for, but she would when she saw it.

She had intentionally kept her attention away from the wider room until Roper arrived.

He walked slowly around the table, staring at the mug. 'Still some left,' Roper mused, looking into it.

Jamie was more focused on the chairs now. The one in front of the coffee cup was pushed out from the table, almost to a right-angle, and another was at a slight angle. Not quite tucked in.

The other two were perfectly square. As Mimi liked them.

Jamie went to the slightly off-angle chair and leaned in to look more closely at the wooden table top. 'Here,' she said, pointing to a faint water ring. 'Mimi wouldn't have left this. It's from another cup.' She went to the sink now, but there wasn't one there. Nothing in the drying rack, either.

And yet there were water droplets around the plug from that morning.

Jamie pulled on a pair of gloves herself and started opening the cupboards above the units.

'You think Mimi's hiding in there?' Roper called.

She ignored it, finding what she wanted. 'Cups,' she said, pulling the three that were there out. All white, all matching. Pink flowers. Same as the one on the table.

Jamie turned them upright and put them down, looking inside the cupboard, seeing what she'd hoped she would. 'Water, here,' she announced, running her finger through the ring on the white veneer. 'This cup was washed recently.

Roper and Hassan both came closer, arching eyebrows incredulously.

'The killer did the washing up?' Hassan asked.

Jamie squinted down at the cups. They were spotless. No staining inside, no hint of discolouration. Mimi was definitely anal retentive about this sort of thing.

'Yes,' she said. 'I think he did.'

'That's a new one,' Roper laughed. 'Why the hell would he do that?'

Jamie didn't answer, going back to the cup on the table now. She sat in Mimi's chair, open from the line of the table.

It faced her bedroom door.

It faced Delgado.

She looked ahead, and then moved her arm for the cup, unable to get to it, her elbow knocking on the side of the back of the chair. 'She didn't move her chair like this.' Jamie was putting it together in her head. 'The killer did.' She reached over now, dipped her index and middle finger into the cold liquid, holding it to her nose. There was something odd in it. Something sharp. A tinge of chemical that shouldn't be there. 'He drugged her,' Jamie said, her mouth getting there before her mind. 'The tea – and then turned her chair so she was facing the bedroom.'

Roper and Hassan hovered, watching as Jamie laid it out.

'He knew Mimi – Alyssa too. And Delgado. He knew them well.' She turned to face Roper. 'That's why he washed his cup.' She confirmed it to herself, nodding. It fit. 'He drops in to see Mimi, unannounced. But he knows her schedule. Knows she'll be here. Knows she'll be up, no doubt. Knows that she'll be alone. Delgado doesn't sleep here. He slept in his own bed last night. But he won't take Mimi there. He comes here, they have sex, then he goes home. It's cleaner that way. Cleaner for him.'

Roper shook his head, turned out his bottom lip a little in disapproval.

'The killer arrives, knocks at the door. Mimi answers,' Jamie went on.

'She knows him well enough to not think anything of it, lets him in. Offers him a cup of tea.' She looked at the cup. 'He knew she would.' Jamie swallowed, wondering what kind of person would look someone in the eye like that, knowing they were going to abduct and mutilate them. 'He sits there,' she said, looking at the other chair. 'She sits here. Then he puts something in her drink – spikes it.' This was getting clearer by the second. 'There's no sign of a struggle. She doesn't even know. They sit, they talk for a while. He finishes his tea. Says he'll clean his cup – knows that's what Mimi wants… He knows that's what she wants…'

Roper and Hassan leaned in more.

'He not only knows her, he respects her. Likes her. He liked Alyssa, too. That's why he left her hands like that, positioned her body that way. Apologising.' She exhaled. 'This isn't about the girls for him, it's about their hands.' She looked at hers. 'A means to an end. A necessary evil.'

'What is?' Hassan asked, trying to keep up.

'Killing them,' Jamie said gravely. 'He waits for the drug to start to kick in, and then he calls Delgado. That's how he handles them both. Mimi is out of it.'

Roper hung his head a little.

Jamie looked around and then got up. 'He waits here,' she said. 'Behind the door.' Jamie positioned herself so that anyone coming in wouldn't see her. She looked down at the ground, at the trail of blood-splatter. It was thicker in places. Smeared like Roper said, hard to follow.

'Delgado rushes in, the killer charges him, grabs him here' — Jamie stepped forward until she was over the blood — 'puts the knife into him. Once. Twice.' She walked forward. 'Drives him backwards through the open door, and to the ground.' She exhaled, at the bedroom doorway now.

The SOCOs looked up at her.

'Three, four,' she said, feeling that same detached coldness coming over her that she'd observed in Roper earlier. 'And then pushes him down, turns back to Mimi, walks out to her, dripping with Delgado's blood.' She glanced back over her shoulder at the dead man. 'Turns to face him, as he's dying.' She drew one last breath. 'And shuts the door on him.'

'Fuck,' Hassan muttered, shuddering.

'Fuck is right,' Roper added. 'That's brutal.'

Jamie swallowed, feeling a knot in her throat. 'Yeah. From cleaning a cup of tea out of respect, to… *that…'* She nodded over her shoulder at Delgado now, unable to look at him again. 'I don't know who we're dealing with, but something inside them is broken.'

Roper let out a long sigh. 'And then he throws Mimi over his shoulder and carries her down four flights of stairs.'

Jamie cleared her throat. The knot didn't move. 'I guess so.'

'Unless he's not working alone,' Hassan added.

Jamie shivered. It hadn't occurred to her. But it was possible. This would have been easier with two people. That's for sure. But they both would have had to have known Mimi – or one would have called the other in.

'Or he was just a big guy,' Roper mused. 'It's a lot of stairs, after all. If he knew Mimi, knew where she lived, then he'd know about the stairs. If he couldn't carry her, he could have taken her somewhere more accessible.'

Jamie didn't know. It was getting muddy again. The snapshot of clarity was fading. 'Maybe.'

'To which?' Hassan asked.

'Both,' she said, looking at Mimi's empty chair. Wondering if she was still alive. If she was already dead. Or if, as they spoke, she was having her hands cut off. 'And honestly,' Jamie muttered, rubbing her forehead. 'I don't know which would be worse.'

20

SMITH, as always, did not look happy.

Jamie normally thought of his office as spacious, but with four people crammed in there rather than three, it felt snug.

She was between Roper and Hassan, and their elbows were all touching.

Jamie couldn't see Smith's face directly. He was facing the window, his hands massaging his cheeks. But the reflection in the polished glass gave him away.

It had been a full three minutes that they had been sitting in silence, and Jamie was beginning to get anxious.

Alyssa Doran was dead, attacked, stabbed, dismembered. Gilbgerto Delgado was dead, brutalised, stabbed and left to bleed out. Mimi Paganelli was missing without a trace. And Chessie Fowler was in custody awaiting questioning.

The whole thing was a mess.

Smith drew a long breath in and then swivelled back around.

'Roper,' he said, leaning forward and putting his elbows on his desk. 'I want you to push ahead with the Fowler interview.'

Roper? This was her case. But she knew better than to question Smith. He didn't do anything without thinking about it first, and the last three minutes of silence told her he'd definitely thought about this.

'Go easy on her,' Smith cautioned. 'She's scared, her best friend is dead, and people around her are dropping like flies. But I bet she can point us in the right direction. So go for names – anyone who had a score to settle with Delgado. He's our way into this now.'

Roper nodded, got up without a word, and walked out.

'Hassan,' Smith went on, turning to him. 'I want you to head back out to the college. From what Johansson said, the head of student services – Eleanor Phillips, was it?'

He glanced at Jamie and she nodded to confirm.

'Sounds like she was close to Delgado. See what she's willing to tell you. And don't tell her he's dead. Hold that back, if you can.'

Hassan looked at Jamie, but Smith was still looking at him. He'd not addressed her yet, and wasn't about to send her with him.

That's what he was waiting for, but after a second or two, he got the picture and stood up.

The door closed behind him and then Jamie and Smith were alone.

She licked her bottom lip slowly.

'I want to see how he handles it,' Smith said, answering the question she hadn't asked.

'I wasn't—'

'Hassan is smart, but he's no detective. Not yet.'

'Sir?'

'Did he tell you that he passed his physical last week?'

'No,' Jamie said, trying not to sound shocked at the news.

'Yes. Cleared for active duty again.'

'Armed response?'

'Yes, but I gave him the option to stay on as your second – finish out the investigation into Amherst and Brock.'

'And he accepted?'

'Well, he hasn't put in his papers to transfer back.'

Jamie processed. 'You think he's done with AR?'

Smith stuck out his bottom lip, rocked gently on his chair. 'Maybe. He's not as young as he used to be. Got two little ones, and maybe taking that hit during the trafficking case put things into perspective for him. It was the first time he sustained a serious injury in the line of duty, if you can believe that.'

'And you think he's going to push for detective?'

'Maybe. I know you and he are close.'

'I wouldn't say close.'

Smith smiled at her like he knew something she didn't. 'Well, he's not being kept here against his will. He seems to like the position he's in. Is he being useful?'

'Surprisingly.'

'What about Roper?'

'What about him?'

'Johansson,' Smith said, looking at her with hard eyes.

'He's okay. He doesn't like being sidelined – but I think he'll adapt.'

'I don't know that he'll have to.'

Jamie stared at him, trying to decode the riddle.

'He's entitled to a fairly large payout after what happened. And at his age, he could opt for early retirement if he wanted.'

That was news to Jamie. She guessed she hadn't been paying that much attention since their last case together. They'd stopped carpooling, stopped 'catching up.' As far as she knew, he was still going to AA and wasn't smoking again. His newfound independence had taken him away from her. She inhaled, thought about what it would be like if he did retire. 'I'll support him, whatever he decides to do,' Jamie said diplomatically.

Smith was amused by that. 'Well, let's not jump to any assumptions just yet, but bear in mind that detectives work in pairs, not trios.'

'Are you asking me to choose between Roper and Hassan?'

'No,' he said lightly, rolling a pen back and forth with his fingers. 'But just bear what I said in mind.'

'Okay.' Jamie didn't know where this was going now. 'Do you want me to assist Roper with the interview? Or catch up with Hassan and head to the…' She trailed off, reading the look on Smith's face. 'Is this a test or something?'

'No, Johansson,' Smith said, cracking his neck. 'They can handle this. It will be good to give Roper the lead on Fowler. Might help him make up his mind. And Hassan needs to stretch his legs, see if this is something he's going to want to pursue, too.'

'And me, sir?'

'You, Johansson, should get a drink.'

Jamie narrowed her eyes at him. 'I don't think I understand.'

'Roper told me that Brock cornered you, asked you to go for a drink with her.'

Jamie felt a little anger towards Roper suddenly. 'I don't think that's a good idea.'

'Why not?' Smith asked. 'We've been at a dead-end with this case for the last few months, and now Brock wants to take you for a drink?'

'Doesn't that seem odd to you?'

'Very. But I also think it provides an avenue of entry.'

'It's not exactly good timing, is it.' That one was more a statement of fact than a question.

'I think it's perfect timing. A young DS in charge of a gristly murder case that's quickly rippling out. Two dead. One missing. And you've not exactly had an easy start to the year, either. These sorts of thing take their toll. Are cause to blow off some steam.'

Jamie scowled. 'You're not honestly suggesting that I step back from the case to *grab a drink* with Amy Brock?'

'You're right, I'm not suggesting it.'

Jamie sighed with relief.

'I'm ordering it.'

She screwed her eyes closed. 'And what should I be looking for?'

'You're a detective, Johansson. Work it out.'

Jamie finished her paperwork, spent the next twenty minutes wording the text, and just ninety seconds waiting for the response.

'It's Johansson,' the text read. 'Still keen for that drink?'

She didn't think she'd used the word keen in a text in her life. But Brock didn't seem to mind.

'Sure,' she text back. 'Now?'

Jesus, she *was* keen.

Jamie checked her watch. It was nearly two.

Roper had been questioning Chessie Fowler for over an hour, and Hassan hadn't checked in since sending her a message that said he was meeting with Eleanor Phillips.

'Sounds good. Tell me where.'

Jamie got out of her chair, grabbed her jacket off the back, and headed out.

Brock text her a moment later with the name of a pub just around the corner. Jamie hadn't been in, but Roper used to talk about it so much she felt like she'd closed it out a hundred times right there with him.

It was popular with officers and detectives coming off shift. Though technically neither Jamie nor Brock were finished for the day. Jamie was, in effect, still working. And she just didn't think Brock really cared that much for the rules. It was evident in her cocky swagger as she approached from the opposite side of the pub, as well as in her suspected involvement in corruption at the Met.

'Johansson,' Brock called, grinning.

'Brock,' Jamie said in reply, forcing a smile.

Before Jamie could do anything about it, Brock came in for a hug, squeezing her tightly.

Whether she was reading into it too much or not, she didn't know, but Brock pressed her body against Jamie's and ran her hands down her back. Checking for a wire, or maybe she just thought Jamie liked women.

Did Brock?

As they peeled apart, Brock kept her hands on Jamie's shoulders, staring her right in the eyes.

'It's good to see you,' she said, as though they were friends.

'You too,' Jamie parroted.

'Come on, let's get inside. Before anyone sees us bunking off.' She opened the door for Jamie and ushered her inside, placing her hand in the small of her back.

She let it slide. She was here to try and lull Brock into a false sense of security. To attempt to get some sort of information from her about her and Amherst's involvement with Grigoryan and whoever else he was connected to.

Inside, the pub smelt like old beer.

The floor was all worn out boards, and the bar-top was stained a dark brown.

Polished beer taps gleamed in the lights above them.

There were few people inside. No one looked up.

It was still early yet.

'What are you drinking?' Brock asked, making a beeline for the beer taps.

'Uh,' Jamie said, following. 'I guess I'll get a soda?'

Brock cast a quick glance at her.

'And lime?'

She curled a little smirk. 'You don't drink, right?'

'That's right,' Jamie said, wondering if she'd blown it already.

'I respect that,' Brock said instead. 'How come?'

Jamie shrugged casually. 'Oh, you know how it is. Couple of bad experiences in uni. And now it just gives me a headache.' She'd told lies like that so many times that it felt like the truth.

Embarking down the road of discussing her father with anyone wasn't something she was interested in doing.

'Fair enough,' Brock said, not seeming to care. 'You mind if I…?'

'Go ahead.'

Brock flagged down the bartender, an ancient-looking man with more wrinkles than a Shar Pei, and ordered herself a pint of ale. She fired Jamie another grin. 'Long morning.'

'I bet.'

She led Jamie to a booth in the window and slouched down into it, putting one foot up on the seat so that her leg was stretched out next to Jamie's left knee, and then spread her arms across the backs of the seats, her leather jacket pulling open a little, exposing her well-muscled upper pectorals.

She caught Jamie looking, and let her mouth curl into a coy smile.

Jamie pulled her attention away and sipped her lime and soda. She wasn't interested in Brock, or women, for that matter, but Brock certainly knew how to put someone off-balance.

Jamie spent even less time in the company of women than she did men. So how the hell she was going to trick Brock into telling her about her involvement with Grigoryan, she didn't know.

'Jeez,' Brock said, putting down her pint, having sucked the top third out of it in one go. 'This Grigoryan case is kicking my ass.'

'Oh,' Jamie said. That was easy. 'How come?'

Brock ran her hand through her short hair, the leather of her jacket groaning. 'He's just a real son of a bitch, you know?'

'I kind of got that impression, yeah.'

'Smith put us on him, but you know how hard it is to find dirt on a guy like that?'

'Very?' Jamie hazarded a guess.

'No, actually, it's pretty freaking easy.' Brock laughed heartily, showing off a great, white smile. She threw her head back, exposing her neck to Jamie, and then ran her fingers through her hair, brushing it over her ear. She let her eyes linger on Jamie's, disarming her.

Or at least she thought she was.

One benefit of having a non-existent social life was getting to dive into all sorts of things that no one else had time for. One of which was a tome written by a Canadian psychologist that was all about body language, reading non-verbal signals and cues, and determining if someone was telling the truth or lying by observing them.

Jamie wasn't a human polygraph by any stretch, but she knew when someone was feeding her some hot steaming bullshit.

Though she figured Amherst and Brock had gotten together to decide which of them would have the best chance at befriending Jamie. And they'd both agreed it would be Brock.

She did think Amherst was kind of an asshole.

'But the hard thing,' Brock went on, running her finger around the rim of her glass. 'Is doing it without him getting wind of it. You can't just ask around about a guy like that without it getting back to him. And while he'll sic his attack-solicitors on you in daylight, when the sun goes down…' She trailed off, pulled the corners of her mouth towards the points of her jaw, and then ran her thumb across her throat.

Jamie swallowed, her mind going back to her run-in with Matt, the head bouncer from the Jade Circle. The memory reared its ugly head and Jamie rubbed her cheek instinctively.

It had healed now, but she could still remember the pain of it. And she still carried the sensitivity in the teeth that had been loosened.

'I can imagine,' Jamie said, taking a sip from her drink. The cold liquid made them ache.

She drew breath, realising the only reason she was here was to gather information. Or at least figure out if Brock and Amherst were dirty.

There was really no one else it could be, but the shocking lack of evidence wasn't evidence.

Jamie smirked. 'You could always let me take a run at the case.'

'What, and have you show us up twice?' Brock laughed again.

'Or we could work it together?' Jamie looked right at her now and held her eye.

'Now there's an interesting proposition.'

'Grigoryan's about as crooked as they come, right?'

'As a Z-bar.'

Jamie let that one roll off her shoulders. Brock was appealing to her interests. Mirroring her. NLP. Neurolinguistic programming. 'If he's got his fingers in every pie, stop chasing the baker, and follow the pies.'

'The pies?' Brock laughed again. 'You're cute, Johansson, you know that?'

Jamie did her best not to, but felt herself flush all the same. 'What I'm saying is if you know someone who's involved with Grigoryan's dealings, someone on the periphery, who's a criminal in their own right, bust them instead.'

Brock watched her talk.

'Get them in a room, on the hook for something *they* did, and then once they're behind closed doors, lean on them for the bigger fish. Don't drop his name, but just ask. See what turns up.'

'The bigger fish?'

'There's always a bigger fish.'

'Did you just quote Star Wars?' Brock turned her head slightly, still grinning with those beautiful damn teeth.

Jamie shrugged. 'Maybe.' They were on at Christmas. Playing on repeat. And it wasn't like she had anything else to do. She made a turkey sandwich, dipped it into a pot of instant gravy, and stayed up until three in the morning watching them alone.

'That's a good idea,' Brock said. 'Maybe we'll do that.'

'Want me to help you find the right fish?'

'I think we'll manage.'

Jamie nodded. Yeah, because if you let me help, then you'd have to make progress or show that you were actively trying not to.

Jamie sipped more of her drink. 'Why did you invite me here, Brock?'

'Call me Amy.'

'Amy.' It felt weird calling her that.

'I don't have a lot of friends,' Brock said, seeming vulnerable, suddenly. 'And Amherst isn't exactly a great conversationalist.'

'Yeah, I think he and Roper were assembled in the same factory.'

'Isn't that the truth.' Brock was already two-thirds of the way through her beer. 'And I don't know any women, really. Don't meet many of them in this line of work – at least none I really want to be friends with.'

Friends. Is that what Brock wanted them to be?

'I tend to…' Brock went on, wiggling her boot next to Jamie's knee. The muscles in Brock's quad twitched beneath her tight black jeans, like two billiard balls above her knee. 'Intimidate women.'

'I can see why.'

Brock tried to look bashful. It wasn't really an expression she could pull off. 'But you…'

'Me?' Jamie feigned surprise.

'Yeah, you're not like other women.'

'You and my mother both agree on that.'

'Yours too?' Brock's relentless grinning was infectious.

Jamie couldn't help but crack a real smile.

'I suspect you don't get intimidated easily.'

'What about the women at your gym? There must be other women, other fighters?' Jamie knew that Brock trained at a gym in the city called The Warrior's Club. Jamie had asked Cake about it – apparently it was a big commercial place that churned out fighters by the dozen.

'Hard to strike up a friendship after you've put someone in a triangle choke. Talk about a bruised ego.'

Jamie scoffed. 'I bet you bruise more than egos.' She glanced down at Brock's knuckles, saw the familiar unevenness of well-used fists. 'And plus, anyone who's dumb enough to let you get anywhere near their neck with those thighs deserves to have their ass whooped.'

Brock laughed loudly and the few people in the pub turned to look at them. She drained the last of her beer. 'Right, no more work talk.' She slapped the top. 'We talked about it back in January – me, you, in the ring. What do you say? Amateur gloves, head guards, the works. I'll go easy on you.'

'*You* talked about it back in January,' Jamie said evasively, folding her arms now. The last thing she wanted to do was get in the ring with Brock. She'd have to sign a waver before she did, and that meant that Brock could snap her neck and get off scot-free. 'I don't fight unless I have to.'

'You train, don't you?'

'Yes.'

'Then think of it as training.'

'I've got too much on,' Jamie said, not lying. 'This latest case. It's a real… I don't even know what. But it's bloody, and the bodies are stacking up.' She suddenly felt guilty for not being with Roper or Hassan.

'You won't be able to duck me forever, Jamie,' Brock said, using Jamie's first name for the first time.

'I don't know, I'm pretty fast.'

'I bet you are.' She narrowed her eyes a little, measuring Jamie for every ounce she weighed.

'Who knows, maybe one day our paths will cross and you'll get your fight.'

She let her lip curl. 'Yeah, I hope so.'

That hung there between them for a few seconds, each not sure whether the other one meant that it would be a friendly matchup or something totally different.

'I guess you don't need to fight these days, though, huh?' Brock said lightly, crossing her impressive legs. She nodded to the black butt of the Glock 17 poking out from Jamie's jacket.

'Not if I can help it,' Jamie said, pulling her jacket over the grip. 'Believe me, I don't want to be carrying the thing.'

'Better safe than sorry though, right? The city is a dangerous place.'

'Yeah,' Jamie said, feeling a coolness descend between them. 'It is.'

They stared each other down for a few more seconds, and then Jamie's phone started buzzing.

She pulled it out of her pocket, not breaking eye contact. It was Roper. 'Sorry,' she said to Brock. 'I need to take this.'

'Go ahead,' Brock replied, slouching back into her disarming friendliness. 'I'm gonna grab another one.' She picked up her empty glass. 'Sure I can't tempt you?'

Jamie shook her head, pulling the phone to her ear, and Brock crossed the distance to the bar, taking her time, her hips swinging, for Jamie's benefit, no doubt.

'Roper,' Jamie said.

'I'm not interrupting, am I?'

'The most surreal and weird drink I've ever shared with someone? Yeah, but I'm glad you are. What's up?'

'Fowler sang like a canary.'

'I'll be there in two,' Jamie said, already getting up. 'And Roper?'

'Yeah?'

'Good work.'

'See you soon.'

He hung up and Jamie squeezed the phone in her grip, a little frustrated he seemed to get so much done without her. No, that was just being childish. They were a team, and progress was progress.

Brock was coming back over, beer in hand. She clocked Jamie on her feet. 'Duty calls?'

'Yeah, I've gotta go.'

'Sure – I understand.' She smiled once more and Jamie felt warmth in her neck and cheeks again. 'Go catch a killer.'

'I'll do my best.'

'Let's catch up soon.'

'Okay,' Jamie said, backing towards the door. 'That'd be good.'

Brock raised her glass a little as Jamie slipped through the door back onto the street, annoyed at Smith that she'd been ordered to have a drink with Brock, and more annoyed at herself for having enjoyed it so much.

She let out a long breath, ran her hands through her hair, and picked up to a light jog.

Brock was right, she had a killer to catch.

And everything else could wait.

21

HASSAN WAS STILL OUT, and wasn't answering his phone.

Roper, on the other hand, was back at his desk, typing out his notes from the questioning.

His fingers worked furiously, the index of each hand bouncing up and down on the keys. He'd never master touch-typing. And Jamie doubted he'd want to.

She stepped out of the stairwell, her heart at a steady one-twenty, and approached quickly. 'Roper,' she called out, pulling up short of his desk.

He swivelled round on his chair and looked up at her. He seemed pleased.

It was an odd look on him.

'What'd you get?'

'Oh ho-ho, what didn't I get?' Roper seemed enthusiastic, like he'd finally found some motivation to push forward with the case.

Jamie hooked her toe around her chair and pulled it forward, sitting down on it, never looking away from Roper. 'Impress me.'

'Okay,' he said, turning to face her, both of them leaning in. 'So Chessie Fowler was Alyssa's best friend. They had been roommates since their first year, and pretty much inseparable. Fowler is first cello, and they both played in a string-quartet together during their first and second year in college. But it wasn't until halfway through their second year that Alyssa and Delgado first started…' He trailed off.

'Sleeping together?'

Roper made a strange face. 'Fowler seemed to think it was more than that. She said Delgado was intense – but that before he took on Alyssa as his protege, there was another girl.'

'Oh?'

'A flautist, apparently. Tall, red-head. Attractive. Very talented.' Roper shrugged. 'She was a few years older than Fowler and Alyssa, and graduated as they went into their second year. It took Delgado a few months to get over it by the sounds of the timeline, and then he laid his eyes on Alyssa.'

'So he's got a habit of doing this, then?' Jamie sat back and processed it.

'For his star players – looks like. But Alyssa didn't seem to mind – and despite the guy being seven shades of slimy, Chessie Fowler seemed to think pretty highly of him. She said everyone did.'

Jamie exhaled. 'Sure – why wouldn't they? The college has a stellar orchestra – they tour all over the place, win competitions… They probably think Delgado is a god.'

'Was.'

'Right.' Jamie exhaled. The guy was dead, after all. A great loss to humanity or not.

'And things seemed to be well, Fowler said – they were *happy*. Alyssa wasn't there much, she said – in their room. She would be with Delgado mostly.'

'Did the school know?'

'Fowler wasn't sure. But she said it was no secret.'

The guy was a dirt-ball, but this didn't strike her as creating motive to kill. But judging by the glint in Roper's eye, he was getting to that. 'So what happened last October?'

'This is where things get murky for Fowler,' Roper said, a little restrained now. 'During the summer, Fowler went home to her family, but Alyssa stayed in the city. Shacked up with Delgado.'

'Okay.'

'Come September, then, she moved back in with Fowler, but apparently, something had changed.'

'Changed how?'

'She said Alyssa was distant, withdrawn, suddenly. Afraid.'

'Afraid?' Jamie raised an eyebrow. Now they were getting somewhere. 'Afraid of who?'

He shook his head. 'I don't know. Neither did Fowler. She said that they went back to classes, as normal, but that Alyssa would go from their room to lectures, and then straight back. Didn't want to go out anywhere. And definitely not at night. Refused to. "Afraid for her life", were the words Fowler used.'

'Alyssa said that?'

'Inferred.'

'Delgado?'

'Maybe…' Roper didn't seem convinced. 'Apparently, he wasn't there for the first few weeks of term. Rumour was he was suspended, Fowler said.'

'Any ideas what for?' Jamie asked, reaching over and scribbling down on her desk to reach out to the college and check.

'No one knew. It was kept quite quiet, Fowler said, but when Delgado returned, he was more serious. *On edge.*'

'But we don't know why?'

'Not a clue – but Delgado's return and Alyssa's disappearance seem to coincide. Third week of October. Delgado comes back, Alyssa disappears.' He snapped his fingers. 'Just like that.'

'No warnings? She didn't talk about it with Chessie?'

Roper shook his head, sitting back. He looked perplexed. 'No, nothing. Fowler said she left for lectures one morning, came back in the afternoon, and Alyssa was gone. No note or anything.'

Jamie pulled her plait around to her front and started parting the knotted hairs sticking out the end of the bobble. 'So something happened during that summer that changed everything,' she mused aloud. 'By what you're saying, everything was fine until then. But when they came back in the autumn…'

Roper was watching her.

'We need to get back in touch with the college, find out what the circumstances of Delgado's suspension were.'

'I reached out to Hassan as soon as Chessie said it. He should have everything we need.'

'Oh,' Jamie said, a little taken aback. He hadn't answered when she'd called. 'Right. Good.' She cleared her throat, got back into her stride. She reached for the phone. 'We should also find out whether they were aware of Alyssa and Delgado's relationship. Maybe if they were – if they found out, and that was why Delgado got suspended, then—'

'Already done.'

Jamie paused, the handset halfway to her ear.

'But if you're thinking that could have caused a lovers' quarrel, driven Alyssa to steal Delgado's violin out of spite, and then drop out of school—'

Jamie wasn't – because she hadn't gotten that far with her train of thought yet – but she would have, given enough time.

'—then it still doesn't explain her death, or his. If he hunted her down in revenge, why leave his own violin? And then what, he goes to Mimi's apartment, and stabs himself to cover his tracks?' Roper laughed a little. 'No, I think we're missing a few pieces of the puzzle here.'

Jamie let out a long breath, quashed the strange and jealous little bubble of anger inside her, and replaced the phone. 'So what do you suggest?'

'Well, what do we know?' Roper opened his hands, looking at Jamie like he was back on top. She couldn't help but feel a little bit condescended to. 'Alyssa and Delgado get into a relationship. Something happens. Delgado is suspended. Alyssa runs away. Six months later, Alyssa turns up dead, Delgado is now sleeping with the girl who usurped Alyssa's crown, and within twenty-four hours, Delgado himself is dead, and Mimi is missing. Despite Delgado being an asshole, I think we might need to start viewing him as the victim here.' He blew out a long breath, and then scratched at his cheek. It sounded like he was sanding a table. 'But where we go next, I'm not sure.'

Jamie focused, tried to rewire her brain back to the old way of doing things. When Roper was in charge. 'Okay, then we do nothing. We wait for Hassan to work his magic on Eleanor Phillips, hope he comes up with the goods, and then go from there. We map out every square inch of Delgado's life from May last year through to October, and then we pick it all apart. We find out what happened, when, and what scared Alyssa so badly that she had to run for her life.'

'Fowler said it, but we don't know she was running for her life for sure.'

'We do, Roper.' Jamie rubbed her eyes. She felt tired. 'Because she's dead.'

Jamie finished her paperwork in silence, dropped an email to Gretchen asking her to try and dig into Alyssa's summer, see what she could turn up on Delgado, too – specifically in the months leading up to October – and then clocked off for the day.

It was only just after five, but Jamie was tired.

In fact, she couldn't ever remember a time when she wasn't tired.

Roper was behind with his own reports, as usual, and stayed late.

Hassan had spoken at length to Eleanor, but it was too much to relay over the phone, and she wasn't prepared to discuss the particulars of what happened in regards to Delgado's suspension. That request would have to be referred up the chain to a specific 'representative' of the college who would be at liberty to discuss what happened.

Whatever the hell that meant.

There was also no CCTV in or outside Mimi's building, with the closest being a camera at a cashpoint a few hundred metres away. So scrubbing through footage was a very long long-shot at best.

And on top of that, the SOCO's report on Mimi's and Delgado's, including the toxicology on the tea, and coroner's report on Delgado, and the DNA confirmation from the semen on the bed, wouldn't be with them until the following morning, at the earliest.

All of which meant, far short of walking the streets yelling her name, there was little that Jamie could do.

She needed to go home. To rest. And to eat.

After a good night's sleep, she would be ready to tackle this head on. And armed with more information, find Mimi. Hopefully, before it was too late.

If the killer was intending to take her hands as well, then at least if he had some privacy, he might take his time.

It was a thin assumption to bet Mimi's life on.

Though Jamie didn't really have any other choice.

She was looking forward to a night off. To just being on her own, getting to eat something decent, catch up on some YouTube videos she'd missed.

Jamie craved her own company sometimes, and needed nothing more than to have one night go smoothly. Just one night without something going wrong. She felt she deserved that.

But just like always, what she thought she deserved, and what happened, were two vastly different things.

It was still dark out when the phone rang, buzzing angrily, like a trapped hornet on the bedside table.

'Cake?' Jamie said wearily, pulling it to her ear.

She looked at the clock on her bedside, the numbers no more than a green blur. She wasn't sure whether it was midnight or just before dawn.

She hoped the second.

'Jamie,' Cake said, breathless. 'I'm sorry to wake you.'

'What time is it?'

'Uh, four-something. Almost five, I think.' He sounded near frantic.

Jamie's brain tweaked, kicked into gear, and suddenly she was sitting up, her eyes flashing to the Glock in front of the clock. She could see clearly now. Four-fifty-six. Almost a full night's sleep. 'What's wrong?' she asked.

'Shit, Jamie – someone broke in.'

'Broke in?' She was already on her feet. 'To where? The gym?'

'Yeah,' he was panting. 'I'm outside now – but there's no sign of them.'

'What happened?' she asked, pulling on a pair of jeans.

'I was asleep – and then I heard a noise downstairs. A door slamming. I came running.'

Jamie knew the layout of the gym – it was a large main room, and then at the back there were four ground-floor rooms. The two on the left were modest locker rooms. Men's and women's. White tiles, a few lockers, and a pair of showers in each. The third was Cake's office, the other a storeroom filled with spare barbells, a few old spin bikes. Nothing of any value, really. The latter two rooms were conjoined, as well as accessible from the main floor.

In the storeroom, a ladder-staircase led up to an open-plan space that Cake had made his own. She'd never been up there, but she'd seen a copper pipe joined to the pipe that fed from the boiler in the storeroom into the women's locker room. It ran straight up through the floor, so she guessed he had some sort of bathroom up there.

But otherwise, she couldn't have guessed what it looked like.

Judging by the way Cake talked about money, though, she doubted it was filled with expensive electronics or diamond jewellery. Which made the reasoning for why any thieves would hit the gym practically beyond her.

'See if anything's missing,' Jamie said. 'I'll be there in ten.'

'Okay,' Cake said, sounding rattled. It wasn't a tone his voice often took on.

'It'll be okay.' Jamie took her pistol off the bedside table and hooked it onto her belt, a cold sense of dread creeping up her spine. 'I'm sure it's nothing.'

She took the stairs quickly, hanging the phone up. She hoped she was right.

But she knew she wasn't.

. . .

Cake was standing outside when Jamie pulled in.

He waved her down as she bumped her hatchback up onto the curb and killed the engine.

The building was an old industrial brick slab set back off the road a little, surrounded by an electrical substation on one side, and a block of apartments on the other that faced away. The street was a narrow one that cut between two residential roads. Opposite the gym was a patch of scrubland before an overland railway line burst from the ground.

Inside you could barely hear the trains. But it was one more reason the rent was as low as it was.

Jamie opened the door and stepped into the cool morning air, her leather jacket squeaking as she walked. Things were quiet.

'Cake,' Jamie said, smiling at him. He looked distraught. Grave, even.

'Jamie,' he said, exhaling hard. He ran his hands through his hair. 'I'm so sorry.'

'It's not your fault, Cake.'

He pulled his lips into a wide line and looked at the ground.

Jamie paused, knowing there was more to this than he was telling here. 'What is it, Cake?'

'I know what they took,' he said quietly.

'What, Cake?' Jamie swallowed, that same feeling of dread creeping deeper into her. 'Rowing machines? Your laptop?' she said, almost hopefully.

'No, they only took one thing,' he practically mumbled. 'Come inside, I'll show you.' He turned and stepped through the open door.

Jamie paused at the frame, looking for signs of forced entry. She couldn't see any.

It was a fire door with a bolt-lock. But the bolt was pushed out of the body – like it had been locked with the door open.

The thing wouldn't snap closed – just bang on the frame.

Jamie frowned, then went inside. She'd ask him about it.

'In here,' Cake said, going towards the office.

She didn't like this.

'Here,' he said, stopping at the filing cabinet.

The top drawer was open.

Inside, a series of hanging files sat in a rough order.

At the back, she could see the word "Tax" written on a label sticking out of a file. And at the front were files with names on their tabs. "A. Benson", "R. Clarke", "T. Fraiser", "J. Johansson."

Members.

Jamie froze, her eyes falling on it.

Had cake opened the drawer?

'What did they take, Cake?' she asked, her voice low.

He reached into the cabinet and pulled out Jamie's file. It was plain brown card.

'Here,' he said, handing it to her.

She took it, felt it light in her hands, and opened it, her heart picking up its pace.

'It's empty,' she said, confused for a second, looking up. 'This is what they took? What was in here?'

'Just paperwork – not much. Two, three sheets was all. Your membership form, your insurance waiver. And a contact sheet.'

Jamie's grip tightened around it. 'A contact sheet?' she said, teeth gritted suddenly. 'With my contact information on it?' She felt sick.

He nodded. 'Yeah.'

Jamie exhaled, hoping, for once in his life, Cake hadn't been efficient with his paperwork. He'd always been lax, ever since she'd known him. 'Please tell me that you still had my old address down.'

He met her eyes now and she already knew the answer.

'I knew that I'd forget if I didn't change it right away,' he said apologetically. 'I'm sorry, Jamie.' He really did sound it.

She hadn't told him about Elliot. Not the truth. But he knew what happened with Matt outside her last apartment. That she now carried a gun in case they were hunting her. That she'd had him install security measures – the motion sensors – because she half-expected someone to turn up looking for her in the dead of night.

But the reality was much, much worse than one of Zhou or Grigoryan's goons with a score to settle.

Jamie wanted to vomit. She wanted to keel over and empty her stomach all over the concrete floor.

Cake was silent.

She felt her cheeks burn then, her throat constrict.

Jamie took a breath, handed him the file without meeting his eye, and stepped back into the gym.

'Did you lock the door?' Jamie asked aloud, putting her hands on her hips.

'Last night? Of course,' Cake said, stepping out behind her, file still in his hands.

'No, I mean this morning – the bolt was out of the lock.'

He looked confused. 'No, it was like that when I came down,' he said.

'It wouldn't shut,' Jamie said, as much a statement as a question.

'Yeah, it was open – that's how I knew something was wrong,' Cake said, not making the same connection that Jamie was.

She took a slow breath, looking at it, knowing that Elliot was an expert at getting through doors. It still baffled Jamie how he'd managed to get into her old apartment. How he'd gotten through a laser-cut-key door.

But he had, and she was sure he had his ways.

'What exactly did you hear? Moving around – the filing cabinet, what?'

Cake shook his head. 'I was sleeping, didn't hear anything, and then *bang!*' He nodded along with the word. 'I rushed down, and could see the door open – a glow from the streetlight coming in.'

'The door banging against the frame on the way out.' Jamie laughed sardonically. 'Son of a bitch.'

'I'm sorry, Jamie,' Cake said. He was really distraught about the whole thing. 'If I'd have thought…' he started.

'No, no, it's fine,' she said now, finally looking at him. 'If they couldn't get the information from my file, they might have come to you directly. It's better this way.'

But there was no 'they'. It was Elliot. He'd known. Somehow, he'd known. And he'd waited until Cake had updated her information, and then he'd snuck in in the middle of the night, found her file, taken it. No more than ten feet from where Cake was sleeping, and slipped out without a sound. And only then, when he was out the door, did he flick the bolt out, and slam it behind him to make sure Cake knew what had happened.

Jamie wondered if he was out there now, watching her.

What the point of this whole exercise was.

He could have just followed her home. Found out that way.

And then it occurred to her.

'The filing cabinet,' she said. 'Was it left open?' She knew the answer.

'Yeah, it was – that's how I knew what was taken.'

He wanted her to know. That was the point of it all. He knew Cake would call her, knew that she'd come running. Knew that she'd put it together like this.

He wanted her to know, without seeing her, without contacting her, that there was no escape.

Hell, for all she knew, he could still be here. Lurking somewhere, watching her.

He could be anywhere.

He could even be…

Shit. Jamie's heart seized in her chest.

'What's wrong?' Cake asked, reading the sudden tension in her body.

She dragged her phone from her pocket and stared at the black lock screen, willing it to stay that way.

Jamie and Cake both looked at it, the former hoping it didn't light up, and the latter not realising what it would mean if it did.

The clock above Cake's office ticked by, the only sound in the silence.

She didn't know how long she'd wait.

But she didn't have to wait long.

She felt it vibrate before the screen flashed red and then yellow. Her motion detectors. Number one, the one above the stairs, had been triggered.

Elliot was in her apartment.

'Shit,' Cake muttered behind her, looking at it.

Jamie narrowed her eyes, a sense of calm coming over her all of a sudden. She pushed her phone back into her jeans and drew a slow breath.

'What are you going to do?' Cake asked, putting a hand on her shoulder.

Jamie popped the Glock from its holster on her hip, ejected the magazine, checked that it was full, and then slotted it back into the grip, banging it into place with the heel of her hand.

The metal felt cool in her hands as she took hold of the slide and pulled it back until it clicked.

She released it, feeling the smooth clunk of a bullet hitting the chamber under her touch.

Cake let go of her shoulder, her actions enough of an answer. 'I'm coming with you,' he said, fear and decisiveness fighting in his voice.

'No, Cake, you're not.'

'You can't go back alone,' he urged her.

'If you're there,' Jamie said. 'Then you're a witness.'

'A witness to what?' Cake asked, his voice strained in his throat.

Jamie turned to him, smiled, and then stepped towards the door. 'I'll call you, alright?'

'And if you don't?'

Jamie sighed. 'Then I'm probably dead.'

What was intended as a dark joke rang in Jamie's head.

As she turned the key in the ignition, it felt more like a bitter truth.

Was she really going to her death here? Was that what this was? Elliot – was he waiting for her to come home? So he could kill her there, harvest her in her own bed?

She shook her head, driving back into the night, dawn still a little ways off.

Her fingers felt slick around the wheel.

Jamie looked up, seeing the outline of her father in the backseat, reflected in the rear-view.

She didn't have to speak for him to hear her.

No, he said. *I don't think you're an idiot. I think that this has gone on too long. And you can end it. Right here. Now. Finish it, finally.*

She nodded. 'You're right,' she said out loud this time, feeling the Glock digging into her side. 'For once' — she met his eye in the darkness — 'you're damn right.'

Jamie pulled up outside her apartment just as the sky was beginning to curdle.

The clouds had that distant glow of almost-dawn and twisted like knots above her.

She killed the engine and got out, the trees rustling quietly, the birds not yet singing.

Everything was quiet.

Jamie crossed the street quickly and headed for her door, keys shaking in her grip, Glock perched at her hip, ready to spread its wings.

22

UPSTAIRS WAS QUIET.

Nothing moved and Jamie's phone had gone quiet, too. There was no sound coming from the top of the stairs as she hung at the bottom, no movement above her. Just the soft snoring of Mrs Iwankowski through the wall touching her right elbow.

Jamie calmed her beating heart and mounted the stairs, ready to cover the room and put three bullets into Elliot the second she saw him. She wasn't about to let him open his mouth again.

The stairs seemed to creak under her and stretch on forever ahead.

Her legs felt heavy, ungainly as she lifted them, clipping her toes on every step.

The gun rattled in her grip, slick in her hands.

Halfway now. She tweaked her ears furiously, straining them for any sense of disturbance upstairs. A quiet breath. A shift of weight on the boards. The slither of a blade through the air.

But there was nothing.

And that terrified Jamie the most.

Her head crested the steps and she turned to look across the landing.

Nothing moved. Dust motes floated in the dim glow of almost-day spilling in through the window.

She exhaled, swept across the space with the muzzle of her pistol and got onto flat ground, forcing her breath to stop rattling in her chest.

The bathroom door was right ahead, and open. The room was small, there was nowhere to hide and the shower curtain was pulled right back, exposing the old claw-foot tub in all its discoloured glory.

He wasn't in there.

Jamie clamped her jaw and moved on, stepping through the open door into her living room, covering the corners.

Clear.

Upstairs.

Her bedroom.

It's the only place he could be.

She went faster now, deciding she was the predator here, suddenly. There was no way he was going to get the drop on her.

Jamie was on the stairs and moving quickly. One, two, three, she counted the steps going up until she could see the floor of her room.

She wasn't breathing, just moving on instinct.

But as she drew level with her bed, she saw it, and knew he wasn't there. The empty room told her that. Her bed sat lonely against the wall. And unless he was folded up into one of the cardboard boxes opposite, she was safe. For now at least.

Her heart slowed immediately, the bead of sweat on her temple running down her cheek and onto her neck.

Jamie sighed and lowered the gun.

Shit.

She swapped the pistol into her off-hand and flexed her knuckles. They were aching she'd been gripping so hard.

Her bed was made neatly.

She had left it a mess of rumpled sheets when she'd run out to Cake's. Which she now realised was a diversion. A way to get her out of the house. Hell, she'd probably driven right by him on the way here.

Jamie approached it and stared down at the brown file that had been left on top. It was bulging with papers and bound with two thick rubber bands.

There was a time and address written on a post-it note trapped beneath one of the bands. She didn't know the street, but the time said eight a.m. plainly enough.

Did he want her to meet him there at that time?

Jamie holstered her pistol, checked over her shoulder once just to make sure, and then lifted the file, turning to sit on the bed as she did.

She tried not to think about the fact that he'd touched the sheets where she slept. Probably ran his hands over the still-warm mattress.

Jamie grimaced and made a mental note to wash them.

And then maybe burn the whole fucking thing.

The band rolled up over the slightly damp-feeling file and Jamie looped it around her wrist, lifting the cover.

Inside was a stack of photos, and beneath it were what looked like photocopies of invoices and bank transfers, as well as credit-card and bank statements. Jamie didn't recognise any of the names on the top as she spidered over the corners of the pages with her fingers.

She went back to the photos and looked down at the top one.

It was a slightly grainy photo of a newer-model BMW. Silver, a saloon. The picture had been taken with a long lens and the lighting was poor.

The car had pulled up in an alleyway, in front of a large steel roller door.

The time-stamp in the corner said that it was three weeks ago, at five-past-eight in the morning.

Jamie lifted the photo, exposing the one below it.

A figure had opened the car door.

In the next he was getting out.

A big guy in a big coat.

Jamie's fingers moved faster, her brain putting together what she was seeing here.

He was on his feet now, walking around the bonnet. The photos were all a few seconds apart.

The metal roller churned upwards.

Three figures materialised from inside.

Two tall, one shorter.

The two on either side of the shorter guy Jamie didn't recognise. But the one in the middle, she did. He was average height, impeccably dressed.

She'd never forget his face.

Ho Zhou.

Manager of the Jade Circle.

The one who ran the casino-cum-sex-slavery-ring.

The one who had dispatched Matthew Tan to kill her.

Jamie rubbed her cheek, flicking through the photographs.

They showed him and Amherst shaking hands, and then Amherst was handed an envelope.

He opened it, pulling papers from the top.

And then he got back in the car and backed away.

But the photos kept going.

They leapt forward a week.

Same thing.

The car pulls up, Amherst gets out. Then the door goes up, Zhou comes out, hands him an envelope, and then he leaves.

The next batch the same.

Three weeks ago. Two weeks ago. Last week. To the day.

Jamie's breath was small and sharp. The address on the front. The time. It was this morning. In just over two hours.

Amherst would be there, meeting Zhou. It was enough to nail the both of them. Shit.

She let the photos fall onto her lap. But how the hell was she going to sell this to Smith? How did she come into possession of this information?

And why did Elliot want to give it to her? What did he have to gain from it?

Jamie went back to the statements. Were they what was in the envelopes? No, that didn't make sense. What would Zhou be giving Amherst envelopes with bank statements in them for?

She started going through them again.

The top few were statements from the last few months for a company called *Integral Logistics Ltd.* Every few days there were payments between a few hundred and a few thousand going in. And then every month, a payment for around ten grand going out. Which was going to an account… She lifted the page and saw that the account number that it had been sent to was circled on both the Integral Logistics statement and at the top of the next batch.

It was a credit account – registered to a Vikram Bakshi – registered with the National Bank of Luxembourg. And the statements showed that over the last three months there had been three cash-withdrawals, bringing the credit balance back down to zero. More than thirty thousand Euros' worth.

Was this the money-trail they couldn't find?

Jamie kept leafing through the statements and saw that the credit withdrawals went as far back as two years ago. And she expected that they didn't just start then.

But what Amherst was doing for the money was of more concern. He was on Zhou's payroll by the look of it. Obfuscated as it was. And she doubted that the corruption stopped there.

Zhou was a sizeable fish. But he wasn't at Grigoryan's level. He was still someone's lackey. And if Amherst was this ingrained, getting him to roll would be a big break in the war that they didn't have enough information to even wage yet.

But this could be it.

Grigoryan. Zhou. Amherst. Brock. She could take them all down in one fell swoop and then blow the whole thing wide open.

Elliot had said there was a criminal network out there – more than one – vying for control of the city. Using the Met to do their bidding. How deep did it go?

Jamie licked her lips, closing the file. The time, the address… She should call Smith, tell him about it. Get Armed Response out there to take them all into custody.

But she couldn't, not without letting slip about Elliot. So what could she do? What would happen if she went?

Would Elliot be there, or just her? She could wait until the meet was going down and then intercept – but those two heavies with Zhou would be armed, no doubt. And Amherst wouldn't have any qualms about watching her go down.

She could case the place, see what was going on there and then move in quietly, try and arrest Zhou after Amherst left… But then it was whether she was going to go it alone or have to make up some excuse to get Smith in on it without incriminating herself.

The file she was holding would be more than enough to take Amherst apart legally, but there was no way it was all obtained through proper channels, and if it wasn't, then it could easily be argued as fabricated. And it definitely wouldn't be admissible in court.

The photographs were enough to get Smith's back up, but yesterday they had exactly nothing, and now suddenly weeks of evidence that he was on the take?

She drew a long breath. No, she had to go, had to corner Amherst. That was the only way she could do it. Maybe she could say that Brock had tipped her off – but then if she argued that she didn't… But why would she? She'd turn tail and run the second Amherst got caught, surely? Unless she wasn't in on it… No, she had to be. Didn't she?

Jamie ground her teeth, exhausting every avenue and always coming back to the same conclusion. Elliot or not, she had to go there at eight, wait for the hand-off, get her own photos, video if she could – and then take him in. At gunpoint if need be. She could say she'd been tailing him… No, Smith wouldn't buy that.

Jamie pulled the file off her lap and slapped it down in between her boots in anger. The photos spilled out into a sprawling mess and faced the cracked plaster of the ceiling.

Could she just ignore this? She asked the question but knew that she couldn't. That she would have to go. Have to see for herself.

She took her Glock from the holster and held it in her hands, staring down at it.

Elliot had been in her apartment. In her bedroom.

She shivered, watched her fingers curl around the cool piece of metal still laying in her grasp.

If he was going to be there, then that was enough. She would go there for him. And put him down, once and for all.

She would shoot him.

She would kill him.

It was the only way she was going to be rid of him forever.

And she could live with that.

Couldn't she?

Jamie looked up, saw her father leaning against the doorframe, smirking at her. And then she was on her feet, shoving past him, pounding down the stairs and running for the bathroom.

She sank to her knees and emptied her stomach into the toilet.

She wretched, flushed, and then slumped sideways onto her hip, breathing hard, the loaded pistol still in her grip.

23

It was seven a.m. when Jamie set off.

She'd scrubbed her teeth, then her body, and then forced herself to eat breakfast. Muesli and skimmed milk. It had stung on the way down and her stomach had clamped shut around it.

Her belly ached as she drove.

Though she'd showered and the morning air was cool, a cold sweat had broken out on her skin. It pushed through her pores and made her feel damp and uncomfortable.

The Glock stared up at her from the passenger seat, her father's grin bearing down on her as she drove towards Elliot's death.

The address was in a decent part of the city, and looked to be at the back of a French restaurant. A service alleyway stretched around behind and the meeting place that Amherst had been photographed in was a dead-end, positioned around a dogleg. Only one way in, and one way out.

As Jamie sat opposite the entrance to the alleyway, still thirty minutes before Amherst was due to arrive, she looked up, trying to visualise where the photos had been taken from. The satellite map on her phone told her that the alleyway was fairly long, so she guessed judging by the angle they showed it had been from the second or third floor of the commercial building next door. There was a shop on the ground floor, and above looked like old offices. Maybe storage. Jamie squinted up at them but the old windows were dark, boarded over or covered from the inside.

That's where Elliot would be.

Jamie watched the shop, but it was completely quiet. Closed.

Shit. How had Elliot gotten in?

She shook her head at that thought and remembered a documentary she'd watched once about rats, which explained how they could shove themselves through a keyhole if they had to. That their bones would all rearrange and then reform. She wondered if Elliot was like that.

A man and a woman walking past the entrance to the shop snapped her out of the train of thought and she grabbed her pistol off the passenger seat, slotting it into her holster.

They paused at a service entrance near the corner of the building and Jamie exited the car and dashed across the road to catch them before they went inside. She managed to catch up just as the door was closing and threw her hand into the gap, opening it behind them.

They both turned in surprise, looking afraid. She must have been in her fifties, he in his twenties. Neither looked ready to give up anything to protect their place of work.

Jamie had her warrant card out just a second later, pulling her hem over the grip of her pistol with the other hand. 'It's okay, I'm a police officer,' she said quickly.

Neither of them seemed especially put at ease by that.

'Detective Sergeant Jamie Johansson,' Jamie added, just to get it out of the way. 'Sorry to catch you like this, but I was hoping I could take a look around upstairs?' She didn't know quite how else to say it.

'Er, why?' the boy asked.

'Yes,' the woman chimed in, turning fully on now. 'What's upstairs?'

Jamie swallowed, pulling the door a little wider, realising she was sort of wedged in the gap. She let it bang against her heel on the spring and straightened herself so that she at least looked like she was supposed to be there. 'I'm not quite sure,' Jamie answered truthfully. A serial organ harvester perhaps? She didn't say that, but gave them both a smile instead. 'But I have reason to believe that one of the surrounding buildings may be involved in an ongoing investigation, and I'd just like to check it out.'

The boy's brow crumpled. 'Wouldn't it be better to check out that building instead then?'

Jamie forced herself to hold onto her smile, and took a breath. 'I would if I didn't think it would compromise the investigation. I'd like to see if there's a vantage point to observe from. And if your upstairs storage space is unused, it may make—'

'Don't you need a warrant for that?' the woman asked, narrowing her eyes.

Jamie hated TV and what it had done to people. Those words came out of the mouth of so many people, and it made her job so much harder. And a lot more tedious, too. 'No, not unless you want to refuse me entry. But as I'm not suspecting anyone here of a crime, or expecting to find anything illegal, and nor am I looking for anything illegal, there's no real grounds for me to either obtain a warrant to enter or a significant reason for you to ask me not to. So which will it be?'

'Uh,' the woman said, blinking at Jamie. She was trying to decode the words she'd just said and it looked like her brain had just shut down in the process.

'What'd they do?' the boy said from behind.

'Who?' Jamie asked.

'The people you're investigating?'

Jamie looked down at her watch. She didn't have time for this. Amherst wouldn't be far away and if she couldn't get upstairs, she needed to figure something else out. 'I can't tell you that – but what I can tell you is that I'm a detective working to stop some bad people from doing a bad thing, and if you want to stop me from looking around, then I'll be holding you responsible for these guys staying on the streets. And, you know, doing what they're doing right next door.' Jamie dipped her head sideways a little and both the man and the woman looked at the wall. 'So what do you say?'

Jamie was shown to a fire-exit stairwell that ran up to the fourth floor of the building, and then left alone.

The door closed heavily behind her, and the sound of her breath was immediately in her ears.

It was nearly ten-to-eight now, and as if Amherst wasn't Jamie's main problem, she wasn't sure if she was about to come face to face with Elliot Day.

The first floor came up too quickly and Jamie was at the door before she even realised, her mind racing.

With a shaking hand she reached for the handle, popping her Glock from the holster.

It came smoothly into the air as the door opened.

The space behind was big. Bigger than Jamie thought it would be.

She hadn't even taken notice of what the shop downstairs was, but judging by the mannequins and rails and boxes full of clothing, it wasn't hard to guess.

It wasn't right, though. There wasn't any dust here, and there was a door at the other end, near the windows. This was all fresh storage, and would be walked far too often by employees. There was no way Elliot would risk it. He was too smart.

Jamie shrank back through the door, even more nervous now.

She turned and took the stairs again, not daring to replace her pistol.

It shook in her hand, hovering in front of her chest.

Her heels squeaked on the concrete as she circled upwards.

The second floor looked more promising. The sign on the door said 'Caution' and speckles of rust around the metal frame gave the appearance that it was used far less often.

Jamie held her breath and took the last few steps slowly, her hand stretching towards the handle.

She pushed it down as quietly as she could, listening to the old mechanism groan.

It clicked open and swung towards her, the smell of musty air following.

A plume of dust rose out of the gap and Jamie slipped inside, into the shadow within.

The last thing she wanted to do was get caught standing in the doorway.

Her eyes stung, the thick air telling her that this was a far more likely place to be able to set up shop without getting caught.

In front of her old cardboard boxes had been stacked up. Christmas decorations overflowed from the one nearest to her, and on her right a one-armed mannequin posed strangely in the darkness. The windows on the far side had been covered up with old and yellowed newspaper and the light pushing through it was diffused and dirty.

Most of it got caught up on the heaped debris that seemed to build towards the centre – years, decades of shop inventory that had been moved up here bit by bit. Boxes and boxes of who-knows-what sealed away as the lease changed hands.

It wasn't the hidden junk that interested her, though. But rather the cover this place would afford. The way that you could crouch down and disappear in here. The way that you could hide and not be found for hours, days… weeks, even.

Jamie picked her head up and sniffed the air, unsure if she was catching just the tiniest essence of food or if that was just the staleness of the place.

She filled her lungs and restrained a cough, then moved on. There seemed to be a corridor of space running around the circumference of the room and then every so often a new avenue would snake into the middle.

There was no sense that anyone else was in there. But then again she didn't think Elliot was the sort of man to be seen or heard unless he wanted to be. All she could do was watch her back and keep her pistol raised.

Having Hassan with her, or even Roper, would have been good. Would have been something. Someone to watch her back. Someone to make sure she didn't get killed. Or abducted. Or cut up for parts.

She grimaced at the thought and pressed on, listening to the sound of her footsteps, dampened on the ancient carpet.

Would she even hear someone coming up behind her?

Jamie felt a cold sensation on the back of her neck and spun round, just to check, covering an empty space with her weapon. Shit, she was wasting too much time. Amherst would be there and gone by the time she even got to the windows.

Jamie paused, tweaked her ears again, and turned back, forcing herself to calm down. Come on, you have to keep moving.

She stepped past the shadowed outline of her father and he fell into step on her shoulder, walking with his big hands buried in the pockets of his peacoat.

Who's hunting who, Jamie?

That was the problem. She didn't know.

Jamie pulled away from him and rounded the corner stepping as quickly as she dared now.

The windows swam in the dust in front of her, the light making her eyes ache in the gloom.

As Jamie got closer, faded headlines blurred into view. They must have been from the eighties, nineties maybe. Corners had flapped down, letting shards of light in from the alleyway outside. Jamie approached and looked through one, seeing the brick wall of the building next door staring back at her.

She was too far across to see down the alleyway, but she got the sense that she was right where she was supposed to be above the entrance to the alley.

If she tilted her head and looked as far right as she could, she could just make out the corner of the street. Her car was parked out of view.

Jamie stepped back, glanced down the long corridor between the boxes and the windows, and froze. There was something at the far end – not a person, not Elliot, but a shape – what looked like a tripod with something on top of it. It was no more than a series of dark lines on a dark background. Shadows on shadows, highlighted by the light coming through the window.

She closed in on it carefully, pistol hanging at stomach-height, clasped tightly in her hands.

Her heart began to pick up.

It beat fast and quiet and Jamie could feel it in her cheeks.

The shape came into view but Jamie's brain wouldn't make sense of it. Not until she was standing right in front of it.

'Jesus,' she muttered, letting her gun fall and hang next to her thigh. Her eyes moved from the stock over the scope and down the long, sleek barrel.

Jamie clenched her teeth to stop her jaw from quivering and stared down at the weapon in front of her, sat on a marksman's tripod, aimed through a circular hole in the newspaper covering the window. It was angled perfectly, set up to face the exact spot that Amherst's car would be in in just a few minutes.

And Jamie didn't even need to look down the scope to know that.

It was an Accuracy International Arctic Warfare, or an AX308 sniper rifle with an attached suppressor. British Military standard-issue. She'd seen them during her firearms training. It was bolt-action, high powered. Enough to blow a hole through anything from this range.

There was no magazine in it, but the bolt had been pulled back, and she could see a single brass round sitting in the body, ready to be chambered. And then fired.

'Beautiful, isn't it?'

His voice barely broke the silence before Jamie turned, throwing her pistol up.

Elliot was standing there in the gloom, hands in his pockets.

He studied her face for a few seconds, and then broke into an amused smile. 'It's good to see you, Jamie.'

She should have shot him right then. Three in the chest. Like she'd promised she would.

But she couldn't. Her finger wouldn't pull the trigger.

'Are you going to shoot me?' he asked, voice barely above a whisper, not a hint of fear in it.

Jamie kept her pistol on centre mass. 'What is this?' she asked, dipping her head towards the rifle, avoiding the question.

'It's a gun, Jamie.'

She jerked the Glock at him. 'Don't screw with me.'

'It's a loaded rifle that's pointed at the spot in which a corrupt detective will stop in, oh, I don't know,' he said, checking his watch. 'Two or three minutes.'

'You're going to kill him?' Jamie flexed her fingers on the grip.

'Me? No.'

She felt a cold sense of dread creep up her spine. 'What am I doing here, Elliot?' she asked, finding her teeth had glued themselves together.

'You're here to step outside of your badge.'

She dragged in a slow breath, her lungs near refusing to inflate. 'I'm not killing Amherst.'

'But you'll shoot me?'

'You're a murderer.'

'So is he.' His eyes flashed in the darkness and he took a step forward.

Jamie backed up a little, her heel hitting the leg of the tripod. It clicked softly and she glanced down, seeing it was screwed to the floor for stability. 'You're lying,' Jamie said reflexively. 'He's a detective – he wouldn't.'

'With friends like Ho Zhou and Jonathan Grigoryan,' Elliot said lightly, taking another step, 'he doesn't have much of a choice.'

'Stop,' Jamie said, her voice cracking. She jerked the gun again. 'Just fucking stop!'

'I'm not going to hurt you, Jamie,' he said.

That wasn't what she meant. She just wanted him to *stop*. Everything.

'But I brought you here to see. That girl – Qiang – her murder would have gone unsolved if you hadn't hounded Amherst for it. Don't you ever wonder *why* they weren't getting anywhere with the investigation?'

'No,' Jamie said, not wanting to hear the answer.

'There's a reason that Detective Amherst either solves cases, or hits impassable walls with them.' Elliot looked disgustingly relaxed. 'You think Qiang was the first investigation he let slide for money? The only reason he let you take it was because if he didn't and still didn't get anywhere it could have raised too many questions.'

'Shut up.'

'How was he when he found you were making progress? Was he happy? Or was he angry?'

Jamie remembered the way he'd been when she'd managed to get into Grigoryan's apartment. How furious he'd been when she'd called him. And how quickly the whole mess got mopped up. 'Just shut up.' She was almost pleading now.

'Zhou has something on him, and uses him to kill the cases that he wants to go under the radar. Sometimes it's as easy as losing some evidence, overlooking a lead… intentionally screwing up the translation of the name of a Chinese merchant ship that just happens to be carrying a dozen women ready to be sold into sex slavery. But sometimes it's more. You look into his cases, and you'll see it – the missing witnesses. Ones that just seem to… disappear.'

Jamie felt bile rise in her throat.

'He's good Jamie. And now he's got you in his sights, too.'

The gun was shaking in her hands now.

'He sent Detective Brock to you, didn't he? One last attempt to see what you knew, to see whether you could be swayed – *bought.* Before he comes for you.'

'Get back,' Jamie said, her voice strangled in her throat.

Elliot was moving closer.

'I'll shoot.'

'No you won't, Jamie. Not me. Because you know I'm right.' He was right in front of her now, close enough to smell. 'And you know I'm here because I want to help you.'

His fingers closed around the muzzle of her pistol, his eyes glinting in the half-light, every line and pore on his face shadowed in vivid definition.

'Kill him before he kills you, Jamie. Keep yourself in the game, and take Amherst out. Strike a blow to Zhou, and Grigoryan, and loosen their hold on the Met.' His eyes drifted from hers over her shoulder and she followed his gaze to the gleaming bullet sitting in the rifle. 'One bullet, one shot. So much good will come of it.'

'I can't,' Jamie whispered, looking at it. 'I can't kill someone.'

'Have you ever tried?'

Jamie glanced down at the body of the Glock in her hand, Elliot's fingers still over the barrel. No. No she hadn't. Not really. But her finger was on the trigger, she could do it now. Move the gun so it faced him, pull the trigger. Put those three bullets into him like she'd promised herself she would over and over again. Get rid of him. Get him out of her life.

For good.

But how would she explain it? She'd been seen by the two workers downstairs. They could place her there. No, she couldn't. She couldn't kill Elliot and she couldn't kill Amherst.

If Elliot was in her apartment, that would be different. Unforeseen. Unanticipated. Without witnesses. She could kill him and peddle whatever story she wanted. But here? No. She had decided. She wouldn't do it.

'Let go,' Jamie said, her voice hard suddenly.

Elliot uncurled his fingers and the pistol came free.

'Get back.' She motioned him backwards with the nose of her Glock.

Elliot let himself smile again, seemingly still amused, and raised his hands until they hovered next to his shoulders. 'You've decided you'd like to try?' Elliot asked.

'No,' Jamie said. 'But I want this to stop.'

He turned his head slightly, measuring her.

'This… whatever *this* is. The contact, the postcards, the stalking, the breaking into the gym… All of it.'

'I can't do that.'

'You have to. I can't arrest you – not without going down myself. You've made sure of that.'

He cracked a little smile, proud of himself. 'And I don't want to kill you…' She paused, took a breath. 'But I will if you push me. Not here, not now. But if I see you again – if you come near me, I'll do it.' She locked her grip tighter around the pistol, aimed it right at his heart.

'I'm not the one you should be afraid of, Jamie.'

'I'm not afraid of you.'

He narrowed his eyes a touch.

'Or of Amherst.'

'You should be.'

'He's not bulletproof.'

He laughed a little. 'No, probably not. But would you really be able to shoot him?'

'If I have to.'

'Then why not do it now, while you have the chance?'

'I'm leaving.' She shook her head. 'In fact, I don't even know why I came.'

'You do,' Elliot said, lowering his hands. 'You just didn't have the guts to do it.'

Jamie dropped her gun and let it fall to her side. 'I don't want to have to kill you.' She felt her eyes heavy then. She was tired suddenly. She hadn't eaten or drunk anything since she'd gotten up and the dust in the room was making her throat sting. 'Just please leave me alone.' Jamie swallowed, turned, and began to walk away.

'How do you know I won't shoot Amherst the second he arrives?' Elliot called after her.

Jamie laughed sardonically, pushing the pistol back into her holster. 'Because it's not your style.'

'People can change, Jamie.'

She reached the other door and paused, laying her hands on the steel bar running across it. 'No,' she said, pushing through. 'They don't.'

24

'KEEPING YOU AWAKE ARE WE, JOHANSSON?'

Jamie lifted her head up and dragged in a sharp breath. They were back in the meeting room, and she must have all-but nodded off. 'No, sir,' Jamie said, looking at Smith. 'Of course not.' Hassan had been regaling them with the story of how he wooed Eleanor Phillips into spilling the beans on Delgado – at least up until the point where he'd asked about the suspension and she'd slammed the door in his face. The college were staying quiet on that front and though Roper and Hassan had both called that morning, neither had gotten anything other than 'A PR representative will contact you as soon as they are able.'

Hassan seemed to have finished now, his case-update complete. The long and short of it was that Eleanor Phillips, along with several other female staff, and several students, all had been involved with, or wanted to be involved with Gilberto Delgado. He seemed have no real regard for women, but Jamie didn't see his murder as any or all of them seeking revenge.

Roper had gotten everyone back up to speed on Fowler, too. She had been released from custody, and had gone back to stay with her parents temporarily. Jamie wanted her out of the city until they knew she wasn't a target.

Smith's eyes lingered on Jamie as she pulled herself more upright in her chair, and then turned to Gretchen. 'Miss Fischer – what do you know?'

Gretchen made no attempt to cut whatever she was typing short, finished after a few seconds, and then looked up, pushing her glasses up her nose. 'About what?'

'The case. Alyssa Doran, Mimi Paganelli, Gilberto Delgado…' Smith counted them off on his fingers.

'Two are dead, one's missing, and the guy who killed them is probably a Sagittarius.'

Smith narrowed his eyes.

'That was a joke.' Gretchen raised an eyebrow above the frame of her glasses, but Smith didn't look impressed. 'Detective Roper asked me to dig into Alyssa's phone, specifically looking for information from last year, circa July-October. But tough tits,' she said, leaning back and lacing her hands behind her head. 'Like I said before. Phone's clean. Nothing on it.' She made a fart sound with her lips to illustrate the lack of information she'd found.

'Shit,' Smith said, hanging his head and ignoring the sound effects.

Jamie looked at Roper, who was looking at Gretchen. It had been her order to get Gretchen to look into that, not his.

She kept quiet though. If Roper needed that credit, she could stomach it.

Gretchen went on. 'It's like she was trying to stay under the radar, you know? The deleted Facebook and socials, nothing. No contact with former classmates. No deleted histories or texts. Even her rent was paid from her parents' account – she was staying in an apartment not too far from where she was killed. Renting a spare room off a woman called Jennifer… something or other. She works away mostly – I found an ad on the local free-ads that was advertising for a house-sitter to look after her cat and water her plants. That was in November. Looks like Alyssa has been there since.'

Smith glanced up. 'Roper?'

'On it,' Roper said, nodding, confirming he'd look into her.

'Get SOCOs out there ASAP to go over the place. Pick it clean.'

'Got it.'

Why hadn't Smith asked Jamie?

She looked back and forth between them.

'But she's got a rock-solid alibi,' Gretchen added.

'How rock-solid?' Smith asked.

'She's in the US and has been for the last three weeks.'

He drew a slow breath in. 'Alright. Roper, try and get hold of her, see if we can't gain access, look around. Fischer, what else?'

'There's really not much to tell.' Gretchen let out a long breath. 'Alyssa was making a point of staying hidden. And you can't read into what's not there.'

Jamie disagreed. 'I think that tells us more than you realise,' she said without meaning to interject as matter-of-factly as she did. She cleared her throat. 'Were there texts or phone calls to her parents?'

'Texts.'

'Saying what?'

Gretchen looked back at her screen, flashed through a series of pages, tapped on the keyboard, and then read some of them. 'Small stuff. "I'm okay" mostly. Couple of words every week or two, mostly replies to texts from her mum saying, "Still alive!?!?".'

Hassan leaned forward now, resting on his elbows. 'Think the mum knew something was up? That Alyssa was in danger?'

Jamie pressed her lips into a line. 'No – I think that's just mumness. I know a thing or two about passive-aggressive parents.'

Hassan looked at the table.

'Still worth checking out though,' Jamie said, forcing a smile. She was in charge here and Smith seemed to have forgotten that. She needed to show him she could lead. 'Why don't you use your manly charms, speak to her, see if you can't find out whether she knew anything about the October incident with Delgado.'

Hassan seemed to brighten a little, and then nodded.

Jamie returned it. 'Coordinate with Roper, he's already spoken to them about coming down to the city to give us a positive ID' — she turned to look at him — 'right?'

He averted his eyes, expressionless, and then gave the vaguest hint of a nod as though it was insulting that Jamie even asked.

Jamie ignored the off-handed pettiness and carried on.

'Gretchen,' she said, 'what about Delgado's phone? Did we get anything from that?'

'The handset was new in February – just a few months old, so no texts, photos, nothing like that from the summer. I've got a request in with the provider for his phone records now. He doesn't maintain a Facebook account either. No socials other than an unused Twitter account and a LinkedIn profile that hasn't been touched since last spring. No stories to tell there. But I can tell you he hasn't been in touch with Alyssa since he got his new phone. There was a single phone call made to his number at nine-twenty-four yesterday morning. I suspect that's from Mimi's number. Though I won't know for sure until I get those records. Once I do, I'll run a track-and-trace, see if I can get a hit on her phone. Until then…'

Jamie clamped her teeth together. On the off chance it wasn't Mimi's phone they couldn't just run an invasive track on a random number. Once they had confirmation, there would be cause. But right now…

She sighed, shook it off, and took a breath, determined to take the helm now. 'Okay, thanks. Stay on it, and get that search run the second we get those records.'

Fischer nodded.

Jamie took stock of the room. Of the situation. It felt like she'd sufficiently compartmentalised the morning's craziness, and no calls had come in saying that Detective Amherst had had his head blown off by a sniper rifle, so Jamie guessed that Elliot hadn't followed through on his plan. What Jamie was going to do about Amherst, Brock, and the tendrils that Zhou and Grigoryan, and whoever else was out there had around their throats, was still unclear. But this case right here? This was real, and she didn't think the killer was about to let up. 'Alyssa was hiding – for six months. Which meant that whatever scared her in October was still a threat. We need to find out what went on during those summer months, and we need to do it now. If Delgado's suspension is tied up with the college, and Alyssa is a dead end' — Smith fired her a cold look at the turn of phrase, though she didn't bother to stop and tell him she hadn't said it intentionally — 'then it's time we look at Mimi. She might still be alive, and the killer knew her. Enough to get into her apartment. We can use that. I want to know where Mimi was last summer, what she was doing, who she was doing it with, and I want to know now. Roper, I want you to get a list of her friends, classmates, everything. Find them, contact them, pull them in here for questioning. Hassan, you contact her parents, they need to know what's going on. Ask them whether she told them about anyone bothering her recently, anything like that. I want to know whether she had a boyfriend, where she liked to hang out at night, where she shopped, everything. Gretchen, Mimi was active on socials, more so than Alyssa, so scour them. I want her life timelined from last spring through to now in excruciating detail. Where was she over the summer? Did she go home? Did she stay in the city? I want every name and every face of every person she crossed paths with laid out for us to see. Ping her phone, too, see if you can get anything back from it.' Jamie finished and looked at each of them in turn, settling on Smith finally. 'Okay?'

He nodded almost imperceptibly, looked for just the briefest second like he was trying to restrain a smile, and then stood up. 'Well,' he said. 'You have your mandates. Find this son of a bitch.'

Hassan, Roper, and Gretchen pushed back and left the briefing room. But Smith's eyes on her told Jamie that she needed to stay right where she was.

When the door closed, he wasted no time.

'You good, Johansson?' he asked.

'I am.'

'Are you sure? Because you look like shit.'

'Thank you, sir.'

'I'm not trying to offend you, and I know this job takes a toll. Are you sleeping?' He sounded genuinely concerned.

'I am.'

'How much?'

'Enough.'

'Johansson.'

'I'm fine, sir,' Jamie insisted. 'I was up this morning for an early trip to the gym.' She wasn't lying. 'It's stressful, I won't lie – this case, Amherst and Brock – but I'm good. I can handle it.'

He narrowed his eyes and measured her. 'I can ask Roper to shoulder some more respons—'

'No,' Jamie said more definitively this time. 'This is my case.'

He nodded slowly. 'You need to look after yourself, Johansson. The last two big cases you had… One got you a broken arm. The other… I don't even know what happened. And I'm guessing you're not going to tell me?'

Jamie stayed quiet.

He sighed. 'You know, putting everything you have into cases… It's not always the best thing to do.'

Jamie eyed him.

'This job takes a lot from you. It takes everything you give it, and then a little more, too. So if you let it, it will take, and take, and take, until you have nothing else left in the world.'

Jamie thought on that. On her non-existent relationships. On her non-existent social life. Of her terrible apartment. Of the serial killer stalking her every move.

She drew in a slow breath and got up. 'Is there anything else?'

'Hold something back, Johansson. That's all I'm saying.'

She smiled a little. Sadly. 'Sir, honestly, I wish I had a reason to.'

When Jamie got to her desk, Roper was already at his, going through records from the college, cross-referencing names of Mimi's classmates, who she'd shared rooms with, trips she'd been on with the college. Anything that could help. The majority of murders and kidnappings were committed by people the victims knew.

Jamie didn't think this one was any different, and she wanted to break open this dome of silence that was surrounding the October incident. Both Alyssa and Delgado, the two people involved, were now dead. And that couldn't be a coincidence. Something happened during those months.

'Forensics report,' Jamie said aloud, spotting the file just as she sat down. It had been put in her documents tray.

Roper peeled his eyes from his screen and slid back on his chair, the old wheels grinding through the carpet. 'From Mimi's apartment?'

Jamie nodded, pulling it in front of her and opening the cover. 'Yep.'

'What's it say?'

Jamie scanned the pages carefully. 'Labs show that the blood was all Delgado's. No other blood samples recovered at the scene.'

'That's good, right?'

'Well it means he hasn't hurt Mimi – or at least he didn't before they left the apartment. Looks like even the blood trail was all Delgado. Dripping off the killer.'

Roper pulled in a slow breath. There was plenty of blood. It wasn't a shocking revelation really. 'What about the cup?'

'Positive for gamma-hydroxybutyrate,' Jamie said, reading it fluidly. She'd done it a hundred times.

'GHB?' Roper clicked his tongue and began fidgeting. That was usually what he did right before going for a cigarette, but Jamie was impressed with his fortitude. He'd been a smoker as long as she'd known him. Never thought he'd quit. But maybe that close call with De Voge really scared him. Maybe it changed him. She studied him for a second, and realised that she'd not really spoken to him in months. Not about anything serious. They'd been friends before the attack. Even after. But now…

She cleared her throat. 'Yeah, which makes sense. The guy comes in, gets tea made for him, slips something into Mimi's, calls Delgado in…' She rolled her hand through the air. 'We've got the picture, right.'

Roper nodded, and then sighed. 'Doesn't make it any better.'

'That it doesn't,' Jamie mused, going through the report. Delgado had been killed by a blade – same dimensions as the one that killed Alyssa. That tracked, too. Same area – right in the abdomen. Another personal attack. He wanted to look Delgado in the eye while he did it.

Jamie shuddered.

'So it tells us nothing?' Roper asked. 'Or at least nothing we didn't already know.'

Jamie bit her lip, looking for anything else of use.

Damn, was he right? Was this just another dead-end?

'Wait,' she said suddenly, homing in on something on page five. 'The bed.'

'What about it?'

'A semen sample was recovered.'

Roper perked up. 'Delgado's? Yeah, we knew he was messing around with Mimi already.'

'It's not Delgado's.'

'Then whose is it?'

Jamie screwed up her face, not liking the place her mind was going. The DNA didn't match Delgado's.

Roper read her expression. 'Jesus, you don't think the killer...?'

Jamie closed the file and laid it back on the desk, placing her hands flat on top of it. 'What I think, is that we need to find Mimi, and fast.'

25

ROPER'S PHONE rang almost as soon as Jamie had put her own down, asking for the DNA collected from the bed to be run through their database.

Neither of them had said it – because so far there was no concrete evidence to suggest it – but if the semen belonged to the killer, then that brought a whole new element into play here. One that made Jamie feel sick to think about.

Jamie closed her eyes and ran her hands over her head, brushing back the loose strands of hair. She was struggling to keep the image of what happened in Mimi's room out of her head… The sort of person who would do what he did. Who *could* do what he did. Amherst, Zhou, Grigoryan, they were bad enough… But then there were people like this. Like De Voge… Like *Elliot.* She shuddered and then pricked her ears without thinking, a tone in Roper's voice striking a discord in her head,

'…Jesus, yeah, alright… Okay – sure. We're on the way.'

Jamie opened her eyes and leaned forward, seeing Roper grave. 'What is it?' she asked, voice catching in her throat.

He exhaled and then heaved himself to his feet. 'We've got another one.'

'A body?' Jamie asked, on her feet already.

'Worse.' Roper shook his head. 'It's another pair of hands.'

Jamie's blood ran cold. 'Mimi's?'

He shook his head. 'I don't know. But the scene is fresh – uniforms are on their way.' Roper was reaching for his coat when he paused, looking up at Jamie. 'Do you want me to…?'

She glanced at Hassan, who'd turned around on his chair to look at them. 'Yeah,' she said, nodding to Roper. 'And you too,' she added, looking at Hassan. 'I think we need all the eyes we can get on this one.'

Roper's car had blown a head gasket and Jamie's had no hope of squeezing both Roper and Hassan into it – at least not without the rear arches scrubbing on the tires. Which left Hassan's car.

Roper took one look at the two booster seats in the back of Hassan's four-by-four, and then climbed into the front without saying a word.

Hassan paused, realised that his two kids' seats took up most of the room in there, and pulled the door open in front of Jamie. 'Hang on,' he said, trying to undo the fasteners for the seats. 'Just a second – I think these do something… like… clip… unclip? With this button or is this a…'

Jamie clicked her teeth together watching Hassan loosen and unloosen a strap that adjusted the height of the headrest on the baby seat, came to the conclusion that he'd never taken them out of there before – and that he probably hadn't put them in in the first place – and tapped him on the shoulder. 'It's fine – come on, just get in. I'll squeeze in the middle.'

'You sure?' he asked, turning to her, looking sorry, but already moving for the front door.

Yeah, otherwise we'll be here until Sunday, she felt like saying. 'Sure,' she actually said, clambering up and across the seat.

She squashed herself down into the small gap in the middle so that the edges of both baby seats dug awkwardly into her hips, and pulled her gun off her belt so that it didn't poke her in the back.

Jamie held her tongue as Hassan got in and looked at her in the rear-view. 'You okay?'

'Let's just go,' she said sourly.

Roper stayed facing front as they backed into the underground carpark and then pulled away smoothly.

Jamie grunted and shifted herself a little, moving from one painful position to another. 'So where are we going?' she asked, trying not to sound strained.

'An old theatre,' Roper said, still not meeting her eye. 'It's been abandoned for a few years, about to be renovated. Someone came in to do a pest-inspection – the breakers were off. He flipped them on and found them…'

'The hands?' Jamie asked, reaching down underneath her, fishing a dummy out. She grimaced and dropped it into the baby seat on her right. 'Where were they?'

Roper sucked air in through his teeth. 'I didn't get much in the way of details, but they'd been… arranged?'

'Arranged?' Jamie arched an eyebrow as they slowed into traffic.

'"Strung up" was what the initial report said.'

Jamie pinched the bridge of her nose and closed her eyes. 'Jesus. Like hung up to dry, or what? What are we looking at here?'

'You tell me,' Roper said, glancing in the mirror at her for the first time. 'You're the one running this show.'

Jamie let the slight air of scorn roll off her back and leaned back instead. She was still tired, and she didn't think she could keep being polite with the plastic corners punching her in the bottom with every jostle. So she stayed quiet, let Hassan drive, and tried to keep an open mind. But whatever lay ahead, she knew that it wasn't going to be pretty.

. . .

Hassan eased up to the police cordon and showed the uniform at his window his warrant card. She lifted the tape and the four-by-four scraped under it, the plastic flapping across the roof as they did.

He pulled in at the curb between two marked cars and killed the engine.

Jamie's left leg was completely numb by now, but she levered herself up and was out of the car before either of them anyway.

She shook some blood back into it and then repositioned her holster, looking up at the darkened building ahead.

It was old, with ornate stonework. Weeds grew out of the rotten window frames and the main door, a big, heavy wooden thing stained near-black sat like a stone barrier. Someone had spray-painted something ugly over it and the stone slabs at its flanks. The word *Chiggsy* was written in white, curling letters, with a series of 'X's and dots surrounding it. A tag. And a pretty crappy one.

Jamie's eyes drifted up to the huge for-sale sign above it, and the 'SOLD' banner stretched across that.

Some scaffolding was constructed around the left-hand corner, and a sign hanging off it said 'Hanover Construction'. Jamie made a mental note of it.

The uniform who'd lifted the tape came over, looked at the three of them now standing in front of the car, and smiled. She couldn't have been more than mid-twenties.

'Detectives?' she said, almost too enthusiastically.

They all nodded.

'Good – Dana Lyle,' she said, extending her hand to Roper first.

It wasn't a given, but Jamie knew addressing the most senior detective first was good manners.

He shook and Jamie restrained a scowl.

Then Dana went for Hassan's hand next. Then finally Jamie's.

'DS Jamie Johansson,' Jamie said, taking it firmly. 'I'm the lead on this case.'

Dana paused for a second, then blushed a little. 'Oh,' she said, 'Great. I was first on the scene – the guy who found them, or, uh, it?' She cleared her throat. 'The inspector who first discovered the scene is over there,' she said, pointing to another uniformed officer speaking to a guy in workman's trousers and heavy boots.

'Okay,' Jamie said, keeping her tone firm. The ride had done nothing for her mood. 'I'll speak to him after I've seen inside. Can you take us?'

Dana nodded. 'Of course,' she said. 'This way.'

They followed in silence, and Jamie made sure to go first.

Roper rolled his eyes in her peripheral vision and Jamie sighed away the annoyance. She was tempted to stick him on the inspector, let her get some breathing room in there. But this wasn't about her, and definitely not about whatever juvenile power struggle was going on. There were people being killed, cut up, and now *strung up*. This was bigger than them. And anyway, by what Smith was saying, Roper would be gone soon enough anyway.

Jamie doubted he would stick around if he could get his hands on a payout.

She smirked at that for a second, then felt bad about it. Jamie shook off both the smile and the feeling and pressed on, listening to Roper limp behind her. He'd probably never walk right again. And she shouldn't be feeling any sort of good about that.

Dana took them down the side alley and around to an open fire escape. A thick chain hung from the door, the gleaming steel of fresh bolt-cutter marks exposed at the rusted ends of a broken link.

'In here,' Dana said, her boots crunching on the stone chippings under foot.

Jamie ducked inside, swallowed by the gloom.

Hassan and Roper followed them in and Dana led them through what would have once been the back-stage corridors.

There were no lights on, just the light spilling in from the open door behind them.

They passed dressing and store rooms on both sides, some empty, some filled with old chairs, rolls of carpet or rolled up stage curtains, random props… Jamie caught glimpses as she passed, following right on Dana's heels as she led them to a door that said 'STAGE'.

'Through here,' she said, motioning up a pair of well-worn steps.

Jamie nodded her thanks, dug in her pocket for gloves, and pulled them out.

She snapped them on, not offering Roper a pair in who-knew-how-long and then pushed the door open.

Both Hassan and Roper followed her up and onto the stage which was bathed in a harsh light.

A portable flood-lamp had been positioned in the corner, facing towards the door, and outlined one of the cruellest and strangest scenes Jamie had even laid her eyes on.

She lifted her arm to shield herself from the glare and traced a circle around the main attraction.

'Did, uh,' she said, squinting back at Dana, who was still hovering in the shadow of the doorway. 'Did you put the light here?' She nodded towards it.

'No,' Dana said, shaking her head. 'We haven't touched anything. The inspector who came in said he flipped the main breaker, and it came on. A bunch of lights did – which led here.'

Jamie squinted back at her, not even taking in the horror of what was hanging centre stage. 'What do you mean led?'

'He said that the only lights that were on led down a corridor, and into the main hall here,' Dana said, trying not to look at the exhibition arranged before them. She pointed off up the room towards the back rows of seats. The hall was a mess of broken chairs and other debris just laid in the aisle. Jamie could see a main door in the gloom, light burning behind it.

There were no lights on back stage. Just this portable lamp here, and the ones from the breaker to the main hall. Jamie bit her lip. 'How long has this place been empty?'

Dana shook her head. 'I don't know, years?'

'Were the bulbs new?' Jamie asked.

'Sorry?' Dana replied.

'The bulbs leading from the breakers to here.'

'I don't know.'

'And was the chain on the back-door cut when you arrived?'

'Yes, it was.'

'And the inspector, did he come in through the back?'

'No, through the front door. He had keys.'

'So why did we come through the back?'

'The back door was already open, and you can't exactly climb over all that,' Dana said, nodding out at the mountain of overturned and ripped out chairs. It looked like they'd already started dismantling the room for the renovation.

Jamie nodded processing. 'Thank you,' she said, allowing her eyes to drift to the middle of the stage.

The killer had come through the back as well then – didn't want whoever was coming in to know the theatre had been broken into. Then he took the time to find the fusebox, make sure that the only lights burning led to the main hall. Anyone with any sense of curiosity, morbid or otherwise, would follow the trail.

Roper and Hassan were standing back, viewing from the rear of the stage.

But Jamie knew that this wasn't meant to be seen from back there.

She circled around to the front until her back was pointed directly at the front door, and took it in, in all its gruesome majesty.

There, in the middle of the stage, bathed in all but a spotlight, were two hands.

They were suspended in the air, perfectly shaped and placed at head height. As Jamie looked at it, the left hand was pointing away, knuckles raised towards her, curled over. The right was positioned just next to it, facing towards her, fingers arranged at different heights.

They looked pristine, alabaster almost in the light. The pale white skin was faultless, the nails trimmed, shaped, the cuticles treated and groomed. And the cuts, this time, were clean and precise. Severed right at the wrist bone.

There was no blood on the stage, and the hands seemed to float ethereally, suspended by thin wires – fishing wire, Jamie guessed.

She looked upwards, seeing that there was a lighting rig overhead, the wires running to it. It must have taken hours to position. The killer would have climbed up there, tied off the lines, draped them all down, then come down, hung the hands, hooked through the skin with a fine stitching needle, and tied each off.

Jamie stepped closer.

They looked like spider's silk.

There must have been eight per hand – maybe more.

From any distance, they were invisible.

But Jamie guessed that was the point.

When the inspector came in, he would have seen them just floating there. Two hands, positioned like this, against the black curtain behind.

Jamie took a long breath in and then let it out.

The theatre, the hands, the positioning… It was a performance. He wanted them to be seen, to be witnessed here. This was the killer's show. And he was putting it on for whoever would watch.

'Is it Paganelli?' Hassan asked, breaking the interminable silence.

'No,' Jamie said, barely above a whisper. 'I don't think so.' She sighed and looked away. 'But I think I know who it is.' She looked at Roper now. 'You said Chessie talked about Delgado's old favourite, before Alyssa?'

'The redhead – the flautist—' he cut the word off sharply, realising what he was looking at, the way the hands were set, as though clutching an invisible flute. 'Jesus Christ,' he muttered. 'It's her.'

'Yeah,' Jamie said, turning to face the open room. 'It's her.'

Jamie had been on hold for thirty-five minutes.

She'd spoken to a young woman at the reception of the College, and had demanded to be put through to *someone* with the authority to divulge what had happened over the summer last year. They were getting the run-around, and now it really was costing lives.

They could get a court order, force the college to release the information, but Jamie wanted to take one last swing at it. Two dead former students, one current student missing, a dead lecturer. What the hell were they trying to keep quiet?

Roper came up behind Jamie and cleared his throat.

She opened her eyes, the spring sun burning orange behind her lids, and turned to face him. 'What'd you find?' she asked.

'The pest inspector has no links to Delgado, to Alyssa Doran, or our new victim. He's never heard of the college, let alone been there. He's not from London, not had any contact with the theatre or the company renovating it before he was booked for this appointment. I don't think he was targeted here to find the body. Not specifically.'

Jamie drew a slow breath in. 'Alright, good work. What about the victim?'

'Rachel Bartlett, twenty-three – not reported missing, but her roommate said she hasn't come home for a few nights.' Jamie had asked him to run down Delgado's old flame while Jamie called the college. 'Her roommate said she stays with her boyfriend a few nights a week, so it's not unusual for her to be over there for a few days at a time.'

Jamie nodded, holding her phone against her collarbone. 'Okay, good. You got an address?'

'For the roommate?'

'For the boyfriend. I want to talk to him.'

'I'll get one.'

'Good,' Jamie said, pulling the phone back to her ear. The holding music was still blaring, tinny and annoying. Roper moved off and Jamie waved at Hassan. He looked up from his phone and came over slowly. It was at moments like this that she saw the inexperience in him. Roper was busy, so was she, and without direction, he was lost.

SOCOs moved around, in their white suits, photographing everything, and a sea of blue lights flashed silently at their flanks. And in the middle of it was Nasir Hassan, rookie detective. Out of his depth. But he'd get there.

After Roper was gone, he would be all she'd have.

She shook that thought off and lowered her phone again.

'Roper is following up a lead – the victim's boyfriend.'

'You like him for this?'

She shook her head. 'I don't know – unlikely. But maybe. If it is him, I'll feel better that you're with Roper.'

Hassan smiled a little, unsure if it was a compliment.

Jamie didn't even think about it. 'Just stay with him, okay, watch, listen, learn. Find out what you can about Rachel – the victim – whether she had any enemies, anything like that. Anyone she'd had trouble with at the college – that's the link here.'

He nodded. 'What are you going to do?'

'I'm going to the college,' Jamie said, finally hanging up. 'This is getting ridiculous now. They've got a hand in this somehow – and whatever they're trying to bury, I'm going to find it.'

Hassan inspected the lines of her face. She felt like she looked tired, and turned her head away.

'You sure you don't need me to come with you?' he asked. 'Roper can handle himself.'

'No,' Jamie said, trying to stay pragmatic. 'You can learn more from Roper than from me. It'll be good for you to go with him. Plus,' she said, putting on a smile, 'the principle of the college is probably some stuffy old guy – and no offence, but I don't think your charms would work on him.'

Hassan laughed and held his hands out. 'What, you don't think guys want a piece of this too?'

She couldn't help but smile for real now. 'Get out of here,' she said, waving him off. 'Find Rachel's boyfriend before he gets killed too.'

'You got it,' Hassan said, nodding to her and then walking off to find Roper.

Jamie watched him go. The last bit had been a joke, but as she watched Hassan melt into the crowd of white jumpsuits and marked cars, she couldn't help but wonder if they would find another body when they got there. The killer was smart, and he wasn't wasting any time. And he sure as shit didn't have any qualms about killing. He was mopping up as he went, and leaving a trail of bodies in his wake.

Jamie felt her fist curl around her phone and an anger well up inside her.

She lifted it again and redialled the college. She wasn't going to wait on hold to speak to someone this time. She just wanted a name. And an office number.

And then she was going.

Jamie was tired of being on the back foot.

It was time to go on the offensive, hunt this son of a bitch down.

She felt her pistol heavy on her hip.

And if necessary, *put* him down.

Jamie was sick of letting serial killers dictate her life.

It was time to take it back.

No matter the cost.

26

Jamie pulled in at the college for the third time and was out of the car before it had even stopped rolling.

She didn't have the time or the patience this morning to deal with traffic wardens, and didn't even bother to check whether they were hovering.

The reception building came up quickly and she shoved through the front doors and into the foyer.

'Ah,' Scott, the kid behind the desk, said, a grin slicing its way into his cheeks. 'Detective, nice to see you again.'

She found it difficult to return. 'Hi,' she replied, coming right up to it. 'Scott, I need your help.'

He looked a little taken aback, and then a little proud. 'Uh, of course. What can I do for you?'

'Who's in charge of PR for the college?'

'PR?' He looked confused.

'Public relations.'

'Uh,' he said again. He seemed to start every sentence with it. 'I'm not too sure. But I could make some calls, find out for you?'

Jamie shook her head. 'No, it's fine.' She didn't want them to know she was coming. 'What about the principal?'

'Of the whole college?'

'Yeah,' Jamie said. 'What's his name?'

'It's, uh, Terry? Or Terence, I mean – Brownmiller, I think?'

'Terence Brownmiller?'

Scott nodded. 'I think so. I see him walking around sometimes.'

'And where's his office?'

'Uh, it's in Thornton.'

'That a building?'

'Oh, yeah,' he said with a nervous laugh. 'It's out the door, right, all the way to the end, and the last building on the right. If you hit the gates, you've gone too far.'

'He in his office?'

'Uh, I can check?' he began reaching for the phone.

'No, don't bother,' Jamie said, moving again. 'I'll see for myself. Don't call.'

He replaced the receiver tentatively. 'Okay? Do you need—'

But she was already out the door and jogging. Her boots clipped on the concrete as she headed for Thornton, determined to get out of Brownmiller what she needed.

The door opened automatically to accept Jamie, but despite the glass frontage, the interior was dated – antique, almost. Thornton was an old building – eighteen-hundreds by the feel of the place. There was wood panelling on the walls, thick red carpet on the floor, and every scrap of painted wall was that rustic off-white that made it look like a thousand cigars had been smoked in there.

Jamie glanced around, clocking the three corridors. One ahead, one left, one right.

'Can I help you?' a woman in thin glasses called from behind a desk against the wall.

She was tall, mid-fifties, with a pointed chin and long, blood-red fingernails. She looked Jamie up and down, the dirtied boots, skinny jeans, and long sleeve t-shirt – not quite the usual apparel that came rolling through that door to meet with the brass of the school.

'Terence Brownmiller,' Jamie said flatly. 'He in his office?'

'The *principal,*' the woman said haughtily, straightening her blazer, 'is seen by appointment only. And not just by anyone, *either.*'

Jamie took a few steps forwards, reached into her pocket so that the hem of her jacket was brushed back over the butt of her pistol and pulled out her warrant card.

The woman's eyes flashed to it and she stiffened in her chair.

'DS Jamie Johansson, London Metropolitan Police. Want to try that again?'

She cleared her throat. 'My apologies.' She seemed slightly more reserved now, but still didn't look like she was about to give in to Jamie's request. 'But I can't just let you walk in there and see him.'

'So he is in there?' Jamie narrowed her eyes. That confirmed that.

The woman drew in a long breath and lifted her chin. 'Mr Brownmiller is very busy and— where do you think you're going?'

Jamie didn't have time for this and wasn't about to stand here and exchange terse words with the woman. Not when the killer had Mimi locked up somewhere, ready to kill. Hell, maybe he already *had* killed her and they just hadn't stumbled across her dismembered remains yet.

Jamie's fist tightened around her warrant card as she reached the end of the left-hand corridor and doubled back. Not down here.

She read the brass nameplates on each of the polished wooden doors, double checking them as she headed back.

The woman was out of her seat now, standing with her hands on her hips. 'I don't know who you think you are, but I'll have your warrant card number if—'

'Sit down,' Jamie commanded her, her voice like iron. She breezed past and cut left up the central corridor now, her head swinging back and forth, searching for the right name.

The woman took a step back and seethed. She was probably used to the students here paling and quivering as she approached. These kinds of places were built on tradition, founded on respect. No one would dare speak out of turn against a lecturer or staff member.

But Jamie was all out of patience, and wasn't about to let some beanpole in a skirt-suit derail the little progress she was actually making.

Jamie paused at a door on the left, the tarnished nameplate displaying the words 'Terence Brownmiller – PRINCIPAL' etched into the metal. She didn't bother knocking. The extra few seconds would have allowed the beanpole in the heels to come tottering into grabbing range. And she didn't feel like being manhandled. Especially not with her claws.

Jamie twisted the knob and stepped inside, her warrant card already coming up.

The room was spacious, regal, even. The floor was oak boards with a big, Persian-style rug, and an enormous desk was backed by a tall window. It was littered with little sculptures and framed photographs showing Terence Brownmiller in various places, holding a trombone, and grinning. Jamie took stock of the room quickly – the shelves with the antique books, the instruments mounted, the framed posters for orchestral performances, and the man at the centre of it all. Principal Terence Brownmiller.

He was short, easily in his early sixties, with a receding hairline, and a shirt that was two inches too small on the collar. His throat budged over it like uncooked bread dough.

Brownmiller muttered something into the phone he was holding to his ear and replaced it on the desk, clasping his hands together. His watch clinked softly on the wood as he put his arms down, his round fingers strangled by a series of gold rings. One wedding band, one signet ring, one mason's ring.

He looked up at Jamie with beady eyes, his false, welcoming smile making her skin crawl just a little bit.

'Hello,' he said measuredly as she approached.

Before Jamie could speak, the woman who had tried to stop Jamie squawked from behind her. 'I'm sorry, Mr Brownmiller, I tried to stop her, but—'

'It's fine, Vee,' he said, his soft voice carrying in the silent room. 'That will be all.'

She nodded diligently and then backed out of the room like he was damn royalty, pulling the door behind her.

It shut and Brownmiller's eyes flitted from Jamie's face to her dirty boots on his clean carpet and back.

His smile remained, but Jamie could tell there wasn't a hint of sincerity in it.

'DS Jamie Johansson,' she said formally, her warrant card still raised.

He gestured to one of the two leather seats positioned at perfect forty-five-degree angles to the desk.

'I'll stand,' she replied.

He lowered his own hand, put it back into the other on his desk in front of him and waited for her to speak.

'Alyssa Doran.'

The name hung in the air, but Brownmiller didn't flinch.

'She's dead.'

He looked down, perfectly rehearsed, and took a moment, before looking up. 'I'm sorry to hear that. She was a wonderful student. We're remiss to have lost her, both from our halls, and from the world.'

'Cut the bullshit,' Jamie growled.

Brownmiller looked at her like a waxwork.

'Rachel Bartlett.'

'Another former student of ours,' Brownmiller said, this time a little thrown by the name. 'Is she…?'

'Dead? Yeah, she is.' Jamie was struggling to keep the scorn from her voice. 'Gilberto Delgado, too.'

Brownmiller swallowed, then cleared his throat. 'Mr Delgado was a valued—'

'Oh, shut up,' Jamie said, sighing. 'They're all dead, and now Mimi Paganelli is missing.'

'Miss Paganelli?' Brownmiller's mask finally slipped.

'Yeah, for more than twenty-four hours now. And judging by the time between Alyssa Doran's death and Rachel Bartlett's, the killer isn't hanging around. If she's not dead already, she will be soon.'

He licked his thin lips. 'We'll of course do anything we can to—'

'Last summer – between July and October. Alyssa Doran, Gilberto Delgado. What happened?'

His eyes twitched a little but he fell quiet. 'I don't know that I can—'

'Something happened, and we need to know what. Right now.' Jamie stepped forward. 'I don't care what you did, what the college did, but there's a girl out there who's about to lose her life because of it. And after her, another one. And after her, another. And another. This guy isn't going to stop, and if you don't tell me—'

'Aaron McElroy.'

Jamie stopped speaking. 'What?'

'Aaron McElroy.' He seemed to squeeze the words out reluctantly.

'Who's that?'

'I fear…' He said, lowering his voice and sucking in a thin stream of air between his teeth, 'he is the man you're looking for.'

'You *knew?*' Jamie's voice was little more than a hiss. 'And you did nothing?'

'No – of course not,' Brownmiller said, looking older suddenly. 'We weren't aware that Miss Doran and Miss Bartlett were dead. Gilberto' — he stopped himself quickly and started again, masking the strain in his voice — 'Mr Delgado, has missed a day of classes, but again, we weren't aware that he was…' He couldn't say *dead.* 'But those names… Those poor girls…' He shook his head. 'It has to be.'

Jamie took a long breath, tried to let some of the anger drain out of her. It was her call when to release the names of the victims. She'd been holding back on it, keeping her cards close to her chest. She needed positive IDs, needed to have the parents, next of kin, confirm their identities before she could have… this wasn't her fault, was it? No, she couldn't think like that. She followed protocol. She did the right thing.

'Wha—' she began, her voice catching in her throat. 'What happened last summer – with Alyssa, with Delgado, with Aaron McElroy.'

Brownmiller sat back in his chair and it groaned softly. 'The college has always been a philanthropic establishment.'

Jamie folded her arms.

'We've always run programs to help those who were less fortunate, less privileged... Those with *talent* that the world would miss if it was wasted.'

Jamie felt her fists curl. She didn't like where this was going.

'We trialled a program last year that allowed for young offenders to seriously pursue a career in music.'

'Young offenders?'

'Youths who had committed a crime, or had been previously imprisoned. Aaron McElroy was one such young man.'

'Jesus,' Jamie muttered.

'He applied for the program under the guidance of his case worker. He wanted to become a conductor. A talented musician by all accounts, but his passion lay with conducting.' Brownmiller stopped for another moment, looked at the wall on his left, taking stock of his thoughts, and then looked back at Jamie. 'He was brought here to study under Delgado, to participate in a summer internship.'

Jamie swallowed. 'What did he do?'

Brownmiller tapped his thumbs together, his hands still clasped. 'We... didn't know. The crime he committed wasn't able to be divulged due to his age at the time. The case was sealed, and we were told that... But his audition video, it was... *promising.'*

Jamie closed her eyes. If she'd had this information thirty-six hours ago.

'Gilberto saw something in him – something special, he said. So we accepted him, and he arrived in early July on a twelve-week basis. He was due to leave at the end of September, before the students came back.'

'What happened with Delgado and Alyssa?'

Brownmiller fell quiet again.

'We know they were in a relationship – we know Delgado was suspended, that Doran was afraid for her life.' A picture was already beginning to form in Jamie's head, and she didn't like it. Not one bit.

'Gilberto and Aaron hit it off immediately. The boy was charming, clean-cut, intelligent. He seemed so innocent. So innocuous. And he was dedicated, too. He threw himself into the work, thankful for the opportunity – though that was the point of the program.'

'I don't care about the program. Just tell me what happened.'

'At this point, we were unaware, of course, of the relationship that had formed between Gilberto and Miss Doran. We knew, previously, that Gilberto had been... *involved'* — he took a few seconds choosing that word — 'with another student.'

'Rachel Bartlett.'

He nodded slightly. 'But after the warning he was given then, we thought that he had gotten the message.'

'Apparently not.' Jamie didn't buy it for a second. They just looked the other way because Delgado made their orchestra one of the best in the country.

Brownmiller met her eyes and his narrowed for an instant. 'Yes. And we were not aware that they were cohabiting either.'

Fowler had already confirmed that to Roper, so it wasn't news to her. Jamie desperately wanted him to talk faster, but every word he said was carefully chosen. Brownmiller was smart, and he was well aware that withholding this information was obstruction – he was just trying his best not to incriminate the college or himself.

'Gilberto's relationship with McElroy continued to blossom. They met often, spent hours practicing. In the college, and outside it. Gilberto invited him to his home, to practice, to learn. To study.'

'Where Doran was.'

'McElroy developed an attachment to her, it seems.'

Jamie felt her jaw tighten.

'He became infatuated, obsessed, even. And then, there was an *incident.'*

'An incident?'

'McElroy confronted Doran, not on college grounds – but things became heated. McElroy attempted to assault her—'

'Sexually?' She thought back to the semen in Mimi's bed.

He shook his head. 'I don't know. She believed so. She screamed. And McElroy fled.'

Jamie processed it.

'When Gilberto found out, he was enraged. He was always a passionate man. So he went to McElory, confronted him about it.

Things escalated. Delgado said that McElory claimed it was innocent, but he didn't believe him. They exchanged harsh words, McElroy said that Miss Doran had led him on. Gilberto and he fought.'

'Physically?'

'Yes.'

'When was this?' Jamie swallowed. She needed to know everything about this McElroy kid. Who he was, what he'd done. She was already going through the motions in her head of how to track him down and get his case file unsealed.

Brownmiller swallowed and smacked his lips. 'Late September.'

'Just before the term started?'

'Yes. Delgado sustained some injuries – but the confrontation ended with him terminating McElroy's internship. He ended it a week early, and threatened him.'

'Physically? If he ever came near Alyssa again?'

'Professionally. That he would never work in music.'

'How did McElroy take it?'

Brownmiller shook his head. 'I don't know – we never heard from him again. He disappeared. He was very involved with the college, with Delgado, with the idea of working with him, under him. Of doing something real with his life.' He sounded almost wistful about it.

Jamie let it roll over in her head. 'Did Delgado come forward about all this?'

'There were rumours that he and Miss Doran were in a relationship. She had bruises on her wrists, her throat, from the assault.' He cleared his own throat, loosened his over-tight collar slightly with his finger. 'Delgado had a black eye, a cut cheek – we brought him in the moment we saw it. We couldn't let him teach like that.'

'So you suspended him while you investigated?' This was starting to add up.

'Yes, we did. We launched a formal, *internal* investigation into the whole incident.'

'Why wasn't it reported to the police? Why didn't Alyssa come forward?'

Brownmiller quietened again, looking nervous.

'You buried it, didn't you.' It was a statement more than a question.

'Miss Doran had a bright future ahead of her here. And Gilberto Delgado was an asset to the school. If we had reported it, then it would have blown up, become a media frenzy. We couldn't afford that sort of attention. A respected teacher sleeping with a student?' He scoffed a little. 'And if Miss Bartlett came forward, if others did…'

'There were others?'

'There would have been pressure to have him removed. It was something we couldn't let happen.'

'So you forced Alyssa to keep quiet about it?'

'Forced is a strong word. We merely suggested that the unwanted attention may prevent her from pursuing her career in its fullest capacity.'

Jamie's blood ran cold. 'So you threatened her.'

Brownmiller stayed quiet.

'What happened then?'

'Everything went back to normal.' Brownmiller stated it as though he expected that to have been the end of the whole thing. 'Miss Doran returned to her student accommodation, Gilberto remained on leave until his face no longer showed signs of the exchange, and then…'

'Everything went back to normal.' Jamie spat the words. 'Except it didn't, did it? Because Chessie Fowler, Alyssa's room mate said that she was scared for her bloody life.'

'We weren't aware of any ongoing—'

'Bullshit. You knew, but you were too afraid to lose your star violinist, and too afraid to lose the piece of shit sleeping with her. So you looked the other way while she went to sleep terrified every night of the monster you invited in the front door.'

Brownmiller's mask had resumed itself now. He was back to the waxwork.

Jamie pressed him. 'Delgado ripped his one shot from him, and then he sought revenge. He came after Alyssa, didn't he?'

Brownmiller looked at her but said nothing.

'McElroy was coming after Alyssa, and she knew it. That's why she fled. Why she left school, disappeared.'

He just stared up at her.

Jamie shook her head. 'And you let it happen.'

'Is there anything else I can do for you, detective?' Brownmiller asked politely.

'No,' she said, shaking her head. 'This guy was dangerous, and you knew it. You could have stopped this. Before it ever started.' Jamie turned to leave, seething, her shoulders rising and falling, nails digging into her palms.

'We can all only do what we believe is right in the moment,' he said to her back.

Jamie paused for a second on the threshold, thought about saying something else, decided against it, and then the door snapped shut behind her.

27

Aaron McElroy was twenty-three years old.

He was five feet and eleven inches tall, of average build. He had brown hair, brown eyes, and was neither handsome nor unattractive.

There was nothing remarkable about him.

Except that he felt nothing when he took a life.

Nothing except the subtle thrill of watching the light go out from behind their eyes.

Jamie stared at his picture on her screen. The photograph was from a year and a half ago, an update to his file as the previous one had been taken when he was just thirteen. The age he was when he stabbed his father to death.

He stared at the camera with indifference at twenty-two. The age he had been when the courts had decided he was *rehabilitated.* The case had been sealed as he was a juvenile at the time. His sentence had been twenty years, cut down to just eight.

When he was released from prison his mother was nowhere to be found. She had fled. No one knew where.

The file contained no current address, no current phone number. The next of kin was listed as an auntie who lived in Scotland. McElroy was from Yorkshire.

He didn't have anyone except his case worker.

Before applying to the college for the mentorship position he had been living at a half-way house, working sporadically as a pot washer in the kitchen of a local Indian restaurant.

The file made no mention of music, no mention of him being talented in the slightest. It just said that he was an exemplary prisoner, and that he showed true remorse for his crimes.

She practically scoffed at that.

Jamie leant back and let out a long breath, picking up her phone. Still nothing from Roper and Hassan. They'd been with Rachel Bartlett's boyfriend for hours now and hadn't returned any of Jamie's calls.

She was beginning to get worried.

When her phone rang, she almost tore it off the hook. She was waiting on a call back from McElroy's case worker, from the pathologist regarding Rachel Bartlett's hands, from Gretchen about Mimi's phone, and from the media liaison about putting out a statement. She had to get out ahead of this now. Neither her or the Met could afford a scandal. And if there was a serial killer on the loose in the city and the press got wind of it before they made an announcement. Well, Jamie didn't want to be on the wrong end of that.

'DS Johansson,' Jamie said, pulling the phone to her ear.

There was a loud sigh from the other end.

'Gretchen?' Jamie asked.

'Paganelli's phone is a no-go. Sim-card was pulled before it left the apartment. Can't get a trace on it. But I did match the number to the one that called Delgado. So we know it was her – or at least that the killer called Delgado from her phone.'

'Shit,' Jamie muttered.

'What do you want me to do now?'

Jamie shook her head to herself, wondering where to go from here.

'Detective Johansson?'

She swallowed. They had McElroy's name now, his face, his history. But where he was, and where he was going to strike next, she couldn't say. But he'd hit the ground running. Three kills, one kidnapping, all in the space of days. This was nothing short of a bloody rampage.

Jamie put the phone down without saying another word and leaned forward, resting her elbows on the desk.

She jammed the heels of her hands into her eye sockets and pressed until they hurt.

It was rare that she felt the urge to cry. Sometimes it came on in a surge after a phone call with her mother. But rarely did it come for her over work. And even rarer at work.

And yet that familiar, sickening grip had come once again and taken hold of her throat. She dragged in a few, ragged breaths, and wondered how it had gotten so bad so fast. How someone with such rage could stew on it for six months, and then suddenly snap. How they could wait for so long, and then let it all out now, in one horrific, unstoppable torrent. His floodgates had broken, and now he was unhinged.

Jamie stopped massaging her eyeballs and sat up suddenly. Except he wasn't.

He had *chanced* across Alyssa in that tunnel – he hadn't planned to kill her. Not there at least. The hastiness of the attack. It didn't fit his MO. Which was planning. Careful execution. The way he displayed the hands and arranged for them to be found. The way he planned Mimi's abduction and lured Delgado to her apartment. They were all expertly planned and carried out. But Alyssa? That was just a crime of passion. When something inside him snapped.

Jamie shook her head more violently this time. How could she have been so blind? Alyssa wasn't the *first*. She was just the sloppiest. The one that put him on the map.

He had a thirst for it – of course he did. It's why he couldn't control himself. But McElroy wasn't stupid. He knew who would come forward… Who would link him to the crime.

Delgado.

So he killed him.

Part-revenge, part self-preservation. Hell, he probably stood over him as he was breathing his last and told him that he'd killed Alyssa. That he'd butchered her.

And then he told him he was going to do the same to Mimi, sitting there, unconscious at her kitchen table… And closed the door on him.

Jamie shuddered.

He'd been watching Delgado, she bet. Stalking him. Waiting for the right time. That's how he knew Mimi would bring him there…

And Mimi? She wasn't Alyssa, but she was good. Almost as good.

She would do.

Jamie swallowed, watching as all of the pieces snapped together in her head.

Jamie kept her eyes closed, moving outwards from the eye of this storm. Rachel Bartlett – how did she figure into it? Revenge? If this was revenge for the way Delgado treated him, he could kill her, but what good would that do his vendetta if Delgado was already dead? No, Bartlett's room mate said she hadn't come home for a few days. He could have taken her before he killed Delgado. Told him about both Alyssa and Rachel. I have both of them… And now Mimi. But how would he know about Bartlett in the first place?

Her phone rang. It was Roper. 'What have you got?' she asked, her eyes flashing open, the phone flying to her ear.

'Rachel Bartlett is alive.'

Jamie tensed her jaw. She was surprised for only an instant. 'At her boyfriend's?'

'Yeah – took us hours to find them. They were out together – at first we thought they'd both been taken. But Bartlett is alive and well.'

Jamie breathed a sigh of relief. 'That's something.'

'But then who's hands were in the theatre?'

Jamie drew a slow breath. 'I don't know, Roper.'

'Jesus. Where do you want us to go now?'

'I'll meet you at the coroner's office. I have a hunch that I'm hoping isn't about to pan out.'

'Okay, we'll see you there.'

Jamie hung up the phone and dialled Gretchen back. 'Gretchen,' she said as soon as it connected. 'I do have something for you.'

'Sounds exhilarating.'

'I want you to compile all of the missing persons reports filed in the last six months for women under the age of… thirty…' she said, trying to build a profile in her mind.

'That's not exactly my area of—'

'Once you have their names, I want you to look them up online, separate all the ones who are musicians.'

'Musicians?'

'Classical. Prominent ones.'

'You think our killer has a type?'

'I do.' She drew a breath. 'I'm heading to meet Roper and Hassan, but I want this list as quickly as you can. Names, addresses, when they went missing. And especially what they'd accomplished musically. Put it in a timeline. And earmark any flautists you find – caucasian, pale skinned.'

Gretchen sighed. 'Okay. Sure. Guess I'll cancel my dinner plans, then.'

'Depends how fast you work.'

She laughed sardonically. 'You're funny, Detective Johansson, anyone ever told you that?'

'No,' Jamie said. 'They haven't.'

Jamie pulled up outside the coroner's office and whirled into reception.

Roper and Hassan were waiting by the door that led down to the examination rooms.

Roper pushed it open and Jamie fell into step with them.

'Which room?' she asked.

'Five,' Roper said, reading the seriousness on her face. 'You going to tell me what your hunch is?'

'I don't think you'd like it if I did.'

'Surprise me.'

Jamie stopped at five, planted her hand on the wood. 'I don't think Alyssa Doran was his first kill.'

Hassan's mouth fell open. 'You're shitting me?'

Jamie shook her head, keeping her eyes fixed on Roper, who looked stony. 'That's a big hunch, Jamie,' he said quietly. 'You know what you're suggesting?'

'That a serial killer has been operating with impunity in the city for god-knows how long and we've had no idea?'

'This fucking city,' Roper said, shaking his head. 'First Day, now this—'

'Let's just see what the coroner has to say first, alright?' Jamie said, cutting in. The last thing she wanted to be reminded of right now was Elliot Day.

She pushed the door open and an older guy with wispy grey hair and a long nose that seemed to occupy a lot of space on his face looked up from the tablet he was holding.

He was bathed in a bright light and on the metal table before him lay a pair of severed hands, still in the shape they'd been arranged in at the theatre.

Jamie glanced down at them and then locked onto the coroner, trying not to grimace.

'Detectives, I presume,' he said tiredly. 'I told you that I would send my report over when it was done. And standing here and badgering me is not going to make it go any faster.'

'I'd just like to ask some questions,' Jamie asked. 'Preliminary enquiries to speed things along.'

He let out a long breath and lowered the tablet. 'I suppose I don't have much of a choice, do I?' He looked at his watch emphatically.

Jamie knew it to be after three from the clock on the wall behind him. 'Not if you want to help us catch a killer.'

He grinned at her falsely. 'I'm at your service.'

Jamie shrugged off the passive aggression and cleared her throat, trying to dislodge the taste of bleach. 'When do you think she was killed?'

He looked down at the severed hands. 'That's difficult to say.'

'Because they've been embalmed?'

He looked at her, eyes twitching. 'Yes. How did you know?'

'Call it a hunch.'

Roper huffed behind her. A little laugh of semi-surprise.

'Yes, the victim was embalmed using a mixture of formaldehyde, glutaraldehyde, and methanol. Standard embalming fluid used in every funeral home in the developed world. So if you were hoping to narrow it down from—'

'I wasn't.' Jamie cut him off. 'How long can someone keep a body preserved like this?'

'In the right conditions?'

'Sure.'

'Weeks, if they have access to a chilled room and are able to regulate and adapt the fluid. But are we talking about the entire body, or just the hands?'

Roper interjected. 'Does it make a difference?'

'Oh yes,' the pathologist said. 'Preserving a whole body requires arterial injection. Preserving a pair of hands would be as easy as… putting them in a jar of dilute solution and placing them in a cold fridge.'

'Great,' Roper grunted. 'Lots of space in a fridge for jars.'

Jamie ignored him. 'Is there any way to tell when they were severed?'

'Not really. There's slight decomposition here, around the cuts, but that is natural for this sort of thing.'

Roper interjected again. 'There's a natural for this sort of thing?'

'I just meant that exposed tissue like this will degrade first. But that's likely due to them being presented as they were, rather than occurring during the preservation.'

Jamie nodded. 'Can you tell us anything else?'

'The hands appear to have been worked on – the nails trimmed and shaped. The skin is smooth and moist – but this can be achieved with embalming fluid. It gives them a lifelike appearance. Though I suspect they were cleaned and then treated afterwards in order to remove the smell.' He sniffed the air. 'Mostly.'

Jamie tried not to stare at them. They were still locked in shape, still holding that invisible flute. 'What about the arrangement? They were meant to look as though they were holding an instrument.'

'The killer removed them from the fluid, allowed them to dry, and for rigor mortis to set in. Then he made the incisions for the fishing line. By the looks of it with a stitching needle. Very neatly done. He has steady hands. And this doesn't look like a first attempt.'

Jamie's heart sank a little. 'Thank you, doctor,' she said, turning to look at Roper.

He had his arms folded. He looked grave.

Hassan looked anxious. This was a hell of a ride for his first time out of the gate.

'Come on,' Jamie said, nodding towards the door. 'We'd better get going.'

'Where?' Roper asked.

She ran her hands through her hair and headed for the door, dying to be out of the bleach stench. 'I don't know yet. But I know the killer isn't here. And that crosses off at least one building in the city.'

'It's a start, I suppose,' Roper replied, falling into step, albeit with a limp.

She glanced over at him, smiling just a little. It was moments like this that it felt like they were their old selves again.

Fleeting as they were.

28

McElroy's flat was a tiny studio located nearly ten kilometres from the college.

He had to take a bus, a tube, and then walk the last two just to get there every day.

But he'd been insistent on living on his own, his case worker had told Jamie.

The application for the mentorship scheme had come with a housing subsidy, and he'd just been able to afford the rent with what little money he had saved up working at the Indian restaurant.

His case worker, a friendly sounding woman by the name of Tara, had said she couldn't believe he'd fallen foul of the police again. That Aaron was one of the nicest, smartest young men she'd met. And she'd had no doubt that he was going to put his life back together. She said that what had happened all those years ago was a misunderstanding, that he had been protecting his mother. That he loved her.

Jamie didn't think luring his father into the woods at the bottom of their garden and stabbing him seven times with a kitchen knife sounded much like defence of anything.

And if she was just being protected, then why flee from your son before he gets out of prison?

Aaron McElroy was a manipulator and a psychopath by the sounds of it. He'd got his case-worker believing his story. Had Brownmiller choking it down to. Even Delgado thought highly of him. Until he tried to attack Alyssa, at least. No, McElroy was good at this. He knew how to get into people's heads.

Just like Elliot.

Jamie screwed her eyes closed and dislodged that thought. She couldn't think about him right now.

McElroy's mother had run for her life, though. Like Alyssa.

What had driven him then, Jamie didn't know. What had his father done? Had he done anything?

What drove him now? She still couldn't say. But she hoped that some answers would lay beyond this door.

Roper hung back at the stairwell while Jamie and Hassan approached, pistols in hand.

Hassan was leading, back in the groove like he'd never left. They had ballistic vests, but nothing else. Jamie didn't want to risk a full armed response. That had a strange way of tipping off the media, and she wanted to at least see if he was here or had been recently before they barrelled into that buzzsaw. There was nothing more damning than a fleet of journalists asking about leads, suspects, victims, and all you could tell them was, *we don't know, sorry.*

Jamie exhaled, shaking it off, and watched as Hassan crossed the front of the door and paused.

She lifted the key they'd gotten from the landlord, whose number Tara had given them, and worked it into the rusted lock.

The whole building looked like it was on the verge of falling down. The hallway carpet was ratty, and Jamie was glad she was wearing skinny jeans. Made it harder for the fleas to jump up them.

Hassan nodded to her, and she turned the key.

The latch clicked and he pushed through the door, covering the room with his pistol in an instant.

Jamie came in after him, stepping straight into the bathroom, finding exactly the same as Hassan.

Nothing.

She clicked her Glock back into its holster and sighed, loosening her vest.

The studio was grubby, with water marks running down the peeling walls and creaking boards underfoot, but otherwise, it was stark, and kept in good order.

It didn't look like McElroy had been there in weeks. Maybe longer. And there was certainly no sign of a fridge big enough to store body-parts in.

'Clear,' Hassan called over his shoulder.

Roper's thu-thunking limp echoed dully in Jamie's ears as she scanned the room.

'What a shit-hole,' he said, coming in behind them.

'Ain't it just,' Hassan added.

Jamie stared around. A single bed against the wall next to the window, a tiny desk with an old dining chair and a single draw. A kitchenette that was more like a counter-top balancing on one leg. It was shoved into what was more like an alcove than anything else. A square of prep space no wider than two feet, with a microwave on it, a tiny plug-in kettle next to it. A small sink that looked like it was made out of tinfoil sat next to them, and above a single, tired cabinet clung to the wall.

Jamie's eyes drifted over it, cataloguing everything.

She could see under the bed, the desk – there were no personal effects, no clothing.

A clothing rail stood empty next to the door. There was no wardrobe.

And the bathroom – Jamie walked in – was a cupboard.

A shower cubicle an average human would struggle to turn in, and a toilet you could barely sit on. There was no basin. She guessed tenants had to wash their hands in the kitchen sink.

And yet – Jamie ran her finger along the top of the toilet cistern. Clean. No dust. The old lino on the floor, too, looked clean. Old, but clean.

She went into the kitchen, found it the same. The counter chipped, the sink discoloured by time, but everything clean.

Jamie approached the bed last, and pulled back the covers. Clean again. She sighed.

'There's nothing here,' Roper said astutely, opening and closing the empty desk drawer. 'Not a fucking thing.'

'But do you notice how clean it all is?' Jamie asked absently, tweaked by it.

'Classic psychopathic tendency,' Roper mused. 'What was Day's apartment like?'

Jamie turned, stared at him with narrow eyes. It was the second time he'd brought Elliot up in nearly as many hours.

'Clean too, I bet?' Roper asked, his expression unreadable.

'Yeah…' Jamie said slowly. 'I suppose.'

Roper walked in circles. 'I'm not surprised. The way the hands were arranged – the guy is fastidious.'

'Big word for you,' Jamie said bitterly.

Roper glared at her. 'All I'm saying is that this guy wouldn't be stupid enough to shit where he eats. No,' he said with a sigh, wobbling the clothes rail. 'He's got himself a nice serial killer dungeon somewhere. Somewhere where it's quiet, where he can work in peace.'

'Somewhere with electricity,' Jamie added, wanting desperately to navigate away from the rapids her and Roper seemed to be steering down. It felt like scorn coming off him. In waves.

She looked at his bad leg – it was fine physically, but the nerve damage from his back meant he couldn't lift it normally. That it hurt with every step – and they'd climbed a lot of them getting up here.

Did he blame her for that?

Did he have a right to?

He nodded at her input. 'Yeah, he'll be working under lights.'

Hassan jumped in. 'And he needs to run a fridge.'

Jamie was trying to imagine it. 'Somewhere tucked away – somewhere he can easily dispose of the bodies.'

'What,' Roper said with a laugh, 'you don't think he's holding onto them? As a memento?'

'No,' Jamie replied. 'I don't. I don't think he likes the killing. It's about the hands for him. It's always been about the hands. The music – he's fascinated by them.'

'Maybe.' Roper stuck his bottom lip out, rolling his head back and forth.

'The bodies are… incidental.' Jamie was musing. 'He doesn't like people. But he loves the music they make. For him, the hands are what's special, what create the music. The people he could do without.'

'So why kill them? That stops them from creating it, surely?'

'He wanted to be a conductor, a maestro. If he's a psychopath, then he craves control. And what offers that more than posing a body part? He's creating his own music. Each kill and posing is a symphony for him. A carefully executed series of acts, ending with the big reveal. His crescendo.'

Roper wanted to argue for argument's sake but couldn't find anything wrong with her reasoning. 'So we know who he is, we know what he's doing. What's next, *boss?'* He eyed her with a bubbling anger.

She couldn't wait to be away from him, and at the same time, wanted him to stay. For a long time. She wasn't sure if she was ready to lose him. As a partner, or as a friend.

Jamie broke their awkward stare and checked her watch. 'It's almost six. Hassan, you probably want to get home to your kids.'

He held his hand up flat and shook it in the air. 'Eh.'

Jamie had to give it to him, he knew how to lighten a mood.

'And you, Roper,' she met his eye again, realising she knew nothing about his life anymore. What he did with his time, who he did it with.

'Yeah,' he answered, putting his hands in his pocket. 'I've probably got stuff to do.'

'Go,' Jamie said, motioning them both towards the door. 'I'll lock up, put in a request for SOCOs to come and sweep the place.'

Roper was out the door first, without a word.

Smith was right. He was getting out. And he couldn't wait to be gone.

'You coming?' Hassan asked, pausing at the door.

'In a minute,' Jamie said, turning and sitting down on the bed.

The springs squeaked underneath her.

'You want me to stick around?'

She shook her head. 'No, it's fine. I just need to think.'

He watched her for a moment. 'You should go home. Get some rest.'

She smiled at him, hiding the same resurgent fear of impending tears. It took everything she had not to scream as loud as her lungs would allow. 'I will.'

Except that was the last thing she wanted to do. To go home to find Elliot waiting there for her. Or worse, to go home to an empty apartment. To be alone with it all – with what she'd done, what she knew.

She had nothing to go home for. Nothing to go home to. Nothing except the job. And the floor under her boots. The floor a serial killer had walked a thousand times.

No, she wouldn't go home. Couldn't.

Not yet. Not with him out there. Not with so much of the city left to search, and lives hanging in the balance.

If he'd taken Mimi, and he had a process, then maybe there was still time. Maybe she was tied up somewhere while he found the right place to mount her.

Jamie swallowed, saw that Hassan was still watching her. 'Go, honestly,' she said, feeling her voice begin to crack. 'I'm fine.'

He lingered, balled his fist, and knocked it on the doorframe twice. 'Okay, Jamie,' he said. 'Call me if you need anything.'

'I will,' she said, willing him to leave.

She watched as he faded from the frame and listened to his steps in the corridor.

When he was gone, she leaned forward, let her body begin to shudder, and watched as a silent tear made a single dark blot between her heels.

She made a fist and squeezed hard. And then punched herself in the thigh.

And then again.

The pain shot through her knee and down into her ankle.

She hit it again, right in the same spot, felt the pain surge in her leg. Felt anger come with it. Let it drown the fear. The tears.

She let it fill her, and then she got up, roughly wiped her cheeks with her sleeve, and headed for the door.

It was going to be a long night.

And she had lots of ground to cover.

29

JAMIE WAS SITTING in a twenty-four-hour Starbucks, stirring her second large Americano.

The wooden stick turned slowly in the black liquid, her eyes cutting through the steam to her phone screen on the far side.

It was nearly seven now, and she'd been driving for an hour.

She didn't know where, but traffic oozed through the city at this time, and you could move endlessly without getting anywhere.

Going home wasn't something she was interested in. Not until she couldn't stand anymore at least.

Sleep would come fitfully, or not at all. And lying there thinking about its absence would only make things worse.

Jamie sucked in a long breath, felt her eyes ache with waking, and then blinked a few times, willing her coffee to cool enough to drink.

She'd spend the last thirty minutes going through listings for old theatres and halls that had been abandoned in the city on her phone. But what was readily available on Google wasn't exactly comprehensive and she didn't think she could face going back to HQ just to trawl through pages and pages of public records.

But then again, she didn't have to.

Her phone vibrated in her grip and she pulled it to her ear. 'Gretchen,' she said quickly. 'What have you got?'

She sighed emphatically. 'Okay, so three women match your criteria. All disappeared in the last six months – all prominent musicians in the city working with classical outfits. Amelie Dovak, Hungarian, twenty-six, cellist. First chair with the London Symphony Orchestra, disappeared in late December. She was walking home after a performance, but never got there. Her roommates reported her missing the next morning when they couldn't get hold of her.

'Daisy Hardwick, British, twenty-three, pianist. Played with the London Philharmonic Orchestra. She was reported missing in February by her sister. She missed a lunch date and when she went to her apartment to check on her, there was no trace.

'And then there's Kathryn Orlov, Russian-British, twenty-seven years old. Flautist. First chair with the National Orchestra.'

Jamie stopped stirring. 'Do we have a description? A photograph?'

'Yup,' Fischer said plainly. 'Pale skinned, black hair, blue eyes.'

Jamie closed her eyes. 'Jesus. I'd bet that's her.'

Fischer was silent on the other end.

'Can you, uh, print their files, any information we have, and put it on my desk for the morning?'

She sighed again. 'Sure.'

'And Fischer?'

'Yeah?' she asked, not even trying to keep the tiredness out of her voice.

Jamie checked her watch and ignored the fact that it was late. 'Can you check out the theatre where we found her? All previous performances by prominent orchestras.'

A second of silence. 'Sure.'

'Specifically performances of concertos. *Flute* concertos.'

'Right.' She either didn't care why she was being asked, or was just too tired to bother.

'And then can you compile a list of other prominent theatres or halls that are currently being renovated?'

'How would I do that?'

Jamie shook her head. 'I don't know – just see what you can dig up. Look for articles, which buildings have been sold, anything like that.'

She made a sort of grunting sound that probably came instead of a facetious answer. *I'll just wave my magic wand, shall I? Check my crystal ball?*

'Thanks, Gretchen, this is a big help.'

'What am I looking for, specifically? That would *actually* help.'

'He's choosing these women based on their skill, on how good they are. I don't think he'd just display them anywhere. Not with this much care and attention to detail. He's choosing the venues as carefully as he is the victims.' Jamie had done nothing but think about him for the last two hours. Had done nothing but picture those hands, suspended in the floodlight. Had done nothing but picture him bringing them there. Taking her. Cutting her. Preserving her. Preparing her. Shaping her. Displaying her there.

He wanted them seen in all their glory. Perfect.

He wouldn't just put them anywhere, it would have to be *perfect.* And he would have to ensure they were found quickly. He wouldn't risk decomp, any wasted time or effort.

Did he make the call himself? Report rats or vermin?

Hell, he probably had.

She'd need a log of that call. Would need to follow up on that.

There was method in his madness. In his evil. And Jamie felt like she was getting closer to it. Getting deeper into his mind. Sinking deeper into it. Into what was driving him.

The toll it was taking on her was evidence of that.

She watched her own hand, frozen above the coffee cup, clutching at the stirrer.

'That all?' Fischer asked.

'Drop an email to the pest-control company that made the discovery this morning. See if we can't find out who made the call.'

Gretchen sighed loudly in her ear. 'Anything else?' she asked curtly.

Jamie swallowed. 'Yeah, thank you.'

Fischer put the phone down without another word and Jamie picked up her coffee and took a sip.

Cold.

She grimaced and put it down, dropping her phone on the counter as she did.

The sky had grown dark now, the city lights a sea of fire behind the polished window she was sitting in.

Her focus drew closer and her own reflection swam from the darkness, tired and thin.

When had she last eaten?

She couldn't tell, but her stomach was full of bile and bitterness. Full of evil and sadness.

She couldn't eat.

She could only work.

Bradbury Hall. Stanley Hall. Royal Wellington Hall.

All three were known music venues.

All three had hosted performances by orchestras from around the world.

All three were now disused.

All three were currently undergoing renovation work.

Jamie sat in her car, looking at the photograph of Bradbury Hall in its hay-day on her laptop, the stonework that perfect colour of sand, the walls clean, the doors polished. Posters hanging from the Greek-style porch way. Excited people milling around outside it, waiting for the doors.

She let her eyes drift upwards from the screen at the semi-derelict building across the road.

Its exterior was a criss-cross of scaffolding and red netting, its doors boarded over.

A banner hung from the top saying 'A new performance venue coming this Autumn'.

Looking at the state of the place, she didn't believe it.

She spent a long time over her coffee, going through it again and again. Trying to get into McElroy's head. His method.

Everything had to be perfect.

He was meticulous. She knew that from his presentation and from his apartment.

The presentation had to be right, but then, there was only a small window for his displays to be found before the hands were past their best. Before the whole effort would be *wasted.* No, it had to be fresh.

McElroy wasn't going to leave it to chance.

He had to be going in at night, knowing the body would be discovered by *someone* the following morning.

Jamie still hadn't heard back from Gretchen on who called the pest-control company. But Jamie had a strong hunch it was him. And she wondered whether another call would be placed in any day now. A different company, probably – maybe someone reporting the smell of gas. A burst pipe. Whatever it took to get someone out there…

Jamie sighed. She could conjecture over it all night but it would get her exactly nowhere. All she could do was wonder.

She checked her watch – a little after nine p.m.

She didn't know how she felt about that.

Could she really just drive around aimlessly, checking on the venues until sleep threatened to run her off the road?

No, she had to think. Had to come up with something better than a scattergun approach.

Up until now they had been working under the assumption that McElroy was operating on raw emotion. That his kills had been a violent rampage. A flood of anger uncorked by chancing across Alyssa.

But that was wrong.

Jamie knew now that he was as cool and calculating as they came.

He had always had the violence in him, and the college had defined it. They had given him that thing he had been missing, shown him the beauty in violence that he had been searching for.

Alyssa had just been unfortunate. The one that got away.

Jamie had no doubt that had she not run for her life she would have been his first victim.

His first kill here in the city.

But if McElroy and Delgado were close, and Alyssa was there, it wasn't a far stretch to think that they knew each other. That she had shared intimate details she didn't realise would seal her fate. A simple, *so where are you from?* provides enough information for a killer to hunt someone down back to their childhood home.

If Alyssa had fled there, he could have followed. Her hiding in the city like this suggested he *would* have. Or at least Alyssa thought so.

But she couldn't give up the music. Couldn't stop playing.

And McElory probably heard that mournful cry of a violin carried on the city air and was drawn to it, moth to a flame.

That older couple had said it – the music ended. Then the scream.

He had gone to her, been in awe. Enamoured. Had waited. Listened. Languished in her music. And then given in.

As soon as she'd struck that last note he'd rushed her and shoved a knife into her gut.

Twisted.

Wrenched.

And then in a moment of blind passion, hacked her hands clean from her wrists.

He noticed just after that he'd mauled her.

That he'd ruined it. That he'd ruined her.

And recognised that.

That's why he placed her in that pose.

That praying, sorrowful pose.

He liked her.

Felt something for her.

Perhaps it was not hate that drove him to murder. No, Jamie didn't think it was.

It was love – the love of what they could do.

Alyssa was his first. He loved her music. What she could create.

Did he feel guilt for it?

No. She didn't think so.

Remorse?

She made a face to herself.

No that wasn't quite right either.

A certain sadness, perhaps.

But he was only sorry that he'd done it *like that,* not that he'd done it.

He was overcome by his urges, a surprise to him, Jamie thought.

He was a planner. His attention to detail was amazing.

But Alyssa was an anomaly.

But how would he do this now, then? How would he go on from here?

Jamie closed her eyes.

Why choose just then to present Kathryn Orlov?

What was he waiting for before? What was his intent?

He had taken three women over the course of five months. Quietly, too. No blood. No public mutilation. No bodies.

And now he was killing frenziedly, leaving victims in his wake, working to display his previous kills at the same time?

Was he just unhinged suddenly, or did he have a plan that Jamie just couldn't see?

She tapped her knuckles on her steering wheel.

What was the end-goal here?

She worked backwards.

What did he want from life? To be a conductor. To be in control? No. It wasn't just about that. He could exercise control in a million other ways.

What did she know about psychopaths? They were narcissists. Vain. He wanted then, maybe, not just to control, but also to be seen controlling.

A conductor stands at the centre of it all.

A hundred and two sets of eyes on him.

Following his every movement.

He wanted to be seen controlling, as well as to control.

The performer craves an audience.

She opened her eyes and drew in a slow breath.

This was getting out of hand. Five deaths. One kidnap.

Jamie ground her teeth.

Six deaths.

She couldn't bank on Mimi being alive still.

The girl was as good as dead, her hands in a fridge somewhere.

That made Jamie feel a little sick. Then a little cold.

He was ramping up here.

And the press would come sniffing. Hell, they probably already were.

With a known serial killer on the loose they would have to issue a statement. Jamie had already written it in her head.

They knew his type, too, knew that he was active. *Very* active. They would have to inform his victim-type, warn them not to travel alone. To be aware.

Jesus, is that what he wanted? For this to be dragged into the spotlight right now? A gristly, violent murder – Alyssa Doran – poorly executed but serving a purpose nonetheless. Had this just moved up his timetable? Thrust him into the spotlight a moment too early?

Was this his chance? One he intended not to squander?

He wouldn't go quiet now.

Not while the spotlight was falling on him.

Finally on him.

Revealing his work in all its morbid, macabre glory.

Jamie was trapped then, in the car, stifled.

Three girls. Three venues. Amelie Dovak, cello. Daisy Hardwick, piano. Kathryn Orlov, flute.

Orlov had been presented at the Old Cambridge Theatre – a former concert venue, among other things. Fischer had dug up an old listing for a performance of Mozart's Flute Concerto No. 1 and then cross-referenced it against Kathryn Orlov's previous performances. Her orchestra had been touring it when she was abducted.

In fact, she was abducted the night she performed it at the Barbican.

The attention to detail was excruciating.

McElroy chose the player, chose the venue. Arranged her to be playing that piece of music forever. For it to be immortalised in her hands.

And Jamie had the sickening feeling he was doing the same here.

Fischer had finished for the night and Jamie couldn't well ask her to work until midnight based on a vague hunch.

But she intended to.

All she needed was a hint that he was going to be, or had been, here.

Maybe she would discover another body.

She hoped not.

Jamie sighed, checked her pistol was tight in its holster, and then kicked the door of her car open, stepping into the cool night air.

It was one of those evenings where there was no wind, the sounds of the city echoing through the stillness.

The street she was on was empty and quiet. Shops closed up on one side, the scaffolded behemoth on the other, sucking up most of the space between the two corners.

She stood on the tarmac, staring up at it.

It waited silently to be reborn.

Jamie sighed, wondering what the hell she was doing, her hands shaking from the caffeine overload.

She pulled up her phone, saw that Cake had text her again asking if everything was okay. She'd not spoken to him since that morning. Since Elliot. Since the rifle and Amherst and the crime scene and the college and McElroy's apartment and…

Jamie shook her head, dizzy from it all.

Jesus, had that all been one day?

She was running on fumes, fuelled by the fear of going to sleep.

Jamie glanced left and right. There was no one on the road and no clear means of access into the building itself.

She began to take a slow circle around, heading for a narrow walkway that led down the side of the building, remembering the other theatre.

A steel fence with a padlocked gate spanned the small gap.

There was no sign of forced entry.

But the fence was useless. No more than a visual dissuasion.

It had a support strut running across the mid-point, and a square frame around the lock itself.

Jamie felt the cool, flaking metal under her fingers as she levered herself upwards, her boot firmly planted on the steel.

She swung over and landed like a cat, ignoring the slight jolt in her knees.

A horn blared somewhere in the distance, a near miss in night-time traffic, and Jamie turned back, seeing the world through bars.

She shuddered a little and clenched her hands, exhaling the breath she was keeping in her chest.

Gravel crunched under her heels as she walked down the pathway, keen just to cross this place off her list for peace of mind if nothing else. Exhausting all avenues of investigation seemed to be a reasonable reason to fall into bed.

Jamie rounded a dog-leg in the building and felt the dim light from the streetlamp behind her fade.

She pressed on into the darkness, patting her jacket pocket, searching for the multitool she always used to carry. It had a torch on it.

She didn't have it.

Hell, she didn't even know where it was.

Was it in her jacket when she got Simon Paxton's blood all over it? Had it gone in the bin?

No.

Had she boxed it up during the move?

She couldn't remember.

What was wrong with her? She used to be so organised. So focused. So sure.

On the left, the wall rose up, impenetrable and slick.

On the right, the fence persisted. It had become barbed-wire topped and brambles swung in long, fierce loops between the bars. Beyond them the wall of the next building was a black veil.

Jamie kept moving, unsure where the path would lead, if it led anywhere.

As she approached the back of the building, she saw that ahead there was another gate. Similar to the one at the front.

Black bars. A padlock. A chain.

She got closer, seeing a door leading into the hall itself. It was a fire escape. She could see the little blue sign on the outside of the door, barely visible in the darkness.

The tension began to drain from her shoulders.

And then she slowed, something catching her eye in the darkness.

The doors, two of them – double fire doors – normal double fire doors. No handles on the outside, just slabs of wood.

Except they were ajar.

One was overlapping the other slightly. Barely an inch, if that.

She drew closer, still unsure if it was a trick of the light or not.

At the threshold she paused, looked down, saw that the loose gravel under her feet had been swept back.

She knelt, ran her fingers over the cool painted surface of the door, felt a hole the size of a five-pence piece under her touch.

She stuck her finger in it. The edges were smooth, the hole perfectly round.

Jamie squinted, reaching down to the floor, and pinched some wood-shavings between her fingers.

She rolled them there, feeling the grain, smelling the fresh cut wood.

A drill.

Someone had drilled through this door – right through the bolt by the looks of it.

Jamie stood up and looked at the gate. An access lane ran across the back of the hall.

It would give more cover to someone coming up on foot.

Jamie glanced at the door again, then at the gate, then at her hip. She lifted the hem of her jacket to double-check her pistol was there, and then exhaled, trying to stay quiet.

Someone. She kept thinking that. But it wasn't *someone.* It was McElroy. It had to be.

Her hunch was right. He was moving up his timetable. One last night, one tonight… He was going three nights in a row with his three kills.

Four maybe, with Mimi. He'd wanted Alyssa, but he'd spoiled her. Mimi was almost as talented. Number two to her. Number one since she left.

She was a fitting replacement.

Jamie grimaced, wondering who would be inside. Whose hands he had brought.

There was no sound coming from the door so Jamie risked a step into the shadow of the building, pressed herself against the wall, and pulled her phone from her pocket.

She unlocked it and went to her messages, not wanting to risk a call. She didn't want to alert McElroy. Not with something as stupid as a phone-call.

Her thumb hovered over Roper's name, but she couldn't bring herself to press it.

Beyond the tension between them, could she really drag him into this? Did he deserve that? He'd come, sure. He would never leave her. She knew that, but she didn't know what she'd do with herself if he got hurt again. If he got killed.

She'd already dragged him into the line of fire once and it had nearly cost him his life.

She wouldn't do that twice.

If he wanted out, then he should have it.

Jamie exhaled and thumbed down to Hassan.

He'd already taken a bullet when he was with her. And now he was getting out of Armed Response. Wanted to become a detective. But could she pull him away from his kids? And how long would that take? McElroy could escape. A thousand things could happen.

Hassan had a lot to learn still. And while he was probably the number one person she wanted watching her back, she knew that she wasn't going to call him.

She knew she was going in alone, even if the reasons weren't wholly clear to her.

Jamie pushed her phone back into her jeans, clicked the Glock out of its holster, and ducked inside, pulling the door open just enough to slip through the gap.

And then she was in darkness.

In an unfamiliar building.

With ruthless killer.

And yet she was still moving, still digging deeper into the interior.

Still hunting McElroy.

30

Stay calm, Jamie.

It unnerved her how much her own voice inside her head sounded like her father's.

How close at hand he always seemed.

How she could feel the weight of his body pressing down on her if she thought about it, like when she was a little girl and he would stand behind her, his arms around her shoulder as the rifle waved in her grip.

It was too heavy for her, but he told her she would get stronger.

And she did.

He held her there, not breathing, not pushing, just waiting for her to pull that trigger.

She always hated hunting. Killing felt senseless to her when you could buy meat at the supermarket, but those times with her father had been the best of her childhood.

Hold it softly, don't grip too hard.

Jamie flexed her fingers around her pistol creeping forward in the darkness.

He's more afraid of you than you are of him.

She smirked abjectly at that. Yeah, right.

Don't rush. Don't want to spook him.

No, I don't.

Don't just use your eyes. You have five senses, so does he. What do you see? What do you hear? What do you smell? What do you feel?

Fear.

Crushing, twisting, knotting, punching fear.

I hear nothing. Just deafening silence.

I smell mould. Damp. Rotting wood. The sickly-sweet smell of bleach. No, not bleach… paint thinner? Just a whiff on the air. Faint. Barely detectable.

Jamie closed her eyes.

She couldn't see shit anyway.

Yes, there again. Paint thinner?

She reached out and touched the wall, felt peeling wallpaper. Anaglypta. No paint.

What smells like paint thinner?

She raced back to her childhood again. The stench of cheap vodka.

Had someone been drinking in here?

Jamie's mind whirled in the darkness. Alcohol. Ethanol. Ethanol and methanol. And formaldehyde.

Embalming fluid.

Jamie stopped and looked up, picking out the near-invisible edge of a wall ahead as the corridor turned a corner.

She could smell embalming fluid.

Shit, she wished she had looked up the layout to this building before coming in here.

Jamie glanced over her shoulder. Could she go back?

Her father's shape barred the way.

You think I would?

She gritted her teeth and pressed on, shuffling forward on the old carpet, thankful that it was deadening the sound of her boots.

The corridor wound forward, right, then left, the smell of embalming fluid still lingering in the air.

Jamie couldn't hear anything, couldn't see anything either. She just kept her right elbow brushing the wall.

Ahead, a thin square outline of light swam into view.

Jamie slowed, tried to keep her heart from leaping out of her throat.

She felt her father's arms around her again, guiding her aim as she approached, touched the muzzle of her pistol against the flaking white paint, and nosed the door open an inch at a time.

It didn't squeak, and opened into the empty space behind the stage. A wide, concrete area that was no doubt used for prep, set storage, positioning, and everything else that went on behind the curtain.

Miraculously, it was still hanging.

Thirty feet in front of her, it was draping down from the lighting rigs attached to the ceiling. It was black, heavy cloth, but it was moth-eaten and frayed. Holes speckled it, and through them light shone.

It flooded the wall above Jamie's head with stars.

She stepped cautiously into the splintering shafts, holding her hand up to shield her eyes.

The light coming through was bright. Blindingly so.

A powerful floodlight.

He needed it to work. To see the threads. To get everything *right.*

Breathe, Jamie.

Her father's voice never left her.

Just aim and squeeze.

She looked down at the gun in her hands. It was a deterrent. For protection. She wasn't going to kill McElroy, that's not how this worked.

She was going to take him in, alive.

Get on the floor, right now.

That what you're going to say to him?

Yeah, I am.

She blinked herself clear, the voices getting muddled. Hers. Her fathers.

She needed to focus.

Shit she was tired.

But she had come too far now.

Jamie looked left and right and chose.

McElroy would be centre-stage.

Though she didn't know what she was walking into. Or what she would walk in on.

She hooked to the left and made a wide circle sticking to the back wall, listening for any sounds coming from beyond.

There was nothing. But the curtain was heavy and designed to deaden any noise.

It was doing its job.

Though Jamie was still terrified that he would hear her heart beating against her ribs.

It was the only sound in her head.

Whack. Whack. Whack.

It was about to burst through.

Her fingers rolled on the grip, tightened, and she moved quickly, determined to confront him before she lost her nerve.

Stalling for time would do nothing. She had to take him, and she had to do it now.

The steps came out to meet her, and she stepped up into the brilliance streaming down from the stage.

McElroy had set up a portable floodlight.

It sat on the floor, no larger than a toaster, but the light it gave off was achingly bright.

Jamie squinted, blinded for a moment as her eyes adjusted.

Her toe banged against the step in front of her and she stumbled a little.

The gun dropped six inches and she sank into her knee, banging it on the corner of the top concrete step.

Jamie hissed through her teeth, recovered her balance, and then jumped up them and onto the stage, levelling her pistol at the figure in front of her.

'Stop!' she yelled, willing her eyes to focus. 'Don't move!'

Nothing did. And no sound came from the stage.

Jamie was squinting through her eyelashes now, standing in the glare of the lamp.

The man in front of her, no more than a shadow, looked up.

Jamie could see lines draping in front of him, like spider-webs, catching the light.

'Aaron McElroy,' she called, watching him swim into focus with each second.

Aaron McElroy looked back at her, his face expressionless.

His brown hair was longer than in his photo, naturally curly. His brown eyes tired.

He wasn't unhandsome, his features masculine and symmetrical.

McElroy stood there in a pair of dirty chinos, trainers, and a sweat-shirt, a worn satchel hanging from his shoulder. She shuddered to think what was in it.

Though it wasn't hard to guess.

He narrowed his eyes at her and slowly lifted his latex-gloved hands, not saying a word.

The thin length of fishing wire he was holding swung freely and settled among the others hanging before him.

'Get down on the ground,' Jamie ordered, motioning down with her pistol.

'Who are you?' he asked carefully, not moving a muscle.

Jamie's mind raced. She didn't have cuffs on her, no zip-ties. Nothing. And he didn't look like he was going to oblige. He didn't seem phased in the slightest by the gun pointed at him.

She swallowed, seeing Elliot there for a second, his hands up too, for his own amusement rather than from serious fear.

McElroy blinked back into view, waiting for his answer.

'I'm Detective Sergeant Jamie Johansson,' Jamie announced. 'London Metropolitan Police. Now get on the ground.'

'Were you looking for me?'

'Get on the ground, McElroy.' She jerked the gun.

'How did you find me?'

'You left a trail,' Jamie growled. 'Now get down.'

He took a step sideways, around the lines, lowering his arms. 'No I didn't.'

She raised the gun so it was levelled at his head now. Even in the glare of the lamp, from this range, she could blow the back of his skull out. There was no question of her aim.

But of her nerve to do it?

'Stop. I'm warning you.' She tried to keep her voice even.

'Shoot if you want.' He took another step, forward this time.

'I don't want to shoot,' Jamie admitted. 'I want you to get down on the floor.'

'I'm intrigued,' he said, eyes flashing.

Jamie didn't say another word. She just felt the trigger heavy against her finger.

'What do you think of my work?'

'Your *work?'* Jamie spat through gritted teeth, feeling the anger rising in her.

He nodded, moving another pace. 'Yes, you are the one chasing me, aren't you? The person working this *case?'*

He emphasised the word as though it was funny to him that it wasn't being considered art.

Jamie forced out an *mmm* sound.

'So, what do you think?' He grinned now, his face shadowed by the lamp at his back, all carved and dark. He was right in front of it now.

'I think you're sick,' Jamie muttered. 'And you're not going to get away with it.'

'Getting away with it was never my intention,' he said, barely above a whisper. The acoustics in the room carried his voice across the ten feet between them. 'The music is for the listener, not for the artist.'

God how she wanted to pull this trigger.

She looked at McElory, his forehead hovering between the sights.

Why couldn't she?

Why couldn't she just scrub him from the world?

'You see, detective,' he said, taking one more step. 'It's not about what comes after for me. It's about the act.'

'The act of killing?' Her eyes began to twitch, aching in the light.

He let his grin widen into an axe wound in his face. 'You wouldn't understand.'

'Try me.'

He paused, stood stone still, almost in lunging distance. 'I think I will.'

The world lurched, and he pounced.

Jamie's finger hit the trigger.

The lamp died behind him.

The muzzle flashed.

It lit the room in a violent strobe.

Aaron was there, on her, hands raised, face blasted in the fire, burned into her retinas.

She felt his weight hit her.

Jamie stumbled, thrown backwards.

The pistol came out of her grip and her heels caught on the wooden floor.

They squeaked, rubber on varnish, and she fell backwards, landing on her hip.

Her gun skittered into the darkness and her brain faltered.

Jamie swore and rolled instinctively to the side, got onto her hands and knees and spun around towards what she thought was the middle of the stage, ready to take McElroy on.

Ready to face him in the darkness.

But her readied hands touched nothing but the air.

Jamie held her breath, listening, but there was nothing.

No sound, no feeling of presence there.

She was alone.

Jamie's mind churned, her brain lighting up without any input from her senses. The last few seconds replayed in her head and she remembered the floodlight at the corner of the stage, the cable trailing across, in front of McElroy, how he'd moved over it…

Jamie, still on her hands and knees, crawled forward, sweeping her hands back and forth on the dusty wooden boards until she found it, and then quickly followed it back to the foot-switch McElroy had triggered.

That she'd let him trigger.

She smacked it with the heel of her hand, growling in frustration, and then blinded herself as it came to life.

Jamie threw her hands up to protect her eyes and squinted around, confirming what she already knew.

There was no sign of him

'Shit,' Jamie muttered, trying to blink herself clear.

McElroy was gone. Escaped.

She looked around for her pistol, saw it lying on the ground a few feet away, and reached for it.

Jamie stood awkwardly, her hip throbbing, and went for the steps.

She could see now that the wire for the lamp ran across the stage and under the back curtain. A foot-switch was sitting on the marked floorboards.

She'd let him move right over the top of it.

She clambered down the stairs and loped towards the back door. He'd shoulder-barged her, right in the chest, and she was wheezing.

He wasn't big but he'd put power into the shove.

By the time she reached the back door, he was gone. Which way, she didn't know. It was pitch dark, and he had a head-start.

Jamie sighed and fell against the doorframe, breathing hard.

Her father came up behind her. *You should have just shot him.*

She lifted her head and stared into the turbulent night sky. 'I know.'

31

JAMIE GOT HER WISH.

It was two in the morning by the time she left the crime scene.

She'd put a call in a few minutes after she'd caught her breath and stopped kicking herself and SOCOs had been on scene within the hour.

They'd logged and inventoried everything, dusted everything for prints – though it seemed pointless considering Jamie knew who it was – and photographed every square inch of the place.

It all seemed tedious and pointless at this point.

McElroy was out there, and now he knew he was being hunted.

What was worse was that she knew where he wanted to go, what he wanted to do. Knew that he *had* to finish.

Smith hadn't bothered to call her after she'd called in the scene. He just text her the words, 'Go home' and then swiftly after in another text, 'my office, 8 a.m.'

She looked at it, and then quickly sent a text back with the addresses of the other locations. Tried to explain the situation as best she could.

It was almost midnight by then.

He was probably in bed.

She didn't want to call him.

His wife was probably nagging him to go to sleep, sighing and tutting next to him.

He ignored it and just repeated the first text.

Go home.

Jamie left, head hung, and drove back to her apartment in silence. She didn't even have the radio on.

She just kept thinking about McElroy. That he could have killed her.

That he could have kept the lights out, could have put a knife in her, too.

That she could have stopped him. From doing that, from doing what he was doing. From killing again.

If she'd just pulled that fucking trigger.

Her grip tightened on the wheel as she drove, on autopilot.

She let herself into her apartment, thinking she wouldn't sleep, and dragged her laptop onto the kitchen table.

There was a lot of paperwork to do. Which now included a firearm discharge report, too. She'd fired her weapon, and that needed to be explained and accounted for.

How she was going to make it sound like she wasn't completely inept, she didn't know.

The word counter told her that she'd made it to two thousand and some change before she'd fallen asleep.

She picked her head up off the table as the first rays of sunlight bled in through the front window, and blinked hard, her neck aching more than her hip.

She'd pushed the laptop away at some point, laid her head on her arm, and slept.

Jamie didn't remember that.

She walked with legs not her own to the bathroom and showered, leaving her clothes in a pile on the floor.

When she got to her bedroom, she stopped, eyeing the file that Elliot had left, the photographs still spread out on the floor.

She didn't have the patience or the nerve to deal with it.

Not just then.

Jamie dressed with her back to the bed and then left the room as quickly as she could.

Her stomach felt like it had shrivelled up and eating was painful.

But she had to.

Had to force herself to.

She was no good to anyone, let alone herself, if she couldn't function.

Aaron McElroy was out there, and now he knew he was being hunted.

That put her on the back foot.

Which meant if that son of a bitch was going to be hard to catch before, now it was going to be a whole lot harder.

He'd wait for his moment now, and then he'd strike. Fast, and hard.

And Jamie needed to be ready.

She sat at her table, staring into space, forcing down muesli with soya milk, chewing thoughtfully, counting down the minutes until she left, headed to work, and faced Smith, again.

Jamie missed the days of being a uniform. Go here. Do this. Man this post. Secure this scene. Stop people from doing *X*. It was never this difficult. Never this heavy.

She grimaced, the food in her mouth like chalk-flavoured mulch, and pushed the bowl away. The contents had turned to slop and time had run thin.

It was time to go.

Jamie got in before eight and climbed to four.

Smith was sitting in his office, looking over a stack of papers on his desk.

He looked up as she walked between the desks, seeing two new manilla folders in her document tray. Forensics reports from the SOCOs. The confirmation of McElroy's semen in Mimi's bed. The confirmation that they were Katheryn Orlov's hands.

She kept walking. Smith was locked onto her now. She couldn't stop.

His door was open and he watched her enter. She didn't need an offer to sit down.

'Johansson,' he said quietly. He looked as tired as Jamie felt.

'Sir, before you—'

'Just shut up, Jamie.' He leaned back and rubbed his eyes. He never used her first name.

'You keep pulling yourself in here,' he muttered. She barely caught it. 'And it's always for the same damn reason. Because you over-reached, you acted recklessly, and you're too damn good at what you do. You could have skulked around a hundred buildings last night and never seen McElroy, and neither you or I would be sitting here right now. But you didn't. You sent Roper and Hassan home, you pushed Fischer to stay on late, to get you information vital to the case, and then you went it alone.' He leaned forward on his chair now. 'Jesus, Jamie – what if he'd killed you?'

Jamie opened her mouth to speak, then fell quiet. 'I'm sorry, sir.'

'You know I'm not pulling you in here to reprimand you, because it never seems to work. You're like a dog who never learns – I scald you and you slink away with your tail between your legs, and then when I turn around you're pulling the same shit again. We have protocol for a reason, Jamie.'

'I caught him in the act,' Jamie interjected, trying to keep the stern-ness out of her voice. 'I was right, and—'

'And McElroy is not in custody, not behind bars, and the forensic prelim shows that gunshot residue was found at the scene. Did you discharge your weapon?'

Jamie swallowed. 'Yes.'

'So you sent your partners home, then proceeded to track down a serial killer with a known tendency for sudden violence, and confront him without thinking to call it in? And then, you went through with it, presumably *did* confront him, pointed your weapon at him, and then what?' He stared right at her.

'I didn't try to kill him.'

Smith licked his lips, studying her face.

'He rushed me.'

His jaw flexed.

'The lights went out, he came at me, I fired, missed, and he escaped.'

Smith drew a long breath in and rubbed his head. 'This is getting out of hand, Johansson. You should have waited. Called for backup. Secured the building. Observed. Followed him. You should have done any number of things other than going in there with your gun out.'

'I know.'

'If you know, then why did you do it?'

Jamie didn't have an answer for that.

He looked grave now. 'And if you were going to go in there with your gun out, then you should have been prepared to use it.'

'Sir?' Jamie looked up now and met his eye.

'Jesus, Jamie, what if he'd killed you? Frankly, I'm surprised he didn't. You let him get the drop on you, and that's even stupider than going in there alone. If your weapon is out, then commit to using it.'

'Are you suggesting…?'

'That you premeditated killing him?' There wasn't a hint of quaver in his face. 'No. But I would rather be sitting here filling in a report to explain why you shot and killed a serial killer than one explaining why you were in there alone when he killed you.'

Jamie drew a breath. 'I'm sorry.'

'One of these days, I see it coming to that. First with the Jane Doe case and Zhou, and now with this?'

Jamie kept her face straight, but she knew he was right.

'I keep telling people, and myself, that you're a good detective. And I need you to start acting like one.' He cracked his neck. 'There are two forensics reports on your desk. Both of which have been sitting there since yesterday afternoon. And if you'd bothered to read them, to take the time to come back, do your paperwork, get everyone else up to speed on what the hell is going on here, then you may have had second thoughts about barrelling in there.

'Hell, if you'd have just gone *home* last night when Roper and Hassan did, you'd have come in this morning, seen them, and been able to do exactly what you did last night, but with a fresh head on your shoulders, and Hassan and Roper at your back.'

Jamie grit her teeth. 'And we would have missed McElroy.'

'And he still wouldn't be in custody, and the girl would still be dead. You fucked up, Johansson. Own it.'

Jamie nodded, her throat constricting around any words she might have tried to form.

'Now,' he said, looking over her shoulder briefly to check they were still alone. 'You look like shit.'

Jamie felt a twinge in her guts. 'I didn't realise this was a beauty contest.'

'It's not. But when you're getting a thousand photographs taken in a few hours, I want you looking like you've slept in the last three days.'

Jamie licked her teeth inside her lip, feeling the same anger bubbling in her that seemed to come during those sparse lunches with her mother. 'I haven't. And what do you mean a thousand photographs?'

'We have a serial killer loose in the city. And now we know who he is. For certain. And we know his victim type. And we know the type of location he's intending to present his victims in.' He paused for a second. 'It's uncharted territory for you, but you'll be heading the press conference.'

'Press conference? I don't think that's necessary – I already have a statement planned which—'

'It is necessary, Johansson. A statement isn't going to cut it. Will that be a problem?'

'I just think we've got bigger—'

'I've spoken to PR, they've arranged it. We need to get out ahead of this. Rumours are swirling. We need to get McElroy's face out there. We need to make him famous. We need to close down his options. I've already got a surveillance requests in on the properties you gave me, and I've got officers doing stop-and-searches around all popular music venues in the city, at busking spots, in music shops. There's not a place in this city that this guy is going to be able to hide.'

'But why me, Sir?' Jamie was even more afraid of facing a wall of journalists than she was going toe-to-toe with McElroy again.

'You spoke to him, correct?' He knew she had. She'd given a prelim to one of the SOCOs last night and Smith had been through the report that morning. *Early* that morning by the bags under his eyes.

'McElroy? Yes,' Jamie answered, trying to be conservative.

'What did he say?'

'That, uh,' Jamie began, trying to recall the conversation as best she could. 'That it wasn't about the killing, that it was about the… *act.* That the music was for the listener, not the performer.'

'What the hell is that supposed to mean?'

Jamie shook her head. 'I don't know – that he doesn't intend to stop?'

Smith held his hands up and shook his head. 'It doesn't matter right now. Make sure to put in your report.' He glanced over her shoulder again.

Jamie didn't get the feeling he was checking that they were still alone.

He beckoned someone into the office and a woman entered.

She was in her forties, wearing a skirt-suit, with red hair pulled into a large, frizzy bunch at the crown of her head.

Smith motioned her towards the chair next to Jamie and she sat.

'This is Ms Lewis. She's an HR representative, and will be coaching you through the press conference.'

Jamie had stiffened visibly. She hated having her photograph taken, and public speaking was not her strong suit either. There was nothing worse she could imagine, in fact, than getting up on stage in front of a room full of cameras.

'Jamie,' she said, her voice soft, hints of a Scottish accent dripping through. She placed a hand on Jamie's, which was rested on her leg. 'It's important that the Met maintain a good working relationship with the press. And conferences are a key way to do that when it comes to big cases like this.'

Jamie said nothing.

'And as you're not as senior as most of the detectives heading cases like this, there'll be a lot of questions surrounding that. Surrounding your…'

'Ineptitude?' Jamie asked coldly.

'Age, experience, handling of the case,' she replied diplomatically, not even addressing the question. 'We're going to run through how it will work, the sorts of things you'll be asked, and some answers we'd like you to memorise for when these questions do arise.'

Smith chimed in. 'You have nothing to worry about, Johansson. I'll be right there with you. I'll present the facts of the case, and then it will be up to you to reveal McElroy to the public, give a brief summary of things, and then appeal for information. We'll be in and out in under twenty minutes.' He smiled, but Jamie wasn't buying it.

She sighed. 'There's no getting out of this, is there?'

Smith's smile faded. 'No, Johansson. There isn't.'

It had been three hours since the end of the press conference, and Jamie was still seeing spots from the camera flashes.

When she'd said McElroy's name, pens scribbled fiercely on notepads in front of her. And then again when they'd given Alyssa Doran's name, Gilberto Delgado's. Both had been formally identified. The rest were more difficult.

Though Jamie knew they was Kathryn Orlov's hands lying in the coroner's office, a next-of-kin ID would be impossible, not to mention highly distressing for the family.

Instead, all she could do was name her as missing. Along with Mimi Paganelli, Daisy Hardwick, and Amelie Dovak.

Though Jamie had no reason to believe any of them were still alive.

It was made excruciatingly clear to her by the PR rep and Smith that she not box herself in by answering questions on the subject.

So she ignored them and pressed quickly on.

Smith had talked about McElroy's victim type – prominent classical musicians – and asked anyone who'd seen anything strange or disconcerting, or knew of anyone who was missing, to come forward. They had given the locations of the attacks, talked about theatres and performance halls as places he might go. They'd done everything except discuss how he threaded fishing line through their hands and hung them on stage for the world to see.

No, they refused to give him that pleasure. That satisfaction. No one would know what he had done.

And yet, with all the information out there, they'd received nothing back.

At least nothing had come through to Jamie.

And there was no sign of Roper or Hassan, either.

She didn't know where they were, and Smith wasn't in his office, either.

After they'd left the conference, he had told her to go back to her desk, finish her paperwork, and wait for him.

And she was.

She'd completed all her reports, read the forensics reports front to back – on both the theatre where they'd found Kathryn Orlov's remains, and the Bradbury Hall scene.

Just like Doran's murder, the places were clean. He'd not left anything behind. And both swab-tests of the foods revealed the same stuff – dust, traces of rat poison, traces of mud, traces of faecal matter. But hell, where in London couldn't you swab and come up with traces of rat poison and shit? If nine out of ten shopping trolley handles tested positive for it, she shuddered to think what got trampled under people's feet.

She grimaced, recalling the article about the trolleys, and looked around.

Still no hint of Roper or Hassan. Jamie tapped her foot nervously, knowing there was something going on.

She expected her phone to be going crazy. To be inundated with tips, leads, and people calling to say they thought their next-door neighbour was McElroy in disguise.

But there was nothing.

And that was making things worse.

The lift opened behind her and Smith walked out.

She craned her neck to watch him come, hoping, for the first time since she'd started working for him, that he was coming towards her.

And he was.

'Johansson,' he said, stopping at her desk. 'I'll make this quick.'

'Sir?'

'The McElroy response has been sizeable.'

'I haven't had any calls, or—'

'And that's because I told no one to contact you. I've set up a task force to deal with the—'

'A task force? Where? I should—'

'You should go home, get some rest.'

'But, Sir—'

'For once, Johansson, don't argue with me. Roper and Hassan are down there now. They have been since first thing this morning. Roper has worked these sorts of things before. He knows what he's doing.'

'He's running it?'

'Yes.'

'This is *my* case.'

'I never said it wasn't. But Roper has the experience, and you need to sleep. Eat something. Get your head right. Let Hassan and Roper handle the leads, sort all of them out. The good from the bad. Then you come back tomorrow, rested and ready to work.' He wasn't asking.

'McElroy is out there right now, and—'

'And he'll be there tomorrow.' Smith cut her off. 'If anything solid comes in, we'll call you.'

'But—'

'Get out of here, Johansson. Now.' Smith was already heading for his office.

Jamie stood. 'Sir, if I could—'

'You can't. Now go home. And if I see you or hear your name before the morning, you can consider yourself suspended. *Indefinitely*.' The door to his office shut behind him and Jamie was left standing there in silence, her fists clenched so tightly at her sides her nails were threatening to draw blood from her palms.

32

SHE KNEW IT.

She knew Smith wouldn't let her have it.

But then again, if she were in his shoes, would she?

Jamie knew that she had been reckless. That since the Oliver Hammond case things hadn't been the same.

Since Elliot.

She ground her teeth, walking in circles around her apartment.

He was invading her life, dominating it. And all she was trying to do was escape him. It had screwed with her brain. She used to be so collected. So logical.

And now…

Jamie was a tempest on her living room floor. She'd been driven from her home and from work.

One chance.

That's what she'd been given and she'd all but blown it.

She couldn't believe how impulsive she'd been. How narrow-minded. How tunnel visioned.

She couldn't believe she didn't have the brass to just put a bullet in Aaron McElroy when he would have killed her in a second.

Why had she been so scared?

It's never a level playing field.

'Not now,' she growled, ignoring her father, leaning, arms folded, against her kitchen counter.

If you're not prepared to pull the trigger but they are it's not a fair fight.

'Shut up.'

Why do you even carry that thing if you're not going to use it?

'Be quiet, please.'

It's time to choose, Jamie. Choose what kind of person you're going to be. Shooter or target. Hunter or hunted. Predator or prey. Lion or sheep. Strong or—

'I said shut up!' Jamie yelled this time, the pistol flashing from her hip and into her hand, levelled at thin air.

Her father was a memory she refused to let go of. He was a worm that had burrowed so deep into her brain that he would never come out.

She spent so long wanting to be like him. So long wanting to be him.

So long hearing her mother telling her never to be.

That he was worthless, that he was a terrible father, a terrible husband.

Her mother couldn't fathom what he went through.

What Jamie had gone through.

Was going through.

Enough to tear her apart.

Physically, mentally. Emotionally.

Jamie was exhausted. Exhausted of fighting it. Of fighting the urge to let go of that softer side, to embrace the memory of her father. To embrace the darker part of her that was always clawing for the surface. To embrace the piece of cool steel in her hand and finally step up to the mark. Finally be the person that pulls that trigger. That chooses life in those life or death situations. Who fires first. Who kicks their hardest and worries about how much it's going to hurt them after.

It's what her father had always said. That this job takes everything from you.

And she was finally beginning to understand that.

Jamie opened her eyes, not realising they were closed, and looked around.

This place was a wreck. Damp walls, dirty kitchen. She had come here to hide. Crawled into a hole to hide from a man there was no hiding from.

Elliot was too smart, too ruthless, and too well connected.

But he wasn't interested in killing her. He was interested in something else.

Roper and Hassan were under Smith's purview now. They were running the task force, fielding calls and drowning in paperwork.

Jamie had felt confined before, but now she realised that Smith had done the opposite. He hadn't tied her hands. He'd cut her loose.

And now she was free. Free to operate however she wanted. As far as he was concerned she was on bedrest. Which meant she could go hunting.

And so long as he didn't find out, then he'd never know.

And she wasn't going to tell him. She'd add it to the list of things she'd keep secret.

One more wouldn't weigh on her any more.

Jamie slotted her pistol back into her holster and exhaled.

She was hungry.

The fridge had some eggs that were just in date and there were oats in the cupboard. It was the afternoon, but that didn't stop her from making a three-egg omelette, eating two pieces of stale toast and then heating up a bowl of oats in the microwave.

Her mind had emptied itself now and she was finally thinking clearly.

Food was first. She needed fuel.

Water next. She was dehydrated and not working at full capacity.

Jamie headed for the stairs with a two-litre bottle of water in hand, taking mouthfuls as she climbed.

McElroy had scurried back to his hole. Wherever that was.

He was smart. Too smart to show his face again until his next big reveal.

There were still a lot of places in the city that money talked. That you could rent or use if you had the cash and no one would ask questions. Too many, in fact. And the people running them knew it wasn't above board so they weren't likely to come forward and tell the Met that they'd illegally rented a murder-dungeon to a serial killer.

But, that didn't mean that the information couldn't be found by other means. You just needed the right connections.

Jamie breezed past the files still strewn on her bedroom floor and went towards the wardrobe.

She knew what box she was looking for.

It was in the middle stack, on the bottom. She took hold of it and yanked it out without moving the others.

They dropped into place behind it and she slid the one in her hand into the middle of the floor, kneeling in front of it.

Her hair fell in front of her eyes and she brushed it back off her face, stripping off the tape and lifting the lid.

There, on top of a folded-up world map – which hid Elliot's post cards – was the flip-phone.

Small, dated, black. Untraceable.

She reached for it, her hand pausing just before she took hold.

This was it.

No going back now.

Jamie exhaled and pulled it out, opening it up.

The old black-and-green display shone dimly and she pressed the green button to pull up the phone book.

There was only one number programmed into it and it had a three-digit prefix that was anything but British.

Jamie felt her heart beat a little harder as she hit the green button to call and held it to her ear.

The line crackled for a few seconds, then there was silence, a click, and a discordant beep.

Jamie winced at the tone, waiting for it to ring, but it didn't. She wasn't sure if it was connected to someone, or she was leaving a message, or the phone it was calling wasn't even in service anymore.

She sighed. 'It's, uh… me.' Jamie cleared her throat. 'I need…' Shit, this was harder than she thought. 'Help.' She squeezed it out between her teeth. 'I need you to…' She swallowed, letting herself trail off. This was bad enough but she didn't want to incriminate herself further. Instead she cleared her throat.

And then she hung up.

If he was even going to get the message that would be enough for him to call her back.

For now, there was nothing else she could do. At least when it came to the case.

Jamie had been neglecting herself, though.

She pocketed the flip-phone and pulled her own out, pulling up a new message to Cake. It was getting late in the afternoon now but she wanted to try her luck anyway.

'Afternoon bag session?'

She sat and waited for a minute or two, hoping he'd text back, but there was nothing.

Probably busy.

Jamie stood anyway and gathered up the photos and files from Elliot's delivery.

She got them together neatly and put them on top of the map, sealed the box, and then pushed it back into her wardrobe.

Quick phone check.

Nothing.

She kept moving, stripped off, and got into some gym gear. Leggings, a sports bra, a zip-through hoodie.

If Cake didn't reply, she'd go for a run.

Jamie forced down as much water as she could from her two-litre and headed for the stairs.

Her phone pinged as she got to the living room. It was Cake.

'Can't. Got a date.'

She stopped dead in her tracks, felt a smile creep over her face.

Good for him.

'Good luck,' she texted back. And then added, 'We need to get back to training…' She looked up at the spot where her father had been, resting against the counter, and saw nothing but her run-down kitchen.

She missed her old place. Her clean, neat, modern apartment. She wanted to go back. Or maybe somewhere else. Somewhere better.

She loved the city, but that didn't mean she didn't miss the wide-open spaces of her childhood.

Jamie had been thinking about it a lot recently.

She finished the text. 'Maybe we should talk about a fight.'

Her thumb hovered over the send button, and then she hit it.

Screw it.

It was time to take charge. Time to stop being afraid of losing control.

Maybe that's what she needed.

He text back almost immediately. 'Seriously? Okay, let's talk soon. g2g.'

That made her grin. g2g. Got to go. She didn't take him as the text-speak type. But then again, if he'd wrangled a date from somewhere, maybe he was changing.

Did anyone ever really stay the same?

As she headed for the door, she really was happy for him. He'd had a tough year or two. She was glad he was getting a win.

Jamie did nearly twenty kilometres.

Her chest was burning by the time she got back to her street, her collar soaked with sweat, her feet aching, knees throbbing.

She hadn't run in a while. At least not like that.

Jamie's chest burned as she let herself back into her apartment. She had a running belt with a pouch on her waist that she put her phone in, along with a water bottle. Neither her normal phone or Elliot's had rung on the run.

She was starting to lose hope that he'd get the message.

It had been months since he'd given it to her.

There was no wonder it was dead. He'd probably been through ten new numbers by now.

Jamie let herself into her apartment, planning on doing exactly what Smith had ordered. Get some rest. Ready herself for the day ahead.

She had just got onto the stairs when the floorboards above her creaked.

Jamie paused and looked up.

Nothing moved.

Shit. She glanced at the motion sensor at the top of the stairs, the light dark. She hadn't turned it on when she'd left.

Elliot.

She had to stop herself from smirking.

That slippery son of a bitch.

He'd obviously gotten her message. And instead of calling her back, he'd broken in.

Again.

She hated that, but under it was a rising sense of something else. A churning tide of something that resembled a dark excitement. Trepidation, maybe. Nervousness. But there was an eagerness there, too.

If she could tame him into helping her on her terms, then maybe, just *maybe* something good, usable even, could come of his fixation.

She needed to stop being the victim here. There were worse people out there – ones like Zhou, and De Voge, and all the others that Amherst had helped slip through the net.

And if Elliot really did want to help, then maybe it was about time she put him to work.

It twisted her guts up thinking about it, but Jamie couldn't remember a time when she didn't feel like this.

There came a point where you had to stop swimming against the current.

And Jamie had reached it.

She got to the top of the stairs, her breath settling, heart returning to her resting rate, and wiped the sweat from her forehead.

He was in the living room.

'Jesus,' she said, stepping in. 'You ever hear of a phone call?'

'I prefer the personal touch.'

Jamie froze, almost tripping, and looked up.

She knew that voice.

But it wasn't Elliot.

Her heart wasted no time kicking back into overdrive.

Detective Amherst was sitting on the arm of her sofa. He was perched, the hood of his thick parker slumped around his head like a dead wolf, his big hand on his thigh, the gleaming body of a silver pistol jutting out from under it, his finger resting on the trigger.

'Amherst,' Jamie breathed, her feet rooted to the ground. 'What are you—'

'It's best if you just come with me, Johansson,' he said, his voice even. He looked unphased by the encounter, but his eyes held something that contrasted with his cold demeanour.

She could tell he didn't want to be there.

But he was.

And there was no getting away from that fact.

Jamie slid her feet slightly wider apart, counting the steps to him. Wondering how quickly he could get that pistol up. How good his aim was.

She didn't really like the odds of charging him down, but she thought she could dive for the door. Go for the stairs, get to her bedroom, to the pistol she'd put on her nightstand when she'd changed.

Though he'd probably swept the apartment for it.

Jamie's mind turned.

If she went with him she wasn't coming back.

All she could do was run.

'Don't even think about it,' Amherst said, reading her, his grip flexing on the gun.

Jamie swallowed.

They locked eyes.

Each waiting for the other to make the first move.

Jamie tensed. She would jump first.

Everything stopped. Just for an instant. Her muscles surged, her toes digging into the soles of her shoes, the soles digging into the floorboards, and she twisted.

Her head spun around and she lunged, straight into Amy Brock.

Brock's fist came up in a steep uppercut, right into her gut and Jamie curled over the top of it, her own momentum impaling her on Brock's arm.

She made a high-pitched whining noise as the wind was blown out of her lungs, her feet leaving the ground.

Jamie's eyes pulsed black and she landed, her knees buckling, pain surging through her stomach and back.

She staggered backwards, fighting for breath, clutching her midriff, and turned on unsteady feet.

Amherst was on his feet now, sidling towards her. He straightened his belt, pistol still in hand. He sighed loudly. 'You should have just come with us.' And then he raised the pistol, showed the butt to Jamie, and brought it down hard above her left eyebrow.

Then there was darkness.

33

When Jamie regained consciousness, she couldn’t see anything.

Her hands were bent down behind her back, her wrists bound together. She struggled, feeling the sharp edge of plastic dig into her skin. Zip-tie.

Jamie grimaced, feeling the pain in her head suddenly.

Like broken glass against her skull

She groaned, her voice reverberating in her ears.

She was aware suddenly of the fabric against her cheeks, her head. A bag.

And she was sitting.

Jesus, she was tied to a fucking chair with a bag over her head.

She tried to calm herself but it was no good.

The stench of old sweat coming off her neck told her she’d been out for a while. But what had happened during that time and where she was now remained a mystery.

She couldn’t see anything through the bag, couldn’t taste anything except copper.

Her shoulders ached, her knees too.

‘Don’t struggle.’ Amherst's voice rang in the darkness.

‘Amherst, you piece of shit,’ Jamie spat, her mouth dry.

'It's nothing personal, Johansson,' he said, his boot steps ringing around her.

She felt him take hold of a fistful of bag, along with some of her hair, and roughly pull it off.

The light stung her eyes and she screwed them shut, feeling matted strands of hair clinging to her face.

When she forced them open she could see that she was in what looked like a storage room. And she was most definitely tied to a chair.

One ankle to each leg, hands behind her back.

A bulb was burning overhead, throwing light on the blue steel shelving hugging the walls. Jamie squinted around, seeing clear plastic boxes full of what looked like appliances – toasters, blenders, food processors. She kept looking, seeing sacks of potatoes and flour, rice. Tinned goods. Food and foodstuffs.

Her mind tried to work.

A restaurant?

The French restaurant that Amherst and Zhou had met behind.

It had to be. But what good did knowing that really do her?

She swallowed, her throat full of razors.

Amherst walked backwards towards the door, banged on it with his fist, and then sat down on the folding steel chair he'd been perched on when Jamie came to.

The door opened a second later and Brock came in, wearing her ever-present leather jacket and black jeans.

Neither she or Amherst looked happy about the situation.

Jamie squinted up at them, her head stinging. She could feel the dry discomfort of blood down the left side of her face and it had run into her eye. It was making it difficult to see.

Brock came forward slowly.

'That's close enough,' Amherst growled as she got near.

Brock slowed, staring down at Jamie, and bit her lip. 'She's tied to a fucking chair,' Brock said back.

'Yeah,' he replied. 'And she's going to stay that way. Now back off, Brock.'

She clenched her fists, her nostrils flaring, and stepped back.

There was compassion in her eyes.

But Jamie didn't think that was going to get her out of the situation.

Somehow, she didn't feel like pleading, either.

There was more noise outside the door now. Footsteps, shuffling. And then it opened.

Jamie could see two guys outside, tall, in black suits, their backs to the door.

But her eyes went to the man in the middle.

The man in the paisley tie.

Ho Zhou, the former manager of the Jade Circle.

Jamie swallowed as he walked towards her and stopped about six feet away. He put his hands behind his back, studying her.

Brock moved out of the way and leaned against the wall, folding her arms. She refused to look at Jamie.

After a few seconds Zhou began to smile wryly. 'Detective Sergeant Jamie Johansson.' He tutted slowly. 'What a mess you've got yourself into.'

Jamie coughed, hawked, and then spat on the floor between her knees. She could still taste the bag. 'If you say so,' she muttered.

'You know, Detective Brock held out hope that you could be swayed.'

'Oh yeah?' Jamie asked, not bothering to look up.

'That you could be bought.' Zhou paused for effect. 'But it seems that Amherst was the better judge of character.' He chuckled a little. 'But I guess that comes with the territory, right *Detective*?' he asked, turning to Amherst.

The big man in the parka grunted.

'He said,' Zhou went on. 'That you were far too honourable for your own good.'

Jamie scoffed at that, laughing abjectly. That was kind of funny considering the relationship she maintained with a wanted serial killer.

'I hope that honour was worth dying for,' Zhou said, letting his hands drop to his sides.

He kept his eyes fixed on Jamie, who was staring up at him from under her bloodied eyebrow.

Zhou raised his left hand to his side, palm out.

Amherst got to his feet and approached slowly, pulling that sleek silver pistol from one pocket of his coat, and a suppressor from the other.

He looked right at Jamie as he pushed them together and screwed.

The sound of metal scraping on metal as the threads bit was the only sound in the room.

It hit the stop and Amherst turned it over, placing the grip into Zhou's hand.

His pudgy fingers curled around it and let it hang at his hip again.

He was drawing this out, taking pleasure in it.

He wanted to see fear in Jamie. For her to beg.

But she just didn't fucking feel like.

After all that had happened, she just didn't really care any more. At least not enough to ask this piece of shit for mercy.

If she was going to get her brains blown out here in this grubby store room, then she at least wanted to go out with dignity.

Her father's words rang in her head, as true as they did that first day working the Oliver Hammond case. *Don't give them a fucking inch.*

I won't.

I bloody well won't.

Jamie lifted her head now and stared right at Zhou, expressionless.

In her peripheral, Brock folded her arms, looked at the ceiling.

Her eyes seemed to glimmer in the light, but Jamie couldn't have said if it was anything other than just their natural shine.

Amherst had turned half on now, facing Brock.

He stared silently at her, a stone monolith behind the small but terrible Zhou.

Jamie wondered if their pay packets were thick enough to make any of this worthwhile.

Zhou held the gun in his hands, staring down at it, and then raised it, levelling it at Jamie's head.

This was it.

She looked from Amherst to Brock again, and then right down the barrel of the pistol.

She couldn't get over how dark it was.

Everything else faded away.

All she could hear was the distant throb of her heart somewhere inside her chest.

The rest was static.

Brock and Amherst both turned their heads in unison to look at the door.

Jamie didn't hear anything above the roar. Like an ocean in her ears.

Brock pushed off the wall and walked towards it.

She pulled it open and slipped through.

Jamie couldn't see anything past the gun.

Amherst started after her, but only made it two steps.

The door flung open in the background, banging dully on the frame.

The noise was muted in Jamie's ears.

Amherst staggered backwards suddenly, and then fell, landing flat on his back with a loud thunk.

Zhou jolted, twisted, raised the pistol, and then convulsed.

He staggered, body shuddering violently, and took three steps backwards.

His heel hooked over Jamie's foot and he tumbled sideways, a flurry of bloody holes in his pristine black suit.

He thudded to the ground and lay still, the pistol still in his grip.

Jamie blinked, a spattering of fresh blood on her face, and looked up at the doorway, the roar now turned to a piercing whine in her ears.

A surge of sudden joy and violent anger raged in her.

'Elliot.' Her mouth formed the word without her meaning to.

He stepped through the door, his right hand raised, his well-muscled forearm stretching from the sleeve of his shirt like a lance. In his hand was a suppressed pistol, the muzzle still smoking.

Jamie could see the shapes of Zhou's two bodyguards outside, slumped against the wall, a dark pool of blood forming around each of them.

Amherst lay on her right, riddled with bullets, and Zhou on her left, his chest a mess of deep craters.

Elliot couldn't have been further from the man Jamie met in the homeless shelter six months ago as she watched him push the pistol into the back of his belt, approaching quickly and wordlessly.

A knife was in his hand before Jamie even saw him draw it, but she didn't flinch as he closed in on her.

The blade sliced through the ties at her feet and then he was leaning around her, his collar pressed against her chin as he lifted her hands and cut the final tie.

He smelled good.

Jamie screwed her eyes shut, stamping that thought out.

Elliot retracted and stood in front of her. His hand lingered in the air, as if he were about to offer it, and then he didn't, letting it hang at his side instead. 'You weren't kidding,' he said quietly.

Jamie looked up at him quizzically, rubbing her wrists.

'You really did need help.'

She made a disapproving sound and got to a shaky stance. She counted four bodies. 'Where's Brock?'

Elliot looked at her for a second. 'Come on, we should go.'

He turned to leave and Jamie thought about whether she should go with him.

Then she decided.

And started walking.

34

THE GRAND REGENT Hotel was five stars.

When Elliot had pulled up outside it, she'd been surprised.

People thronged in the street before the doors.

He stopped at the curb and let the car idle.

The sun had gone down now and traffic oozed past them on the drivers' side.

Jamie didn't know why, but she'd expected an abandoned warehouse, or some slum. Somewhere that didn't ask questions when someone turned up with a fistful of cash.

But then again, they were in a Mercedes. A new one.

A rental, of course, but it was still plush, with pale leather seats and all the chrome trimmings.

He was hardly low-profile. But then again, in a city of nine million people, did he really need to be? Elliot wasn't a common criminal. He was smart, and smart enough not to get caught. As well as well connected. And better financed.

Jamie stared up at the fancy hotel from the fancy car.

They'd rode in silence, Jamie deathly aware that she was sitting next to a monster.

And yet there was no fear in her.

It was like a dangerous dog you knew wouldn't bite you.

He'd saved her life.

There was no two-ways about that.

Elliot looked ahead, totally relaxed. One of the most-wanted men in the country. 'It's room six-twelve,' he said quietly, holding up a white keycard, the thick window glass deadening the sound of the city outside.

Jamie kept looking at the hotel, wondering how it would be to know that you were being hunted by one of the most sophisticated and tenacious law enforcement agencies in the world, and still have the balls to walk into a five-star hotel with forged ID and pay for a room.

She swallowed.

'I won't come back,' Elliot said, reading the silence, the card still held between them. 'Don't worry.'

'Where are you going?' she asked absently, not sure she wanted to get out of the car and desperate to at the same time.

She felt ill, her wrists and throat still raw, her neck still speckled with Zhou's blood.

'I have some things to attend to,' he said vaguely. 'I need to go back, sweep the scene, make sure there's nothing that can tie you to it.'

'Me?' Jamie asked, her face screwing itself up. She turned to look at him now, his cold eyes staring back.

He nodded. 'You were never there, Jamie. I need to make sure of that.'

She didn't have anything to say back. She was afraid if she opened her mouth again vomit would shoot out of it.

He wagged the card slowly. 'Six-twelve. Get showered, get cleaned up, order some food. New clothes. Whatever you want.'

'New clothes?' Jamie whispered the words, looking down at her leggings and hoodie, a thin spray of blood still clinging to them.

'Bag those up. Get rid of them.' He paused for a moment, checked the street. 'I don't need to tell you why you need to do that.'

She stared down at her body, could smell the mixture of sweat and blood on the fabric and her skin.

'Jamie?'

She exhaled, took hold of herself, and then pulled the card from his grasp.

'The room is paid for, they have my card. Speak to the manager, she'll get you what you need. *Whatever* you need.'

Jamie didn't even want to ask.

She pushed the door open and shouldered through the crowd, the people bumping into her no more than dark blobs in her periphery.

The doorman opened the door for her and she stepped into the quiet lobby.

For a moment she paused, struck by the sudden vastness in front of her, and then looked back through the doors.

Elliot was gone, a taxi now in the spot he'd been in.

Jamie turned back, looked around, felt eyes upon her, and made for the stairs.

The sharp corners of the keycard in her hand told her that all of this was actually real. Though her mind was struggling to comprehend.

Her legs ached, but she kept pounding up the flights, turning left and left and left and left until the numbers began to start with six.

She stepped into the corridor, out of breath, the smell of fresh sweat layered on old sweat invading her senses.

The doors seemed strangely spaced.

It took a while to reach six-twelve, at which point she paused, wondering what lay beyond.

The card flashed in the reader and she pushed through, the desire to get Zhou's blood scrubbed off her skin overriding the desire to not be in the same space that Elliot had walked.

The room was closer to a suite than anything else.

It stretched away in front of her, a living room with two leather sofas, a huge flat-screen tv, and a wide set of windows that overlooked the city.

The sky was bruised and darkening and the lights burned like jewels on the skyline.

Her footsteps were quiet on the thick carpet as she crept deeper.

There was no sign that Elliot had been there. No personal effects, no suitcase. No clothing. Nothing.

She passed a marbled bathroom on her right and stepped into a double-doorway on her left that opened into a palatial bedroom.

A four-poster bed stood on a raised platform and she stared at it longingly.

No, she couldn't sleep here.

Wouldn't.

Jamie turned, looking at the front door, and went back to it, grabbing the chain and sliding it into place.

She didn't want *anyone* coming in.

Jamie stopped there, rested her forehead against the cool grain of the wood and rattled a few breaths into her lungs, summoning what strength she had left.

She reached down, took hold of the hem of her hoodie and dragged it up over her head.

It pulled on her hair as it did and she tore her bobble out with hurried fingers, eyes screwed closed, the door still six inches from her nose.

She shook her plait loose and scratched at her ribs for the band of her sports bra, tearing it off.

Jamie stepped into the bathroom, shedding the remainder of her clothes as she went, and reached for the taps above the bath, throwing them both open.

Water streamed into the tub and she climbed in without checking the temperature, feeling herself shiver despite the warmth in the room.

She lowered herself down, watching as the water splattered on her ankles, taking the spots of red caked on her skin away and down the plug hole.

Jamie scrubbed at her shins with her hands, feeling the water burn, and moved upwards, raking over her thighs, pulling at her belly. She ran her palms over her shoulders and biceps, her fingers through her hair, feeling them catch on the knots there.

Jamie pushed the plug down and slid down onto her back, the water lapping at the arch of her back, climbing her ribs up towards her chest.

It lapped around her ears and then drowned out the world.

She could hear her blood moving in her veins, the coolness of a tear on her cheek.

And then the water was at the corners of her mouth, her hair floating around her head in long strands.

Her nose stung as the water crept inside and she breathed out, emptying her lungs, felt her body sink beneath the surface.

Her eyes closed and she lay there, submerged, wondering how long she could stay like that.

Thirty seconds?

A minute?

Forever?

Jamie rose slowly to the surface, her body floating in the water, and she let her eyes open, her nose breaking into the air.

She took a slow breath and tried to replay the last few hours over in her head.

But it had already become a fog.

A dark fog punctuated by the shockwaves of gunfire.

The hiss and spit of the muzzle, the dull thump of bullets hitting flesh.

The rolling of force through the body.

Each time it felt like she was the one getting hit.

But it wasn't her.

She was alive.

Jamie floated there, holding her naked body, and let the water cocoon her.

She felt as far from home as anyone ever had.

But she knew there was nowhere to go back to.

She was a tourist in her own life, an imposter in her own body.

Jamie Johansson did not know who she was any more.

And she didn't think anyone was about to tell her, either.

35

THE PHONE RANG NEXT to the bed and Jamie looked up, pulling on a knitted sweater and straightening it around her waist.

It was a little *designer* for her tastes – and snug, too – but she couldn't fault the quality or the softness of the wool.

She'd sized up from her norm and embraced the bagginess as it hung off her shoulder, bunching around her forearms where she'd rolled it up.

Elliot was right, the manager had been obliging. She'd asked Jamie a dozen questions about her size and preference, and then dispatched someone to hunt down some new clothes for her.

She grabbed the tag that was sticking in the back of her neck and pulled it off, feeling the stiffness of new jeans around her knees. She was disappointed to learn there was no elastane in the fabric.

Jamie lifted the receiver to her ear, expecting it to be the manager again, checking that everything was okay this time around. 'Hello?'

She'd sent back most of the things that had been delivered and changed sizes on the jumper.

But it wasn't the manager this time.

'Jamie,' Elliot said.

She felt tension in her shoulders, her damp hair cold around her ears. She brushed it back over them with her free hand. 'Yeah,' she said quietly.

'How are you feeling?'

She bit her lip, not sure whether talking on the phone with a wanted murderer was a good idea. Then she realised where she was, checked in under a false name. The manager had called her Mrs Hirsch. She hadn't corrected her, and had been trying not to think about the fact she was posing as Elliot's wife. 'I'm fine,' she lied.

'Good. It's done.'

There was silence.

'You'll be safe from now on.'

She set her jaw. 'Is that all?' Jamie asked after what seemed like too long.

'You tell me,' Elliot said casually.

Jamie faced the window and let her hand fall across her stomach, her fingers clenching the fabric.

Was he watching her?

She shivered at the thought.

'You called me, asking for help,' he went on, his voice as smooth and easy as it had always been.

'It's nothing,' Jamie said, reaching out and closing the curtains.

'It didn't sound like nothing.'

'I've changed my mind.'

'About needing help, or about seeking it from me?'

'Both.'

He chuckled a little on the other end of the phone and the hair on the nape of her neck stood on end.

Jamie tried not to gag at how that made her feel. At how quickly her mind seemed to slingshot between pure loathing and something far more painful to confront.

She so wanted him to be someone else, and hated that she did.

Hated him for being who he was, rather than hating him.

'What is it, Jamie?'

She wished he'd stop saying her name.

Jamie shook her head, turning back to the room in front of her. Could she just hang up? Then what?

'This case,' she started, letting her mind run free, her mouth following.

He listened intently.

'There's a man – a killer – he's out there, somewhere, in the city.'

He didn't interrupt.

'We're looking for him.' She took a breath. 'He's hurting women.'

Elliot processed.

'He's taking them, he's killing them, and then he's…' She held back an abject laugh, feeling almost absurd saying it. 'Cutting their hands off and displaying them as though they're playing instruments.'

'What kind of instruments?'

'Violins, flutes…'

'These women,' Elliot said astutely. 'Are they musicians?'

'Good ones. The best.'

'Is he a musician?'

'Conductor – or wanted to be.'

He made an, 'mm,' sound. 'Classical.' More a statement than a question.

'That's right.'

'What drives him? What does he want from it?'

Jamie shook her head. 'I don't know – to immortalise them? To… to…'

'Remove everything but their music.'

Jamie swallowed.

'It makes sense.'

Did it?

'You need help finding him?'

Jamie sank her teeth deeper into her lip.

'Where has he displayed their hands?' He asked it with brutal pragmatism.

'Concert halls, theatres.'

Elliot processed. 'You believe he's hiding in the city?'

'I do.'

'Why?'

'The display sites, the abductions… They're all in the city. And he doesn't have a car or even a license. I don't think he's using public transport, too much of a risk carrying…' She trailed off and grimaced. 'The hands.'

'And he's killing them?'

'The women?' Jamie sat on the bed. 'Yes.'

He made the 'mm,' sound again. 'Discards the bodies.'

Jamie grimaced.

'I'll do what I can.'

Jamie narrowed her eyes. 'Don't you want to know his name?'

There was silence on the line for a moment and Jamie imagined him smiling, amused. 'Sure,' he said after a second.'

'McElroy. Aaron McElroy.'

'I'll let you know what I find.'

What are you going to do? What *can* you do? She wanted to ask him. But she doubted he'd tell her. She didn't know if she even wanted to know.

Jamie gripped the receiver more tightly. 'I'll, uh, leave. Soon.' She couldn't bring herself to thank him.

'Why?'

'I can't just… *stay* here,' she said, looking around.

'Rest. Eat. Stay until morning, at least. I won't come there, I promise.'

A shiver ran down her spine. He kept saying that. But he'd never had boundaries before. Why start now? And what did a promise from a killer mean anyway?

'I, uh,' she said, clearing her throat. 'I have to go.'

'Sleep well.'

The line clicked and went dead before she could say anything else, his words ringing in her ears.

Jamie put the phone down and walked out into the living room, glancing at the empty plate on the table in front of the sofa.

She'd felt bad for all of three seconds when she'd ordered the sirloin off the room-service menu, charging it to the card Elliot had used. And then she'd felt horrible after eating it, realising where the money for that card had come from.

Then she ignored it.

Then it came back.

Tourist.

Who the fuck was she anymore?

She pulled her eyes from the tray and went to the windows. They were cracked a little to let the smell of the food out and a cool breeze was blowing in.

Jamie approached, laid her hand on the handle to close it, and paused. She could hear music drifting up from below. Echoing through the streets.

An entrance to the underground burrowed through the pavement across the road.

A few lonely souls walked in and out.

he couldn't see the player, but she could hear the distant groans of a cello being sawed at.

The music rose from the mouth of the tunnel, magnified by the smooth walls inside.

She listened for a moment, and then closed the window and locked it.

Jamie'd had enough of music.

All she wanted now was silence.

Inside her own head.

And out.

36

Jamie was halfway across the lobby when the night-porter called her over.

She stopped, hoping that she'd see no one considering it was just after six in the morning.

She just wanted to get out of there, get to work. Report her phone and wallet as stolen. Start over, and forget this ever happened.

'Excuse me,' he said, his voice carrying across the deserted lobby. 'Mrs Hirsch?'

She did a double-take, then remembered, forcing a smile.

Jamie wanted as few people to be able to place her there as was possible. 'Yes,' she said, looking up.

He could only have been in his twenties, and he looked tired.

Night shifts were no fun. Jamie could attest to that.

The boy approached at speed, holding his hand out, a thick brown envelope in it. 'Your husband dropped this off for you early this morning,' he said, grinning.

She looked at it from the corner of her eye, keeping the far-side of her face pointed away from him. A bruise had begun to swell on her forehead from where she was struck, the thin split in her skin at the centre of the impact mark hidden in her hairline.

Jamie took it, trying not to look too cautious or disgusted by the fact that Elliot had introduced himself as her husband.

She couldn't be out of there quick enough.

The envelope was weighty in her hand, and she leafed it open and reached inside.

She let out a single note of a disbelieving laugh. 'Thanks,' she said to the porter, and turned away, pulling out her watch.

The one that she'd been wearing during her run.

She stared down at it, the joy at having it back overriding the thought of Elliot pulling it out of the pocket of one of Zhou's dead cronies.

It was the same one Hassan had worn on the docks when they'd taken De Voge and Kosiah down.

She loved that watch.

Under it she found her car keys, a paper tag affixed to them with 612 written on it. The space he'd parked it downstairs in the hotel car park.

Her wallet came out next. A lightweight leather thing that held three cards and a few folded up notes. She only had two cards in it. Her debit card and her driver's license.

There was one more thing in the envelope.

Her phone.

She pulled it out and swiped the screen to life.

Jesus Christ, he'd even charged it.

Jamie stuffed it into her jeans and pushed the loose strands of hair she'd purposely left out of her plait to cover her forehead out of her eyes.

The night-porter still lingered.

She gave him another quick sidewards glance and turned back, heading for the stairs to the car park.

'We hope you enjoyed your stay!' he called after her.

But she was already gone.

She found her car quickly and got in.

Her boots were sitting on the passenger seat, perched on top of her leather jacket. It was folded neatly.

Jamie ground her teeth, annoyed by the fact that just before she'd got in she'd been thinking how she'd have to drive home to get them.

She reached over and lifted them off, dropped them into the footwell, and noticed the uneven shape of her jacket.

Under the top fold she found her pistol and warrant card, and scoffed to herself.

Whether they'd been in her apartment along with her boots, or Amherst had taken them when they'd broken in, she didn't know. But Elliot had found them, and now they were here.

Here everything was.

Her car, her phone, her boots. Even her damn watch.

Whether he was trying to be nice in his own twisted way or this was just him reminding her that he knew her, that he could go wherever he pleased, that she could run, but there was nowhere to hide – she didn't know.

Jamie decided now wasn't the time to try and get inside the mind of a serial killer.

At least not *this* serial killer.

She swallowed, jammed the key into the ignition, and peeled out of the hotel without looking back.

37

In the four years that Roper and Jamie had been partners, he'd never once been early.

Not once.

And yet at ten past eight he came strolling into the task room with a cup of coffee in hand.

Jamie looked up from the desk at the far end, her pen stopping on the page, and looked at him.

She quickly reached up and released the hair from behind her ear so it covered her face.

Roper approached slowly, sucking his breakfast from his teeth, and cast an eye over the papers spread out around Jamie.

Tips that had come in. Possible sightings. Potential leads. Maps. Crime scene photographs. Information from McElroy's caseworker and from the juvenile facility that he was held in before prison. Everything they had so far on the case.

Jamie had spent the best part of the last two hours reacquainting herself with it all.

'Solve it yet?' Roper asked.

'Good morning to you to,' Jamie said, keeping her head down, focusing on the page in front of her. It was a list of purchases from a funeral home wholesaler. The biggest seller of embalming fluids in the city. So far nothing was standing out to her.

'Smith know you're here?' Roper took a loud slurp of coffee, making sure to stand close enough to Jamie so his shadow rolled over the page she was working on.

'No,' Jamie said, sighing. 'Why should he?' She risked a glance up. 'This is still my case.'

Roper didn't respond, just sort of lifted his eyebrows and tilted his head.

He took another sip.

'So, you going to fill me in on what you've got so far?' Jamie asked after a few seconds.

'Thought this was your case?' Roper asked absently, still just standing in front of her.

Jamie let out a long breath and wondered when Roper had turned into such an asshole.

He read the lack of patience in her sigh and put his coffee down. 'McElroy's not using his or any of the victim's cards, he's not flagged on any traffic cams' — he counted them on his fingers — 'analysis of the scenes has come back with nothing conclusive that points us at where he could be—'

'Just dirt and rat poison,' Jamie finished.

'Which narrows it down to all of fucking London.'

'Mm.'

'We think he's travelling on foot,' Roper said.

'Why?'

'He never passed his driving test. Doesn't even have a license,' Roper said.

Jamie already knew that from her own research on McElroy.

He read the unimpressed look on her face. 'And CCTV clocks him moving to and from scenes on foot. Plus, we don't have him at any gates for the underground stations near the display sites around the time of the incidents. Nothing on facial rec. We're still scouring footage, but so far… He's either walking, or taking the bus.'

Jamie turned in her chair, making sure her cheek was facing away from Roper, and looked at the map spread across the back wall, the crime scenes all marked out on it. 'He gets around.'

'Yeah. Miles between them at times. Especially Doran and…' Roper snapped his fingers, trying to recall the name.

'Orlov. Kathryn Orlov.'

'Right.'

'With the college right in the middle.'

Roper nodded.

'The places are that important,' Jamie mused, 'that he's willing to walk halfway across the city with a pair of severed hands in his satchel…' She shook her head.

'Deranged,' Roper added.

She couldn't help but agree. 'Any word on Mimi Paganelli?'

'Well, her hands haven't shown up tied to a rafter, if that's what you mean.'

Jamie grimaced. 'Did you manage to get hold of her parents yet?'

Roper was silent.

'Roper?'

'No,' he said. 'Left a message.'

'When?'

'The afternoon after she disappeared.'

'Did you follow up?'

Silence again.

'Roper?' Jamie turned on her chair now and Roper looked down at her, his eyes moving to her forehead. 'Did you call them again?'

'No,' he said.

'Why not?'

He seemed to puff his chest out. 'I'm a little busy, if you didn't notice. Running *your* case.'

'I never asked you too—'

'No, *Smith* did. Because you seem incapable of doing it yourself.' That bite was back in his voice again. Gone, and back just as suddenly.

Jamie did her best to rein her anger in. 'Tread carefully, Roper,' Jamie said coldly. She was done taking shit from him. She'd been through too much, and faced down ten times worse than him in the last twenty-four hours alone. 'Because whether taking orders from me rubs you up the wrong way or not, you've still got to do your damn job. I asked you to inform Mimi's parents of her disappearance, and leaving a bloody message doesn't cut it.'

He let a thin smile spread across his face. 'Why don't you do it yourself, then? Instead of running off on whatever fucking crusade you think you're fighting.' He flicked a hand at her and turned away, limping to another desk.

Jamie thought he made a point of doing so, to emphasise the damage the blade had done.

She shrugged it off.

He'd only be able to throw it in her face if she let him.

'Crusade?' she scoffed. 'Jesus Roper, you need a head torch to see when you're this far up your own ass?'

He sat down with a groan and glared at her.

'You've fought me at every turn on this case. If you've got a problem, then just come out and say it. I'm sick of this hot-and-cold bullshit.'

'I *have* to fight you at every turn. When I don't, I get a knife in the fucking back.' He jerked a thumb over his shoulder, his voice rising.

'And what, you don't think I feel horrific about that? You don't think it keeps me up at night?'

'I think that I spent six weeks in hospital just to get told I'll probably never walk right again, while you strolled into Smith's good graces without a mark on you.'

She raised her eyebrows. 'Not a mark on me? I got the living shit kicked into me, Roper. Or don't you remember that?'

'I thought that was a sparring accident?' he asked lightly.

Jamie bit down on her tongue. Shit. He was right. That's what she'd told Smith.

'And I suppose the mess on your face right now is from the same thing, huh?' He shook his head. 'Either learn to fucking duck, or get a better story.' He waved her off.

'I'm sorry that hunting criminals is too dangerous for your liking,' Jamie said, the bile really coming out now. 'Guess life was easier when you were pounding ten pints a night and following up on outstanding parking tickets because you couldn't be trusted with anything else.'

He stared at her, his jaw quivering with rage. 'You know, maybe I'll call Cake,' he said, voice dripping with venom. 'See if he'll corroborate your stories. I bet Smith would love to hear that.' He sat back on his chair. 'Or maybe I'll just pull some CCTV footage from the nights in question. See if he's prepared to lie for you then.'

Every shred of respect had left Jamie now. 'I don't know why it fucking matters, Roper,' she said, laying her hand flat on the desk. 'Not like you're sticking around anyway. I hear you're waiting on a fat payout and then it's nothing but white sandy beaches and all the fucking rum-filled coconuts you can force down your neck.'

He narrowed his eyes at her.

'So don't fucking threaten me.' She met his stare. 'Unless you're willing to make good on it. Seems like you forgot all the times I dragged your sorry ass out of bed, shit-faced drunk, and drove you here because you weren't fit to be behind the wheel yourself. Or does that not even matter now that you're some white fucking knight, a paragon of self-discipline and virtue?'

Roper's fist balled on his thigh. 'It's not even in the same fucking league.'

They eyed each other, the silence between them deafening.

Footsteps echoed in the corridor outside and then the door opened.

Neither of them looked up.

'Uh,' the voice came. 'Roper?' It was a young detective constable. She must have been just pushing thirty. One of Roper's task force, Jamie guessed.

He turned his head, letting his eyes rest on Jamie until the angle moved them away. 'Yeah?' he said gruffly.

'The DCI wanted me to find you.'

'What for?' Roper asked, not ready to lower his gloves yet.

She swallowed. 'It's, uh…' She cleared her throat. 'Detective Amherst. He was found dead this morning.'

Roper cast Jamie a cold look and she held her face straight and emotionless, looking up at the constable.

'And do you know where I can find a Detective Sergeant Johansson?' the young DS asked. 'The DCI asked me to inform her, as well.'

'I'm Detective Sergeant Johansson,' Jamie answered.

'Oh,' she said, smiling awkwardly. 'I didn't – it's... Sorry.' She shrank from the doorway and disappeared.

Roper turned slowly on his chair towards Jamie and eyed her. 'How did you say you got that bruise again?'

Jamie drew in a deep breath, unable to stop her nostrils from flaring, and then she pushed to her feet. 'Fuck you, Roper,' she growled, desiring nothing more than to not be in the same room as him.

And then she headed for the door.

38

Jamie was seething.

She hated Roper.

But she hated herself, too.

What a damn mess.

She got ten steps across the room before her phone buzzed in her pocket.

Jamie pulled it out on the move and stared at the screen, seeing it was an email from a strange address that was a jumble of random letters and numbers, the server displaying what looked like Russian characters.

She slowed down, seeing '(no subject)' as the header, and swiped to unlock it.

The email opened on screen as she reached the door and she stared down at it.

There was only one thing written. The number '6'. And then a link.

She didn't make a habit of clicking strange links on random emails, but when she read the URL, she made a judgement call.

It was from the Guardian newspaper, the title of the article; 'Ten Unconventional Classical Music Venues Hidden In The City'.

She swallowed and hit it with her thumb, willing the HQ WiFi to load the page faster.

This was Elliot, it had to be.

Number one was an outdoor amphitheatre in a park to the north of the city, the second a square in the south. She kept going down the list, seeing old warehouses, palaces, public gardens, and then she got to number six.

It was called Halliday Station. Jamie had never heard of it.

She read the snippet under the picture, which displayed a vaulted room decorated with enamel tiles.

'Originally built as a storehouse and emergency shelter during World War II, Halliday Station was then expanded and was set to form the central station for a new proposed rail line. Ground instability proved too great and after much testing, construction was abandoned. The station now sits vacant, but during the early two-thousands was used as a bespoke music venue, the natural shape of the main hall providing excellent acoustic properties for both classical and modern performances.' Jamie licked her lips, still frozen at the door. 'Halliday Station has now been closed due to structural issues, but retains its current setup in hopes that one day music will return to these ornate tunnels.'

Jamie swallowed, her thumb shaking as she opened up her browser and typed the words Halliday Station into the nav bar.

The screen reloaded and brought up a map, a red pin dropping itself right in the middle of the city.

Jamie stared at it, scanning the surrounding street names, and froze.

She turned slowly and stared back across the room at the map.

Roper was still sat at his desk, filling in some paperwork, and looked up. 'What is it?' he asked, the note of anger still in his voice.

Jamie ignored him, homing in on the display sites.

Halliday fell between them.

She then zeroed in on the Doran site, her mind racing.

He'd been on foot.

It had been a spontaneous crime.

Unplanned.

Rash.

Which direction was he coming in from?

She took one step forward.

'Jamie?' Roper called, laying his pen down.

Where were Alyssa's hands found?

In a bin… Jamie traced a line from the tunnel to the street where they were found.

She held the phone up, matching the map to her screen. If you drew a straight line from the tunnel to the bin and kept going…

Jesus.

It practically rolled right over the top of Halliday Station.

That had to be it.

He'd been going back there, had come across Alyssa – maybe heard the notes on the air like Jamie had last night, and was drawn to it.

He found Alyssa, couldn't help but gut her.

Tried to immortalise her, as with the others, failed…

Didn't have time to take her like the others.

Didn't have time to do it right.

He knew her, liked her… *loved* her, even.

That's why she was posed like that.

Praying.

For forgiveness.

Jamie felt her back tense, her muscles pulling at her spine.

Then he ran home – to Halliday.

But the hands were ruined. He'd ruined them. Ruined her. Ruined everything.

He couldn't bear to even think of using them.

So he left them, wrapped in a damn violin handkerchief, in a bin. Discarded like the off-cuts they'd become.

And then scurried back to his hole.

Jamie felt her fist tighten around her phone, her teeth grinding together as she glared at the map.

That's where he was – that was his hole. It would have what he needed. Electricity, space to work. It had the heritage, too. It was out of the way, he wouldn't be bothered there. And it would be cool – perfect to preserve his creations. To make a final display…

She swallowed, feeling her throat tighten.

The dirt, the rat-poison left at the scenes.

It was probably rife down there.

All the pieces slotted into place and snapped together.

'Jamie!' Roper nearly yelled this time and she looked over now.

'What?'

'What have you found?'

She opened her mouth and then stopped. 'Nothing.' She said, not even thinking about it.

Roper began to rise from his chair. But Jamie was already out the door.

She wasn't going to get into another argument.

She wasn't going to let Roper muscle in on this collar.

And there was no way in hell she was going to let McElroy slip through her fingers twice.

It was still before nine, and Jamie knew two things.

She wasn't going to repeat the same mistakes as at Bradbury Hall.

One, she'd shoot first, and two – she wouldn't be alone.

Hassan would still be heading in. His wife usually did the school-run with the kids, but she knew they tag-teamed to get them ready in the morning, which meant they rarely left the house before quarter-past eight.

Which meant he rarely arrived before nine.

She had time.

Jamie swung past the nearest coffee machine, got him his usual, and then headed to the car park.

She waited at the bottom of the entrance ramp and flagged him down as he pulled in in his four-by-four.

He rolled to a stop and wound down his window with a questioning look.

Jamie handed him the coffee and smiled as best she could. 'Park up, we've got to go.'

'Go where?'

'Some sites I want to check out.'

He lifted the coffee up and nodded a thanks, and then took a mouthful, wincing at the heat. 'McElroy?'

'What else?'

He looked around. 'No Roper?'

'He's enjoying trying on daddy's trousers upstairs.'

Hassan gave her a quizzical grin. 'Uh, alright? You two okay?'

He must have read the contempt in her voice.

'Who knows.' She shrugged. 'Who fucking cares. He's on his way out.'

Hassan's eyes twitched as he tried to work that out, but he didn't say anything about it. 'Where we going?'

Jamie glanced over her shoulder, concerned that Roper might actually show up and start asking questions.

McElroy was slippery and the last thing she wanted was sirens and a fleet of police officers barrelling down there yelling his name.

Those tunnels were probably a labyrinth and if he knew they were coming he'd slip out the back door no doubt. Or disappear into the underground.

No, prep on a full-scale assault like this would take too much time.

She had the info, she had Hassan, and she had a pistol on her hip.

That was everything they needed to take him down, and she wanted to be the one to slap cuffs on him.

'You know what,' Jamie said quickly, circling the bonnet. 'You drive. It'll be easier.'

She climbed in before he could protest, and pulled the door behind her.

'Okay, let's go.'

Hassan eyed her for a second, and then let off the brake.

The car sidled forward and he circled the car park in silence before heading back into the city streets.

. . .

They drove slowly through the city.

Hassan kept looking over and Jamie kept looking away, conscious that her hair wasn't doing enough to hide the bruise on her forehead.

'You going to tell me where we're going?' Hassan asked after twenty solid minutes of silence.

They'd barely moved in the morning traffic.

Jamie lifted her phone so Hassan could see. She had a Wikipedia page on Halliday Station up. 'Here,' she said.

'Halliday Station,' he read, the brakes under the car squealing as he eased to a stop just short of an Audi's bumper. 'That where McElroy's holed up, you think?

'Could be,' Jamie said, trying to play it down.

'Roper know?' Hassan asked lightly.

She shrugged. 'I don't know. He made a pretty big point of telling me where to shove it when I asked him to bring me up to speed on this.'

Hassan drummed the wheel with his thumb. 'I don't know what's going on with you two, but you should probably still discuss leads like this.'

'He disagrees with how I come up with them and how I chase them down. I think this is worth pursuing, and I don't want him trying to cut my legs out from under me.'

'You think he'd let his own… *whatever* get in the way of the case?'

'Grudge, vendetta?' Jamie offered.

'Bit strong, don't you think?'

She shook her head. 'He's pissed off, and he's got every right to be. He took a knife in the back, and I can't do anything about it. He sees it as my fault, and if he needs to put that on someone…' She trailed off, and then shrugged again.

'Give it time.'

'Yeah, sure,' Jamie laughed. 'I've known Roper a while. He's not the forgiving sort.' She thought on it. 'I think he's just trying to close a chapter in his life. And I'm included in it.'

'He'll come around,' Hassan said.

Jamie couldn't help but smile at his positivity. A few years as a detective in this city would scrub that out of him for sure.

'If you say so.' She exhaled. 'All I know is that we have differing opinions on how to handle this case, and if this lead pans out, I want to be holding the reins on it.'

Hassan said nothing this time.

They just kept rolling forward.

Inch by inch.

Towards Halliday Station, and whatever evil it held.

39

THEY PULLED up across the street from Halliday Station.

It was set off the corner of a T-junction.

The entrance to the station was set among a copse of trees that sprawled back into a park. Steps led down to a flat section, which then fed through a set of doors into the station itself.

At ground level, the station had been surrounded by a high fence with spikes running along the top.

And at the bottom of the stairs, the doors had been covered over with steel sheeting.

'Looks pretty locked up to me,' Hassan observed, scratching his chin.

'I think it's supposed to,' Jamie said. 'But let's check it out. If the locks are tight and nothing seems off, we'll head back to HQ.' She said it as casually as she could, but in her mind, everything was resting on this. And if Hassan dragged her away, she'd be back tonight with bolt-cutters.

He relented, knowing that when Jamie got like this there was no arguing with her. Not until she was appeased at least.

They exited the car at the same time and headed across the road towards the station.

The streets were busy, but few people were walking here.

The entrance to the park was on the next road over and the buildings along this street were mainly upmarket apartments. Which meant all the residents would be in work.

Halliday Station lay quiet, tucked away, and largely unnoticed.

Jamie and Hassan mounted the curb on the far side and drew closer to the locked gates.

The thick black paint had begun to flake, showing red spots of rust underneath.

Hassan put his hands on his hips and looked up at the metal spikes on top.

Jamie inspected the gate itself instead.

It was solid, with two bolts lancing into the concrete at the bottom.

A chain was wrapped around the centre seam, a heavy padlock securing it.

Neither looked touched. They were both old, and perfectly secure.

The gate didn't seem like it had been opened in years.

'Nothing,' Hassan said, letting his hands drop.

Jamie clicked her teeth together, not ready to give up just yet.

The gates around Bradbury Hall had been closed and chained too.

She leaned in closer and inspected the cross-bar above the chain.

Rust showed through more prominently than in other spots.

Like the paint had been scrubbed off.

She pulled a pair of gloves from her pocket and snapped them on, running her finger along the surface.

The paint came away onto the pad of her finger and she lifted it to look.

Flakes, rust – but also… she rubbed it between her fingers – dirt. Grime.

She sniffed it.

And something harsher.

Something that smelt off. A chemical tinge.

Rat poison.

She looked up at the spikes on the fence, too, then reached up, grabbed the bars, and planted her foot on the same cross-member that

McElroy had when he'd rubbed the shit off his treads and onto the gate.

Jamie levered herself up and stepped in between the spikes, dropping down the other side before Hassan could say anything.

'What are you doing?' he hissed, coming up to the fence.

Jamie dusted herself off and looked around. No one was watching. 'Someone's climbed this gate recently,' Jamie said, pointing to the crossmember. 'I just want to check the doors.'

'We can't just jump fences and—'

'If anyone comes, just show them your warrant card,' Jamie said, brushing him off. 'If the doors are locked, then we know it's just kids.' She gave him a reassuring smile. 'I'm sure it's nothing, but I just want to make sure.' She walked backwards, turned, and then jogged down the steps, ignoring Hassan's panicked muttering behind her.

She got down to the flat in seconds and slowed, scanning the ground for any signs of recent activity.

A few empty plastic bottles, crisp packets. Some smashed glass. Leaves from the surrounding trees.

She pursed her lips. The wind would move this stuff all around continually.

It didn't tell her anything.

Over her shoulder she could see Hassan leaning against the fence, staring down at her.

She exhaled and got closer to the steel cladding over the doors – thin sheets riveted to the frames.

Three sets of double doors sat abreast and she moved from left to right.

Jamie inspected them quickly – no locks, no means of easy ingress.

She looked at the frames now, stopping as she reached the one on the far right.

There were rivets in the steel, but they seemed to be missing on the right-hand side of the sheet, next to the outer wall.

Jamie inspected the wood around it more closely and could see that the material was old and cracked.

Someone had jammed a crowbar or screwdriver behind it and jimmied the thing loose.

She could see undulations in the metal, too, where it had been pulled on, and looking at her feet, the bottom corner was hanging away from the frame entirely.

Not by much, but it wasn't attached.

Jamie knelt and hooked her fingers behind it gently, pulling.

The thin sheet of metal bent and warped as she lifted it.

It came so far and then pulled against the rivets on the left and top of the frame.

Jamie peered underneath and into the darkness. Through a gap that was big enough for her to squeeze through.

She exhaled and then drew a slow breath in through her nose, trusting her senses.

Mould. Dust. Dirt. Rat Poison. Embalming fluid.

Her eyes opened and she laid the flap back, her heart beating quiet and fast, and turned to the stairs, walking back up to Hassan.

'Well?' he asked before she'd even reached the top.

Jamie wasn't sure how to play this. Gentle or firm?

She made the decision.

'He's in there,' she said decisively. 'So get your ass over this fence.'

He narrowed his eyes at her as she came up to the bars.

'We can't just go barrelling in there without due cause.'

'Due cause?' Jamie spat. 'We're well within our rights to go wherever we please in pursuit of someone who's committed a crime. And last time I checked, murdering four women and abducting a fifth is definitely a crime.'

'In pursuit means you *follow* someone in there,' Hassan replied, folding his arms. 'Get out of there, we'll call this in. We'll tell Roper, and—'

'Roper's not going to do shit except fuck this up,' Jamie said coldly. 'This show he's putting on, like he gives a shit? He's gunning for his payout, that's all.'

Hassan met her eyes.

'Roper is leaving, Hassan. Early retirement. He's just biding his time, is all.'

'It doesn't matter,' he said quietly. 'This isn't the right way to do this.'

'Right?' Jamie shook her head. 'No, *right* is making sure that bastard doesn't slip away. Right is putting him in cuffs and then behind bars. Right would be putting five bullets in his fucking chest.' She scoffed. 'There's nothing right about leaving this piece of shit on the streets for a second longer than we absolutely have to.'

Hassan was standing firm.

'Do you want to be a detective?'

'What?' He feigned surprise at the question.

'Smith told me – you had the all clear to return to AR. You turned it down.'

'I…'

'I know. Your family. But if you want to be a detective, you have to learn to think for yourself.'

He looked like he was taking offence.

'In AR you had your plan, your target. Parameters. Rules. Shoot on sight. Don't shoot. You had it all laid out. With this… it's different. It's more about reaction than action. Roper taught me that, back when we were first partnered. He knew how it worked.'

'And he doesn't any more?'

'His priorities have changed. Mine haven't.' Jamie bit her lip, knowing she was wasting too much time. 'I let one murderer get away, I'm not letting another.'

Hassan measured her.

'If you're really done with AR and you want to be a detective, then you're going to need a partner.' She met his eye. 'I'd be proud to have you as mine.'

He didn't know whether to say thanks or not.

'Roper,' she said, quietening, 'always had my back. He knew that when I asked, it was because I needed it. And when he asked, I was always there. It's how it works.'

His jaw tensed.

'You work together, you back each other, and you never let your partner go in alone.'

Hassan shifted from one foot to the other. 'You're really not coming out of there, are you?'

'No.'

He blew a long stream of air out through his nose and looked left and right. 'Fucking hell,' he muttered, climbing the fence. 'Smith told me not to let you talk me into doing anything stupid.'

'You think this is stupid?' Jamie asked as Hassan landed heavily next to her.

He straightened the Glock on his belt and looked at her. 'Stupid, no. Reckless and dangerous? Definitely.'

She laid her hand on his should and squeezed. 'Well then it's a good thing you're with me.'

He tsked and shook his head. 'Yeah, then you can be the one who explains that to my wife.'

40

HASSAN PULLED the steel sheet away from the frame and Jamie ducked inside.

The darkness swallowed her up and she paused for a second, her breath loud in her ears.

She turned, aware of her steps echoing in the space and held it open for Hassan to squeeze through.

He had considerably more trouble fitting than her.

But then, they were both inside, the sheet was falling flush to the wood, and they were in total darkness.

Jamie's hand went to her hip and she slid the pistol from its holster.

She didn't dare pull the slide back and risk the click as a round snapped into the chamber.

Hassan's outline came into view, dim and dark. Tiny splinters of light bled in around the frames, cutting him out from the black veil across Jamie's eyes.

He lifted his own pistol and nodded to her.

Your lead.

She took it, feeling a thousand times better that she had Hassan at her shoulder this time around.

They traced their way down into the old station, sliding their heels over the lips of each step so they didn't fall.

Jamie led them down, squinting ahead, into a deeper patch of black on the black backdrop.

Whatever meagre light there was at the top of the steps had long since abandoned them.

'Shit,' Hassan hissed, stumbling.

His heel caught a loose brick and it tumbled forward off the step and thudded into the one below it, flipping to a stop on the third.

Jamie froze, tweaking her ears furiously, feeling Hassan's bulk behind her, standing awkwardly with his legs splayed, breathing harder than she would have liked.

'You good?' she all but mouthed.

He nodded, made a low *mm* sound and Jamie pressed on.

Her knee jarred as she got to the flat ground and she fought back a grunt, regaining her balance. 'Watch it.' She muttered over her shoulder and she presumed Hassan nodded back as he took the final step with more grace than she did.

Ahead of them the tunnel stretched out and then carved around to the right.

Jamie squinted, not sure if it was a trick of her eyes or if she could see a faint light bleeding back towards them.

She took a few more steps and glanced at Hassan, his face shadowed but visible now.

There was definitely light ahead.

Hassan nodded her on and she forced her feet to move, her muscles all tightening, stiffening her joints.

She exhaled, forcing herself to breathe, and kept moving, following the vaulted tunnel as it meandered around.

Ten people could stand in it abreast.

The place was huge, the walls covered with enamel tiles.

You could drop a pin and hear it echo. There was no wonder it was perfect for concerts.

Or for murderous psychopaths.

She shivered, adjusted her grip on the pistol, and kept going.

The air was cold and damp, the smell of embalming fluid growing more pungent with each step.

She felt a hand on her shoulder and jumped a little.

It was Hassan.

She looked over at him and he lifted his hand to his ear and grabbed his lobe, then motioned to his eyes with his two forefingers and pointed to the source of light.

Jamie stopped and listened, watching as the faint light on the wall ahead danced.

A shadow flitted across it and Jamie waited for more movement.

None came.

Hassan touched her shoulder again and leaned in so his chin was practically on his knuckles. He whispered, the words barely audible. 'Once we confirm McElroy's presence, we should back off and call it—'

Jamie had heard enough.

She shrugged him off and kept moving.

Hassan waited for a moment, and then followed.

Good.

He did have her back.

She breathed a silent sigh of relief and approached the corner.

The tunnel cut right and Jamie pressed herself into the shadow, peaking out.

Halliday Station lay ahead, cavernous and grand.

On the left, the platform fell away into a deep, black trench, the tracks already laid, ready for a train that would never arrive.

Pillars rose towards the ceiling, covered with odd-shaped mosaic tiles, the same off-white enamel colour as the walls.

The ceiling curved overhead and dove into the ground on the other side, wide stone slabs spanning the gap.

Old, standing floodlights were set up at the far end, casting a shadowless light over the area.

They lit up the remains of a raised stage – interlocking platforms two feet high.

Cables snaked across the floor, the space between Jamie and the stage not empty in any sense.

Along the wall Jamie could see makeshift shelving with jars and chemicals in cans and bottles lined up.

There was a cot-bed, too. Blankets and pillows on it.

Food was piled up on top of pallets. Tins and bottles of water.

On the other side, between the pillars, his work station.

A long bench – two saw horses topped with sheets of plywood – had been set up. On top of it, Jamie could see a few appliances, various tools. She squinted, everything too far away to make out in detail.

From here it looked like a leatherworkers table, and above it, a rope had been strung between two of the pillars, various spools of fishing line suspended from it, the wires hanging from them, glowing in the floodlight.

This is where he prepared the hands.

Jamie grimaced and pulled back behind the corner, taking a deep breath.

Hassan was next to her now, nodding reassuringly.

McElroy was in there.

Somewhere.

'On three,' she whispered. 'One, two…'

They both moved swiftly from cover, Jamie staying tight and Hassan going wide.

She headed straight down the centre while he swung out towards the pillars, covering the tracks.

Jamie kept her gun steady, her heart beating evenly.

She'd descended into a sort of zen state. A coolness that had her moving precisely.

A hyperawareness had seized her mind and the air seemed to fizz and vibrate around her, her eyes darting from every corner to the table and back.

Where was he?

Hassan disappeared behind the first pillar and then reappeared in the gap as they worked their way forward down the platform.

Jamie slowed, glancing up at an ancient sign above a doorway cut into the righthand wall. Two faded icons of a man and a woman were painted onto the tiles.

She stopped, looking around.

There was nowhere else he could be.

Hassan came to a stop between two pillars and looked over.

Jamie raised her chin at the doorway and Hassan followed her gesture, stepping backwards until he was hidden behind the support strut.

She followed his lead and stepped sideways until she was next to the shelves full of the embalming fluids.

And then they waited.

A flush echoed around the station and Jamie squeezed herself into the gap between the shelf and McElroy's camping cot.

The sheets were crumpled, a faint odour of sweat mingling with the chemicals in the air.

It was enough to make her head swim.

Jamie blinked twice and saw a shape appear in her vision.

She forced her eyes to focus, lifting her gun slowly.

Aaron McElroy stepped into the middle of the platform, drying his hands with an old, tattered towel, and stopped, lifting his head up.

Jamie moved into the open and trained her muzzle on him, centre mass, keeping her distance. 'Aaron McElroy,' she announced, more firmly than last time.

He turned his head slightly, a smile creeping into his cheek, and turned. 'Detective,' he said, narrowing his eyes a little, studying her.

'Get down on the ground,' Jamie ordered, motioning to the floor.

'We've been through this dance before, haven't we?' he asked, his eyes alight, the floodlight behind him throwing a white halo around his head.

He took one step forward.

Jamie held firm.

'I'm arresting you for the murder of Alyssa Doran,' she said, her voice echoing around the room. It resonated and sustained.

He took another step.

'For the murder of Gilberto Delgado, Amelie Dovak, Daisy Hardwick, and Kathryn Orlov.'

'My my,' he said, grinning wider. 'You have done your homework.'

'And for the abduction of Mimi Paganelli.'

His grin slipped into a wry smirk. 'What, you think I haven't killed her, too?'

Jamie widened her stance. 'Last chance, McElroy.'

He dropped the towel between his feet and brushed his brown curls out of his eyes, cracking his neck. 'You're going to have to shoot me, Detective,' he said, tilting his head to the side. 'I'm not going back to prison.' He licked his lips. 'And I'm not stopping.'

Jamie filled her chest and took a step back towards the tunnel. 'Don't make me shoot you.'

'Oh, you're not going to shoot me. You don't have it in you.' He took another step, lowering his chin. 'I can see it in your eyes.'

Jamie swallowed, met his cold gaze, and let her pistol fall. 'You're right,' she muttered. 'I don't. But I don't have to.'

His eyes twitched in realisation, but it was already too late.

Hassan had circled into his blindspot, moving remarkably lightly for a man of his size, and swept up behind McElroy before he could react.

Hassan's arms encircled McElroy, one against his ribs, the other around his neck.

McElroy bucked, threw his free elbow back hard, the sound of it hitting Hassan's chest a dull thud like a timpani drum.

Hassan released him for an instant and Jamie's pistol flew back up, ready to put him down, but before he could even take a single step, Hassan's elbow flew over McElroy's right shoulder and connected squarely with his ear.

McElroy's feet left the ground and he flew sideways, slingshotting to the floor.

He landed hard and twisted into a pile, mewling, his right ear bleeding, the cartilage split above the lobe.

He rolled onto his front and coughed, spitting blood onto the stones.

Jamie wouldn't be surprised if he'd knocked some teeth loose with a blow like that.

Hassan cleared his throat and rubbed his chest. 'Now you're really under arrest,' he squeezed out, wincing.

Jamie breathed a sigh of relief and holstered her pistol. 'Good job,' she said.

He nodded to her, bending down and putting his knee in the middle of McElroy's back to stop him from crawling away. 'You want the collar?'

'No, you take him,' she said, scanning the room. 'Cuff him and drag him up top – call it in.'

'What are you going to do?'

'I'll sweep the area.' Her eyes had already fallen on several things that we making her skin crawl.

McElroy had a board leaned against one of the pillars, a series of stitching needles hanging from it. Different sizes and gauges.

She looked away.

'Alright,' Hassan said, pulling a pair of zip-cuffs from his pocket. 'And Jamie?'

'Yeah?'

'I'll always have your back.'

She smiled. 'Thanks.'

He meant it, and so did she.

Partners changed, but the necessity for them didn't. And she couldn't think of anyone else she'd want looking out for her.

Hassan slapped the cuffs on him and wrestled him to his feet.

By the way his eyes were lolling, Hassan had damn-near knocked him unconscious. But all the same Jamie could hear him reading him his rights as the dragged him back down the tunnel and towards the surface.

She exhaled. It was hasty, but clean. They'd got McElroy, and that was all that mattered.

Jamie paced forward into the room, wanting to call out.

But it seemed wrong, almost, to break the silence in here.

The worktable beckoned and she approached, still wearing her nitrile gloves.

The surface had been sanded smooth, a work-lamp hanging from the rope suspended above.

Jamie looked up at it, at the different thickness fishing lines on offer.

She looked down and paused, seeing a framed photograph sitting at the back of the bench.

McElroy was standing on the left, grinning, holding a conductor's baton.

In the middle, Delgado stood, looking proud. He had a wide smile cut into his cheeks, his arms around McElroy and the person on the right.

Alyssa Doran stared back, smiling warmly, holding the 1909 Hofner Violin that Delgado had given her.

She held it as one would a child.

Jamie's eyes lingered, inspecting the photograph.

This must have been last summer, before everything.

Before McElroy's obsession set in.

Before the October incident.

Jamie licked her lips, remembering Delgado's house, the missing photograph in the attic.

This was it.

McElroy had been there, had taken it. Probably minutes before she'd arrived.

Her blood ran cold.

Maybe he was *there* when she arrived.

She thought back – the open door, the warm milk in the microwave.

Jesus, she'd interrupted him.

The front door. It was open when she circled back to the stairs. Had she left it wide open? She didn't think so.

Had he slipped out when she was in the kitchen? Was he that arrogant? To kill a man and then go to his house, let himself in, and make a fresh pot of coffee?

Jamie swallowed hard, trying to make sense of that.

He wanted Delgado's life, didn't he? He saw what he had – the house, Alyssa. He wanted it.

Then Delgado took it away.

He wanted to know what that felt like – what being *him* felt like.

Jamie remembered what Brownmiller, the principal of the college had said – that he and Delgado had been close.

She stared down at the photograph.

Delgado and McElroy could have been father and son in it.

Her mind went to all of the mythological fables that seemed to include a son killing his father and raping the mother.

Jamie grimaced.

She could think of McElroy's motives all day long, but she wouldn't know for certain until she got in a room with him.

Which wouldn't be long.

Jamie carried on, dragging her eyes from the photograph, turning her attention to the rest of the effects.

On the surface she could see his tools lined up neatly.

Craft scalpels, nail scissors, emery boards.

Moisturisers. Cuticle oils.

Clear Nail varnish.

A white linen cloth was folded in the centre, its surface shiny with the liquids he'd applied to the hands to make them look pristine.

And the knife.

The brutal hunting knife with the six-inch blade.

The one that had been driven into Alyssa Doran and used to hack her hands off. The one that had killed Gilberto Delgado, the others. And Mimi Paganelli.

Would Jamie find her body down here?

She stared down with disgust, feeling her face contort, and then pressed on.

All of this would be catalogued as evidence, bagged, tagged, and presented in court.

Jamie's head still swam from the fumes but she needed to secure the area.

Ahead, next to the stage, she could see a storage crate. It looked like it would have held speakers at one time.

Everything here was cobbled together from what was left behind or from what he could drag through the small opening on the surface.

Jamie approached the crate, looking down at the water leaking from the bottom.

It had formed a dark puddle, a thin stream dripping down onto the tracks.

The faint noise filled the otherwise impenetrable silence.

Jamie exhaled, feeling the cold on her skin again.

The smell of embalming fluids grew stronger as she closed the gap, knowing what she'd find in there before she even unlatched the lid.

Her hand reached out, stopped, and then took hold, throwing it back.

It hinged upwards and fell away from her, revealing bags upon bags of supermarket ice cubes. A polar bear in sunglasses grinned up from the front of each, but Jamie's eyes homed in on something else.

Three zip-lock food bags nestled down among the melting ice, the ghostly visage of pink skin peaking through the condensation.

No way to get a fridge down here.

He had to make do.

Jamie leaned down, plucking the corner of one from between the bags and turned it slightly, being careful not to disturb the ice.

SOCOs would want the scene as fresh as possible.

Jamie swallowed, seeing a finger poking out.

She released it and the embalming fluid inside the bag sloshed gently and then settled, the temperature in the crate keeping them perfectly preserved.

How could someone do this?

How could someone do this to another human being? Abduct them, cut them apart, and treat their body with such—

The skin on the back of Jamie's neck hackled and the world slowed down around her.

She looked up, feeling a disturbance in the air behind her, and twisted.

Something flashed in her peripheral, metal catching the light.

And then pain erupted from Jamie's right shoulder.

She wheeled sideways, the knife missing its mark by inches and slicing across the nape of her neck instead.

The blade dug through the collar of her leather jacket and into her skin, cutting a line from below her ear down her shoulder until it bit into flesh.

It had been meant for the square of her back.

Jamie howled, stumbled and threw herself backwards, managing to stay on her feet, the searing pain roaring through her back and up into her jaw.

The cut was deep.

Her right hand spasmed and locked, the knife striking nerves, and her jaw clamped together so hard her teeth nearly split.

Jamie looked down at it, gnarled like a claw, and then faced her attacker.

Mimi Paganelli charged forward, knife raised, and leapt at Jamie.

She didn't have time to think, to even realise what was going on.

Mimi's right arm flew up, knife glinting in the floodlights, and then brought it down. Jamie's left fist shot upwards, grabbing her wrist out of the air.

The edge of the knife scratched at Jamie's sleeve as Mimi's weight drove her backwards, her heels catching the edge of the uneven stones.

They landed hard, together, locked in an embrace.

Jamie's right arm, slick with blood and half-lame came up under Mimi's chest, the girl's collarbone pressed hard to her forearm, the point of Jamie's elbow tight against her throat.

Mimi bore down, bedraggled and deranged, her right hand still firm around the hilt of the knife, Jamie's left quivering around her wrist, trying to keep the blade from plunging into her chest.

'Give him back!' she hissed, spitting flecks of saliva onto Jamie's face.

Jamie growled, the pain in her shoulder blinding, and fought the girl back. 'Mimi!' she squeezed out through gritted teeth.

She recognised the girl from the social media photographs, but the once slim build was now skinny, the once luxuriant black hair now matted into strands. Her eyes, once kind, were now cold and changed.

But her hands? Jamie's eyes went to her hand. Her nails perfectly cut and shaped, her cuticles moisturised and soft, the same scent of cocoa butter fighting through the stench of blood.

Jesus – it was her. She'd prepared the hands…

Jamie thought back to Alyssa's, dumped and discarded. The uneven cuts, the badly filed nails… That was him. The rest? It was Mimi. But why?

Mimi writhed on top of her, reaching over with her left hand, slamming her palm into the bottom of the knife, driving it down, yelling madly as she did.

Jamie's elbow smacked against the stones and send a bolt of electricity up through her wrist.

The blade descended, the tip hovering just inside Jamie's shoulder.

Mimi bucked again and Jamie's hand bend over, the ligaments straining.

The tip of the blade pressed into the leather.

Jamie's jaw quivered, her teeth bared, lips pulled back as she tried to fight.

She only had one arm, she couldn't push her off like this. She had to think, and fast.

Mimi let out a guttural cry and flopped up and down, shoving the knife against Jamie as hard as she could.

Something popped in Jamie's wrist and the tip of the knife sank its teeth into her skin.

Their position shifted slightly and Jamie's leg slipped inside Mimi's.

She felt it move, just enough, and instinctually threw it upwards, driving the point of her knee into Mimi's groin.

The girl's eyes widened and she let out a high-pitched grunt, the impact sending her sprawling.

Jamie rolled as hard as she could and threw the girl to the ground, leaving a scarlet print on the stone where her back had been.

The air was thick with blood.

Mimi landed and the knife clattered against the stone.

Jamie scrambled to her knees and reached across her body with her left hand, wrestling her pistol awkwardly from the holster.

Mimi regained herself, scrabbled to her feet.

Jamie's pistol swung wide as she drew, the breath caught in her throat.

Mimi drew a sharp lungful of air.

Jamie pulled the trigger, barely aiming.

There was no time to.

The muzzle flashed, the noise bouncing around the room, singing off the walls.

Spots danced in her vision, but she didn't hit anything.

Mimi was gone.

Jamie's blood ran down her right arm, streaming from the gash on her back.

Stones crunched as Mimi jumped down onto the tracks, and then footsteps echoed all around.

Jamie groaned, swore, and tried to stand up, forcing her right hand to move under her for support.

She put it on the stones and pressed into it.

It wouldn't take her weight, her fingers tingling.

Blood ran down her sleeve and made a puddle around her wrist.

The pain was blinding.

Jamie hissed, let go of the gun, and dragged her phone from her pocket, dropping it onto the floor under her.

The screen lit up.

No fucking service.

Of course. They were fifty feet underground.

Jamie growled, glancing up at the far end of the room – it was easily eighty feet to the tunnel, and another few hundred to the surface. If Hassan was at the gates… Shit, what if he didn't hear the shot?

Mimi's footsteps began to die away.

She couldn't let her escape.

Jamie took her gun in her good hand and forced herself to her feet, using what little response she had in her right to grip a fistful of leather jacket, cradling her arm across her stomach.

She loped at first, looking for balance, and then found it, leaving footprints in her own blood as she approached the edge and then dropped down onto the tracks.

Black stones crunched under her heels as she landed, glancing left and right as she did.

Three mounds in the stones caught the light from above, nestled next to the tracks.

Kathryn Orlov. Daisy Hardwick. Amelie Dovak.

The discarded remains.

She ground her teeth, spat out the taste in her mouth, and then pushed forward, taking off down the tunnel after Mimi.

In seconds, she was swallowed up by the darkness, with nothing but the sound of her ragged breath and uneven footsteps in her ears.

41

Jamie slowed and glanced over her shoulder, the station behind her a circle of light in the distance.

The filthy stone walls around her seemed to eat what little light was bleeding down.

Jamie sloshed through the chipped stones, seeing the tracks disappear underfoot.

They'd only laid them just beyond the station.

She squinted ahead, wondering where this tunnel led.

Her mind raced, rearranging all the pieces of the case she had in her head.

The place where Alyssa's hands had been discarded. It was almost between the kill site and Halliday station. Almost. But Mimi's apartment wasn't on Roper's map. And the hands were left in the *morning,* after they'd been worked on.

He'd brought them back here that night – tried to work on them – tried to make them *right.* But he couldn't. That was Mimi's part.

She swallowed, tracing a line from Halliday Station to Mimi's apartment in her mind.

That's where he was going. That's when he left them.

Jamie tried to settle herself.

But how did her and McElroy meet? How did this happen?

Jamie slowed, taking long strides, listening for any sign of Mimi, but there was nothing but silence.

Her skin hackled, the faintest outlines of the stones around her just visible in the gloom.

'Mimi?' Jamie called softly, lifting her pistol.

It felt heavy and unwieldy in her left hand.

It shook wildly, the near-inaudible click of the components rattling just reaching her ears.

There was no response.

Jamie's shoulder throbbed, the blood hot down her back under her jacket.

She tried to ignore the pain, forcing herself not to collapse and curl into a ball.

'Mimi Paganelli?' She called more definitively now.

Still nothing.

And then she saw it and stopped.

Ahead, the tunnel ended in solid stone.

A dead end.

Jamie swallowed, just seeing the lines of the scarred stonework from ancient blades.

A blade glinted.

Jamie tried to hold her gun firm, giving herself as much space as she dared while keeping her aim true.

Mimi stood there, facing the wall, hands pressed flat to it, looking for a door that wasn't there.

The knife was still in her grip, raised over her head, drenched in Jamie's blood.

'Don't move,' Jamie said, her voice echoing in the darkness.

She wasn't sure if Mimi could hear her heart hammering against her ribs.

But it was just about all Jamie could.

Mimi lowered her hands slowly and turned, looking down at the knife. Its polished blade caught the thin strands of light fighting down the tunnel.

Otherwise, she was just a shadow.

'Drop the knife,' Jamie demanded.

Mimi didn't even seem to hear her.

'You wouldn't understand,' Mimi said quietly. 'No one will ever understand.'

Jamie tightened her grip on the pistol, her eyes stinging from the dust in the tunnel. 'It's not too late,' Jamie said evenly. 'You can still get out of this. Just drop the knife and get down on the ground.'

Mimi's eyes flashed in the darkness. 'It is,' she whispered, her voice carrying.

'You haven't done anything wrong,' Jamie said. She had to try. She knew what men like McElroy could be like – smart, charming. They could say all the right things. Make you believe whatever they wanted. *Do* whatever they wanted.

The bed at Mimi's apartment. The semen.

McElroy's. But he hadn't forced himself on her.

She wanted it. Or at least thought she did. Was made to think she did.

Mimi was the victim here. Not like the others, but just like the others at the same time.

Jamie knew the truth of it.

She'd almost lived it.

'I have,' Mimi said, lifting the knife and studying it. There wasn't a hint of fear in her voice.

'What are you talking about?'

'I killed him.'

Jamie's fingers readjusted on the grip, the trigger alien under her left index finger. 'Who, Mimi? Who did you kill?'

'Gilberto.'

'Delgado?' Jamie's brow furrowed. 'No – McElroy…'

She laughed. 'He didn't want me to. But I did. I did it anyway!'

A shiver ran down Jamie's spine.

'I was just supposed to keep him busy, give him the tea. But he wanted more. He wanted me.'

Jamie swallowed.

'Like he'd had the others – Rachel, then Alyssa…' She laughed again. 'They all wanted him. But *we* knew the truth about him.' She nodded fiercely. 'He came at me—'

'Mimi, listen to me. We can help you. *I* can help you.'

'So I killed him. With Aaron's knife.' She lifted it into the air like it was some holy relic. 'It was easy. Easier than I thought it would be. I put it right in his belly, like Aaron showed me. And twisted.'

Jamie's mouth had gone dry.

'There was so much blood.'

Jamie felt Mimi's gaze cold on her skin.

'But he deserved it. For what he did. To Aaron. Do you know what he did to Aaron?'

'I do,' Jamie said, her voice a croak in the ocean of ink.

'No you don't,' Mimi said, laughing. 'You couldn't know. Not really. Not what it's like to be us.'

Us? 'You're not like him, Mimi,' Jamie forced out.

'You don't know what it's like to never get what you worked for. To be cut down at every turn. To always be second best. To never be *that* person. To watch everyone else get what you deserve.' She balled her fists and threw them down at her sides. 'To get what's *yours!*'

Jamie jolted, felt the stones shift under her.

Her right arm was aching now, the blood soaking down the back of her jeans.

She was feeling faint.

Her jaw began to quiver.

'They made it all about them – *they* had to be the best. *They* had to win. *They* had the talent. *They* had it all handed to them while the rest of us' — her voice began to crack — 'were left to fight for what was left! They said it was about the music! Always about the music, but they lied… But we fixed that.' Mimi laughed, loudly, her shrill tones echoing in the tunnel.

'They were selfish. They didn't know what they had, how lucky they were.' Mimi's cheeks glittered with tears.

'Mimi…'

'But we fixed that…'

'Mimi?'

'Aaron saw me… when no one else did.'

'Mimi,' Jamie said more assertively.

'He got rid of Alyssa for me – made it so I could be first.'

Jamie forced herself to breathe. They knew each other before the October incident. Mimi must have stayed in the city over the summer. Jesus, if Roper had got hold of her parents… If she'd followed up with Gretchen… If she'd waited, like Smith had said…

Jamie shook those thoughts from her head. She couldn't think about that now.

'Mimi?'

She wasn't listening anymore.

'And then we made it so nothing else mattered. We made it about the music, don't you see? We made it so there was no best or worst, no first and second chair, no tears and pain, no… no… nothing else! We did that.' She took a step forward.

'Stop. Don't move, Mimi.'

'It's not too late,' she said, taking another step.

'I mean it.'

'Please,' Mimi said, raising the knife. 'We can keep going. We can fix them all.'

'Mimi!'

Everything stood still.

The air around them froze.

The stones crunched under the girl, an ear-splitting shriek filling the tunnel.

She charged, blade forward, right at Jamie.

The pistol waved, steadied, and then kicked back against Jamie's hand.

The muzzle flashed.

Once.

Twice.

She fought the recoil, the light painting everything in a vivid snapshot.

The first – Mimi leaping, mouth open, teeth bared, eyes wide, knife raised.

The second – a pair of red roses in the middle of her chest, her face contorted in shock, the blade spilling from her grasp.

The was a second of silence, and then a loud crunch as Mimi landed at Jamie's feet, face down, and slid to a halt in the stones.

They cascaded around her, the knife bouncing to a rest somewhere on Jamie's right.

Mimi let out a low hiss of air and then fell still, Jamie's still smoking muzzle hovering above her prostrate body.

She looked at it, faint blue curls drifting into the thick air.

Jamie's stomach knotted, her balance left her and she wobbled, staggering backwards.

She fell, landing hard, and rolled onto her side, the blood still pouring from her shoulder.

Jamie kept her eyes on Mimi's still outline.

She couldn't look away.

The pistol fell against Jamie's thigh and she breathed raggedly, still cradling her right arm.

Her chest felt heavy.

She shivered, feeling cold.

Somewhere behind her, she heard her name echoing down the tunnel.

Someone calling for her.

She looked up, her father's broad shoulders filling her vision. She felt his rough hand at her face, smoothing the tears from her cheeks. *It's okay, Jamie,* he said. *It's over now. It's all over.*

42

The sun was setting on the final day of September.

It sank low over the water, the sea still for the first time since Jamie had arrived.

She stood on the beach at Machir Bay on the isle of Islay, as far from the darkness of the city as she could get.

The cold air that whipped across the Scottish wilds was as close to home as she'd felt in a long time.

She folded her arms, her right shoulder twinging as she did, and locked in what little warmth she still had.

Her hair blew loose around her head, the quiet lapping of waves punctuating the desolate coo of the breeze.

It had been more than five months since the tunnel.

Since she'd been put on administrative leave.

Since McElroy and Mimi Paganelli and their dungeon of twisted love and horrors.

She didn't know if she wanted to go back.

She wasn't strong enough yet.

And didn't know if she ever would be.

Those snapshots, painted in the light of her muzzle were burned into her eyes.

Every time she closed them they played on repeat. Over and over.

Mimi's death weighed on her.

It should have gone differently.

She should have made sure of that. But she didn't.

She fucked up. And now she had to live with it.

In her mind, it could have gone a thousand ways, and only one of those ended with her shooting Mimi twice in the chest.

Jamie looked at the wet sand between her boots, willing the sun to cling to the sky just a little longer.

It was getting dark faster now.

The summer was fading, and winter was closing in.

Jamie could feel it in the air.

She'd been thinking a lot recently.

And things had become clearer. Perhaps clearer than they'd ever been.

The thick collar of her pea coat caught the wind and pressed around her head, and then the wind died.

The sky ahead was streaked with red and purple.

'Beautiful.' A voice rang from behind her.

She'd not heard it for a long time, but she knew it instantly.

'Elliot,' she said, not looking away.

He walked across the beach and stood next to her, hands in the pockets of his jeans, pushing an overcoat back over his wrists.

'I was surprised to get your call,' he said.

The beach was empty, the nearest house nearly a mile away.

Jamie liked the remoteness of it.

It made her feel safe, even now.

'I'm surprised you came.'

'I wanted to make sure you were okay.'

She let a strange smile creep over her lips. 'That's funny.'

'Is it? Why?'

She didn't answer his question. 'Do you think our lives are left to chance?'

'What do you mean?'

'Is everything predetermined? Do we follow a path set out for us, the outcomes unavoidable, free will nothing more than an illusion? Or do we have control over what we do? True control.'

Elliot stared at the horizon. 'I don't think we can ever know. To know that would erase the very question.'

She thought on that, and then nodded.

He went on. 'But I believe that there are things that we must do. Things in each of us we cannot ignore. Things we are driven to, eventually, no matter how much we resist.'

'To kill?'

He looked at her.

She kept looking at the sea.

It was so still.

She'd never seen it like this.

'Are you driven to kill? Is it something that you have to do?'

He kept looking at her, and then nodded. 'Yes.' He paused for a moment. 'But the method, the means, the outcome… They are mine. I choose to channel it in a way that I believe is right.'

She let out a low *humph.* 'That's a weak justification.'

He didn't respond.

'Would you stop?' she asked.

'No.'

'Not even if I asked you to?'

'No.' Quieter this time.

'Why me?'

He narrowed his eyes a little.

'Why choose me?'

'You fascinate me.'

'Why?'

'Because you understand me.'

'No I don't.'

'I think you do. It just scares you to admit.'

'Nothing scares me anymore.'

He inspected the lines of her face, silhouetted in the liquid gold of the fading sun.

'Are you going to kill me?' Jamie asked after a minute of silence.

'Not unless I have to,' he answered, no hint of emotion in his voice.

She swallowed. 'I never thanked you for saving my life. From Zhou. From Amherst.'

'Are you thanking me now?'

'Yes.'

'You're welcome.'

'But there's still something I don't understand. Something I can't put my finger on.'

'What is it?'

Jamie drew a slow breath. 'How did Amherst know where I lived?'

Elliot turned back to the sea.

The sun was halved by the horizon now.

'He must have gotten your address from the Met database.'

Jamie smiled again. 'I never changed my home address.' She turned to him. 'Because I suspected that was how you'd find me. I kept my old address listed.'

Elliot was silent.

'But you found me anyway, didn't you.'

He kept his eyes fixed on the sun.

'You told me that Zhou was powerful,' Jamie started, unfolding her arms and pushing them into the deep pockets of her coat. 'But that there were people controlling him. That there was a power struggle in the city and there were those looking to change that. Do you remember that conversation, Elliot?' She looked at him.

'Yes,' he said.

'I know it was you.'

He didn't look at her.

'I don't know how, but I know. You orchestrated it. To draw Zhou out, to force Amherst and Brock into that position. So you could kill them, there, in front of me. So you could eliminate them to make way for whatever it is you're planning, and *save* me at the same time…' She trailed off, laughing a little.

The sun sank lower.

'You killed Zhou, Amherst, two of Zhou's bodyguards. I watched you do it. You murdered them.'

Elliot was stone.

'And God-knows what you did with Brock.' She shook her head. 'I don't even want to imagine it. But I guess she fetched a high price in parts.'

He didn't move a muscle.

'But I can't arrest you for it. For any of it. Can I?'

He wouldn't look at her.

'Because you made me complicit. In all of it.' She felt her eyes begin to fill. She still couldn't believe how stupid she'd been. 'The rifle above the alleyway – all for show. You knew I wouldn't kill Amherst. But you had to show me – what he was doing. It was all ground work, wasn't it. The files, the pay-offs. And then, when they took me, from my apartment, you knew when it was going to happen and where they were going to take me. And when you came in and killed them… with a gun?' She shook her head. 'That's not your style. You prefer the *personal touch.* And anyway, where would you even get a police-issue Glock 17? Other than my nightstand, of course.'

The muscles in his cheeks twitched almost imperceptibly.

'You killed them with my gun, didn't you. Broke into my apartment, took it from my nightstand, watched as they took me. Waited, right there, until the last moment. So it was believable. So it was *really* believable. And then you came in and killed them.

'Already had the hotel room booked and prepaid for. Already had it all worked out. Put me there with no phone, no money, no other options. Manipulating me, shaping me, ready to repay the debt when you needed it.'

'It wasn't like that,' he said.

'And then you had the balls to give my gun back to me. The murder weapon. So that if you ever felt I was getting cold feet, or plotting something, you could tip them off, put the spotlight on me. Or at least threaten it to get your way. You're a clever son of a bitch, you know that?'

'What are you going to do?' Elliot asked.

The sun was all but gone from the sky.

'I could kill you.'

'But you won't.'

Jamie let one final smile spread across her lips, her fingers opening in her deep pocket.

She felt them slide around the grip of the snub nose Smith & Wesson Model 36 revolver hidden there and tighten.

'Things change, Elliot,' she said quietly, watching the final rays of light fade from the sky. 'People change.'

AUTHOR'S NOTE

There comes a time for all writers when they're asked why they write. A lot of us say things like, *it's a compulsion*, or because *I must.* For me, it's just a way to express myself. I'm a creative person, always have been. I've always liked to make things, draw things, write things. But there exists a conflict within that creativity. A part of myself that wants to create for me, make things, lock them in a box, and never show anyone. And then another part which wants to create things for others. To share what I believe is worthy of being *out there* for people who I think might enjoy it.

The dream of 'making it' as a writer is one that of course exists for me, but it's not why I'm doing this. If it was about the money, I probably would have given up ten years ago when my first novel fell flat on its face. And yet, even that has changed. For me, now, making it doesn't mean making money. It's about reaching, and connecting with readers.

It's about having the things I've written read and enjoyed by those on the other side of the page.

And for the first time, I feel like I'm close to that.

This is book three in a series that I hope will grow and grow.

But saying that, this is the end of a chapter. A chapter of Jamie's life, at least.

The thing I get asked about most from my readers is why I portray Jamie's father as an apparition, or ghost, or hallucination – or whatever he's supposed to be.

I'm glad, though, that it's unclear.

Someone even asked me whether Jamie was mad. Was she delusional or insane?

I can say that she's not. But she's filled with guilt and anger.

Her frosty (at best) relationship with her mother, and the lost relationship she had with her father spur her on. She looks back on her childhood with difficulty, but the memories she has of her father are warm, the ones of her mother cold. And yet, she can't deny the way that her father treated her mother, either. Which places Jamie in this difficult position of hating her father for tearing their family apart, but at the same time, always wondering if she made the right decision to leave her with her mother.

Just fourteen at the time, she didn't have a lot of choice.

But that doesn't stop her from thinking about it. And thinking about whether she could have done anything to save her father had she stayed.

His appearing to her, his voice in her head, it's all just a way of keeping him with her. Everything she learned as a girl about detecting she learned from him. His lessons echo in her head, and she does her best to imagine him so that she doesn't forget. His words of wisdom, as revealed in the latter half of this book, are just her own thoughts reverberating in her head.

It's been so much fun writing these three novels. And even more fun taking Jamie from that straight-laced, happy-go-lucky, got-her-life-together DS to someone pushed to the limits of their sanity and psyche. If you have Bare Skin, go back, read those first few chapters, and you'll see that Jamie is now a different person. For me, that's rewarding to write. And I hope it's been rewarding to read.

Each book, too, has offered a new challenge to Jamie, and has forced her to face the darkness of her job. The eternal struggle between what's right and what constitutes justice has been a driving force in the narratives, and to be able to allow it to culminate in Jamie finally pulling that trigger was bittersweet – but also necessary.

People have told me that I focus too much on Jamie's internal development, but it's always been my goal to do that with these novels. To craft a story that focuses on Jamie, and really fleshes her out in a way that shows all of her cracks and flaws. That makes her feel like a strong detective who also struggles with her parents, and with her social life, and with everything. So many famous detectives seem to be broken, but never to show that. They carry on quipping one liners and taking down baddies with no seeming toll taken on them.

Jamie will always carry her wounds forward, both mental and otherwise.

But now what? The sun has set on a difficult year of Jamie's life. She's been tricked, lied to, tested, manipulated, stalked, forced to run and hide, forced to harm, to kill… And now what? Can she come back from this, and if so, who will she be on the other side of it?

I've been ruminating on that for a while now, and while I originally planned to have a fourth book begin immediately after this one, I think that it will only serve to undo what we've done so far.

This leg of the journey is over, and as Jamie tries to put her mind back together in this remote wilderness, a place closer to her childhood home than any she's had since leaving, another evil gestates.

One that only Jamie can defeat.

To me, Jamie is real. The world she lives in is real. These killers, the people in the books, the places, they all continue to exist even when Jamie's not there to witness it.

Smith, Gretchen, Roper, Hassan, Cake… These are the people who have helped and shaped Jamie through these novels, and they'll be around in the future. But perhaps just not as you remember them. I can safely say, at the moment the book ends, Jamie doesn't know what lies ahead. But she doesn't think it includes the Met anymore. Perhaps it doesn't. Maybe she'll stay in Scotland forever, meet a guy, settle down, raise a family. Maybe she won't. Maybe she'll get back to policing in the Highlands. She hasn't planned that far ahead.

But I have.

You have all shown me a tremendous amount of support. Whether you've reached out in the form of a comment on Facebook, you've sent me an email through my website, you've left a review on Amazon or Goodreads, or whether you simply read the books and enjoyed them. All of these things help to no end, and allow me to keep doing what I'm doing.

So, where to next? Are you hungry for more Jamie Johansson? Well, you won't have to wait too long.

Jamie is already being dragged into her next case, kicking and screaming, albeit.

The icy, frozen north is calling her back. Fresh blood is staining the snow of her childhood home.

The last case her father worked before she was taken to England has reared its head, and Jamie might just be the only one who can help.

Time has moved on, Jamie has moved on. The events of this book have landed her with a promotion, as well as a heavy burden to carry. She may not be the same person she was, and as these books are written through her eyes, the world may look different, too.

But one thing hasn't changed. And that is that there is evil out there. Evil which can't be stopped until someone stops it.

Jamie may not be ready to go back. She may not even be willing. But there's something deep inside her that won't let her just stand by when she can do something.

She'll be forced to confront difficult memories, a painful childhood, and a killer who's had twenty years to prepare for what comes next…

Thank you, for everything. I hope you're sticking along for the ride. It's going to be a wild one!

My best,

Morgan

ANGEL MAKER

Book 1 in the DI Jamie Johansson Series

It's January and the snow falls thickly over Stockholm.

A man jailed twenty years ago for the murder of seven teenage girls lies dying in his cell.

News of his death finally brings comfort and closure to the families of his victims.

But then, three days later, a body is found in the woods north of the city.

A young girl has been suffocated, bathed, and mounted in the forest, boughs of a birch tree driven through her back, the branches spreading into the air above her like wings threatening to take flight.

The Angel Maker is back.

A thousand miles away, DI Jamie Johansson receives the call. One of the biggest cases her father ever closed has just been reopened. The details of the murders were never released to the press or public, the nature of the kills kept secret. And now, the original case files are missing, along with Jamie's father's former partner.

The Stockholm Polis believe a copycat has emerged… The other option is much, much worse.

The detective working the case needs Jamie's help to retrace her father's footsteps, to see where he went wrong. What he missed. Did he catch the real Angel Maker all those years ago, or did he get the wrong man?

Jamie must confront the childhood she left behind and exhume all of the painful memories she ever buried.

She always wanted to return home.

But she never thought it would be like this…

Angel Maker is the fourth novel in the Jamie Johansson series, and the first novel in the DI Jamie Johansson series.

The runaway bestseller, Angel Maker has cemented Jamie Johansson as a reader-favourite detective.

Get your copy on Amazon today.

Printed in Great Britain
by Amazon

78458105R00203